BRIGHTEST KIND OF DARKNESS

BOOK I

NEW YORK TIMES BESTSELLING AUTHOR

P.T. MICHELLE

BRIGHTEST KIND OF DARKNESS

Print ISBN-10: 1939672104
Print ISBN-13: 9781939672100

To stay informed when the next **P.T. Michelle** book will be released, join P.T.'s free newsletter http://bit.ly/11tqAQN

V011419

Cover credit: Cover designed by P.T. Michelle
Graphic credit: Corvus symbol designed by Keith Draws

SERIES READING ORDER

Brightest Kind of Darkness Series

ETHAN *
BRIGHTEST KIND OF DARKNESS
LUCID
DESTINY
DESIRE
AWAKEN

ETHAN is a prequel that delves deeper into Ethan's background. It's best read* ***after* *BRIGHTEST KIND OF DARKNESS.*

The Brightest Kind of Darkness series is best suited for readers 16+.

CHAPTER 1

For me, being surprised was like wearing my best friend's favorite shirt, cherished for its borrowed uniqueness. Some people loved potty humor. I loved watching life's surprises happening all around me. It was so rare that I got to experience them myself.

But after last night, I've decided I hate surprises.

Before I fell asleep, I'd whispered, "Can I just have *one* surprising day?" And four short hours later, I was zooming across an empty Walmart parking lot in my car, shoulders knotting with each spin of my wheels. "I should've defined 'surprising'," I muttered as I squealed to a stop in a parking spot. Grabbing my white-framed sunglasses, I jerked them toward my face, then slowly lowered the shades back to the dash. *What was I thinking? The sun wasn't even up yet.*

Could I be wrong? I glanced at my mom's favorite wool scarf sitting on top of my jacket in the passenger seat. I'd brought it for practical reasons, but I'd also wanted a part of her with me, as if her scarf riding shotgun meant she'd approve of my decision. How would she react if I was wrong and got arrested for reporting a false crime? Would she be shocked? Disappointed? Think I've lost my mind? Would she show any emotion? Or would she wait until the end of the day—after her last meeting was over—to check her messages and then come post my bail? It'd almost be worth the risk to find out.

With a heavy sigh, I cocooned myself in a layer of winter clothes. Halfway across the parking lot, sweat began to coat my skin under the thick jacket. The scratchy scarf only made it worse. All I could think about was clawing my irritated neck, but the building's security cameras hung like gargoyle guardians nesting on the shoulders of a red and blue striped elephant. Tucking my chin into the scarf's folds, I pulled my knit cap lower. I didn't care if I looked like an idiot dressed like the boy from *A Christmas Story* in fifty-degree fall weather. Anonymity was my top priority.

Near the payphone, a blast of frigid air whisked dead leaves along the edge of the building, turning my sweat to chill bumps. Wind whistled and tunneled, pitching low and then high. "No!" brushed past my ear in a harsh, grating whisper, and the top layer of my hair charged, floating above the scarf. I froze and smacked my hair down as I scoured the area for the source. Wind and leaves battled the empty space on both sides of the building. My car sat alone in the dark lot, yet I couldn't shake the feeling I was being watched…or reminded of the past.

I have no idea how many times I've forced myself to stand back and just be a knowing observer. But I couldn't today. When I stepped toward the building, an invisible weight began to crush my head and shoulders, compressing my spine. I tried to inhale calming breaths, but thick, icy moisture swept into my lungs, stealing my air.

My vision blurred and I stumbled forward, my feet heavy weights dragging across the asphalt. Falling against the building, I pressed my cheek against the cool rough bricks and wheezed. I wasn't certain things would go right, but there was one truth I knew for sure. "I can't ignore this," I whispered harshly.

As the crushing sensation slowly tapered off, I sucked in lungfuls of air, my gaze glued to the building's sharp edge. Would someone come around the corner and tell me I was wrong? I waited. A minute passed. And then another. I was running out of time. Blowing out a breath, I pushed away from the wall. At least I wouldn't have to peel off the wad of turquoise gum covering the phone's coin slot. This call was free.

I picked up the grungy handset and dialed.

"911 Operator. What's the nature of your emergency?" an older woman's gravelly voice shot across the line.

God, what if I got it wrong somehow? Palm sweat soaked my gloves. "I—I want to report a potential threat to Blue Ridge High School."

"Speak up," the operator pitched higher.

Clearing my throat, I spoke again, my words huskier. "I think someone's going to bomb Blue Ridge High today. A student who was recently expelled."

Typing sounded at rapid speed. "Your name?" The woman demanded.

I hung up and ran on shaky legs to my car. I hated that I didn't know what would happen next.

MY CAR SCREECHED into the school's back parking lot seven minutes before first bell, the smell of burned rubber my constant perfume. Mom was going to be pissed if she had to get me new tires and brakes in the same year. Sliding on my narrow-framed black and red shades, I surveyed the ordered chaos. Police cars and fire trucks surrounded Blue Ridge High, their lights blinking in a strobed rhythm of red and blue. More students seemed to be leaving than arriving.

Digging my fingers into my backpack strap, I started toward the school with a clueless, but curious expression on my face.

The loner guy from my History and Trig classes headed toward me, hands shoved in his jeans pockets. "What's happening?" I called out.

When he didn't respond, annoyance kicked in.

I remember the day he'd transferred in a couple weeks ago.

It was the end of the day, and Lainey and I were goofing around in the hall with the soccer ball. I'd just passed the ball to Lainey when Sophia jumped in and punted it past me. Not to be outdone by Sophia, I'd gunned for the ball and looked up in time to see I was about to collide with the new guy.

"Look out!" I warned.

Blue eyes, framed with circles of exhaustion, flashed behind longish black bangs. At the last second, he'd jerked sideways and I slid past. Just as I regained my footing and turned around, he'd snagged the ball with lightning speed and sent it back to me, then continued down the hall without a word.

In the brief glance he'd passed my way that day, I'd noticed his hollowed cheeks and the blank "no one cares, why should I give a shit" look. Since then, I'd heard rumors that he'd been kicked out of his last school, so I'd tried to be nice and say "hey" to him in the hall a couple of times, but he'd ignored my attempts, brushing past me as if I hadn't spoken.

From his first day at school, he'd parked in the back of the classroom and scribbled on a notepad, ignoring everyone. And here he'd done it again. I was just about to yell, "Hey, rude guy," when I saw ear bud wires dangling in front of him. Had I missed seeing them in the past too?

As he started to pass me, the wind blew his unbuttoned flannel shirt open, revealing a vintage black Rush t-shirt. Cool. A band with deep lyrics. The dark circles under his eyes had faded somewhat, but his gaze never engaged with anyone's, like he totally existed in his own world. I moved to tap him on the shoulder, but he jerked out of my reach before I connected. What was his deal? Frowning, I lowered my hand.

"Sorry," he mumbled. Pulling the ear buds out, he shook his black hair away from his eyes. "What'd you say?"

His deep voice stunned me. Though I wasn't sure what I expected him to sound like, husky wasn't it. Maybe grittier to go with his indie look. "What's happening?"

"Bomb threat."

"Are you serious?"

"Someone called it in." His blue eyes held mine longer than he'd ever done before.

My shades were dark, but I felt as if he could see right past the lenses. *God, I hope my eyes didn't give me away.* Curling my nails into my palms, I tried to keep my expression and voice even. "As in…someone called in a bomb threat?"

He shoved his hands back in his jeans and continued to stare. Was he expecting me to say something else? To confess I already knew the truth? Not in this lifetime.

"Don't know," he finally said with a shrug. "I just heard the principal say school's cancelled and others talking about a bomb."

Exhaling a pent-up breath, I forced a calm tone. "Thanks."

When he walked away, I called after him, "I'm Nara. What's your—" but he'd already put his ear buds back in as he headed toward an old black Mustang in need of a paint job.

"Off!" he barked at a black bird sitting on the car's roof, then shook his fist as it took flight.

Guess it left a present. As I snickered, a blonde girl from my Spanish class passed me. "Hey, school's canceled," I told her. "Some kind of a bomb threat."

"A bomb?" Her eyes widened. "Thanks for letting me know."

While she hurried back toward her car, I tried to recall her name. Sarah? No Shannon? Something like that. I could name every girl on my soccer team, but outside of that realm, I wasn't the best at remembering names.

"Nara," someone called out when I opened my car door.

Sitting in the long line of cars exiting the school, my friend Lainey leaned out her window, her auburn hair swirling in the wind. She held up her cell phone and a couple seconds later my cell beeped with a text. *I'll call you later.*

I waved, then climbed into my car, welcoming the lingering heat to chase away the chill in the air.

As I set my sunglasses on the rubber mat on my dash, I glanced in the rearview mirror. The guy was still standing beside his Mustang. *He's not looking at you.* But when I pulled out of the parking lot and his attention followed my direction, I glanced away from the mirror, worry echoing in my mind. *He knows I'm the one who called.*

~

SETTING my backpack on our coffee table, I grabbed the remote and clicked on the TV. Our school was the "breaking" news and a blonde reporter held a mic in front of our principal.

"Principal Wallum, can you give us an update?"

Mr. Wallum pushed his thick, black-rimmed glasses up on his bulbous nose and squinted at the bright camera light. "A bomb tip was called in at five this morning—"

"So it wasn't a bomb threat then. Someone tipped the police off?"

My cell phone started ringing Dokken's *Alone Again,* and I turned the TV down, then quickly dug through my backpack.

Emailing and texting were my mom's main form of communication, so hearing the ring tone instead of a text message ping was surprising. Mom cared about my grades and which colleges I was thinking of applying to. Otherwise she depended on me to keep myself together, because...I always had. She had no idea I had my own way of coping. No one did. (Well, except Gran Corda, my seventy-eight-year-old semi-lucid grand aunt, who sequesters herself in a retirement home and has this to say about her name: "*Corda's short for Cordial. I—I mean Cordelia. Or maybe it's Corduroy. Wait, it's....well, hell's bells...I can't remember.*" I'd confided in Gran the year my dreams first started, thinking, "There, I've told *someone*. She'll forget the moment I walk out the door." Oddly, that was one thing she never forgot.)

Pushing my cell phone to my ear, I glanced at the TV. "Hey, Mom."

"Inara, I just heard the news. Where are you?"

The shakiness in her voice startled me. Mom was always in control.

"Inara?"

"I'm fine. They sent us home before school even started."

"I'm glad you're safe." She exhaled, then cleared her throat before her tone went back to the steady one I was used to.

"They said on the news that a student might've planted the bomb."

My eyes darted back to the screen, where Mr. Wallum was nervously adjusting his bowtie. He always looked like he'd stepped right out of a dusty old library book. "Seriously? I haven't had a chance to listen to the news."

"They found an explosive rigged to detonate inside one of the school lockers. Thank God it was caught before school started."

I winced. The thought that a student could've been blown to bits made my stomach queasy. Not to mention all the other people who might've gotten hurt. My instincts had been right. "Yeah. Me too." I turned off the TV and tension released between my shoulders.

"Well, I'm due in another meeting," Mom started to say when my phone beeped.

"That's Lainey calling. See you later." Clicking over, I switched ears as I flopped onto our tartan-patterned couch that desperately needed to be updated to something from this decade. "Hey."

"Did you hear the news? About the bomb?" Lainey sounded breathless.

"Yeah, I just saw—"

"Ohmygoditwasinthelockerrightnexttomine! My dad said they're investigating a couple of suspects. Both are people from school. Can you believe it? I want to kiss whoever called in that tip. I could be in a billion pieces right now!"

Smirking, I blew her a silent kiss. Lainey had been my best friend since she walked up to me on the first day of middle school and announced, "Hi, I'm Lainey O'Neal and we're going to be besties, I just know it." That's what I loved about Lainey. If she wanted something, she marched in and *made* it happen. Rejection/failure didn't compute. Not only had she given me my nickname, Nara, but she'd always been a great source of information. When it came to the latest news, she knew the scoop, since her father was a Central Virginia police officer.

"That was a close call," I agreed.

"No freakin' joke. Dad said that anyone within fifteen feet of that locker could've been killed or seriously injured."

"Good news all the way around then. Since school's out, I guess that means practice is cancelled too," I said.

"Nope. Miranda just called. Coach talked to Principal Wallum about practice. Even though the fall soccer program isn't 'officially' part of the school, Mr. Wallum loves that we're undefeated, so he said we could use one of the back fields furthest from the main building while the police conducted their investigation."

Miranda always conveniently forgot to pass on team news to me. As team captain, she hated that I sometimes ignored her "orders" at practice. I didn't like the sway she seemed to have over my teammates (they were the hive-mind to her queen bee). But right now I didn't have time to be annoyed. I hadn't really thought through what having a "surprising day" would be like. I'd just liked the *idea* of it. I curled my fingers tight around the cell.

The bomb incident in my dream had woken me before I could see how my day would turn out. Once the disaster was averted, I'd planned to ride out the remaining few hours in the predictable confines of my home, where the biggest surprises were when Mom would be home and what we'd have for dinner. That would've been a novelty. But now I was going to have to play soccer? *Be calm. It's just practice. Not a game with more on the line. You'll be back to your old self tomorrow.*

"You there, Nara? My dad says it's safe to practice."

"Yeah, I'm here." *Silently freaking out.*

"The football team will be practicing in the back fields, too," she sing-songed.

Lainey liked to tease me about Jared Polenski. I'd been crushing on the blond quarterback since last year. Well, me and every other girl in school. "Just because I watch him practice doesn't mean he's even aware I exist."

"He's seen us there checking the team out, and I heard him say you're tall."

Five eight isn't that *tall.* "Great, he thinks I'm an Amazon."

"Actually, he said you're tall for a soccer player. Just

pointing out that he knows you're that *star goalie,* who never lets a ball get past—oh, that's Sophia calling. Gotta go. See you at four."

Star goalie, who never lets a ball get past.

If Lainey only knew the truth.

CHAPTER 2

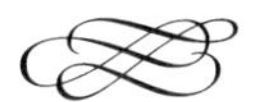

You know that feeling of déjà vu people talk about? I live it. Every. Single. Day. I've dreamed my entire next day since I was seven, so it just became a part of me, like the small scar on my forehead, the dimple on my left cheek and my wide smile.

It's not like I can predict the future or try to win the lottery. That's not how my dreams work. I only dream about things *I* will personally experience in my life…well, a day before they actually happen. That's it. I just get one day ahead. Which sometimes makes life pretty routine and predictable, but there's also an upside. Imagine knowing you're going to have a bad hair day, or that you'll burn the toast for the eighty-zillionth time, or that Mount Everest will appear on the tip of your nose a half hour after lunch. That's when a ponytail, cereal and Benzoyl Peroxide come in handy.

Knowing what's coming can be reassuring somehow. Not to mention, it sure helps with exams, dealing with friend stuff, and definitely playing soccer goalie. Who wouldn't want to know which direction the ball would be kicked *before* it left the player's foot?

I've lived with this odd gift for nine years now, which hasn't always been easy. There've been times when I've woken in tears from a friend's betrayal or been crushed by a slam from a boy I thought was the cutest guy in the entire middle school. "Nara likes me? She's a dog." I'd overheard him tell his friend outside the boys' bathroom.

Growing up, I often choose to avoid the unpleasant stuff I know is coming. Avoiding situations doesn't stop them from happening, but the "out of sight/out of mind" concept mostly works for me. Every once in a while, though, I've challenged a dream.

When I was eight, I'd dreamed that a boy I really liked had given another girl in our class a heart-shaped box of chocolates. All he'd given me was a lousy punch-out Valentine card. As soon as I'd woken that morning, I'd desperately rubbed my Magic Crystal Ball (a birthday present from Aunt Sage, who was clueless about my gift).

"Will he really give her that heart box of candy?" I'd asked the shiny ball. Digital words spelled out across the surface in reply, "Not sure, try again". I immediately rubbed it again and got "Concentrate and ask once more". One more vigorous scrub gave me, "Try again later". So frustrating! At school that day, instead of going to the bathroom to avoid witnessing the hurtful scene, I'd stayed and hoped. And had my heart ripped apart all over again.

My dreams had never been wrong.

Not once.

Which was why today was so out of the norm. I didn't usually change the course of things for people around me. I'd tried once when I was seven, not long after my dreams began. In my dream, a girl named Sadie had fallen from the monkey bars and broken her arm. The next day, as Sadie sprinted off toward the monkey bars, I caught up with her and asked her to do chalk drawings on the asphalt. In my dream, I didn't think much of the over-the-fence "homerun" baseball that had bounced across the asphalt and rolled to a stop in the grass. I'd been too busy watching the teachers hover over Sadie after she'd fallen. But that day, instead of bouncing innocuously, the baseball had clipped Sadie in the head.

Sadie didn't come to school the next day. Instead, she was in the hospital with a blood clot on her brain. I blamed myself for not paying attention to the details. If I had, Sadie wouldn't have had to suffer through brain surgery. The hardest part was wanting to apologize to her but not being able to.

After that experience, any "adaptations" I'd made had been strictly stuff that affected me. And even those weren't often. I'd learned the hard way that altering an event *could* affect how the rest of my day was supposed to unfold. Knowing what was coming—even if I didn't like it—was better than *not* knowing what would happen if I changed something. Avoidance worked for me. But last night was the first time a dream had left me with only one choice.

My dream started out just like any other day—full of screeching tires and normal "I'm running right up until the bell" annoyances...

It's three minutes 'til second bell, and I'm in such a hurry that I rush into the school bathroom and accidentally pick the stall with the lock that never works. Of course I'd pulled on the jeans with the stupid zipper tab that sometimes gets turned sideways. I always have to fiddle with it in order to unzip it. *Not now.* I grind my teeth and flick at the dang metal tab, hoping to get it to cooperate.

After thirty frustrating seconds of flicking, I vow to cut the "jeans of torture" up the moment I get home.

Someone shuts the stall door next to mine. "I'm at school. Where else would I be?"

Still attacking my zipper, I roll my eyes and wonder, *Why do people talk on their cells while in the bathroom? Eww.*

"Yeah, no one's around. What's up? You sound weird. Wha—What'd you say?"

I pause my zipper attack.

"You're serious? Why are you doing this?" she hisses.

A deeper voice comes through the phone, louder now, but I can't make out the guy's words.

"I thought you were blowing off steam last night, bullshitting with Jay and Kurt." Her voice lowers. "Just cause you're pissed at the principal isn't a reason to rig a frakkin' bomb in the school."

God, no! A bomb? My urgent need to go evaporates and my

hands start to tremble. I grip my waistband tight as the guy's voice rumbles, sounding harsher. I strain to hear what he says, but my heart is thudding too loud.

The girl is Lila Jenkins. I recognize her "frakkin" comment. She's a Science Fiction fangirl to the point she even bleached her hair blonde and cut it short like her favorite TV show character. Lila also dates David Donaldson, who was recently expelled for beating up a sophomore because the guy had the nerve to take "his" parking space.

"I won't rat you out. Don't you threaten me, asshole. Everybody in this school's a jerkoff anyway. I'm going out to my car until the fireworks are over. That is far enough away, isn't it?"

A couple seconds later, she flips the phone closed and mumbles, "Idiot" with a heavy sigh.

I clench my jaw and wait for her to discover my presence. By the time she bypasses my stall, I'm so anxious my teeth are hurting. As soon as the bathroom door closes behind her, I count to ten and then burst out of my stall in a full run…only to jerk awake at four this morning.

I didn't bother flipping a coin. Instead, I quickly got dressed, then went hunting for a nearly extinct species—a payphone.

CHAPTER 3

"Don't forget to make that eye doctor appointment, Nara." Miranda wagged her finger toward me as she and Sophia walked down the hall. Sophia snickered, briefly pausing in front of me to cover one eye and squint through the other one, pretending to read an eye chart. "I see…a G, an O, an A, an L and an S."

"Trying to get your own stand-up TV spot, Soph?" I called after my teammates as they continued on their way, "Yesterday was a fluke," I finished as I opened my locker.

Sophia snorted, wrinkling her freckled nose. Miranda cast a captain-like "it'd better be" look, then turned away. Her dark, choppy hair flipped out in all directions—thanks to gobs of pomade. It also never moved an inch. I knew this for a fact, because her hair always looked the exact same *after* practice as it did before. Made me wonder how she got her fingers through the concrete mass to shampoo it.

Sifting through the stack of books in my locker, I jerked out texts for upcoming classes. My teammates had teased me mercilessly yesterday for missing so many balls during practice, but Miranda and Sophia had been the worst. "But Nara, you're so perrrrfect. You never miss," they hissed.

Sophia had especially enjoyed mocking me over and over. Once that girl sensed weakness, she circled like a vulture, ready to peck you *beyond* death. Neither of them would let up anytime soon. At least not until I proved I was back to my old "never let a ball find its way to the back of the net" self, which I was pretty sure Sophia secretly hated as much as Miranda secretly resented.

I tried to refocus on the positive. It was good to get back to my routine. Even though I'd woken feeling drained (an annoying downside of dreaming one's *entire* next day), my dream had also left me feeling tense and upset. People crowded around chitchatting, throwing paper balls and yelling down the hall to each other, but my thoughts were elsewhere. The stricken look on my mom's face in my dream kept replaying over and over in my mind. I hadn't seen emotion like that since I was five.

In my dream, the phone rings around seven in the evening. I pause stirring through a bowl of trail mix for random peanuts and briefly glance at the caller ID. It's a D.C. area code. We don't know anyone in Washington, so I ignore it.

"Inara." Mom fusses and walks from the living room into the kitchen. Shaking her head at my laziness, she scoops up the handset. "Hello?"

Her friendly smile fades and the look on her face gives away the caller's identity as she grabs the counter.

No way. The kitchen stool scrapes as I jump up, every nerve on high alert. *What does he want?* "Mom?"

"Why are you calling, Jonathan?"

My dad, the lowlife who'd walked out on us when I was five, is suddenly calling after eleven years of complete silence? I'm fire and ice, furious and cool. My only memory of him is a hazy collage of images: strong arms hugging me close, a big hand palming my whole head and smiling green eyes framed by dark eyebrows.

My mom's light blue eyes tear up as she glances my way. She presses the phone harder to her ear. "Inara's here. She's fine." Her voice quavers slightly and she shakes her head, running trembling fingers through her blonde chin-length hair. "She's perfectly safe."

Hurt flits across her face and my chest tightens. He didn't

ask about her. He asked about me. My hands begin to shake. I worry Mom will slip back into the near catatonic state she'd wallowed in after he'd left us—the rapid weight loss, endless insomnia and twice-weekly visits to her therapist. She didn't stop wearing her wedding ring until I was twelve.

I'd always thought that if something had happened to him, like if he'd been killed in a car accident, that would've been easier for my mom to deal with.

Mom doesn't demand to know why he left us. Instead, she calmly says, "Please don't call here again." But the moment she hangs up, she bursts into deep, heart-wrenching sobs. I want to hug her, but I know she'll pull away. I refuse to ask what my dad wanted. I don't care. All I could do was helplessly stare in frozen fury.

The moment I opened my eyes this morning, sadness had kicked in. After my dad left, Mom pulled away…until the early memories of her kissing me on the forehead, singing while brushing my hair and snuggling close to read me a story had faded like rock-skipping ripples dissipating in a pond. Mom was as smooth as glass now. She never hugged me. Never showed any emotion, yet I knew she loved me. I thought Mom was impervious, indestructible even, but now I knew that wasn't true. Dad's desertion had left us suspended. On Pause. And all it took was one call to rewind us eleven years.

Tired as usual, I reached for the quarter on my nightstand and instantly thought of my Gran. Mom didn't visit her mother's older sister. She claimed spending time with Corda was a sad reminder of her own mother, who'd died in a car accident with my grandfather when I was a baby. Instead, Mom sent me a few times a year as the family envoy. It was during one of my visits when I was thirteen that I'd complained about my gift.

"There just aren't ever any surprises, Gran."

Gran's wiry eyebrows shot up under puffy gray hair. "What about when you do something different than what happens in your dreams?" she asked as she shoved a couple of rainbow colored gummy worms into a potted plant.

"I think it's going into sugar shock," I said, nodding to the plant's droopy leaves. She'd ignored me and added another worm. Sighing, I answered her question. "It's not the same. Then I *know* I'm going against my dream. Anyway, you know I rarely do that, which means…there are never any unknowns."

"Ha, you think so?" Gran set the bag of gummy worms down, then pulled something out of the pocket of her light blue cardigan sweater. She always wore a cardigan, no matter the time of the year. Her green eyes glistened as she held the quarter up. "Sugar high money", she said with glee. The retirement home vending machines only took quarters. Shuffling over to her desk, she slowly lowered her petite frame into a straight-backed chair. She made a show of flipping the coin, then set it on her desk where she covered it with a piece of paper.

I gestured toward it as she rubbed the quarter's face on the paper with a pencil. "I knew you were going to do that."

"Smarty Pants." Gran made a face and hunched around her rubbing. When she was done, she quickly tucked the folded paper in her cardigan pocket.

"I knew you were going to do that too."

"So, what does it say?" Gran gave me a hoity-toity look (at least that's what she'd call it) "Heads or tails?"

I shrugged. "You didn't tell me in my dream."

Satisfaction flitted across her thin, deeply-lined face. "And I won't tell until the next time I see you. That's *one* thing you don't know about today, Inara Collins."

When Gran was lucid, her insight was razor sharp. As I sat in the morning light, worrying that my Dad would make a random, utterly useless call after all these years, I rubbed the quarter between my fingers. Taking a breath, I thumbed it into the air. Heads meant YES and Tails meant NO.

Slapping the coin between my palms, I slid it from my hand onto my nightstand and covered it with paper from the 3x3 paper cube next to my hand-painted jewelry box. After I'd made my "blind" pencil rubbing, I brushed the quarter into my nightstand drawer, then quickly folded the paper into fourths.

While sliding the folded paper into its slot in my backpack, I realized I didn't have one from yesterday, since I'd rushed off to find a payphone. Now, I desperately wanted to pull the new rubbing out and look at it, but I held off. The question I'd asked of the coin was always the same, *Should I act on something I'd dreamed about?*

As I grew older I'd given Gran's coin-toss a dual purpose. It became my way of asking for an unbiased opinion, even though I never looked at the answer until the following morning. I still wanted at least one tiny thing about my day to be "unknown".

Glancing at the hammered metal wastebasket beside my nightstand, I worried my lip with my teeth. The basket was full of past paper rubbings; every single one was Tails. I hadn't acted on my dreams in so long, it had made sense that they were all Tails. Like the coin agreed with me. But was it possible I'd somehow subconsciously controlled the outcome? If I'd taken the time yesterday morning to flip the quarter, would the rubbing have been Heads?

An image of my sobbing mom reappeared in my mind. I glared at my backpack. "If Tails is on that paper, I'll eat it," I snarled before grabbing the cordless phone and punching the Talk button.

Silence. Had someone left the phone off the hook? "Hello?" I hung up, but before I turned the phone back on, I closed my eyes and tried to visualize the DC phone number from my dream. As all ten digits quickly flashed through my mind, I wrote the phone number on the paper cube. Turning the phone back on, I waited for the dial tone.

"Don't," an eerie whisper threaded through the crackling across the line.

A cold, heavy chill prickled my skin and the tiny hairs around my face began to cling to my skin as if drawn by a magnet. Brushing them away, I immediately punched the End button.

Three seconds passed before I got up the nerve to turn it back on. Oppressiveness still tugged at me, but at least a normal dial tone rang in my ear. I didn't like this newfound guilt that had me imagining weird voices and heavy, cold chills.

My conscience could take a hike. I wasn't letting my mom go through that. Better to have an emotionally distant parent than an emotionally wrecked one. Been there, done that. Squaring my shoulders, I dialed the phone company.

As I pretended to be my mom, unease clung to me like a nauseating perfume. I kept glancing over my shoulder, half-expecting Mom to catch me in the act when I told the operator we were tired of receiving telemarketing calls and I wanted to put a block on all unsolicited calls. After I gave a list of approved phone numbers, I hung up and felt much better. The guilt, worry…whatever it was, had completely disappeared.

At least I'd prevented one tragedy today, even if I couldn't stop the other, considering it had already happened. This afternoon, after fourth period, Lainey would rush up to share the latest gossip. In my dream and even now, the news left my heart heavy with regret and deserved guilt.

Wham. A heavy thump jerked me out of my musings just as something banged my locker door. As the door swung wildly toward me, I reached up to stop it at the same time a hand landed on mine.

"Sorry." Apologetic blue eyes sought mine as the loner guy's hand fell away. "My elbow caught your door."

I eyed the pile of books he'd just dumped onto his locker's metal floor. "Why'd you move lockers?"

"My old locker's been confiscated."

"Confiscated?"

His longish-bangs partially covered his eyes with his nod. "My locker had the bomb in it."

Oh. My. God. "No way! That must've freaked you out."

Pushing his shoe against the tumble of books, he shut his locker door, then tucked a book and notepad under his arm. "No biggie."

"You could've…died." I was babbling, but I couldn't help thinking, *I saved this guy's life yesterday.*

"It's all good. I'm Ethan Harris. You're Nara, right? I think we're in History and Trig together."

I was so thrown off by the fact this entire conversation with him was: one, happening at all, and two, *new* to me, that all I could think to say was, "Yes. Nara."

His eyebrow shot up. "Nara of the no last name?"

He must think I'm a total moron. "Oh, it's Collins. Inara Collins."

"In-ara. I've never heard that name before."

The way my name rolled off his tongue, that deep baritone enunciating each syllable, made my stomach flutter and my heart thump. "My parents intentionally picked a rare name." How lame was that? Why couldn't I have come up with some great philosophical reason?

I missed what he said because the first bell rang. The noise in the hall grew louder and everyone scattered like ants. When a football player zoomed by, bumping Ethan from behind, I realized Ethan's shoulders were almost as wide as the other guy's.

Ethan didn't spare him a glance. Instead, he suddenly zoned as if he were seeing something else instead of me. As he rubbed his left forearm, I could tell he was miles from the locker hall.

"Ethan?"

He blinked, but his gaze remained hyper-focused.

I touched his arm. "Are you okay?"

For a split-second, a face flashed, a lightning blip featuring a gaping maw and…long teeth. Gasping, I pulled away. "Did you see that?"

Ethan's attention snapped back to me. "See what?"

I seriously doubted I could explain it. Maybe what I saw was just in my own mind. "You, uh…kind of zoned out."

"Sorry." Ethan tilted his head and the right corner of his lip lifted in a grim half-smile. "I just remembered I have a test today."

That was some pretty intense zone-age over a forgotten test. Then again, I was hearing voices and seeing things. Who was I to judge "normal" behavior?

The hall was clearing and I was finally able to talk without screaming. "I'd better go. Good luck on your test."

"Thanks. See you in History."

As he walked away, I stared after his long stride. Yesterday, the people I'd saved had been faceless. Today, at least one had a face, making me doubly glad I'd called the police. Ethan seemed like a nice enough guy. He might seem intense, but the way he kept to himself didn't mesh with the kind of behavior that usually got someone kicked out of school. What could he have possibly done to get expelled?

~

HISTORY CLASS WAS RIGHT next door to Homeroom, so I always got there before most everyone else. Pulling out my thick History book, I opened to the section we'd be lectured on today. I never studied (at least not for any school subjects. Teaching myself Latin was a whole other story), but I needed to at least "appear" studious, considering I had a 99% average. Once my desk was set up, I turned to the important stuff—jotting down notes about the rest of my day.

When I couldn't find my purple ballpoint pen, I remembered that I'd used it to write down the phone number on the Caller ID from my dream—just in case the phone company wouldn't let me block *all* unsolicited calls. My favorite pen was on my nightstand instead of where it would normally be, sitting in the third slot in my backpack.

Frowning at the empty slot, I began to dig deep into the bottom of my backpack, even though I knew I wouldn't find a pen. I hated loose pens, change or anything for that matter, rolling around in the bottom of my backpack. I had a pencil, but writing a note on my hand was impossible with No. 2 lead.

I was frantically searching every single zipper, pocket and crevice in my backpack when someone set a blue pen on my desk and kept on walking.

I watched Ethan take his seat at the back of the classroom and open his notepad. He didn't look up or acknowledge what he'd done in any way. Instead, he retrieved a pencil from inside the pad's spiral binding and immediately began to run the dark lead across the paper, completely engrossed.

The blue ink slid across my skin like silk as I wrote the couple of things I wanted to recall on my palm. I never wrote down answers to test questions. My dreams always seared those into my memory. Mostly I just noted other stuff that I didn't want to forget or situations I wanted to avoid. Like coming out of third period today and seeing Lainey whisper something in Jared's ear as he grabbed her around the waist. She *had* stayed after practice yesterday to watch the football players. I'd felt so crappy after letting so many shots into the goal that I'd just gone home.

I wrote two things:

Take long way to 4th pd.

Send flowers.

Curling my fingers closed, I looked up to see Ethan watching me, pencil paused over his paper. I'd never seen him with a pen. From what I could recall, he'd always used a pencil, which meant he knew I was looking for my pen, because…

He'd watched me write on my hand every day.

AFTER THIRD PERIOD, Lainey ran up to me in the hallway, swinging her cowhide designer bag over her shoulder. "There you are. Why'd you go this way?"

When I shrugged, offering no reason, Lainey didn't even notice. Her brown eyes were brimming with anticipation. "Did you hear about, Lila—"

A couple of guys brushed past, one speaking to the other in a loud voice, as if his buddy were across the room instead of right next to him. "What'd you want to do this Friday?"

I frowned after them. "Why's Aaron screaming?"

"I heard him telling someone that he was wearing his headphones yesterday when a high-pitched sound squealed. He said it hurt so much he almost passed out."

I winced. "Ouch."

Lainey pointed to her ear. "Temporary hearing loss. Aaron swears it was interference from an airplane zooming over." Spinning her hand in an impatient circle, she said, "Anyway, did you hear what happened to her?"

My heart hammered like crazy, but I tried to remain calm and not let the guilt show on my face. "Who?"

"Lila Jenkins." Lainey drew closer. "She was admitted to Jefferson hospital last night. Supposedly, she was pretty roughed up and they don't expect her to come back to school for a couple weeks."

Despite my attempt to remain cool, tears burned behind my eyelids. Hearing about Lila all over again only made my guilt ratchet higher. I blinked rapidly to hold my tears back and wished our school didn't have a policy against wearing sunglasses inside. "Do they know who did that to her?"

"Nope. Which brings me to the other news. They arrested David Donaldson for planting the bomb."

"David Donaldson?" I squinted, pretending to remember who he was. "Didn't he get expelled for beating up that guy over a parking spot?"

"Yeah. Lila was dating David." Lainey flipped her wavy red hair over her shoulder. The morning mist had totally ruined her flatiron straightening efforts. "Makes me wonder if she's the one who tipped off the police and that's why she got beat up."

"But you said David's been arrested. Who beat her then?" I desperately hoped that for once my dream was wrong and the police had actually arrested the person responsible for attacking Lila.

Lainey lifted her shoulder, then popped a big pink bubble. "My dad said Lila's refusing to talk about it." Glancing at the students milling around us, she leaned in and whispered, "The police originally suspected that the bomber might be that new guy, since the bomb was in his locker. Plus, the tipper said the person responsible had been expelled."

My eyes bugged. *I meant expelled at* this *school!* I began to cough. I might've saved the new guy's life, but I'd also accidentally pegged him as the bomber.

Lainey pounded my back. "You okay? You choke on your gum or something?"

"I'm good," I croaked and waved for her to continue.

"Turns out David had bomb parts in the back of his car." Snorting, Lainey rolled her eyes. "I knew that creep wasn't right in the head. Can you believe he almost blew up our school?"

I was too busy mentally freaking over the realization that in the conversation I'd had with Lainey in my dream, she hadn't mentioned anything about Ethan. Not the fact that his locker had the bomb in it, nor that he'd been a suspect for a brief time. Just like my whole interchange with Ethan in the hall and him giving me that pen. Things were happening that I wasn't expecting.

Why had none of this stuff shown up in my dream? Trying to muddle through it was making my head hurt, so I changed the subject. "How was football practice?"

Lainey looked away, suddenly interested in the two guys arm wrestling across a table against the wall. "Entertaining as always." After a couple seconds, her attention shifted back to me. "I swear all they do is try to kill each other."

"Did you talk to anyone?" *God, I was so asking to have this rubbed in my face.*

"Just the usual. Miranda and Sophia know the guys on the team better than I do."

Uh huh. Normally Lainey would've followed that sentence with, "You should've come with us." I only tolerated Miranda and Sophia because of Lainey, but it was very telling that she didn't seem to miss me yesterday. At least I knew where she stood on truthfulness between friends.

The bell rang, ending our five-minute break. Even with Lainey standing beside me, I suddenly felt very alone. Sophia walked past us, squinting as if she was having a hard time seeing. *Nice.* "I guess I'd better head off to Biology."

"Drop it, Soph," Lainey called after the curly-haired blonde. Glancing at me, she waved after Sophia. "Don't let her or any of the other girls get to you, Nara. None of them could do a better job as goalie and they know it."

Her comment should've made me feel better, but it didn't. In the past, Lainey always had my back and visa versa. In some ways, I felt she still did, but a part of her seemed to be pulling away—and I didn't know how to get her back.

AFTER A MUCH IMPROVED SOCCER PRACTICE, I sat in my car and checked my cell messages. Aunt Sage had left me a voicemail.

"Inara, sweetie, I heard about your school on the news. How terrifying. I'm glad everything turned out okay and you and your friends are safe. Stop by and see me sometime soon. Miss you."

I sent a text back. *Will do. Miss you too.* Aunt Sage might be my dad's sister, but unlike my father, she'd never stopped caring about our family. Whereas my mom was like the eye of the hurricane—eerily calm and solid in an intangible sort of way—Aunt Sage was the tempest raging all around you. She thrust herself into your life, pulling you into a tight hug before you even had a chance to say, "Welcome to my personal space."

Once I left school, I stopped by a florist. Moisture and perfumed scents hung in the air as I browsed the floral arrangements on display in the tiny shop.

"Can I help you with something?" A young, mousy-faced guy in a green apron droned as he leaned on his elbows across the main counter.

I pointed to the bouquet of wild flowers sitting in the refrigerated case. "I'd like to send those to someone at Jefferson Hospital."

He slowly straightened as if undraping himself from the counter was the last thing he wanted to do. "Do you want them delivered today?"

When I nodded, he lifted a small card and envelope from a plastic holder near the register, setting them on the counter. "Our delivery truck will be leaving in a half hour. Fill the card out and I'll wrap the flowers."

While he pulled the vase from the case, then began to wrap the sides to protect the flowers, my pen hovered over the card. It's not like I was going to sign my name. Finally, I just wrote in indistinguishable print, *I'm sorry. Get well soon* and slipped the card inside the envelope. On the outside, I wrote her name, *Lila Jenkins*.

Setting the wrapped vase on the counter, the guy picked up the envelope I'd just sealed and said in a bored tone, "Will that be cash, check or charge?"

I pulled my checkbook out of my backpack, waving it. I'd have to do extra chores around the house to earn the money to put back in my account, but I didn't care. Sending the flowers lessened my guilt a little.

As I drove home, a part of me was still angry that Lila would've let the bomb go off in the school without warning anyone, but I felt bad about what had happened to her. I never thought how my efforts to save others could've caused Lila to get hurt. In my dream David *had* threatened her when he thought she might rat him out. He might be in jail, but someone had taken his anger out on her. Did it have anything to do with what she knew?

And then there was Ethan. I'd saved lives yesterday, but in the process my phone tip had led the police to him. What if they hadn't found the bomb parts in David's car?

When I turned my car down our tree-lined street—currently an October kaleidoscope of burnt oranges, reds, yellows and deep purples—a concept we'd learned in Physics came back to me with a whole new meaning. *To every action there is an equal and opposite reaction.* Had anyone ever considered applying Newton's 3rd Law of Motion on a metaphysical level? From small actions, other things could happen.

Terrible, unexpected things.

CHAPTER 4

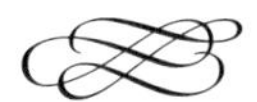

The next morning I woke up feeling refreshed and… completely terrified. Not because some new catastrophe was going to happen, but because I couldn't remember my dream.

My t-shirt crackled with electricity as I shoved my covers away and grabbed the purple pen on my nightstand. I held it poised over my open palm, hoping the familiar ritual would kick my mind into gear. Several seconds passed.

Nothing. Not even a glimmer of a memory.

Ugh. Throwing the pen across the room, I retrieved the blue pen Ethan had given me from my backpack. With a calm breath, I touched the pen to my skin and closed my eyes, beckoning inspiration.

When I opened them, only one word was written on my palm.

Ethan.

A sheen of sweat rose on my skin. Why did *his* name pop up when nothing else came to me? As cool morning air blew against my feverish body, I shivered and whispered, "I didn't dream. At all." And I had two tests and a game today.

My gaze snagged on my backpack and a glimmer of hope lifted my spirits. "Maybe at least one thing will go right," I mumbled. Pulling out the folded piece of paper I'd rubbed yesterday before I blocked my dad from calling, I slowly unfolded it.

Tails! So much for believing all those Tails papers might somehow have been because I influenced the coin's outcome. Fisting my hand around the piece of paper, I crumpled it into a tiny ball, then shoved it in my mouth. *How dare it tell me I shouldn't have interfered.* I chewed with a vengeance. As the paper quickly soaked up my spit, I swiped the ever-present quarter from my nightstand. *What a bunch of crap!* Spitting the wad onto the coin, I tossed them both into the trash. "You don't get an opinion anymore."

Once the quarter wound its way through the mound of Tails papers, hitting the metal bottom with a final plink, I blinked at the trashcan.

An entire day of unknowns? My chest squeezed. Maybe I could crawl under the covers and pretend to have the flu. Several serious seconds of consideration followed, but I had to go to school. No one else was trained as goalie, not at my level. *Any* body was better than *no* body. Pushing the covers back, I murmured, "Today's going to be a total disaster."

"How's school going?" Mom asked when I flopped down at the island a half hour later to pour myself a bowl of cereal.

My fingers tightened around the box. "Fine."

Grabbing the orange juice from the fridge, Mom glanced at the door as it closed. "I see you have a game tonight."

I'd put the schedule up on the fridge several weeks before, hoping she might come. Of all the times for her to notice. She hadn't been to any of my games this year. Usually Mom and I spent our weekends together, but during the week, she worked long hours as her company's CFO, often taking business trips a couple times a month. I never saw her at the end of a financial quarter.

"Uh, yeah." I gulped. *Not tonight. Please.* "It's not a big one though."

Pouring the last of the juice into a glass, she caught my gaze. "I wish I could go, but work's—"

"It's no big deal." I said quickly, both sad and frustrated that I felt relief.

Dead silence hung between us until Mom finally spoke. "I just wanted to wish you luck." She flashed a quick smile. "Though you never seem to need it." Buttoning her suit jacket, she tried to smooth the puckered material, then frowned at the bulging bottom two buttons. "You always come out on top."

My face turned hot. She was so wrong. A half dozen unfinished projects sat in my bedroom: a papier-mâché small-scale model of the lawn area at the CVU (aka Central Virginia University, where I hoped to go to college.), a painting of my favorite playground at Hyde Park, and a hand-stained music recorder—well, the mouthpiece part at least. Another dozen projects took up space in my closet. I loved starting new projects, but quickly lost interest. When I saw myself working on my brand new project in my dreams, the excitement and newness quickly wore off.

Everything was always a do-over. I might be successfully teaching myself Latin—Yey, me. I translate web documents in a language no one speaks just for fun—but doubt always lingered in the back of my mind. Did I have any *original* talent that wasn't perfected by a repeat performance? I started to confess, "You have no idea—"

"You're just like your dad..." she spoke over me, then paused, her lips thinning as her hand fluttered to the counter.

I'd seen the beginnings of that look in my dream night before last. I started to put my hand on hers, but knew better. We were like two icicles dangling from a rooftop, residing side-by-side, but permanently frozen apart. "What's wrong?"

Her unfocused gaze shifted to the wall. "The weirdest thing happened yesterday morning. I was listening to the news station on my way to work when the radio fuzzed in and out and then music came through." Her hand curled into a fist. "It was playing the song your father and I used as our wedding song."

My stomach bottomed out. "Gotta love random music floating around on the air waves," I said in a high-pitched tone as my mind replayed my dream about my dad's call over and over in a torturous loop.

Mom's eyes turned red as if she were trying not to cry.

"What made it even stranger...the radio display flickered in and out. I could've sworn the station numbers were our wedding anniversary."

I swallowed, unsure what to say. The way she'd looked in my dream...so broken, crumbling to pieces. I'd made sure she didn't have to suffer, but sheer happenstance had toyed with her emotions anyway. Great. She might've taken her wedding ring off a few years ago, but it still sat in that stupid soap dish on the back of the kitchen sink—as if she planned to slip it back on any moment.

"You probably saw every radio station number at once because of the mountain's interference with tower signals."

Mom straightened her shoulders and gave a wry smile. "Probably true, but yesterday would've been our twentieth wedding anniversary."

I'd *totally* forgotten the date.

Before I could respond, she pressed her palms to her heart-shaped face like she was hot and spoke in a lighter tone, "He was always so solid." Her cheek-touch was just a cover as she quickly swiped her fingers under her eyes, brushing away unshed tears. "You're just like him."

Yeah, so solid he'd bailed on us. I hated when she compared my dad and me. "But I have your face and hair," I insisted, tension lacing my light words. I didn't want to be *anything* like him.

The radio thing might've shaken my mom, but her smile held a determined edge. She'd bury herself deeper in work this week so she wouldn't have to think about it. I'd seen the pattern often enough.

My gaze slid to the soap dish. Mom needed more than work in her life.

"Anyway," I said lightly. "It's probably a good thing you hadn't planned to come to my game this week, since there's a 'required' parent participation night on Thursday at six."

"Required? This Thursday? Why are you just now telling me?"

Since it just occurred to me that Mr. Dixon is widowed and isn't bad looking in a tall, lanky kind of way. Plus, he has kind eyes. I shrugged. "My Spanish teacher Señor...er, I mean Mr. Dixon is having an international dinner night. I'm supposed to prepare a French dish." Not to mention, I had a feeling I was going to need the extra credit Mr. Dixon was bribing the class with to attend the event. Maybe I could score some extra points for bringing my mom.

Mom's fine blonde eyebrows shot up. "I'm expected to cook something *French*, too?"

I imagined Gran snickering in my ear, *"That'll boil her ice cream."* Meaning, in Gran's unique mashing of words, Mom wouldn't have time to think about the past, since she'd be stressing all week. Spaghetti was the *only* thing she could cook. "Yep."

"I—I'll think of something." Sighing, she turned to toss the empty orange juice carton into the trash, but paused. "Inara—" she began as she dropped the carton, then pulled a pair of jeans from the trash that were Swiss-cheesed with scissor holes. "What in the world?"

Pouring milk into my bowl, I smiled, satisfied with my revenge. "Trust me. They had it coming."

~

Worst. Day. Ever. Slamming open my locker, I quickly exchanged my Spanish book for Trig and English. As I arranged the rest of the books in my locker in order of upcoming classes, I considered the possibility I might've been cursed.

During Homeroom, Sophia gleefully shared the news that Lainey and Jared were dating. Lainey's betrayal hit so hard, bile rose to the back of my throat. Then, at the end of lunch, I found out that Miranda had convinced Coach to train Sophia as a permanent backup goalie. Miranda had Coach so wrapped. I could name at least three people who'd have made better goalies than Sophia....and one of them was in middle school. "Just a few more hours of torture to go," I mumbled.

"What'd you say?"

I jumped at the sound of Ethan's deep voice. "Oh, hi." Ethan stood to my right holding his locker door open. Instead of his usual flannel shirt, he was wearing a navy fleece that zipped at the collar. Where he'd left the zipper open, he had on a black t-shirt underneath, probably another old band tee. "I'm just having a crappy day." *That* was the understatement of my life. Going through the school day blind was sheer agony. What had I been thinking asking for a day of surprises? How did the other people walk around school everyday, never knowing who or what was about to walk up and slam them in the face?

As far as I was concerned, preparation was the key to survival. Of course, the fact that I'd probably just made a low C on my Spanish test—would've been an F without my Latin background—would normally rank as another hellish experience for today, but at least I'd anticipated that one.

Ethan nodded, his look sympathetic. "I've had a few of those."

He'd had the *ultimate* crap day recently, no thanks to me. "I heard that the police gave you a rough time, well, until they discovered David was the one who'd planted the bomb. Sorry about that."

Shrugging, he shut his locker, then pushed his dark hair out of his eyes. "Yeah, *that* day would count, but you don't need to apologize."

My throat went dry and I looked away as I shut my locker door. "Um, well, I feel bad that that even happened to you. I'm sure it's not easy being new, and then to be suspected of—"

Ethan touched my shoulder and I caught a whiff of spicy deodorant. It made my nose tingle and my heart race. "Nara. You don't need to apologize."

His expression was sincere, yet understanding, and the weight of his hand made me jittery with anticipation. Seeking a distraction, I reached into my backpack to retrieve the pen he'd given me. I didn't really want to give it up, but I pushed it toward him. "Thanks again for lending me your pen."

Folding his fingers over mine, he brushed his thumb along the arch on my palm. "You keep it."

My pulse pounded. I'd washed the ink off my hand, but Ethan had just run his finger over the exact place I'd written his name this morning. Goosebumps scattered across my skin.

"Why didn't you show up in my dream night before last?" I wanted to ask.

"I don't use pens," he continued.

"Thanks," was all I could think to say. He'd seen that I used a pen every day, but there was no way he'd carried that pen around just in case I needed one. Right?

Releasing my hand, he shifted his Trig book and notepad under his arm, then leaned against the lockers. "I was wondering...since we've got that Trig test today, would you mind being my partner during study hall? I really need someone to help clear up a couple of points for me."

Heat spread across my face. His quiet, observant personality was so different from the flirtatious, outgoing characteristics I thought made Jared so hot—yet he'd just made me feel special on a day when nothing seemed to be going right. Normally I spent most of study hall chatting with Lainey, but I wasn't in the mood to talk to her right now. Maybe if Ethan and I studied together, I'd have a sliver of hope in passing my Trig test. I smiled. "Thanks for asking. I need a refresher, too."

~

AT THE END of the day, my French teacher, Mrs. Kearney, called me over. "Hey, Nara. Since you don't have practice today, would you mind helping Kenny carry his backpack out to his car?"

As Kenny hobbled along beside me on crutches, I shoved my shades on and tried to balance my backpack strap on one shoulder and his bulging pack on the other. Glancing down at the air cast on his left ankle, I asked, "Did that happen during soccer?"

Kenny's freckled forehead wrinkled as his red eyebrows shot up. "I wish! A sports injury would make a much better story."

"What happened?"

"I tripped over my dog."

I tried not to laugh at the look of total embarrassment on his face, but my lips tilted upward anyway.

He grimaced. "I was doing some drills with the ball in the backyard. One minute Deuce was standing near the deck and the next he was under my feet."

"He doesn't chase after the ball while you practice?" When I saw Lainey's dog jumping in and nudging the ball with his nose, that made me wish for a pet even more, but my mom has allergies so I had to get my animal "fix" volunteering at the Central Virginia Animal Shelter.

"Nah. Deuce never jumps at the ball, but yesterday he yelped and was under my feet cowering. He'd moved so fast I didn't have time to react."

"He was scared?"

"Yeah. I never did figure out what spooked him." Kenny opened his back door, tossed his crutches into the backseat, then leaned on the open door for support. "He's usually fearless."

I set his backpack beside the crutches. "Well, hopefully you're not out too many games."

"Thanks for helping." His smile was sheepish. "Didn't want the guys to think I couldn't handle it by myself."

I grinned. "Now I know why Mrs. Kearney asked me to help you. What story did you tell your team?"

Kenny laughed. "They think I fell off a ladder helping my dad paint the house trim. And uh, can you keep that between us?"

I gave a conspiratorial smile. "No problem. Do you have someone to help you tomorrow?"

"I'm good. Most of my books are in my backpack now. I'll just borrow while I'm at school."

"If you change your mind, let me know." After I left Kenny, I headed out to my car—which I'd parked in the back parking lot since I'd run late for school this morning. If I'd only *known* construction crews would be doing roadwork, I'd have taken another street and only screeched in five minutes before the bell instead of one minute after.

I was halfway across the main parking lot when Lainey called my name. "Nara, wait up."

Pushing my teal sunglasses up my nose, I slowed.

Lainey fell into step beside me, her brow furrowed. "What's up with you?"

"Nothing's up. I just need to get some chores and homework done before I have to be back for the game."

Lainey grabbed my arm and pulled me to a halt. "I'm your best friend, Nara. I can tell something's wrong. You spent the entire study hall avoiding me."

I kept my tone neutral. "I had to study for my Trig test."

Lainey's brown gaze zeroed in. "Since *when* have you *ever* had to study?"

As far as she knew, that was true. I'd told Lainey I have a photographic memory, and that was as close to the truth as I was ever going to tell her.

Huffing at my silence, she continued, "You've heard the rumors going around about that guy, Nara. What's his name? Eli?"

"Ethan."

"Whatever. He's bad news. I don't think you should get tangled up with someone like that."

It's not like anything was going on, yet I had to admit, Ethan was definitely intriguing. Plus, he'd been nothing but nice to me. "I actually was studying. Not that I really think you care who I spend time with, or who I *like*. That didn't stop you from going after Jared."

The color quickly faded from Lainey's face. "Who—"

"Told me?" I stared her down. "Sophia. And she enjoyed every second of it."

Lainey's face pinched and her eyes watered. "Sophia can be so vicious sometimes. I never wanted to hurt you. Jared started flirting with me, not the other way around. Then he called me and...well, it all happened so fast. I swear I was going to tell you."

Yeah, right. I shrugged. "Whatever. I've got to go."

When I started to walk away, she called after me, "Are you mad?"

Her voice hitched, but I didn't turn around. It wasn't so much that I was mad...okay, it stung a little—actually, a lot—

but Lainey was supposed to be my best friend. She should've had the guts to tell me herself. "See you at the game."

I tried not to think about Lainey's migration away from our friendship as I shoved my key in the car's ignition and turned. Nothing happened. Could it be the battery? I reached for the radio button and turned it on. Silence. Glancing at the headlight switch, I groaned when I saw it was still in the On position. It had been foggy when I drove to school. I thought I'd turned them off, but apparently not. "We bought you for your dependability!" I accused, glaring at the unlit instrument display panel.

The parking lot was empty, except for a couple of cars. I did *not* need this. Stress built inside me. Why hadn't I dreamed last night? I would've made sure I turned my lights off. I had very little time to get home and get my stuff done, which now included *studying*, before I had to leave for the game at six. Out of desperation, I turned the ignition once more, *willing* the engine to start. When it didn't, I banged on the steering wheel and yelled, "Come on!" at the same time a car drove up beside mine.

A blond guy leaned out the passenger side window. "Need some help?"

I rolled my window down. "Do you have any jumper cables? I think my battery's dead." I tried to remember his name as I stepped out of my car. I'd seen him in my lunch period, though I didn't recognize the dark-headed guy driving.

The guy behind the steering wheel shook his head. "No, but I can give you a lift if you don't live too far from here. Then your parents can bring you back and jump your car. They always have emergency junk like that."

"My mom's not home. Thanks anyway." I started to dial my aunt's number.

"You're Nara, right? Do you have cables at home?"

"Yeah," I said, punching the End button.

"We don't mind bringing you back to jump your car." The blond guy pushed his beefy frame from the car and opened the back passenger door for me with a friendly smile.

I chewed on the inside of my cheek. I didn't really know these guys, but it was nice of them to offer. Plus, I only lived a couple miles from the school. Aunt Sage would take at least thirty minutes to get here. I really needed the extra time, especially now that I had to come back and jump-start my dead battery. "What are your names?" I asked as I leaned into my car to retrieve my backpack from the passenger seat.

Just when I'd tugged on the strap, another car drove up, the engine loud and rumbling. When wheels ground to a halt in front of my car, I glanced through my windshield to see Ethan roll down his passenger window. "Everything okay, Nara?"

Shutting my car door, I tugged my backpack over my shoulder. "I think my battery's dead."

Ethan eyed the two guys. "I can take you home. It's on my way."

The blond guy said, "Dude, we've already offered her a lift."

I glanced his way and raised my eyebrows at the slight edge in his voice. Ethan's jaw flexed as if he were clenching and unclenching his teeth. What was with guys and their need to "one up" each other? It didn't matter if they were jocks, geeks, emo or even just intense, quiet loner guys, apparently they all operated on the same basic instinct. Testosterone.

A black bird made a gronk-gronk-gronk sound from its perch on one of the parking lot lights. It almost sounded like "Trust your gut".

Ethan might be new, but I felt like I knew him better than the two boys who'd offered a ride, and I still didn't even know their names.

Locking my car door, I told them, "Since Ethan's heading in my direction, I'll catch a ride with him. Thanks for the offer though."

"Whatev," the blond said with a shrug, but he looked pissed at Ethan before he got into the car.

As I opened Ethan's passenger door, he grabbed the stack of school books from the seat and tossed them into the back. A spiral bound notebook dropped out of his hand into the front seat and flipped open, revealing an amazing drawing of a long-horned demon-like creature. I slid my shades down so I could see the detailed artwork. Sheer evil reflected on a demon's snarled face and blood dripped from its razor sharp teeth. When I saw what looked like a human foot grasped in the creature's clawed hand, I thought of that image I'd seen flash in my mind while I was talking to Ethan. It wasn't the same, but I still glanced nervously after the other guys' car pulling out of the school lot.

Ethan quickly tossed the notebook in the back along with his other stuff. "Get in, Nara."

His gaze was focused, his voice so calm that a shiver passed through me. My instincts had chosen him and I would trust them. Pushing my glasses back up my nose, I climbed inside.

He put the car in gear. "Which way to your house?"

I blinked. He'd talked like he knew which direction I lived in. Apparently, he'd said it for the blond guy's benefit. *Trust your gut, Nara.* While I gave him directions to my neighborhood, I noticed his car smelled faintly of pine and I instantly sought the hanging air freshener thingy. I smiled when I finally spied the cardboard pine tree on the floor at my feet. Ethan was an interesting throwback in many ways. Well, except for his music. An MP3 player was docked in its station in the console.

As we drove off, Ethan said, "Those two are dangerous. Don't trust anything they say, and whatever you do, stay away from them."

The guys didn't appear to know Ethan, yet Ethan didn't casually say "they're trouble" or "they're a couple of jerks". He'd said something very specific. *Those two are dangerous.* At least that explained why he lied to them. "How do you know them?"

Ethan gunned his car onto the main road, tires squealing. His hand cinched around the steering wheel. "Let's just say I've seen them in action."

"What did you see them do?"

"Trust me, Nara. Just promise, okay?"

Ethan appeared on edge, like he *needed* to hear me answer "yes". "I promise," I quickly said, then waited for him to tell me what he'd seen, but he kept his gaze on the road.

After a couple minutes, his shoulders relaxed and the deep brackets around his mouth disappeared. As he turned onto my street, he said casually, "I think it's cool that Inara means shining or illumination."

"You looked up my name?" I said as I pointed out my house. Ethan had this knack for leaving me breathless and teetering. Like a chair tilted on two legs, I was never sure if I was going to topple over or land on solid ground. I realized I *liked* this unsettled feeling of exploring the unknown. At least with Ethan.

Pulling into my driveway, he nodded. "It also means 'ray of light'. I like that one better."

Completely floored, I just stared. I'd never heard that meaning for my name, and it sounded like he'd just given me a compliment. I think. "I, um—"

"Do you have some cables?"

"What?" My mind was still spinning as his car idled in my driveway.

He gestured to the garage door. "Jumper cables."

"Oh, right! Cables." I opened the car door and scooted out. "Be right back."

He probably thinks I'm a total dork. I punched in the code to open the door, then grabbed the cables off the top of the utility shelf.

"What year is your car?" I asked once I'd climbed back into his rumbling Mustang.

"Old enough to know better."

"But she does it anyway," I finished with a grin.

He tapped the dashboard. "It's a '69. She might need a new topcoat, but her engine's pristine and she's dependable. I plan to drive her 'til the wheels fall off."

When he put his hand on the headrest behind me and turned to back out of the driveway, the faded scar on the side of his neck, just below his jaw, caught my attention. What had happened to him?

"Have you always lived in Blue Ridge?" I asked, hoping he'd share something about himself.

He pressed on the gas, moving down the street. "No, I'm originally from Chicago, then we lived in Michigan for a couple of years. This small college town took some getting used to, but I like it now."

I nodded. "I love living in the valley with the mountains all around us. I also like that it only takes twenty minutes to get from one side of town to the other, but yeah, I wish we had midnight movies and a big shopping mall. Those are definite downsides in Blue Ridge. What made you decide to move here?"

Flicking on his blinker, he turned out of my neighborhood. "My brother asked if I wanted to live with him." He shrugged like it was no big deal. "So I moved."

What would that be like, not living with a parent? "How much older is your brother?"

"Samson's five years older."

"Samson's an unusual name, too." I smiled and wondered if the brothers looked anything alike.

"Yeah, he's the strong one."

Even though his comment carried an ironic, self-deprecating edge, it also held affection. *He and his brother must be close*. But it seemed strange his parents let him move in with a sibling only a few years older. We'd entered the school's parking lot, and I was a little disappointed the trip was so short. I was finally getting to know a little about him. "So, you didn't like Michigan?"

A guarded look shuttered his face. "My parents like it. Samson thought I could use a change of scenery for my last few years of school."

Samson thought. Not, *my parents* thought. It was as if his parents didn't have any say-so in his life. Or, my heart sank at the other possibility…they didn't care. Mom might keep me at arm's-length, but I couldn't imagine *both* my parents completely ditching me. "Now that you're here, do you plan to go to college in Virginia?"

He slid to a hard stop, his hood facing my car. "Do I look like the college type?"

Wary blue eyes cut into me. He definitely had an edgy vibe, not to mention the rumors about him. Getting expelled from school never looked good on a college application, yet he'd been smarter than me when we studied for Trig. I shrugged and gave a half smile. "I dunno. What does a college kid look like these days?"

Ethan's expression shuttered as he grabbed the cables from my hands. "Not like me."

CHAPTER 5

As the dreamless days continued, things went from bad to worse. During the game against Westland, our biggest rivals, my goalkeeping went beyond epic fail. I'd never let so many balls zoom past, nor had I acquired as many bruises from trying so hard to stop them. Needless to say, my incredibly competitive Coach (though he'd deny it if you said so) was the silent kind of livid and none of my teammates spoke to me. We'd just lost our season's winning streak. And it was completely my fault.

When the game was over, Miranda walked up to Coach. "I think now's as good a time as any. I'd like to recommend Sophia start training as goalie tomorrow." Glancing my way, she continued, "We can't possibly do *any* worse."

Coach patted her shoulder and mumbled something about being Captain and sportsmanship before he lumbered over to me. Resting his crossed arms over a middle-aged paunch, his bushy gray eyebrows drew together in concern. "Hey, Nara. You've had a rough couple of games. I think Miranda's suggestion to train Sophia makes sense. You've obviously been under some pressure the past few days. You and Sophia can switch out to give her more training and that'll give you more time to practice on the field too."

"I understand, Coach." I tried my best to keep from showing how upset I was, but I doubt it worked. I felt defeated.

Miranda waited until Coach was out of hearing range. "What is your deal, Nara? Coach's trying to save your feelings, but I'll tell you straight up. Now that you won't be playing goalie exclusively, you'd better pull your weight on the field or I'll make sure you ride the bench *full time*."

"You're not the coach," I shot back.

"I can *make* it happen!" Glaring at me, she stomped off to the parking lot, where she stopped to announce something to several of our teammates as they changed out of their soccer gear near their cars. The girls kept glancing my way, then chatting with her. The entire scenario made my stomach knot.

Now this? On top of my troubles with Lainey? I'd felt Lainey pulling away, even though I'd tried to ignore it. I blamed myself partially, since I'd kept to myself the past few days and then didn't respond during her lame attempt at a pep talk right after the game was over. It's not like I could've gotten a word in edgewise with Jared hovering in the background, saying, "Come on, Lane. We've gotta go," every two seconds. I didn't think Lainey really wanted to talk to me anyway. She certainly didn't wave Jared away. Instead, she'd shrugged, then took off with him.

So far I'd stumbled through three consecutive days of not knowing what was coming. Three! Grades and soccer were suffering and now my relationships were, too. I was like that wooden tower game, suddenly minus the key piece. Had *every* aspect of my life, even down to my friendships, been held together by a wedge piece with the words "Nara's sight" etched into it? It stung too much to even consider the possibility.

My gift had never helped improve my relationship with my mom, but now that I'd lost my ability to see ahead, everything else I *could* depend on felt like it was falling apart. Leaning against the goalpost, I sniffed back tears, wishing…

I wasn't really sure what to wish for, my dreams to return or to never dream about my future again.

~

A WEEK LATER, as soon as school let out, I headed over to the Central Virginia Animal Shelter. Volunteering at CVAS was a welcome change. Lately my life had been nothing but practice and studying. Rinse. Repeat. I'd had one dream all week, where nothing interesting happened, except a thin girl walking around the halls with a back brace. I'd only noticed because the crowds spread like the red sea the first day she came to school in the odd contraption.

When I walked in the main door, Sally put both feet down, stopping her office roller chair from being hauled around the lobby area by CVAS's mascot, a lab mix, named Roscoe. "Hey, Nara. Thanks for coming. I'm so glad you could fill in at the last minute."

"We didn't have a soccer game this week, which gave me a free day. I'm glad you called." Hearing my voice, Roscoe abandoned his rope tug-of-war game with Sally. As his hundred and twenty pounds of pent-up, wiggly excitement bounded toward me, I braced for impact. Instead of jumping up, Roscoe stopped a foot away and slammed his rear to the ground, panting expectantly. I squatted and gave him a big hug. "Look at you! All manners now, huh boy? Did you miss me?" A thick wet tongue slobbered up the side of my face. I snickered and rubbed my nose in his thick brown fur. "Okay, maybe not *all* manners. I missed you too."

"Come on back, Nara." Sally stood by the door that led to the back rooms. She'd quickly pulled her blonde, out-of-control curls into a ponytail, which looked like someone had glued an oversized craft fuzzy ball to the back of her head. Smiling, I scratched Roscoe behind the ears and straightened. "I can stay until six-thirty. Put me wherever I'll be the most helpful."

As we walked down the hall, past the clinic doors, Sally filled me in. "With the help of local vets, we're doing a big drive this week. Free first round shots! The traffic has been unbelievable, so we need more handlers to work with the influx of lookers. If the pattern holds, they'll be rolling in soon. Most schools are out now."

"I can see why free vaccinations would be a huge draw," I said, shrugging out of my jacket to hang it in a side closet. An animal smell broke through the filtered air and the brief whiff reminded me of the past summer. Even with the random pungent scents, I missed this place. Working here as a volunteer was pure pleasure, whereas my paid summer job at the Pet Food Warehouse next door felt more like work.

Sally opened the door to the kenneled area. The smells were stronger here, but I knew from personal experience the animals were walked and the cages were cleaned often. "We've had more traffic this week then in the last three months combined."

"Wow. That's fantastic." I shut the door behind us and the dogs were already throwing themselves against the kennels, barking and wagging their tails in excitement. My heart lurched for them. I waved and called over the din, "Okay, little sweeties, let's find you some owners today."

I'D STAYED UNTIL SEVEN, because there were so many people wanting to see puppies and kittens. I wanted *all* the animals to have a chance. Multicolored cat and dog fur clung to my shirt, thanks to the crappy dryer sheets Mom had bought. Generic brands. Pfft! My face hurt from smiling so much, but I lingered, doing my routine final walk by each of the cages. Each animal received a nose pat, an ear scratch and the encouraging words, "Next time it's your turn."

I'd helped six families adopt today. A record for me. And even better, three of those adoptions were older pets that had been at the shelter for at least six months.

"Maybe tomorrow," I said to a black ten-month old pup with white socks on three paws.

He panted, his tongue hanging out. Excitement filled his brown eyes as he shoved his nose through the cage, nudging it under my fingers. The unconditional love twisted my chest tight. This was why I loved this place.

The side door that led to the bathing area swept open and a guy backed through, carrying a freshly-washed Retriever mix in his arms. I held the door for him and when he mumbled, "Thanks," I blinked in surprise.

"Ethan?"

"Hey, Nara." Setting the dog down, he leaned over and opened a bottom cage. "In you go." Shutting the cage behind the dog, Ethan brushed dog hair off his damp black t-shirt. "What are you doing here?"

"I work here. Well, technically, I work at the Pet Food Warehouse and volunteer here in the summer, but they asked me to fill in today while they're doing their big drive. How long have you been volunteering?" *I can't believe we seem to keep crossing paths.*

Ethan pushed his hands through his hair, making the disheveled mass even messier. Who'd have thought mussed hair would look so good on someone.

"I've been here a few weeks. I saw a flyer at school and thought it might be interesting—"

"Ethan—" Sally came through the main door being pulled by a huge brown dog. Mud coated his snout, paws and bushy tail. "This one just came in. I swear we're a revolving door some days." The dog jerked to the left, barking at one of the dogs in a cage. She tugged on the leash, but he only shifted to the other side and snarled at another cage. "I know you've been in the back the entire shift, but this guy's too high strung for Emily to bathe. Can you take care of getting him cleaned up before you leave?"

Ethan grabbed the dog's collar, pulled him close and spoke in a forceful tone near his ear, "Settle, boy." The dog's brown eyes snapped to Ethan and he instantly quieted.

Sally smiled and handed the leash over. "I really appreciate it."

"No worries." Ethan looked at me. "Guess I've got another customer. See you tomorrow, Nara."

"Bye," I called after him.

After he'd walked through the swinging door, Sally patted my shoulder. "Thanks so much for all your help, Nara. It always makes me misty when we can find the older ones a home."

"You're welcome. I had a blast." I'd been so busy with the animals, I didn't think about my dreamless situation. Eyeing the swinging door, I said, "That was awesome what Ethan just did. Mr. Jackson was the only person I knew who could calm an animal without knowing it beforehand."

"Yeah, Old Jack's retirement made us all sad." A look of wistfulness crossed Sally's face, then faded with her chuckle. "The day he walked in, Ethan told us straight up, 'I don't want to deal with people. I just want to work with the animals.' He doesn't say much, but he's amazing with the animals. We're going to offer him a trainer position as soon as he's legally eligible for employment."

"Really?" That was a big deal. I didn't know a single trainer under twenty-one. I peered through the glass rectangle in the door, wondering why Ethan was such a loner. He didn't seem to want to interact with the people around him, yet he'd taken the time to talk to me, not just at school, but here, too. The realization made me feel both sad and a bit special. Well, so long as he didn't think of me like a pet.

~

MY WEEKEND PASSED SANS DREAMS, and even my mom had noticed something wasn't right while we were out shopping the fall sales.

"Inara?" Mom asked, lowering a blue sweater I'd normally be oohing and aahhing over back to the display table.

"Huh?" I moved a sweater to the other side of the table.

"What's wrong?" She eyed the clothes with bemusement. "Want to organize the pantry when we get home?"

I glanced at the sweaters. I'd rearranged them in color-wheel order instead of the random selection the sales people had used. I had no idea why. "I…um, no."

Concern furrowed her brow. "I wasn't going to say anything, but Mr. Dixon mentioned you *needing* the extra two points of credit you received for bringing a parent on top of the five points you received for attending the international dinner. You've never needed extra credit before. Is that why I was the only parent there? I thought you loved languages. What's going on with your grades?"

"You seemed to have a good time," I said. She and Mr. Dixon had talked for at least ten minutes.

Mom raised an eyebrow. She was waiting for me to fess up.

Note to self: Next time, wait until you're no longer in the teacher's class before trying to set up a "meet" with your Mom. Sighing, I said, "I screwed up my last test."

"That's not like you to do poorly, Inara. And normally you love shopping with me, but these past couple of weeks you've seemed so…distracted. What's going on?"

I felt like a specimen under a microscope. I jammed my hands deep into my jacket pockets. "I forgot to study, that's all."

"Are you feeling okay?" She reached over to feel my forehead.

I pulled away. "I'm fine. Just a little tired."

Folding the sweater with quick, efficient movements, Mom put it back on the table. "Come on, let's get you something to eat. You'll feel better soon, then we'll check out that Latin compilation you asked for at the book store."

Mom supported my independent study of Latin, because she believed that I wanted to be a doctor. She'd be surprised to learn it was Gran's sassy comment about her neighbor in apartment 304—"That woman's handwriting is atrocious. It's like reading Latin. I have to guess half the words."—that gave me the idea to check out Latin.

As I followed my mom out of the store, I could've predicted her reaction to my out-of-sorts behavior without the benefit of my dreams. Mom might be an executive and boss to hundreds of people, but she'd never let go of her nurturing Southern ways. If you were hurt or feeling bad, she'd feed you—well, pay someone else to feed you. She believed food was the answer to every ailment.

But not knowing what was coming with my mom versus walking around constantly blind at school, were two entirely different scenarios. People at school could be so mean and cliquey, turning on you so fast you're left fluttering in the wind. I didn't think it could get any worse.

I'd forgotten about Murphy's Law.

~

MONDAY HAD BLOWN by in a hurtful blur after I'd overheard Miranda, Sophia, Lainey and several of my other teammates talking about how much fun they'd had at Jared's party the past Friday night. Lainey and I had been to a couple parties at Jared's before, as friends of friends who'd been invited. Apparently this past Friday, most of my soccer team had gone, yet no one had invited me. I guess that meant that I'd been demoted to the "Do Not Invite" list.

That night, I'd finally dreamed again, but instead of being relieved, I walked into school Tuesday morning anxious and on-edge. The whole "on again, off again" stuff with my dreams made me feel like a faulty, flickering light bulb. I kept expecting my head to make a sizzling pop right before my dreams died out completely.

Tension built inside me all day. By the time I reached study hall and then had to pass by Lainey, Miranda and Sophia chatting away at a table, my nerves were shot. I sat at a table alone and stared at my Trig book, while unshed tears blurred my vision. I wanted to go home, to wish away my responsibility of the rest of the day. I didn't want to go to practice and that depressed me even more. Sighing, I closed my eyes, thankful I only had a couple more classes to go.

"You sleeping, Nara?"

I truly loved Ethan's voice. My friendship with Ethan—our study partnership, at least—was the only one that hadn't faltered. I knew for certain our camaraderie wasn't based on my dreams, because he hadn't shown up in the few dreams I'd had so far. I still didn't understand why that was the case, but like a kid clutching her first piece of candy, I wasn't letting go of our friendship.

"Hey," I said softly with a brief smile.

The crinkles around the edges of Ethan's deep blue eyes

smoothed out, along with his faint smile. He touched his thumb to my chin and sat down beside me. "What's wrong?"

The look of concern on his face and the way he touched me made my heart twist. *Someone cared.* Ethan cared. But I wasn't ready to share. I sniffed back tears. "Nothing. I'm just tired from staying up late a couple nights this weekend."

His thumb slid along my jaw, catching the wetness. "Do you always cry when you're tired?"

"Oh, I—" I shoved my palm across my jaw, swiping away the evidence as embarrassed heat shot up my cheeks.

Ethan's gaze was steady and patient.

I stared at my book. "Soccer's not going that well right now."

"I saw the team's loss to Westland last week. Tough break."

"You were there?" I felt completely humiliated. "Then you know it was a slaughter, no thanks to me, but thank you for trying to make me feel better."

"The other goalie didn't do so hot in the last game I saw, either. There are plenty of games left in the season. You'll rally back to your starting goalie spot."

"At least one of us thinks so." I smiled, despite my worries. Whenever Ethan was around, all the screaming doubts in my mind quieted to mere whispers. Sophia had done a terrible job. The team barely squeaked out a win. It should've been a blowout.

Loud whispers drew my attention. Lainey, Miranda and Sophia were staring at us from across the room. Scrunching my face in a light-hearted goofy look, I grabbed my book and said, "You here to study or what?"

Ethan held my gaze for a long second before he slowly opened his book. "Yeah, let's get to it."

~

SIXTH PERIOD CREPT BY. I had such a hard time concentrating. Between furtive glances at my watch, I tore tiny bits of paper from my notebook and stuck them to my static charged sweater. Another quick check of my watch. I needed to leave now to help a girl named Kristin.

I didn't know the girl with dark hair, at all. But after my dream last night, I couldn't *not* help her, not if there was something I could do to prevent what was going to happen in Chemistry class in less than fifteen minutes.

Brushing the clingy paper bits away from my clothes, I flagged the teacher's attention.

He pulled his glasses down his nose. "Yes, Nara?"

"I need to go to the bathroom."

He waved to the pass on his desk and continued droning on as if I'd never interrupted.

Grabbing the pass, I walked out of the room and turned down the hall toward the bathroom, my heart racing. I'd intended to go straight to Kristin's class, but I ducked into the bathroom first to get my act together. I didn't need to walk into her class hyperventilating.

Thankfully, the bathroom was empty and I rushed to the sink to splash some water on my cheeks. The coolness helped, and as I blotted my face with a scratchy brown paper towel, I met my green gaze in the mirror and blew out a breath. *It won't be the same as Sadie. Everything turned out fine after you called in the bomb threat.*

A sudden chill raced along my cheek, then a pressure pushed on my right shoulder as if someone had leaned on me. I glanced over my shoulder, calling out, "Who's there?" Swatting static-charged pieces of floating hair back down, my heart thumped with heavy beats as I scanned the bathroom. Only the sporadic *plunk, plunk* of water hitting the porcelain sink echoed in the room.

"I'm losing it," I murmured, tossing the crumpled paper towel into the trash. As I turned to leave, the tiny hairs on the back of my neck rose. A circle of fog—as if someone had leaned close and breathed heavily—was slowly dissipating from the mirror.

I ran to the door and pulled, but it didn't budge. Fear shuddered through me as I checked to see if I'd somehow been locked in. It wasn't bolted. Yanking the handle with all my might, I yelled, "Let me out!"

The door suddenly swung wide, and I flew back with the force I'd applied. Catching myself, I scrambled around the door, then rushed down the hall toward Kristin's Chemistry class. I was almost out of time.

Peeking in the door, I called to the teacher, "I've been asked to bring Kristin to the office."

The dark-headed girl from my dream glanced up from her lab table, her eyes extra wide behind her safety goggles. "Me?"

"Just leave your stuff," the teacher said.

As she slowly removed her goggles, then her gloves, it was all I could do not to scream, "Hurry up or you'll end up with cuts and burns all over your face." Instead, I said, "Um, I think it was kinda urgent."

"Why didn't they use the intercom?" her teacher asked.

I shrugged. All I cared about was getting her out of the room. Kristin had almost reached the door when a loud pop sounded and glass shattered.

"Everyone clear the room," a stern voice ordered.

Students gathered in the hall around us, all talking at once.

"Did you see what happened?"

"I dunno. Something explod—."

"—teacher's freaked."

"I think it was her experiment," a girl pointed to Kristin's back as Kristin spoke to me over the noise. "Did the office say what it was about?"

I shook my head and picked at my clingy sweater. The static in my hair must've come from my sweater. I so needed to remind Mom to get new dryer sheets. "I've got to get back to class. See you around."

As I walked away, my mind kept skipping back to what happened in the bathroom. It was possible the breath on the mirror could've been mine, but the door had never jammed on me before. Was that just an odd coincidence?

At least I'd made it to Kristin in time. That's all that mattered.

~

LATER THAT AFTERNOON, I slipped on my tortoise shell shades and had just walked out the school's main door, when someone called my name. "Nara, wait up."

I paused outside the door and Lainey stepped beside me. "I wanted to talk to you," she said as people bustled past us. Grabbing my arm, she started to tug me to the side of the building, when Kristin stopped and looked at me with suspicion. "No one from the office called me."

"Really? That's weird." I blinked. "Maybe it was another Kristin."

"There aren't any other Kristin's in my Chemistry class."

"Oh, I guess I got the wrong class then."

Rolling her eyes, she walked off, mumbling, "At least I got out of class early."

"What was that all about?" Lainey asked, staring after Kristin.

"A misunderstanding."

As soon as we were away from the crowd, I gripped my backpack strap tight against my shoulder and said, "That's cool of Jared to come watch you at our games." I hoped my tone sounded light and sincere. I didn't want to lose Lainey.

Lainey smiled. "He wants to support me like I do him with football. Isn't that so sweet?"

Jared spent most of the soccer game goofing off with his friends on the bleachers, but I buried my thoughts and nodded. Our friendship was more important. "I'm glad he makes you happy."

"So, we're okay, then?" she asked, her forehead crinkling.

"Yeah. I was just upset that you didn't tell me. To find out about you and Jared from *Sophia* of all people." I grimaced. Lainey knew Sophia wasn't my favorite person. Sophia had been stirring cauldrons since middle school, and I somehow always ended up an ingredient in her stew.

"Sorry about that." Glancing around, as if making sure no one was listening, Lainey continued, "I'm glad we're okay, but I wanted to talk to you about something else."

Relieved we were on speaking terms once more, my shoulders relaxed and I leaned against the building. "What's up?"

Lainey tucked a strand of hair behind her ear and moved closer. "I saw you with that Ethan guy today," she bit her lip, then plunged on, "It looks like you two are getting pretty close and—"

"It does?" I was surprised she'd noticed, even as a pleased feeling bloomed in my chest.

"You're not?" Lainey didn't wait for my response, but instead waved her hand dismissively. "Whew. That's a relief. I've heard the worst things about him. I didn't want to have to worry about—"

"What have you heard?" I pushed off the wall to move closer. I wanted to know what nasty rumors people were spreading about him. If it was something I could say was a flat-out lie, I would in a heartbeat.

"He's a freak. Did you know black birds hang out on his car, like there's something dead inside." She shivered and wrinkled her nose. "How weird is that?"

"I think you've watched too many paranormal TV shows. Parking so close to the trees probably attracts the birds."

"Seriously, Nara, I think the guy's off. He hardly talks to anyone. All he does is draw in that notepad."

I shrugged. "Maybe he'd rather draw than make friends."

"He's made friends with you." Lainey shook her head. "One of the guys knows some people from his last school. The rumors are true, Nara. He was expelled for beating up a guy in his class. Everyone said the guy didn't provoke it, that Ethan just went nuts and hammered on him."

I thought about how intense Ethan had been about those two boys who'd offered me a ride home, but he was trying to protect me. "How do we know the guy didn't do something to him, but no one saw that part."

Lainey pursed her lips. "That's the thing. Ethan didn't say the guy had provoked him. A person who saw the fight said Ethan said something to the other guy, then threw the first punch. When the principal asked why Ethan beat the other guy up, he wouldn't say."

Why had *Ethan done such a thing?* I couldn't help but wonder, which made me angry all over again, because now *I* was being swayed by the rumor mill. I kept my tone calm. "There are two sides to every story."

Lainey snorted. "All that other stuff aside, what really worries me is the fact he draws very disturbing blood and gore pictures, like something out of a horror movie with demons and stuff—"

She paused when my eyebrows shot up. "Oh, Anton grabbed his notebook and flipped through a couple of pages while he was in the bathroom. Another guy in the class said that was the most he'd heard Ethan say when he came back and saw Anton checking out his stuff. Ethan cussed Anton out like no tomorrow."

I could imagine Ethan in a rage over someone messing with his personal stuff. He seemed so private and contained. Though, learning he had drawn *tons* of disturbing pictures was a little worrisome. Did one of them look like that monster image I'd seen in the hall? Would he tell me about his drawings if I asked?

My heart sank a little, and I was suddenly annoyed that Lainey had burst my bubble. Ethan had been kind, sympathizing with me over soccer stuff and she'd gone and ruined it.

"I think you've got Ethan all wrong, Lainey. He seems like a decent guy. Sure he keeps to himself a lot, but—"

"Nara, what I think is this guy's some kind of psycho. I'm worried something might happen to you if you continue hanging with him."

The tension in her voice scared me a little, but when I pictured Ethan, all I could think about was the kindness in his eyes and the gentle way he'd rubbed my tears away. He'd cared, which was far more than any of my supposed friends had done recently.

"He was there for me, Lainey. You've been so busy with your new boyfriend, you didn't even notice your best friend was going through some stuff. But Ethan did, and that's enough for me."

Lainey's jaw dropped, but before she could say anything, I

stalked off to my car. With each step I took, my stomach wound tighter and tighter. What *did* I really know about Ethan? Not a whole lot, but what I did know, I liked. I hated that people were judging him unfairly. Straightening my spine, I decided I was going to find out more about him.

No one spoke to me during soccer practice, at least not on a social level. For some reason Lainey didn't come to practice, so the entire two hours were torturous. Several times Miranda, Sophia and a couple other girls hammered on me as we ran up and down the field. They'd elbowed and kicked, cutting me off every chance they got. I avoided as many attacks as I could remember from my dream, but I couldn't avoid all of them.

I'd played in my old position in the field the last couple of games. I knew I was rusty, but part of that was due to me spending the majority of my time in the goal, which the team had been fine with so long as I was saving every single ball for them. Apparently now I was lower than dog's poop on their cleats. If Miranda had her way, I would definitely be riding the bench during the next game.

By the end of practice, while the rest of the team and Coach headed off to their cars, I stayed behind on the bench, feeling beaten on top of every single ache and pain. I saw Miranda whispering to the two other girls who'd helped her and Sophia give me hell during practice. When they all nodded in agreement, like they'd formed some kind of pact, I mumbled, "I can't believe it. She's *trying* to get me kicked off the team."

"You're not going to let that happen, are you?" a familiar voice said from behind me.

CHAPTER 6

I turned around and Ethan was standing on the field, balancing a soccer ball on his knee. My heart raced as I watched him bounce the ball up and down. He kept his gaze on me, yet had complete control. Even though Lainey's comments about his drawings and the story of him beating up that guy at his old school itched in the back of my mind, he intrigued me. I wanted to know his side of the story and so much more.

"What are you doing here?"

"I thought you might like to practice with someone who *isn't* trying to get you kicked off the team." Ethan spun the ball, letting it roll up his right arm and across his chest, then back down the other arm where he caught it in his hands. "You up for a practice partner?" he asked as he dropped the ball, trapping it between his foot and ankle. Kicking the ball up over his head, he then leaned forward and caught it behind his neck, an expectant expression on his face.

He looked mouthwatering in black athletic pants with white stripes down the sides and a royal blue long sleeved t-shirt. I was suddenly very conscious of my sweaty face, my hair pulled back in a quick ponytail. I was a mess, but his mere presence made me feel special despite the dirt stains on my knees. He definitely knew his way around a soccer ball. I hadn't imagined the skill I'd seen that day in the hall. "Who's going to teach me? You don't play soccer," I teased, waiting for him to tell me I was wrong.

Shrugging his shoulder, he dropped the ball into his hands and straightened. "I used to play every season: indoor, outdoor, on a travel team. Even taught summer camp, but you're right. I don't play. Not any more."

A look of regret flitted across his face. Ethan was always so controlled; the brief display of raw emotion threw me. Sometimes he seemed much older, like he'd been through a lot. I wanted to ask why he'd quit playing, but he turned and punted the soccer ball toward the goal, calling over his shoulder in an upbeat tone, "Come on, slow poke. We don't have all night."

Grabbing my gloves, I followed him over to the goal. "Okay, let's see your moves."

He gestured for me to get into position in front of the goal, then dropped the ball on the ground and set his cleat on top of it. "I watched you during some games. I could tell you were tense. Half the time your eyes weren't on the ball."

I bristled and started to argue, but Ethan had no reason to lie to me. He was here to help, so I set my jaw and nodded while pulling on my gloves.

As I readied myself for him to kick toward the goal, Ethan set his foot next to the ball. "It's always important to watch the ball first, but don't forget the player's eyes, his hips, his shoulders…and if all else fails," he paused and winked. "Psych him out. Watch my planted foot, Nara." He set his foot down. "Where am I going to kick the ball?"

"To my left."

"High or low?"

"Won't know until it leaves your foot."

"Look at my body." He leaned back slightly. "I'm tilted back, so the ball will be high." He kicked the ball to prove his point. I jumped, snagging the ball above my head, then tossed it to him.

Dribbling the ball back and forth between his feet, he continued, "You're on the tall side, so you'll leave smaller angles or gaps when you go after the ball. That gives you an advantage in covering the entire goal."

I wasn't ready when he slammed the ball hard. I dove too late and it zoomed past me into the net. Retrieving the ball, I kicked it out to him since he'd moved further out into the field.

Dribbling in a wide circle on the field, Ethan said, "Watch my planted foot and where I actually hit the ball with my kicking foot. The direction of my hips will tell you where the ball is going to go."

Everything Ethan was saying were skills I'd learned but never had to worry about using. Now that I focused on what he said, instead of worrying I'd miss every ball that came my way, my confidence began to build.

This time he kicked the ball in one direction, but it curved back toward me. I dove, grabbing onto the ball before it went in the goal. "Except curve balls," I said as I kicked the ball back to him.

"Exactly, but you can watch the players throughout the game to see which ones have the talent to do curved shots with any kind of accuracy."

After that, Ethan just kicked the ball toward me. He changed it up a bit, tasking my ability to watch the signs he'd suggested while I kept my eye on the ball.

At one point, he stopped and just stood there staring me down. Crouched and waiting, I locked my gaze on him, my adrenaline pumping. I got tired of waiting for him to decide which way he'd kick it, so I took a small step to the left, then dove to the right, saving the ball he'd quickly kicked in the opposite direction I'd stepped.

I stood up with a wide grin. "Psyched you!"

Ethan nodded. "You'll be playing goalie full-time again soon."

His reminder that I could be riding the bench half the time rubbed salt in the wound, so I threw the ball his way and asked, "Why did you give up soccer?"

Stopping the ball in the air with his cleat, his gaze followed it to the ground. He stared at it for a couple of seconds, his jaw tense. Glancing up, he said in a gruff tone, "I quit playing when I was fifteen," right before he hammered the ball at me.

I tried to stop it, but the dew-coated ball shot past my gloves into my chest. The impact threw me back and pain splintered as I collapsed on the ground, coughing and wheezing.

I must've zoned out for a second, because when I opened my eyes, Ethan sat beside me. His arm was wrapped around my shoulders as he held me off the ground. "Nara, talk to me. Are you okay?"

I coughed once more. "Ugh, not the best way to find out you've been holding back on me."

Ethan's brows pushed together. "Sorry. I didn't mean to kick the ball that hard."

I gave a wobbly smile. He had a few freckles on his nose and a chicken pox scar next to his left eyebrow, both things I'd never noticed. "I've never caught air like that before, but I'll live."

"Jumping back to soften the blow was pretty smart."

I didn't jump back, I wanted to tell him, but the gentle sweeping brush of his thumb across the hollow of my throat distracted me. Tiny shivers shot through me when I realized his palm was resting on my chest. Holding my breath, I glanced down and saw the dark edge of a tattoo on his arm where his shirt's sleeve had ridden up slightly. Curved and intricately designed, it looked like some kind of tail that curled all the way around his forearm.

Lainey's comment about his scary drawings came back to me, along with that horror image I'd seen in the hall. Secrets swirled in Ethan's eyes, making me shudder with conflicting emotions of hesitation and curiosity.

"You're cold," he said, gripping my hand. "Can you stand now?"

"Yeah." I felt like a complete wuss.

Pulling me to my feet, Ethan scooped up the ball. "We should pack it in anyway. You're probably tired from the extra practice time."

Adrenaline pumped through my veins, whooshing to the rhythm of my thunderous heartbeat. I could do this all night, so long as Ethan was involved. "Thanks for your help, but yeah, I should get home and start on my homework."

As we headed toward the bench, Ethan tossed the ball in the air and caught it. "Want to practice some more tomorrow?"

"That'd be great if it's not too much trouble." A thrill went through me as we stopped at the bench and I kicked off my cleats to slide into my flops. I couldn't believe how much I'd grown to like his company, but I did. A lot.

Ethan grabbed my bag's strap before I could. "It's a good refresher for me, too," he said, hoisting my bag onto his shoulder. "Heads up."

I caught the soccer ball he tossed my way, and then we headed for the parking lot. When we reached my car, he dropped the bag into my trunk and I tossed his ball back to him. "Thanks for everything."

"Anytime," Ethan said.

"See you tomorrow," I called as he walked off toward his car sitting across the parking lot. Why did tomorrow have to be so far away? Climbing into my car, I'd never felt more energized. I wasn't really sure what was going on between Ethan and me, but I definitely wanted to spend more time with him.

After a week and a half of mostly silent dreams, the unknown still scared me on some levels—but, not knowing what to expect had a wonderful, exciting flipside—like opening my eyes to Ethan holding me close. I didn't want to question why he hadn't starred in my dreams, because experiencing "Ethan-related" events for the first time *in person* (and not in a déjà vu scenario) was something I could become addicted to.

I ENJOYED MY "AFTER-PRACTICE" time with Ethan. While we played, he didn't just shoot on me in goal. Part of the time, we chased one another up and down the field, trying to outmaneuver each other's ball-handling skills. He dominated a good bit of the time, but there were times I beat him too.

As Ethan helped me stow my gear in my car, he said,

"Would you mind helping me with a project? I need an accomplice."

"An accomplice?" I laughed nervously. "Sounds illegal."

"I'm fairly certain it is." He leaned on my car door. "Actually, I'm sure it is, but it's something I think you'd understand and agree with."

Adrenaline shot through me, edged by curiosity. "Hmmm. What's the project?"

Ethan rested his chin on his forearm and the brisk wind ruffled his sweaty dark hair. "Rescuing an abused dog."

He knew just how to reel me in. "How do I fit into your illegal activity?"

Excitement filled his eyes and he jerked his head up. "You'll do it?"

"You wouldn't have asked if there was another way."

He nodded, his expression hardening. "I heard someone talking about this dog's sad situation at CVAS. He's a Shepherd mix, chained on a short leash and the links are digging into his neck, causing sores. Patches of bald skin litter his coat and he's malnourished. The owner's a big man, so people are afraid to act. All I need you to do is distract him while I get the dog out of the backyard."

"Is the dog friendly?"

Ethan held my gaze. "Over the past week and a half I've driven by and snuck up to the fence, feeding him hamburger, hotdogs and chicken. He barks until he sees me, but he's not vicious at all."

At least there won't be rabies shots in our future. This probably wasn't going to go off without a hitch, but now that I knew about the abused dog, I was all in. "How much time do you think you'll need?"

"Ten minutes max."

Ten minutes would feel like an eternity. "I'll think of something," I said with more confidence than I felt.

"Thanks, Nara. This dog won't get help without us."

His appreciation bolstered my shaky confidence. Plus, this was an excuse to spend time with Ethan outside of school and soccer. "When do you want to do this?"

He scratched the back of his neck, looking sheepish. "Would you be able to do it tonight?" When I nodded, he continued, "Great. I'll meet you back here in the parking lot in an hour. Does that work for you?"

"Yeah, that works."

~

As I PULLED in beside Ethan's car sitting in the school's empty parking lot, he got out and shut the door. Dressed in dark jeans and a black hoodie jacket, he swept a surprised look over my jeans and Three Wise Monkeys sweatshirt when I stepped out of my car and tugged my backpack over my shoulder. "You changed."

I nodded. "I didn't think it was a good idea to commit my first crime wearing cleats. They're hard to run in on asphalt."

Worry crossed his face. "Are you okay with this, Nara? You don't have to do it."

I gave a reassuring smile. "I'm committed now. Plus, I'm wearing my 'Don't I look trustworthy?' sweatshirt," I said, pointing to the see-no-evil, hear-no-evil, speak-no-evil monkeys emblazoned across my chest.

When his frown curved into a small smile, I unzipped my backpack and pulled a thick coupon book out. "Oh, and I brought this to 'sell' to the man. My mom bought it from some kid selling them for his school last week."

Admiration flickered in his eyes. "That's perfect."

Warmth flooded my face. I was surprised how much I liked his approval. Glancing away, I tucked the book into my backpack. "I'll drive."

"I'd planned to drive."

I pointed to his car. "It's too loud. We need stealth, not startle."

Ethan smirked. "Deal, so long as you don't slam on your brakes when we park."

I couldn't help but chuckle as he opened my car door.

Once we neared the neighborhood, which, as it turned out,

was only a couple miles from CVAS, I glanced at Ethan. "What do you plan to do with the dog?"

"Get him cleaned up and fed."

"Then what?"

He rubbed the back of his neck. "I can keep him for a few days, but my brother's not ready for a dog. Not yet, but I'm working on him."

I parked my car one street over from the owner's house and we set off on foot.

When we turned the corner and I saw the six-foot high chain fence, my insides began to churn. I really wished my dreams hadn't disappeared. I'd like to *know* this abduction rescue was going to go as planned. As I chanted a we-won't-get-caught-and-beaten-to-a-pulp-by-the-mean-owner mantra over and over in my head, it suddenly hit me; even if I'd dreamed about today, I would've never seen this part, since none of my interactions with Ethan showed up in my dreams. Tension made my voice scratchy. "I only see the one gate near the front of the house. Will you be able to get the dog out?"

Ethan shoved a leash in his jeans pocket, then pointed to a shed next to the fence in the back corner of the yard. "I'll use hotdogs to get him to climb up the stack of wood to the shed's roof, then hopefully I can convince him to jump over the fence."

My steps slowed. "How are you getting inside?"

He pointed to the neighbor's fenceless backyard. It had a huge pile of mulch butted against a matching shed located on the other side of the fence. "I'll jump from one shed to the other. Count to thirty slowly before you knock, okay?"

"Be careful," I whispered as he broke off to skirt around to the back. So many things could go wrong: the dog could refuse to budge, Ethan could break a leg, we could get caught. Taking a deep breath, I chanted the mantra once more as I peeked around the edge of the house to check on Ethan.

He was trying to climb up the mulch pile, but it kept spreading under his feet. My stomach tensed when he stepped off the mulch, then turned and ran full speed up the incline. Just as the pile seemed to collapse under him, he somehow caught air and vaulted to the roof. I blinked. Did I just imagine that? That leap wasn't possible. Was it?

When the dog turned and let out a surprised bark at his rooftop landing, my heart jerked. Grabbing the coupon booklet from my backpack, I bolted to the front door, then jammed my finger on the doorbell.

My pulse whooshed in my ears as the dog's bark switched to an "intruder alert" level.

The door jerked open and a huge man filled the doorway. "What do you want?" he said in a gruff voice. His buzz cut shifted forward as he planted his feet and folded his massive arms over a wide chest.

Skimming my gaze from his holey-toed socks to his ragged flannel shirt, I gulped to moisten my suddenly dry throat and held up the coupon booklet. "Hi, how'd you like to save three hundred dollars?" I said, then launched in a friendly, upbeat sales pitch.

Twenty-five pages later, I was in the process of pointing out several great stores and restaurants listed in the booklet, when I saw movement in my peripheral vision. Someone was chasing something near the neighbor's garage.

I couldn't let the man see the movement, so I hurried my wrap-up along. "Well, I guess that's about it. Sorry you're not interested. Have a great night."

Hiking my backpack up my shoulder, I casually walked away. When the man called after me, "Hey, wait." I was thankful his sidewalk pointed in the opposite direction I'd seen Ethan.

After the dog's owner had closed his front door, tension eased from my neck and shoulders. I waited until I reached the end of the street before I doubled back, squinting for signs of Ethan in the darkness.

When I rounded the corner and saw Ethan sitting in my car, I exhaled my pent-up breath. But where was the dog? Opening my door, I started to ask what happened, then saw the dog curled into a tight ball on top of the blanket in my backseat.

"Is he okay?"

Ethan reached back and patted the dog's head. "Yeah, he's

tired. Once he tasted freedom, I uh, had to chase him for a bit before he'd let me put the leash on him." His dark gaze snapped to me as I climbed in. "If you hadn't shown in the next two seconds, I was coming to get you."

"Mission accomplished." I grinned and waved a twenty-dollar bill. "This should help pay for his food."

His lips tilted briefly in amusement. "You actually sold him the booklet?"

"A worthy cause, combined with self-preservation, apparently made me a powerful salesperson," I said with a half laugh as I started the car.

"You're amazing. Thanks, Nara."

Ethan's softly spoken compliment made me feel special. "Where to now?"

"CVAS."

"Um, it's closed."

"I know where they hide a spare key and the alarm codes."

Shaking my head, I said, "All kinds of illegal, huh?"

He cut a sheepish gaze my way. "Yeah. You still in?"

I turned down the street that led to the shelter.

While Ethan bathed the dog, I made a couple of phone calls. One to my mom to let her know I was at Lainey's and would be home late. The second call was to Aunt Sage.

According to Ethan, the dog's collar he'd left behind said the pooch wouldn't need another rabies shot for two years. It took Ethan and me two hours to clean and dress the wounds the collar had inflicted. The poor dog's neck was scarred horribly, but with lots of love and attention, I was pretty sure his black/brown coat would return to its full luster and even cover up the damage on his neck.

As we pulled out of CVAS's lot in the direction of school, I ached all over from our busy night, but I felt good. "We did it."

Ethan looked as tired as I felt. "Yeah, we did." He patted the dog's snout that rested on the console between us. "I couldn't have done this without you."

My aunt's car was parked beside Ethan's Mustang when I turned into the school parking lot. As I rolled to a stop next to her car, Aunt Sage got out, her bohemian-style dress blowing around her legs underneath her long coat.

Ethan sat up straight. "Who's that?"

"Don't worry. It's just my aunt. I hope you're not upset, but since you could only keep the dog for a few days, I called her and told her his situation. She's willing to give him a permanent home."

Relief flitted across his tense features. "Really? She's got space for him?"

I waved to my aunt through the windshield. "Yeah. She lives a half hour away and has other dogs who'll make great companions."

Ethan cupped his hand over the dog's head. "Did you hear that, boy? You've got a home."

Grabbing the dog's leash, Ethan helped our rescuee out of the car and walked him over to my aunt. She rubbed the dog's ears and gently patted his head. "Hi there, Duke. I see you've had a rough time of it. That's about to change."

In response, he instantly sat on his haunches and leaned against my aunt's thigh.

"Are you really going to name him Duke?" I said with a laugh of disbelief.

My aunt pushed her curly red hair away from her eyes, a Cheshire smile lighting her face. "But of course."

When she put her hand out to Ethan, saying, "Hi, I'm Sage Collins," I instantly tensed. *Please, please don't hug him, Aunt Sage.*

Ethan shook her hand. "Ethan Harris, and thank you for taking…Duke."

Releasing his hand, my aunt's smile remained, but her gaze took on a parental edge. "I hope you don't plan to involve my niece in any more illegal activities."

"Aunt Sage!"

Stern eyes met mine. "No more, Inara."

Ethan looked apologetic. "I promise."

Clasping Duke's leash tight, my aunt waved us on. "It's getting late. Go home, you two. Don't worry about Duke. I have salve at home. He'll fit right in with the boys."

"Thank you for taking him in, Aunt Sage. Oh, and..." I handed her the twenty. "Here's some money for food."

"Thank you, Inara." Aunt Sage took the bill and stood there with Duke, staring at us expectantly.

Ethan and I exchanged "see-you-tomorrow" glances, but so much more was silently communicated. We'd bonded over tonight's adventure. Our mission had held loads of potential mishaps and danger, yet we'd accomplished it. Together. Smiling, I waved goodbye and climbed into my car.

~

THE NEXT DAY, when I didn't see Ethan at his locker before Homeroom, I was disappointed. I told myself he was probably running late, but when he didn't show up in Trig and I didn't see him in the halls, I knew he hadn't come to school. Maybe last night had totally worn him out. *How many times had I hit my own alarm this morning?* I thought as I headed out to soccer practice.

"Hey, Nara." Lainey ran over the moment I set my bag on the bench.

"What's up?" Lainey had been spending all her time with Jared or hanging out watching the football team after practice was over.

Just as I pulled my hair up into a rubber band, Lainey sat down on the bench. "I want to talk to you."

She looked so serious, I instantly sat down beside her. "What's wrong? Is everything okay with you and Jared?"

Her ponytail bobbed up and down. "We're fine. I wanted to talk to you about Ethan."

I stilled. "What about him?"

"I had my dad check on him—"

"Lainey!" My hands balled into fists.

She put her hand on my arm. "That's just between you and me. Never repeat that. My dad could get in a lot of trouble for checking on him, but he was trying to help. Just listen, okay?"

Setting my jaw, I mumbled, "Fine."

She blew out a breath, her eyes sympathetic. "He has a juvie record, Nara. The charges were violence and destruction of property."

I curled my fingers around the bench's metal seat. "When were these charges?"

"When he was fourteen."

"Nothing recent then?"

Her grip tightened on my arm. "You mean other than beating that guy up at his last school?"

I stared her down. "Did that student file charges?"

Her hand fell away from my arm. "No, the only thing on Ethan's record was when he was fourteen."

"Like I said, there are two sides to every story. Why didn't that guy he 'beat up for no reason' file charges? If he was totally innocent, he had every right to."

"Nara, you're being so blind. I had my dad check on Ethan because you're my friend and well, I'm worried for you."

"Thanks for worrying, but I'm good."

She furrowed her brow. "Are you? You mentioned going through some stuff the other day and then ran off. You never did say…"

When she trailed off, I let go of the bench and casually brushed away the metal's indentions from my palms. "No worries. Really." Jerking my thumb toward the field, I stood. "We'd better head over."

Lainey stood beside me, then leaned close, slyness curving her lips. "I told you that you were a better goalie than Sophia or anyone else on the team. There's no way Miranda can convince Coach to keep you on the bench tomorrow."

Since I'd been practicing with Ethan, I'd taken back the goalie reins, leaving Sophia in the dust. I was pretty sure I'd be starting at the next game.

"Oh, she'll try. You should've seen how she and some of the girls ganged up on me at practice yesterday."

Lainey rolled her eyes. "She can be such a bitch sometimes. Honestly though, when it comes to the team, Miranda just wants to win, no matter what. She won't sacrifice a 'win' just so she can rub her hands in glee that you sat out of a game."

Smiling, I wrapped my arm around her neck. "Come on, let's get warmed up."

~

TOWARD THE END of an extended practice—Coach wanted to be extra prepared for our next game—I found myself getting excited, my stomach all aflutter. It was silly to expect Ethan to show, since he hadn't been at school, but I couldn't stop myself from glancing toward the parking lot. It was growing dark and the field lights had popped on, making it impossible to see the lot from the field.

Once practice was over, I took my time getting my gear together. Moving slowly, I still held out hope Ethan might surprise me.

"You coming, Nara?" Lainey tugged her bag onto her shoulder. The hot pink fringe on the strap fluttered with her every movement. I'd bought the flamboyant strap cover for her as a surprise birthday present this past summer. Between my work at CVAS, the Pet Food Warehouse, and hanging with Lainey, I'd stayed busy all summer, which made it easier not to dwell on how much time I spent at home alone. I missed our girl chats. I was glad the tension between us had eased.

"I'm going to kick a few more shots, then head home," I said, waving her on.

After everyone drove off, I frowned at the bright lights. I didn't like how they obscured my view of the parking lot. Pulling a ball from my bag, I walked over to the goal and I told myself I'd only give Ethan five more minutes and then I was leaving.

I'd just kicked the second ball into the net when I heard a rumbling car pull into the parking lot. I didn't turn around right away, because I didn't want Ethan to see the huge smile on my face. Composing my expression, I retrieved the ball and turned, surprised to see the two guys who'd offered me a ride home the day my car battery died, standing next to the bench. Dressed in faded jeans, t-shirts and zip up sweat jackets, they looked pretty harmless, but Ethan's words kept pounding into my brain. *They're dangerous…I've seen them in action.*

The blond guy flashed a smile. "You've been hard to catch up with, Nara."

His tone was light, but something in his eyes, a kind of wild excitement, looked off. My fingers tensed around the ball. "Why were you looking for me?"

"I can't believe you picked that new guy over us when we offered you help," he said.

"It wasn't a big deal." I shrugged, trying not to show them how uncomfortable they were making me. "I saved you guys some gas that day."

He rubbed his jaw. "See, that's where I get all bent." His thoughtful look faded as he crossed beefy arms. "We rarely offer to help, but then you went and dissed us."

They thought I'd rejected *them*? "It wasn't like that—"

"Are you saying we misunderstood?" the dark-headed guy interrupted.

"Nah, it looked pretty obvious to me," the blond cut in. His tone was completely different. Now it held a harsh, unforgiving grate.

"That's not it at all," I said, hoping they didn't hear the hitch of apprehension in my voice. Somehow I needed to soothe their seriously whacked egos. Just how many times *had* these guys been rejected in their lives? "Listen, I'm really sorry. It wasn't meant to be a diss. Ethan just happened to be going my way. I didn't mean to insult either of you, I promise."

The blond guy glanced at his buddy, then back to me. "Since you 'didn't mean it' and all, why don't you come hang with us for a while tonight."

This was seriously getting out of hand. I shook my head in fast jerks. "I can't. I have to get home. I'm already late."

"Big surprise." The blond guy threw up his hands and rolled his eyes.

His sarcasm set me even more on edge. "Really, I need to get home."

"Yeah, right." He looked at his friend then back to me, his gaze narrowed. "I'm *so* fucking tired of people's lies."

People? "I'm not ly—" I cut myself off when I saw a vein bulging along his temple and his fist clenched at his side. Everything inside me went cold and internal warning bells screamed, *Run! Get as far away as you can.* Yet my feet seemed to be rooted to the ground.

"Kurt," the dark-headed guy paused and glanced nervously toward the parking lot. "Maybe we should—"

The blond glared at his friend. "Man up, Jay," he said, then started toward me, his stride determined. "We'll get the truth out of her."

They're insane. Terror unlocked my frozen feet. Tossing the ball in their direction, I bolted across the open field toward the dense woods flanking the soccer fields.

CHAPTER 7

"Shit!" One of them yelled as I disappeared into the bank of trees.

"She's just a girl. She can't get far. Go around, I'll follow her," a gruff voice ordered.

I entered the forest on a well-worn path, running straight ahead. When I saw that the woods only went so far in the direction I was headed, I veered off the path. Staying within the thick protection of the trees, I alternately cursed and praised the darkness. I'd run a quarter mile in when I heard the blond guy's gruff voice sing-song "Narrr-ah", then deepened in a growl of anger, "Come here, you little bitch."

Panic shot through me, but my lungs were on fire, so I quickly stopped and threw my back against a thick oak tree, doing my best not to pant or make any noise.

I thought back to the day Ethan had helped jumpstart my car. I'd assumed I'd left my headlights on, but now with these two psychos chasing me, I realized those guys probably turned my lights on to drain my battery so they could "offer" me a ride. That'll teach me to lock my car.

Why were they after me? And why did the names Kurt and Jay sound so familiar? I wracked my brain trying to remember, but the fear pumping through my veins scattered my thoughts like the leaves falling from the trees around me.

The blond one had stopped running. The underbrush rustled as he walked a few steps, then stopped. Probably listening for my footsteps in the thick leaves.

I heard the dark-headed guy running through the woods too, but he'd run the opposite way from me and had apparently doubled back.

"Jay, that you?" The blond, not more than ten feet away from me, yelled out in the dim light.

"Yeah, I haven't seen her yet," Jay answered from afar.

"Go to the edge of the woods and make sure she doesn't come out that way," Kurt said. His friend immediately headed off to his right, away from us.

Rustling kicked up once more. Every leaf-crunching step brought him closer, making my stomach twist. He was less than five feet away now.

"I know you're in here, somewhere between Jay and me," he said. "You've already cost me fifty bucks. Don't piss me off any more." His footsteps stopped, then thumped the ground hard, followed by a grunt of annoyance.

I can't believe he's after me over fifty dollars. So the "pretending to be offended that I'd dissed them" was just an act? Still, I had no clue why I'd cost him any money at all. I scanned the woods, looking for a path I could take that would allow me to work my way around him so I could head back toward the soccer field and my car in the lot beyond.

"I know you're the one who ratted David out," the Kurt guy said, after another thud and huff of frustration.

As soon as he said David's name, I froze. Everything clicked in my brain. Kurt and Jay were the names Lila had mentioned in the bathroom in my dream. I swallowed a gasp of renewed fear. Could these guys have been the ones who beat up Lila?

"I know you can hear me," he hissed, moving faster, closer than I wanted him to be. He was less than two feet away.

I clamped my lips shut and forced air out through my nose. My chest hurt from the effort to remain quiet.

"Wanna know how I found out it was you?"

He sounded so close and…gleeful, like he was enjoying hunting me. Grabbing the rough bark behind me, I bit my lip to keep my whimper locked inside. My pulse spiked, but I tried to keep it together, so I could react when I needed to.

"Lila called, ranting that I had nerve sending her flowers. When I told her I didn't send them, she said 'the real snitch' must've sent them, because nobody at school cared and her family thought flowers were a waste of money. Dork-boy at the florist held out forever. I had to scrounge up fifty bucks before he gave me your name."

Lila called the guy who beat her up? I wanted to scream at the idiotic girl. I'd written a check for the flowers. A check, which had my name on it. I squeezed my eyes shut, cursing my own stupidity.

"But what's been bugging me all this time." The crunch of the leaves was almost on top of me.

My heart pounded, making me lightheaded. I could hear his heavy breathing. I slowly lifted my foot and set it down on the other side of a bulging root, then slid myself slightly around the tree and away from the direction of his voice.

"And what's been driving us nuts..." he continued.

The silence that followed freaked me out more than the noise of his steps closing in. I inched further away from where I'd last heard his voice, praying I could stay out of his line of sight.

A blur crowded my vision as he came around the side of the tree and slammed his hands against the bark, blocking me in. "How did *you* know about the bomb?" Kurt snarled.

I was so shocked he'd caught me, a small scream escaped, but I knew that if I let him grab me, I'd end up like Lila…or worse.

Jerking my leg up, I nailed him in the groin as if I were aiming for a goal three soccer fields away.

As soon as he stumbled back and grabbed his crotch, I turned to run. Tripping over more tree roots, I stumbled, then took off in the direction of the soccer field.

Kurt staggered after me, coughing hard. "Stupid whore," he groaned, then howled, "Jay, she went this way!"

It took all of my willpower not to scream hysterically, but I knew I needed my lungs for running. I ran in terrified silence, ducking past tree branches, jumping over logs, zigzagging around trees, doing my best to make it hard to track me. The darkness cloaked my movements, but also forced me to slow down temporarily when a tree branch sent slicing pain along my cheek. My legs trembled and my lungs burned, but I plunged onward.

As soon as I dodged around a big oak tree, I'd never been happier to see the soccer field lights through the tops of the trees.

A surge of energy jolted through my system, and my feet hammered the ground as I jumped onto the walking path and pushed even harder. I just needed to get to my bag, grab my keys and cell and run to my car. I sent a silent prayer that I could do all those things before the guys caught up with me.

When the edge of the forest came into view, I swallowed a sob. Safety. Soon.

Startled birds scattered out of the trees, flying away in a rush of flapping wings. Their panicked flight heightened my own, and I dug my feet into the underbrush, giving my shaking legs everything I had.

Almost there.

The moment I cleared the woods, someone grabbed my arm and whipped me around.

"No!" I screamed and struck out, hammering his chest with my fist. I didn't make it this far to give up with out a fight. I kicked at his shin, then I swung my other fist. Anything to be free.

He easily deflected my punch and yanked me toward him, folding his arms around mine in a vise-hold.

Panting, I struggled and looked for a place to bite.

Just as I was about to sink my teeth deep, he gritted out, "Nara, it's me."

When Ethan's voice penetrated my mind, the fight drained out of me. Sobbing, I babbled against his chest between gasps of air. "Two…guys…ch—chasing me. Want to...hurt me."

Ethan stroked my ponytail. "You're safe." His fingers slid down the back of my neck cupping it in a protective hold. "I've got you."

Just then, Kurt came thundering into the clearing, yelling, "I'm going to make you pay for—" he halted and looked left, then right. Glancing back, his attention locked on Ethan and me.

Jay ran into the clearing from another area of the woods. "I heard her scream. It came from this direct—" he stopped speaking, then cut his gaze our way.

Kurt nodded to Jay and they started toward us. Trembling, I wrapped my arms around Ethan's waist and pressed against him, trying to absorb his calm strength.

A shadow caught my eye, and a big hulking guy with olive skin and long black hair stepped out from behind one of the trees to our left and then another tall, thin guy with a spiky blond Mohawk followed him. Crunching leaves sounded to our right. Two other rough-looking boys, their jackets' hoods pulled over their heads emerged from the edge of the woods. The field lights reflected their dark, angry eyes. I didn't recognize any of them from our school. All of the newcomers looked fierce and mean, like they'd lived hard, rough lives and wanted the rest of us to experience their pain firsthand.

When the huge, meaty one punched his fist into his open palm, and the tall guy beside him pulled out a switchblade knife, I glanced at Ethan, eyes wide. *Could this nightmare get any worse?*

Ethan stared Kurt and Jay down. "Don't go near Nara again." Nodding to the big guy as well as the other three boys, he said, "My friends will make sure you don't forget my warning."

Wrapping his arm around my shoulder, Ethan led me away from the circle of guys. My legs shook as we walked. I winced when I heard running, then yelling and whoops that sounded much further away. The guys must've chased Kurt and Jay into the woods. I didn't want to think about what was happening behind us, but I had to say something. Someone could get killed if things got out of control.

"They won't hurt them too much, will they?"

Ethan stared straight ahead. "My friends have been in tons of fights. They'll be fine."

"What about the guys who were chasing me?"

Anger lit his eyes. "They deserve much worse than they'll get."

I stopped walking. "Just how far will your friends go? I mean, those two jerks need personality alterations, but I really don't want someone being 'maimed for life' on my conscience."

Ethan rubbed his eyes with his thumb and forefinger, then sighed. "They'll be scraped and bruised but able to walk. Better?"

My mind eased, I nodded and let him lead me to the soccer field.

I tried to pretend my hands weren't shaking while I collected my ball and put it in the bag. If Ethan hadn't shown up…

Once we'd stowed my stuff in the back of my car, Ethan opened the car door and waited for me to get in. Even though I wanted to ask him so many questions, I was afraid to speak. It felt like we'd moved to a whole new level in our friendship, but I wasn't sure what that level was.

Every nerve ending urged me to hug him, to show my appreciation, but I was unsure. Would he pull away? I didn't need any more rejection in my life. "Thank you for being there," I said in an unsteady voice.

Ethan clasped my wrist and pulled me into his arms, holding me close. "I'll always be here for you."

I shuddered against his chest, mumbling into his flannel shirt. "You weren't at school and I didn't see you after practice. I thought for sure no one would hear me scream when those guys finally got their hands on—"

Warm fingers tilted my chin up. "I had something to do today, but I'd never leave you hanging. When I saw your stuff on the field and then I heard a guy yelling, 'She went this way,' in the woods…" he paused, tensing. "I freaked."

"You got to me just in time." I tried to smile but my lips trembled. "Who knew knights wore flannel shirts and Led Zeppelin tees?" I knew I sounded like a goof, but I didn't care. I wanted him to know how much his rescue meant to me.

Ethan leaned close and I closed my eyes as he lightly kissed my cheekbone, then my forehead. He had no idea that his gentle kiss had melted something inside me, how much I craved the physical connection. His warm lips lingered against my skin for a second before he took a step back and shoved his hands in his jean pockets.

"I'm no hero, Nara." His gaze narrowed briefly toward the woods. "Go home. I'll see you tomorrow."

~

I HEADED TOWARD BARBOURSVILLE INSTEAD. I didn't want to go home to an empty house. By the time I turned onto my aunt's long, winding driveway that led way back into the woods, I'd finally quit trembling. Stopping my car at the end of the driveway, I frowned at my sunglasses scattered on the dash.

As soon as I finished rearranging them in a straight line from the biggest frame size to smallest, I shook my head. "Why are you sorting shades? Sheesh!"

Glancing at my aunt's ranch-style house, warm lights glowing from within, I started to relax. With Aunt Sage, I could vent and discuss my worries. I could totally be myself, well... mostly. The thought she might think I was insane if I told her about my dreams—and we'd lose our closeness over it, or even worse, she'd ask me about it every time we saw each other—made me anxious (with Gran, the subject of my ability rarely came up). I just wanted to be a regular person with my aunt.

From the front, Aunt Sage's home looked tiny, but she'd built a studio off the back for her custom design jewelry business. Her house was an eclectic mix of bohemian and down-to-earth, and it always smelled like an intriguing combination of incense and pastries. She made such wonderful pies that I'd become a snob, refusing to eat deserts anywhere but at my aunt's house. My friends thought I was nuts passing up ice cream (I'm the only person I knew who didn't like ice cream. No, I'm not lactose intolerant) and other good desserts, but they hadn't tasted my aunt's pies.

Barking preceded Bo's white snout poking behind the curtains. More barking ensued and two seconds later his small muscular frame dashed out the dog door. Thunderous barks followed, and then Luke's massive black body settled next to Bo's on the porch as I approached. A Jack Russell and a Rottweiler. What a pair.

"Thanks for the welcome, boys." I scratched behind their ears. "How's Duke doing?" Movement caught my eye and Duke was slowly pushing his head and body through the dog door. As he tentatively approached, I reached out my hand. "Hey buddy." He sat and I patted his head. "You look great."

As soon as I stepped onto the porch, Bo leapt into my arms. When Luke panted and raised his ears, his expression hopeful, I shifted Bo to my hip and put my other hand up in warning. "Don't even think about it, big guy."

Aunt Sage opened the door. "Inara, sweetheart. I've been hoping you'd come by," she said and immediately yanked me into a hug. I hugged her quickly, then stepped back. Living with my mom, I always felt a little unsure how to handle my aunt's demonstrative affection, yet every time Sage gathered me close, a hole inside me widened and I found myself wishing, *Why can't Mom hug me like this?*

Taking in my zip-up jacket, athletic shorts and flops, Aunt Sage said, "Practice huh?"

When I nodded, Bo, who didn't like being ignored, began to shove his head back and forth, looking for more pats. I set him on the floor and followed Aunt Sage inside. Bo had already scrambled up the cushioned chair to balance on the back and stare through the curtain. Most likely looking for squirrels to hunt. "I swear that dog acts like a cat."

Aunt Sage patted Luke's thick jowls, then rubbed Duke's soft head, the stack of gold bangles on her arm clinking with the rhythmic movement. "And just like a cat, Bo rules the roost in this house."

"He *thinks* he's the big dog," I said when Bo leapt from the top of the chair to dive-bomb Luke, then took off down the hall with the Rott in fast pursuit. Ever watchful, Duke lumbered behind them in a slow lope.

"Duke seems to be adjusting well."

"He's a sweet dog. He was a bit skittish when I got him

home last night, but Bo and Luke took to him right away." Sage's tone hardened slightly. "It makes me so angry to see the evidence of his mistreatment."

"His situation was pretty awful."

"That was a kind thing you and Ethan did, Inara. Dangerous, but kind. Please don't do that again. Your mother would have a heart attack."

Waving her hand like a magic wand whisking the topic away, she said in a lighter tone, "Guess what I have..." as she walked off toward the kitchen.

I sniffed the air and followed her long-legged stride, smiling at the multi-colored dress swirling around her bare feet. You'd never know she had a willowy figure underneath the baggy clothes she preferred to wear. I was built more like my aunt than my mother's medium, stockier frame, though Aunt Sage was three inches taller than me.

Baked apples and cinnamon floated teasingly in the air the moment I entered the kitchen. "Pie!" I squealed.

Aunt Sage laughed and handed me a napkin before she opened the cabinet and pulled down two mugs. "Coffee?"

When I eyed the napkin, she touched her cheekbone. "War wound from practice?"

I quickly dabbed at my cheek, coming away with a thin streak of blood. I'd forgotten about the tree limb cutting my face. "Yeah." Forcing a laugh, I tossed it into the trashcan, then pulled out a high-backed wicker chair and sat down at the mosaic table. "Coffee would be awesome."

While chewing a bite of pie, Aunt Sage paused briefly and pointed her fork. "Don't tell your mother. She'll be upset you had dessert before dinner."

Shoveling the last piece of warm, gooey apple-crusted goodness into my mouth, I mimed an X over my heart.

Aunt Sage winked and picked up our plates. Setting them in the sink, she settled across from me once more as I stirred more milk into my caramel-colored coffee.

"I can tell you've got something on your mind. Does it have anything to do with the boy I met last night? He's an interesting one."

Her casual comment instantly sidelined my riotous thoughts about the incident in the woods. "What makes you say he's interesting?"

Aunt Sage looked contemplative. "I've never met such an old soul before."

Ethan definitely came across as mature, and my aunt had always had keen intuition about people. "What do you mean by 'old soul'?"

"I can't explain it. He just has a kind of a 'been there, done that' vibe about him."

I stiffened. "I don't think Ethan has a 'know it all' attitude."

She shook her head, her curls bouncing like a soft, red halo. "That's not what I meant. Your friend's power…it's off the charts. I haven't experienced that level of energy before, even in people who claim to have been reincarnated and lived several lifetimes."

My eyes widened and she patted my hand briefly. "It's nothing to worry about. All I was saying is that Ethan has a fascinating inner strength. It's amazing to see in someone so young."

"Yeah, he's a solid friend." That part was definitely true. He'd been there for Duke last night, and then he'd saved me tonight. As for the closeness that was developing between us, I wasn't quite sure what to call it. I just knew that it felt…right. Unlike the rest of my life lately.

I hated feeling so out-of-control. Hated not knowing what was coming. If I'd still had my dreams, I would've known Kurt and Jay would try to attack me, and I would've left practice when the other girls did.

Even though worry over my aunt's reaction to my gift still nagged on my conscience, a part of me believed confiding in her at this point was the right thing to do—I needed advice and guidance.

Sage was into tarot, had done a few séances and had gone ghost hunting with her friends. She also maintained a bookcase full of paranormal and New Age books. In a way, my dreams were similar to the divination she sought in her daily tarot readings. Hopefully she'd understand my gift and how I missed the certainty and comfort it brought me.

Wrapping my hands around the coffee mug, I let the warmth soak into my skin. "I know you're into all this New Age stuff…" I began hesitantly.

She smiled, her hazel green eyes reflecting patience.

"Life's been kind of crazy lately."

"Do you want a reading with the cards?" Sage asked, before taking a sip of her coffee.

I shook my head. "A couple weeks ago I could've told you my own future, but now…"

Aunt Sage's calm expression faded. "What did you say?"

"I said I could've told you my future, but now I can't, and it's really bothering me that I don't know what's going to happen."

She gripped my hand. "Are you telling me you can see the future, Inara?"

I braced myself, surprised by her sudden intensity. *Please don't let her freak out*. "Um, not exactly. I can just see *my* future, but only what was going to happen one day ahead."

She frowned slightly. "I thought I sensed something in you, but convinced myself my mind was playing tricks, because you would've told me if that were the case." Guilt gripped me as she squeezed my fingers and her frown smoothed out. "How long have you been able to see ahead, sweetie?"

At least she seemed to believe me and wasn't freaking out. I withdrew my hand and took a sip of coffee as I considered how much to tell her. Mom would've immediately made an appointment with the family doctor and insisted on a psych referral. Elizabeth Collins saw things in black and white, hence the reason my mom was CFO and worked with numbers all day long.

Setting the cup down, I decided to tell her everything. "Since I was seven."

When she gave a little gasp, I rushed on. "It's no big deal. It helps with school and stuff."

"Why didn't you tell me before now?"

Hunching my shoulders, I sighed. "I'm sorry, Aunt Sage.

Mom doesn't know and I don't plan on telling her." When I saw the hurt look in her eyes, I skipped the confession that Gran knew. "I didn't say anything to you before, because I felt that if I didn't have to talk about it, I could pretend I was the same as every other kid."

She gave a slow nod of understanding, then her brow furrowed. "This gift to see ahead is unusual, Inara. I hope you're not misusing it."

"Misusing it?" I hadn't expected her to take that position about my powers.

"In my studies I've learned to respect the balance of nature, the natural give and take."

Sadie flickered through my mind, but I dismissed the memory. Everything had turned out all right after I'd called in the bomb threat...and Kristin was okay. "I try not to get involved in things, but if I hadn't acted recently, a lot of people at my school could've been hurt."

Puzzlement crossed her face, then realization dawned. "Are you talking about the bomb threat?"

When I nodded, something close to panic flitted through her eyes. "Would you expect me *not* to act, Aunt Sage? Who knows how many people could've been seriously hurt." *And God, Ethan probably would've been killed.* Waving my hand, I continued, "That was an unusual circumstance. Mostly my gift just makes it easier to deal with life stuff. But the reason I'm telling you now is because I stopped having my dreams a couple weeks ago—that's how I see my next day, in my dreams the night before—and I've only had them twice since. Do you think you could help me get them back?"

Aunt Sage looked like she was processing several things at once as she absently stroked the teardrop crystal hanging on her necklace. "When you lost your dreams the first time, had anything in your life changed prior to that?"

You mean like calling in a bomb threat? Screwing up in soccer and having problems talking to my best friend? Oh, and I met Ethan. I shook my head. "No, it's been pretty much the same old, same old."

"Did you hit your head, maybe while playing soccer?

"No. My dreams just stopped. What's weird is that now that I don't have my dreams, I don't dream at all. I'd really, really like them back."

Her hand paused over the necklace. "Is there something else, Inara?"

Her assessing look reminded me that there was more to my aunt than the "free love" persona she projected. She'd made a killing with an internet-based business, and then shrewd investing later that had funded her jewelry business. "I'd just rather know about stuff ahead of time, so I can get back to my old self. That's all."

Aunt Sage pursed her lips. "Mmmm, hmmm. I think you're not telling me everything, but for now I'll do some research to see if I can help you get your dreams back. It could be some kind of mental block. Maybe your body just needs a good cleansing."

I hadn't thought that a mental block could've caused my dreams to flicker in and out, but it was possible the whole bomb incident had messed with me more than I realized. It felt good to finally share my secret with my aunt. And if I did finally get my dreams back, at least I wouldn't have to worry about accidentally mentioning her tarot reading before she'd had a chance to tell me about it. There'd been a few close calls in the past.

~

LATER THAT NIGHT, while taking a shower, I'd just lathered the soap bubbles on my face when a sharp pain radiated across my cheek. Wincing, I moved my hands to avoid my forgotten wound, when a sudden realization made my heart do a crazy staccato dance. Ethan hadn't just been kissing my cheek, he'd kissed my wound.

Holding onto that bone-melting thought, I quickly finished my shower and crawled into bed early. As I lay in the dark, I relived the sensation of Ethan's warm hands on my face, his soft lips on my skin and his hard chest pressed against mine as he held me close, over and over.

I'd been kissed by boys before, even had a boyfriend for a whole week when I was fourteen, but Ethan's kiss didn't feel like the fast spin to thrillsville guys had taken me on in the past. It felt like a road trip, a journey to somewhere entirely different. Somewhere solid and real.

Why had I let my own fears keep me from hugging him back? Everything about him intrigued me. I was falling deeper and deeper for this guy, which made me a little anxious. I knew so little about him. That had to change.

CHAPTER 8

The next morning, as I passed from one class to the next, I felt compelled to scan the crowds in the hallways, looking for Kurt and Jay. I must've held and released my breath a hundred times before I finally spotted each guy. Even though they'd both intentionally turned their swollen and bruised faces away when I passed them at separate times in the hall (I wasn't exactly thrilled to see them either), I was relieved neither was having to use a wheelchair or crutches to get around school.

Gossip flew around that they'd gotten into a knock-down, drag-out fight with each other. Considering I saw them pass one another in the hall later and neither said a word or acknowledged the other guy, I could see why people believed that was the case.

When I saw Ethan's dark head weaving in and out of the students crowding the locker hallway after lunch, I mentally psyched myself up for the challenge. *I will get to know him better today.*

I'd worn a v-neck emerald green sweater with faded jeans and my ankle boots. Wearing a sweater of any kind lately tripped my *argh my clothes won't stop sticking to me* comfort meter. Today was no different. Static city. But I knew this sweater looked best with my eyes. Mascara was normally my only makeup, but today I'd added a bit of eyeliner before I took the time to flip the ends of my hair out. Dealing with the curling iron in the morning usually got on my nerves, but at least my extra efforts seemed to have paid off. A couple of the football players had raised their eyebrows and whistled as I walked past. I'd waved, but didn't stop to talk. I was on a mission.

When Ethan approached, I leaned against his locker. Instead of being surprised by my bold move, his dark blue eyes softened. "You okay?" he asked, grazing his knuckles across my cheekbone near my wound.

"I'm fine." My voice cracked and my skin electrified where he'd touched me. I nearly forgot my goal—that "getting to know him better" vow I'd made—but I forced myself to focus. "I saw my aunt last night. Duke's doing great."

Ethan looked pleased. "I'm glad. Thanks for finding him a good home."

I smiled and my fingers flexed, crinkling the paper in my hand. "Oh, by the way," I handed him the note. "Here's what you missed in History yesterday."

As he glanced down at the paper, I rambled, "We were paired up to work on a paper about war. Since you weren't there, I volunteered to be your partner."

His gaze met mine. "Partners, huh?"

"We study together anyway." I hoped I sounded casual. "The paper can be on any aspect of war. We should probably meet in the library today during study hall time."

Ethan's eyebrows shot up as he moved his book and notepad from one hand to the other. "The library?"

"The project's not due for a while, but I thought maybe we'd see if the school library has anything useful." My heart pounded harder as I continued, "Oh, and I wrote my cell on that paper. What's yours?"

"I don't have one."

He looked slightly amused, but I wasn't sure if it was because I seemed to be taking over our project or that I'd just asked him for his phone number. "You don't have a cell?" *Who doesn't have a cell phone nowadays?*

He shrugged. "I don't like being that easy to track down."

I guess not carrying a cell matched his loner personality, but it left me feeling four steps behind his long-legged stride without a way to catch up. How was I supposed to do that when texting and chatting on my cell were my lifeline? Finally my stalled brain kicked in. "Um, okay. You have a landline phone, right?"

When he smirked and nodded, I felt stupid for asking. "Why don't you call me if you miss class and want your homework assignments and stuff."

"Deal." Just then, the bell rang and the noise in the hall shot up. Leaning close, his lips brushed my ear. "See you in the library."

~

I WAS STANDING between two tall bookshelves in the library, scanning through the books on a shelf when Ethan's delicious smell wrapped around me.

"Hmm, somehow I don't think graphic novels are the teacher's idea of appropriate source material," he said in a low tone.

Grabbing a slim volume called *The Demon's Lair*, I flipped it open, then turned to face him. "I was just killing time until you got here." I tilted the book so he could see the colorful, graphic pictures of a demon fighting a two-tailed scorpion. "You ever read these?"

Ethan's focus locked on the pages long enough that I hoped he'd tell me about the horned creature I'd seen in his notebook. "Nope. I read fantasy books by Salvatore, Jordan and Brooks."

Didn't fantasy books have otherworldly creatures in them? Maybe he created drawings based on figures he'd read about. Sounded logical. I glanced at the demon locked in battle with another equally hideous monster. "There's some great detail in this artwork."

Ethan put his hand on the bookshelf above me and stepped closer, flattening the book against my chest. "Nara, if you have something to ask me, just ask."

What would he say if I asked him about his drawings? Would he push me away because I'd asked something too personal?

"I—" I dropped my gaze to the book and slowly shut it. "No, nothing to ask."

He caught my chin and made me meet his gaze. "You're going to ignore all those nasty rumors about my drawings, the stories that I was expelled from my last school, and the dangerous friends I have without a single question?"

How did he know what I was thinking, the things I wanted to ask, but didn't? I was so blown away, I answered honestly. "Yeah, I guess I am."

His gaze narrowed slightly as he slowly traced his finger down the side of my neck. "Why?"

Everything inside me warmed and jumped to life when he touched my skin. I closed my eyes as goose bumps scattered across my body, electrifying every nerve ending. "Because we all have secrets," I admitted before locking gazes once more. "Our friendship is all that matters to me."

Interest reflected in his steady stare. His finger had stopped on the pulse beating along my throat. "If I asked you your secret, would you tell me?"

My heart rate jumped and I looked away. I didn't want to lose Ethan. The agony I'd feel if he walked away from our friendship told me just how much I'd fallen for him—a boy I didn't know.

Our librarian, Mrs. Honeycutt, walked past, her Q-tip French twist whipping around in a double-take. She waved a finger at us, disapproval reflecting behind the half-moon glasses perched on her nose. Ethan stepped away and the connection between us, the magnetic attraction that had drawn us closer, faded.

Shoving the graphic novel back on the bookshelf, I cleared my throat. "So, wars…"

Ethan searched my face for a moment, then nodded toward the windows at the back of the library. "Right. I think the history books are over there."

~

THAT AFTERNOON, as I was walking out to my car, a sandy-haired guy who'd been walking straight ahead of me, began to drift to the right. I eyed him like a car that's starting to drift into my lane and immediately sped up.

Just as I was about to pass him, he stumbled and rammed into me.

"Ow!" I grabbed my shoulder. "Are you whacked?"

"Sorry." Rubbing his forehead, he blinked as if trying to focus. "I have vertigo. When it hits, it makes me so dizzy, I can barely walk."

And I'll be driving on the same road with this guy? "You're uh, not driving, are you?"

"Nah, I've been banned until it clears up. Hitching a ride with my neighbor—"

"In this lifetime, Alan," a guy impatiently called from across the lot.

"I'm coming," he waved to his neighbor, then slowly turned back to me with a rueful grimace. "Can't jerk my head around too fast or I'll pass out. Anyway, sorry again."

"No worries."

As I watched him stagger toward his friend's car, my gaze snagged on Sophia talking to Jared by his Jeep. I started toward my car and tried not to look obvious that I was watching them through my shades, but seeing Sophia giggling while digging her hand into Jared's front pocket made me halt in disbelief.

Jared was talking and kind of laughing, so I couldn't tell if he was enjoying her flirting or if he was nervous and uncomfortable and trying to laugh it off. A car beeped behind me, and I quickly moved out of the way, continuing on to my car.

I'd just unlocked my door when I looked up to see Sophia staring at me from across the lot. Jared was nowhere in sight. I lowered my glasses and stared hard to let her know I'd seen her with Jared. Her eyes narrowed for a brief second, then her lips curved in a mocking, victorious smile before she got in her car and drove off.

I tried to call Lainey, but got her voicemail, so I sent her a text.

Call me. I need to talk to you.

I didn't hear back from her until a couple hours later, when I was on my way to our game. Grabbing my cell from my bag, I said, "Hey, are you at the field yet?"

A radio blared in the background. "I'm getting ready to turn into the parking lot. What's up?"

I pushed the cell phone closer to my ear. "I just wanted to warn you to keep an eye out for Sophia."

"Sophia? Why?"

I swallowed, not wanting to hurt my friend. She was the happiest I'd seen her. Ever since I'd known Lainey she was a pretty upbeat person, but now she just seemed to glow whenever she was around Jared. She'd spent less time spreading gossip and more time just hanging with him.

"I saw her talking to Jared in the parking lot. Let's just say it looked pretty friendly between them." I really didn't want to tell Lainey that Sophia had her hand in Jared's pants' pocket. That would *not* go over well…and I wasn't exactly positive he hadn't done something goofy like steal her car keys and shove them in his pants, saying, "If you want your keys, you'll have to get them yourself." Guys did crude stuff all the time for attention. But I couldn't quit thinking about the way Sophia stared at me in the parking lot earlier; her smile pretty much said, "I dare you to tell".

Lainey didn't say anything for a second, then she snapped, "I didn't want to believe she was right. Sophia *told* me you'd try to do something like this."

I pulled in a parking spot, then slammed on my brakes harder than I'd meant to. "Try to do something like what?"

"She warned me that you'd try to break Jared and me up. Actually, her exact words were, 'You should've seen Nara's face when I told her about you and Jared. Mark my words, she'll try to break you two up so she can have him.' And then, today, she called and told me you seemed to have it in for Jared." A sniff came across the line. "I was your friend, Nara. I supported you over the whole goalie thing. I even tried to look out for you with that Ethan guy, and this is the thanks I get? Why would you try to make my boyfriend out to be a cheating jerk?"

I couldn't believe she thought I'd try to break them up. I opened my mouth to tell her exactly what went on between Sophia and Jared, but she probably wouldn't believe me now anyway. Plus, I just felt she should believe her *best friend* over a teammate. I was right. Lainey had moved so far away from our friendship, she'd allowed Sophia to stir her into her cauldron of lies. I tried to keep my voice calm. "Do you really believe that?"

Lainey's voice hardened. "Now, I do."

How had Sophia manipulated Lainey so easily? It made me wonder if our friendship had ever been real. "When have I *ever* lied to you?" When she didn't answer right away, I continued, "If you choose to believe Sophia over me, then that's your issue." After I hung up, I was so angry and resentful, I stayed in my car until my hands stopped shaking.

That night, despite my argument with Lainey, I'd played well and only let one ball get past. We won our game against Southern, and hallelujah, I'd done it all on my own (well, with Ethan's practice help and encouragement).

During the game, Sophia and Miranda did their standard "whisper, then glance my way" snicker sessions whenever they got near each other. Lainey didn't speak to me before or after the game. She alternated between slumping her shoulders and holding her chin high. I couldn't tell if she was mad at me or just hurt. I didn't know what to do, but as long as she continued to believe Sophia, she wasn't going to listen to me anyway.

Several girls invited me to a party on Friday night to celebrate, but I couldn't muster the enthusiasm over the win or the realization that I seemed to have moved off the "Do Not Invite" list. My mom hadn't been there, and not that Ethan *had* to come, but after helping me practice this week, the close call last night, and then the "moment" we'd had in the library, I'd secretly hoped he would be in the crowd, cheering me on. Then again, I hadn't answered his question, which probably made him feel like I didn't trust him, even though I did. In so many ways. Just not with this one secret.

As I drove home, my cell phone pinged, letting me know I had a message. Once I'd put all my dirty soccer clothes into the laundry and started the machine, I grabbed my cell and opened the message, expecting a text from my mom.

The text was nothing but garbled letters and numbers. I closed the message and reopened it and my heart nearly stopped.

Please respond to this text, Nari. We need to talk.

I couldn't turn my phone off fast enough. My legs began to wobble and I slowly sank to the hall floor. Leaning against the washing machine in my sports bra and underwear, I couldn't believe it.

Only *one* person called me Nari.

Why was my dad texting me?

CHAPTER 9

I sat along the edge of the stacked bleachers in the gym, listening to the principal drone on. No amount of perfume or cologne coating the press of people sitting around me could cover the strong wax floor and decades old sweat scents that permeated the room. I didn't have a clue what Mr. Wallum was talking about. I'd totally zoned out from the boring words. Then again, I'd spent most of the day in a haze.

Many parts of my life—from losing my dreams and Lainey's friendship, to being attacked in the woods and now my dad texting me—were being tossed and jerked around, just like my dirty clothes in the washer last night. And just like my freshly laundered clothes I'd pulled out of the dryer, I wanted my life to go back to being neat and squeaky clean. Instead, it seemed to be headed in the "wrinkled with set-in stains" direction.

Pretending to be engrossed in the principal's less-than-fascinating speech was easier than thinking too much about Lainey not speaking to me, Ethan ditching my game, or the reason behind that stupid text message. It's not like I hadn't already considered other possibilities for the text I received last night, like maybe it was someone's idea of a sick joke.

Lainey was the only person who knew my dad left us. Everyone else just assumed my parents were divorced and I never corrected the assumption. But no matter how upset

Lainey was with me, I just couldn't see her doing something so cruel. Sophia or Miranda? Probably. But Lainey would have to have told them the truth about my dad for them to know how much it'd upset me to receive any kind of message from him.

"Bored out of your mind yet?" Ethan said from his standing position next to the bleachers.

I slid over to give him room, and as he vaulted up to settle beside me, I kept my gaze on the podium in the center of the gym. "Actually, it's pretty interesting."

"Really? What's he talking about?"

I glanced his way and stared blankly.

Ethan's brows shifted downward. "What's going on? You barely said two words in the hall."

I picked at the splintering step underneath me. "Nothing. We won last night," I said with as much pep as a limp noodle.

The crowd suddenly cheered and clapped as the cheerleaders walked out onto the floor. Oh yeah, I remembered now. This was a pep rally for the football game.

"I knew you could do it," Ethan spoke in my ear over the noise. "Congrats again."

I glommed onto his comment, sitting straighter. "Again?"

"Yeah." He nodded to the pocket where I usually kept my cell. "I left you a message last night. You got it, right?"

"Um, no. I didn't get it." He must've called after I'd turned off my phone. I hadn't turned it back on yet, because I didn't want my dad to try to text me again. My face burned as I pulled out my cell.

"You're just now turning your cell on?"

"Yeah, it's a shocker isn't—" I paused when my dad's text message from last night popped up. I'd shut off my phone without closing out of the text window.

Ethan didn't say anything as I continued to stare. Finally, I turned the phone his way so he could read it and spoke in a low voice, "My dad sent this message from the grave last night."

He scanned it and his brow furrowed in confusion. "If your dad's dead, how can he send you a text?"

"He's not dead." I deleted the message, punching the

buttons hard. "But as far as I'm concerned, he is. He walked out on us when I was five. I have no idea if that text message was real or if someone's screwing with me."

Propping his forearm across his knees, he eyed me. "Aren't you curious why he tried to contact you?"

I pressed my lips together and shook my head. Holding up my finger, I clicked the button to listen to Ethan's voice message and pushed my cell close to drown out the droning microphone in the background. I needed something good to scrub the raging resentment for my father from my brain.

As soon as I closed my phone, Ethan looked apologetic. "I'm sorry I missed your game last night. Something came up or I would've been there to see you rule that goal."

Whenever we talked, he made me feel so good. "Thanks. That means a lot. And now I have your number," I finished with a small smile.

Ethan's attention strayed back to my phone. "Why do you think someone would try to screw with you?"

I slid my gaze to Lainey, Miranda and Sophia chatting with a couple of the football players at the top of the bleachers. "I tried to tell Lainey about something I saw between Jared and Sophia in the parking lot yesterday. Now she thinks I only wanted to make her boyfriend look like a jerk so she'd dump him and then I could have him for myself." I shrugged. "Maybe that text message was some kind of payback."

Ethan stilled. "Do you? Like him?"

"Of course not," I said with a "duh" look, even as I thought, *He's not* you.

He glanced toward the top of the bleachers. "The guy *is* a jerk."

Nodding, I sighed. "Lainey's not talking to me. Right now she's eating up every lie Sophia feeds her. It's like Sophia's her own personal 'happy pill' dispenser."

Amusement sparked briefly in his blue eyes, then he nodded toward my phone. "What if the text is real?"

Music started blaring from the speakers and the cheerleaders began to gyrate on the floor.

"Not interested." I said a little louder over the din. "When my dad left us, it took my mom a long time to snap out of it. I won't go there again." I thought about my mom's reaction in my dream and honestly wondered if she could handle another round of rejection—a reminder he didn't want us.

The cheerleaders had started to build a pyramid.

I didn't think that discussing something so difficult for me would provide a rare opportunity with Ethan, but I realized now was the perfect time for me to ask about him. "Why are you living with your brother? Don't your parents miss you?"

"No. They don't."

Ethan stared straight ahead, but his hand clenched into a fist on top of his knee. "Do you miss them?" I asked tentatively.

His eyes flicked to me briefly. "I miss the way they used to be. I hate that they never trusted or believed me…and that they still don't."

Anger and resentment radiated from his thinned lips and narrowed gaze. He literally vibrated, holding his body perched on the bleacher's edge as if he were going to vault off any moment.

I scooted closer until our thighs almost touched. He needed someone who understood. I wanted to touch him, but was afraid he'd pull away. My stomach tensed as I lightly put my hand over his fist. "I'm sorry, Ethan. Parents can be so clueless sometimes." *Why had my mom never noticed that I just seemed to "know" things? I was different than other kids—too calm, too understanding—yet she'd never said a word.*

When Ethan inhaled deeply and his fist tightened under mine, I realized this was the first time I'd reached out to him. Worried I'd crossed some kind of line, I started to lift my hand, but he quickly slipped his fingers between mine, locking our hands together. "Not yet, Nara," he said in a harsh rasp.

Breathless, I glanced up. The look in his eyes, a mixture of angst, fierce need and hope, made my heart rate surge, battering my chest with hundreds of fist punches. I curled my fingers around his and we sat there in the stinky gym, completely oblivious to all the cheering and hollering around us.

COACH HAD CANCELLED PRACTICE, so Ethan walked me to my car after school. We passed by his car on the way and three black birds stared at us from his car's roof.

"What's with the black birds? You don't have a dead body in the trunk, do ya?" *See, Lainey, I came right out and asked.*

Ethan snorted. "They're ravens, a different species, and I have no idea why my car's their hang out spot." Reaching into his pocket, he tossed something and a few pieces landed on his roof with light plings.

As the birds quickly gobbled the hard bits up, I raised my eyebrows. "You're feeding them? No wonder they're multiplying."

"It's just kibble." He brushed the crumbs off his hand. "They kept pooping on my car when I shooed them away. Now, so long as I feed them, they seem content to poop elsewhere."

I chuckled. "If you can't beat 'em..." We'd just reached my car when my cell phone pinged. My attention automatically strayed to the Caller ID. It was the same as before—a text from an unknown number.

"Is it your dad?" Ethan asked.

Wind blew my hair around my face in a messy mop of blonde strands. I swallowed the lump in my throat and tucked my phone away. "Probably. He hasn't said jack since he left and now he's texting me? I have no idea how he got my cell number."

Ethan released a strand of hair that had snagged in the hinges of my sunglasses, his knuckles brushing my cheek. Sympathy reflected in his eyes. "Maybe you should text him back and tell him not to send you any more messages."

I blinked hard to suppress the tears of anger and worry over my dad's second attempt to contact me. *What if he tried to call my mom's cell? He knows my number. It's possible he might have hers.* Ethan's warm fingers palmed the back of my neck and he pulled me close. I dug my fingers into his jean jacket and buried my nose against his shoulder, soaking up his warmth and inhaling his unique smell.

Rubbing his thumb along the curve of my neck, his deep voice vibrated against my temple. "He's probably not going to stop until you respond."

Pulling back, I knew he was probably right, but I didn't want to face it. Not yet. "Want to go get some pizza?"

Ethan gave a wide-mouthed, gorgeous smile, the kind that made my stomach pitch and my legs shake. Taking a step back, I leaned against my car. No one had a clue how good-looking he was, because he'd never smiled like this at school.

"Wow," I said, yanking off my glasses.

He frowned, glancing down at his jean jacket and then his t-shirt underneath. "What?"

"Um, it's just...I had no idea you had such an awesome smile."

Ethan went red and then coughed a couple times before shoving his hands in his jeans pockets. "Er, thanks. No one's ever said that before."

His sheepish smile made me snicker. "If you smiled like that more often, you'd have the girls crawling all over you. On second thought, no smiling allowed." *I sounded jealous…and probably corny, but I didn't care.*

Stepping close, Ethan grasped a lock of my hair. "You're the only one who makes me smile like this, Nara."

My breath snagged. When he leaned closer and his lips almost touched mine, my fingers curled around my shades. I wanted to start our journey. Every nerve inside me was revved to hit the road.

My cell phone began to play *Witchy Woman* by the Eagles.

Pulling back, I slid my glasses on and tried to keep my voice even-keeled as my heart danced a jig in my chest. "My aunt gets worried when I don't pick up." *And she now officially has the worst timing ever.*

"Hey, Aunt Sage."

"Hey, sweetie." She sounded excited. Well, more than usual. "I think I have a solution to your dream problem."

Glancing surreptitiously at Ethan, I pressed the phone to my ear. "Really? That's great."

"Can you come over for dinner tonight and we can talk about it? I've already started making chicken Marsala."

My aunt only made that dish because she knew it was my favorite. Disappointment bloomed in my chest that I'd have to reschedule with Ethan. I'd asked for my aunt's help and she'd come through. I *had* to go. "Sure. What time should I be there?"

"Why don't you come on now? You can help me work on a new piece of jewelry before dinner. I've already called your mom and cleared it with her."

"Okay, see you in a few."

Once I hung up, Ethan asked, *"Witchy Woman?"*

I put my cell away. "The people I talk to the most get their own ring tone."

"I was referring to the fact you chose a song from the seventies for your ring tone," he said, looking impressed.

I flashed a cheeky grin. "Yeah, all my ring tones are older songs...well, except Lainey's. She'd be totally offended if I used an old song."

"What's hers?"

"Death of a Shopaholic by Psychedelic Rhythm."

Ethan laughed, then sobered. "I take it pizza's off."

"I'm sorry. My aunt's helping me with...a school project. How about on Saturday?" My mom would understand if we postponed our trip to Farmville to get a new couch. I'd been complaining that our old one needed to be replaced since I was ten. What would one more weekend matter?

"I can't. My brother's going out of town on business, so he's taking me to the football game on Saturday. Sunday and Monday are shot. I'm taking Monday off school, since we're doing a big roof repair project before he leaves for a week."

"A week?" I said, eyes wide. "My mom so wouldn't leave me for a week." As it was, when my mom went out of town for a couple of days, my aunt would usually call and check on me.

Ethan shrugged. "I've been on my own for as long as three weeks before. My brother works for the Military Intelligence Agency and has to travel sometimes."

"Do your—" I'd started to ask him if his parents knew he'd been left on his own for almost a month, before I remembered his comments in the assembly. "Do you miss Samson when he's gone?"

"Do you miss your mom?" he countered.

Ethan's question made my chest ache. I'd been missing my mom since my dad left. The truth bottled up inside, like a shaken soda can, ready to explode. "Mom's never gone for very long."

Unaware of my inner turmoil, Ethan pulled my sunglasses off. "You have gorgeous eyes. You shouldn't hide behind your shades, Nara."

Blinking at the sudden brightness, I warmed at his compliment. "Thanks," I said in a small voice. The way he looked at me, like he knew my true thoughts about my mom, made me squirm. Sometimes it felt like he could see right through me. "So, *do* you miss him when he's gone that long?"

Handing me my glasses, he said, "My brother can be such a pain sometimes—getting all parental and bossy—so I don't mind him going out of town once in a while. But after about a week though, I get tired of the same meal over and over."

I laughed, picturing him zapping microwave meals. Poor guy. The school's cafeteria food must've started to look pretty good near the end of his brother's three-week trip. "We'll just have to make sure you have at least one good meal while your brother's gone next week."

His eyebrows shot up in excitement. "Pizza?"

I grinned. He was determined. "We'll think of something."

Ethan opened my car door. "You'd better get going. It'll take a while to get to Barboursville."

The intimate moment we'd shared earlier had passed, but the memory of Ethan's smoldering gaze stayed with me as I drove off.

I'd only driven a few miles down the road when it occurred to me that I'd never told him where my aunt lived.

"THIS IS A SPECIAL PIECE, so let your imagination go wild." Aunt Sage handed me the plier-like tool and then returned to her own stool and counter workspace. I stared at the gorgeous light blue prism-shaped crystal and thin silver wire in my hands, thinking about the pointers she'd given me on twisting the thin threads of metal around the crystal and how to create tiny spirals on the ends to add decorative flair.

For the first several minutes, I gazed out the huge glass windows into the woods, hoping for some inspiration. Leaves were falling from trees like heavy colorful snowflakes, but a cluster of them had gotten caught in the breeze and whipped into a spinning kaleidoscope of brilliant colors. What caught my attention was the odd dark-colored leaf that spun around with them. Another gust of wind slammed the tunnel of leaves into the window and that's when I saw the unusual leaf wasn't a leaf at all, but a black feather.

An hour later, after a few false starts with slippery jewelry pliers, discarded wire and some hair-pulling frustration, I held up a delicate silver chain. "What do you think?"

Aunt Sage inspected the pretty crystal hanging by a swirled bail and its intricate holder I'd painstakingly designed. She smiled with pride as she took the chain from me to inspect the detail. "It's a beautiful feather motif. You're a natural, Inara. I'm so pleased with how it turned out."

When she stepped forward and slipped the chain over my head, I touched the crystal lying on my chest and glanced at her in confusion. "I thought you said this piece was a special project."

Her hazel eyes crinkled. "It was. *You* were the project." Touching the crystal, she continued, "Who better to create this necklace, than the person who would benefit from it? By working with the wire and the crystal, they've absorbed your energy."

"Are you saying this necklace will help my dreams return?"

"That's right. The crystal is a Celestite, and one of its main properties is to reduce stress and settle the mind. It creates stillness, an inner peace that allows for worries to leave the mind, opening it back up. It's associated with astral journeys but most importantly for you, it can also be used for dream recall." Tilting her head, she touched the crystal.

"What?" I asked, curious about the small smile on her lips.

"I wouldn't normally have chosen this crystal. It's not the first one that comes to mind for help with dream recall. Red jasper, agate and rose quartz are better known to help with that."

I rubbed my fingers across the blue crystal. "Then why did you pick this one?"

Her smile widened. "Because this particular crystal appeared in a dream last night. One minute my hand was empty and the next, this blue gemstone was there. And if that wasn't a sign about the best crystal to help with dreams, I don't know what is."

Hope swelled and my fingers folded around the stone. I wasn't much of a believer in the healing power of crystals, but it was worth trying. "Thanks, Aunt Sage."

"You're welcome. Be sure to wear your crystal to bed. Before you close your eyes, tell yourself you're going to dream. *Will* your dreams back."

During dinner, Aunt Sage cut into a piece of chicken and said, "You and Ethan seem to be close. Tell me about him."

Heat filled my face when I thought about our "almost kiss" in the parking lot. Swallowing my food, I said, "Obviously, he loves working with animals. He's a bit of a loner and quiet until you get to know him. He's wicked smart—oh, and he's a fantastic soccer player."

She smiled broadly. "You two sound like a perfect match."

I was afraid to think beyond tomorrow, to hope for too much. I didn't want to jinx anything so I gave a half smile. "Yeah, he's been a good friend."

Dinner zoomed by and as much as I wanted to hang with my aunt, I needed to get home. Mom and I were getting up early tomorrow to drive the hour and a half to the furniture store in Farmville, Virginia.

I stood in the doorway, saying goodbye, when Bo threw himself against my leg, demanding attention. As I bent to scratch his ears, my aunt spoke in a casual tone, "Inara, you should answer that text message."

My hand froze on Bo's head and I slowly lifted my gaze to

hers. The unspoken rule between us had always been that we didn't talk about my dad. Sage might be his sister, but as far as I knew she hadn't forgiven her brother for leaving us, nor had she had any contact with him. She gave us a monthly check that came from my dad's trust fund, and that was the extent of anything related to her brother. At least now I knew how he'd gotten my cell number.

My throat burned as I straightened, but I managed to speak past the anger welling inside me. "Aunt Sage, please don't give my number to strangers."

CHAPTER 10

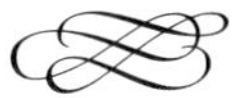

Once I crawled into bed, I slipped my new necklace over my head, then tucked it inside my t-shirt. Clasping my fingers around the crystal, I closed my eyes and concentrated on falling asleep. My mind tried to fight me several times. I kept thinking about my dad texting me and my aunt giving him my number, but I shoved the thoughts to the back of my mind and concentrated my energy on my desire to dream again. As I began to doze, I whispered with conviction, "Come back, dreams."

Claws tore into the warm blackness surrounding me, yanking me from my safe cocoon, tossing me into the air. I landed with a hard thump, skidding across pebbles in a deserted parking lot. Every bone in my body ached and my palms burned from the unforgiving asphalt.

Dust stirred, stinging my eyes and clogging my throat, but I quickly jumped to my feet. Three monsters closed in on me, their dark eyes spewing hatred.

One looked like a wild-eyed Minotaur, moving on cloven hooves and snorting through a curled black snout. Another appeared as a slimy brown blob with no real form other than thick arms, meaty fists and razor sharp teeth hanging in gelatinous goo. The last creature snapped his sharp, pointed teeth at me. It looked like an oversized Pit Bull with a powerful chest, a half-chewed nose and a severely scarred muzzle.

The blood-thirst radiating from the three of them made my stomach churn. I scrambled to my feet, fists raised. My shoes slipped on bits of gravel as I turned in a defensive circle.

The goo creature swiped his claws at me first, shredding my jacket. Gripping my aching, bloody shoulder, I jerked back while tears streaked down my face.

Sharp teeth suddenly dug into the spot between my shoulder and my neck. Crying out, I stumbled forward. The Pit Bull had attacked me from behind. He gave the death shake, inflicting horrific pain as he buried his powerful jaws deeper into my flesh.

I collapsed to my knees but barely felt the tiny rocks digging into my kneecaps. Gritting my teeth, I used all my strength to grab the dog's huge head and yank him forward. My shoulder tendons popped and my bones crunched as I flipped his body over my shoulder, but at least I'd gained my freedom. Pain raged through me as he landed hard on his back. That was about all the fight I had left in me. Blood oozed down my neck and my arm hung like a limp, shredded noodle by my side. As my vision began to blur, the Minotaur dug his claws into my other shoulder and yanked me toward him, his wide, sharp-toothed mouth swooping toward my face.

"I don't want to die," I tried to say, but all that came out was a sticky gurgle.

I woke screaming and drenched in sweat. The moment I sat up, nausea slammed hard. I stumbled for the toilet, tossing last night's dinner. After I'd rinsed my mouth, I walked over to my bed on shaky legs and sat down.

"Are you okay, Inara?" Mom called from downstairs.

Breathing deeply, I tried to calm myself. The scent of burnt bacon registered in my mind, making my stomach roil. Was there ever a piece of bacon my mom hadn't burned? Looked like we'd be stopping at Starbucks on the way out of town. "I'm fine."

"I've made breakfast. Get a quick shower and come on down. We need to hit the road."

"Okay." My voice was hoarse, as if I'd been screaming nonstop, which I had been in my dreams.

Grabbing the crystal from inside my t-shirt, I quickly pulled it off my neck and set the necklace on my nightstand. "Never again," I said with a shudder.

Some of my dreams had been physically violent and others were an emotional wrenching of the mind. Between each dream there was a void of blessed darkness that radiated quiet peacefulness. In the enveloping blackness, I thought I saw an outline of a circle; it was some kind of symbol, but when I tried to focus so I could see it, light began to bleed in and another nightmare began.

Running my hands through my damp hair, I wondered if the dreams I'd had were what other people called nightmares. If so, I never wanted to experience a "normal" dream again.Where had *my* dreams gone? Why had they deserted me?

ON THE WAY TO FARMVILLE, I sipped on my Starbucks mocha, all the while thinking about my dreams. When the sugar and caffeine kicked in, I asked my mom, "Do you ever dream?"

She glanced my way. "All the time."

"Do your dreams make sense?"

"Sometimes they do." She laughed. "Other times they make no sense whatsoever."

"Do you ever have nightmares?"

Mom cut her gaze my way. "Every once in a while. Why?"

I eyed the trees and farmland zooming past. "We talked about dreams in school, so it was on my mind. What are your nightmares like?"

"I don't know really." Lifting her shoulder, she shifted her attention back to the road. "I guess a nightmare would be one where I get lost and can't find my way back. Or when friends or loved ones walk away, leaving me behind."

"You could tell they were your friends or family? I mean, you recognized them?"

"Sure. Though every once in a while I'll dream about

someone I don't know too." She chuckled. "Those dreams fall in the 'weird dreams that make no sense' category. What about you? What do you dream about?"

I dream about getting my dreams back. I shrugged. "I don't dream."

"Of course you dream." Mom snorted. "Everyone dreams. You're such a heavy sleeper, you probably just don't remember yours."

"Yeah, that's probably it."

"That's a shame," she said, thrumming her fingers on the steering wheel.

My stomach dipped. "What's a shame?"

She met my gaze briefly. "The fact you don't remember your dreams. Even the bad ones can be beneficial in a way."

"How?"

"Nothing makes you appreciate life more than when you wake up from a nightmare and realize it was just that. It's a good reality check."

I grunted in response. What I'd dreamed last night could've been ripped from a twisted, mind-freak show. Reality check? More like, pulse check. I was just glad I didn't die in my sleep.

My cell pinged with a text message at the same time Mom patted my leg and nodded encouragingly. "Once you stop keeping zombie hours, you'll probably start remembering your dreams."

When I didn't immediately check my cell, she raised an eyebrow. "Something's definitely on your mind."

I held my breath as I glanced at the sender.

It was from Aunt Sage. *Did your dreams return?*

I quickly typed back. *No. Thanks for trying though* and hit send.

A few seconds later, she sent another message. *I'm sorry about last night.*

I typed back. *Tell him NOT to text me.*

"Must be Sage," Mom said.

My fingers paused over the keypad and my heart began to pound, until I realized Mom wasn't looking at my cell phone display. Quickly hitting send, I put my phone away. "How'd you know?"

She looked smug. "None of your friends get up before eleven on the weekends."

Yawning, I held my coffee up in silent agreement.

~

MONDAY WAS A MIXED BLESSING. I'd finally dreamed again the night before, but as the day wore on, indecision ruled my thoughts. I wished Ethan were there to distract me. While I knew my own day would flow along without a hitch, one of my teammates wouldn't be so lucky.

Tonight, Miranda would send an email to the team.

> *Jody had an accident during tonight's riding lesson. She has a concussion and her doctor banned her from sports for a week. She's upset that she won't be able to play this week, but we'll just have to do the best we can without her. See you at practice.*

Among the flurry of teammate emails asking for details, other tidbits would come through: Jody's saddle had loosened, causing the fall. Yes, she'd cinched it tight. She always did. She'd told Miranda she was so shaken by the accident she didn't know if she'd continue to ride.

The knowledge of Jody's impending accident stayed with me all day at school. Whenever I saw her short, athletic frame strolling down the hall between classes, I couldn't help glancing her way.

As I was pulling my backpack from my locker at the end of the day, I noticed Kristin stop at her locker down the hall to grab a new book. Seeing her notched my guilt higher. I didn't have a choice with the bombing event. I had to try to stop it, and I'd helped Kristin because I couldn't let the girl go through life with a scarred face, not if there was something I could do to prevent it. Thankfully, in both cases everyone had ended up fine, but Jody's injury *was* something she would recover from.

When Kristin walked away from her locker, my line of sight

fell on my teammate opening hers. *Should I or shouldn't I help Jody?* The question ping-ponged through my mind as Kenny, the guy whose backpack I'd carried a couple weeks ago, opened his locker next to Jody's. At least he was finally off his crutches.

Why was everyone's wellbeing suddenly on my radar, anyway? It wasn't fair.

Shutting my own locker hard, I turned and stalked off to my car to get my gear for practice.

~

DURING THE FIRST half of practice, I managed to stay focused and worked extra hard throughout the drills. I'd hoped the exertion would expel some of the frustration that simmered inside me every time Jody entered my line of sight. Then scrimmages started.

Do you have any idea how hard it is to *not* look at a soccer player while you're scrimmaging each other? Especially one who's a leading scorer and you're playing goalie? Watching Jody's dark head buzzing all around was like an annoying hangnail that wouldn't stop snagging on everything, tearing deeper and deeper.

"Nara!" Coach yelled down the field. "Sophia needs some time in the goal. Take the sweeper position."

The change Coach made meant I'd be the last defender between Jody and the goal. As I pulled off my goalie gloves, I realized I'd just been given another way to help my teammate. I was going to yank this hangnail until it bled.

When the opposing players passed the ball down the field and Jody took possession, my heart thudded and my leg muscles tensed. I was ready.

Another player stole the ball from Jody, but then her teammate got it back, punting it down the field to Jody once more.

Jody's shorter stature made her lightning fast on the field. She quickly dodged one of the fullbacks before sprinting straight toward me.

I could've met her head on, but I wanted to approach from behind, so I let her think she'd beat me as she zoomed by.

Pivoting, I quickly sprinted after her, then bent my right leg as I slid my left one between her feet in an aggressive slide tackle. *Yeah, I admit it. I went for her cleats and not so much the ball. Illegal, all the way.*

As Jody tumbled forward, Coach's whistle screeched across the field.

"Nara! What the hell was that?"

"Not cool, Nara," a couple players mumbled as Coach jerked his finger toward the bench with a deep scowl. "You're out the rest of practice for dangerous play."

Glancing at Jody, who was rubbing her ankle and glaring at me with hateful eyes, I stood up and held my hand out to her, saying in a sincere tone, "I'm sorry, Jody. It's been a while since I've slide tackled. Are you okay?" I didn't mean to seriously injure her. I was just hoping to bruise her enough that she'd decide to skip her horseback riding lesson today.

"What does it look like to you?" Ignoring my offer to help her, she pushed herself up. As she began to hobble around and test her ankle, she stopped briefly and snapped at me, "Aren't you supposed to be on the bench?"

AFTER PRACTICE, I sat in my car listening to the radio and worrying my bottom lip until it felt twice the size of my upper one. All I'd accomplished during practice was to piss Jody and Coach off. I'd be lucky if I got to play in the next game.

As I watched Jody kick off her flops and pop open her trunk, tension made my shoulders and neck ache. When my cell phone rang, I turned down the radio and welcomed the distraction that kept me from making a final decision. "Hello?"

"How was school?"

I was surprised to hear from Ethan, but my heart ramped at the sound of his voice. "Boring. How'd the roof repairs go?"

"Done."

He sounded tired and relieved. "Now you can come back to boring old school tomorrow."

"School's never boring with you around."

"Ditto," I said feeling warm inside, but my attention snapped back to Jody when I saw her pull another bag and her riding boots out of the trunk. "Listen, I've got to go. I'll see you at school tomorrow."

"Wait."

I paused. "Yes?"

"I wanted to talk about our history project."

Jody had opened her passenger door and set the bag and boots inside. My stomach churned. "Well…I—"

"I was thinking maybe we should pick a different angle on war than the teacher would expect. The U's library should have resources—"

"Ethan." Jody had opened her car door.

"Yeah?"

"I'm sorry, but I've got something I need to do. We'll talk about this tomorrow in study hall, okay? Bye." I hung up before he could say anything else.

I'd just opened my car door, when my radio's sound bumped up. Frowning, I reached over to turn it off and the digital numbers started flickering in and out. The radio station switched at such a rapid pace that all I heard was a snippet, "Do—" before the station moved again.

"—not."

And another station buzzed in.

"—enter."

Annoyed, I pushed the button, but the radio didn't turn off.

"—ear"

My heart slammed my ribcage and I pounded on the button harder. But the radio kept up its station selection schizophrenia, blaring out in rapid succession.

"Don't."

"Enter."

"Fear."

Freaking, I jerked my keys out of the ignition to cut off the power. Instant silence filled my car, but the hairs on my arms stood on end. I clenched my shaking hands into fists, welcoming the pain as my keys dug into my skin. *What the hell?*

When Jody's car light's flicked on and I heard the engine roar to life, I couldn't let her go without trying. Jumping out of my car, I hurried over and knocked on her window.

Jody jammed her hand through her spiky, sweaty hair, then rolled down the glass with an annoyed grunt. "What do you want?"

Wiping my suddenly damp palms on my shorts, I said, "I'm sorry about practice."

"You did that on purpose, Nara." She scowled. "What's your deal? You've been acting so weird lately."

"Nothing. I just…really am sorry." As Jody started to roll up her window, panic set in. "Um, I also wanted to say—" An icy shaft of air shot through me, stealing my breath and making my scalp itch. I shivered and smoothed the stray hairs floating around my face as I tried to think what to tell her or how to stop it.

"What?"

Her impatience made me anxious. She'd think I was nuts if I told her the truth. "Just…be careful riding."

Rolling her eyes, she zipped the window closed.

When her car shot out of the parking lot, the tire's squealed like she couldn't get away fast enough.

CHAPTER 11

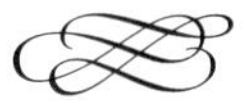

"Nara."

Jody called my name as I walked into school after first bell. I moved to the side and waited for her to catch up.

Stepping beside me, she spoke in a low voice, "You, uh… kinda freaked me out yesterday."

I quickly glanced at her head to see if she had a bandage or a lump on it. "I'm sorry about that, I was just—"

"No, no, that's not it." She waved her hand impatiently. "I'm trying to say thanks. You looked so upset, it bugged me a little, so last night I took it easier than I usually would've." Rubbing her shoulder, she winced. "Good thing, too. My horse's saddle strap slipped and I was thrown."

Feigning surprise, I said, "Oh, no. Are you okay?"

She started to shrug, then flinched. "I landed on my shoulder, but it could've been much worse if I'd been in a full gallop when it happened—" Pausing, her eyes drilled into me. "How'd you know?"

"Know what?"

"How'd you know that I'd get hurt?"

My face heated, but I tried to sound casual. "I—I didn't. I just felt bad that I might've hurt you during practice."

Doubt reflected in her face. "No, you said to be careful—"

"Hey Jody," Janelle from our team called as she walked in the door. "Heard you got hurt yesterday."

Waving to her, Jody returned her attention to me, but I thumbed toward the locker hall and turned in that direction. "Gotta head to my locker. See you later."

Jody frowned after me, but I wasn't hanging around for more questions. It had taken me eons to fall asleep last night. I couldn't quit thinking about what had happened with my car radio, to the point I'd sat up in bed and jotted down what I'd heard: Don't. Enter. Fear. When I read them aloud, that's when the meaning finally lined up in my mind. Don't Interfere!

The words had been purposeful and clear. Had whatever it was also tried to block the bathroom door that day I'd helped Kristin? It was hard to believe I'd imagined a jammed bathroom door suddenly swinging free. *What else could it be?* Questions kept turning over in my mind.

When I did finally fall asleep, I'd dreamed about my day today. Yet again Ethan wasn't in my dream, which put me on edge. I really hoped he'd be here, because my day wasn't going to start off very well.

The moment I saw Ethan leaning against my locker, holding a hardcover binder, pure elation shot through me, chasing away my anxiety about this morning. Instead of his usual Chucks, he wore black army boots, faded jeans, a heather gray t-shirt and an authentic-looking army green jacket. The look was laidback yet tough and it made me want to suggest we ditch school and just hang.

"Hey." I smiled and hitched my heavy backpack higher up my shoulder. "You got some sun. How was the game?"

"The game was great," he said, moving out from in front of my locker. "How was your weekend?"

"We bought a new couch." I kept my tone upbeat, even as I dreaded opening my locker.

"Aren't you going to put your backpack away?" he asked when I just stared at my locker.

I shot a quick glance at the crowd hanging near the other end of the hall, resenting their furtive looks. "Nah. The latch jammed on me yesterday. I'll um, do it later."

Ethan gestured to the door. "Unlock it. Let me see if I can get the latch to work."

I couldn't avoid opening my locker forever. I needed two books for upcoming classes. My stomach cramped as I slowly spun the combination. The moment I started to lift the lock, Ethan stepped close, saying, "Here, let me do it."

"Wait—" I tried to move in front of him, but he crowded me out of the way, pulling up on the latch before I could stop him. When he swung my door open, and I heard a hard thump, I leaned around his broad shoulders. A huge red paint blob covered the hard binder he'd held in front of his chest. Paint was also spattered on his jacket and fingers. My heart tripped with guilt. "Are you okay? I'm so sorry."

Ethan's jaw muscle jumped as he set the paint-stained binder on top of the lockers, then reached inside my locker. Groans of disappointment filtered from down the hall. I turned my narrowed gaze on Jared, Miranda and Sophia standing with a group of football players. Apparently, they weren't happy their paintball booby-trap hadn't pegged me. Lainey had just walked up. She looked confused when she glanced my way, then turned to fuss at Jared.

People's steps slowed. They were intrigued by the growing drama, wanting to know what had captured the popular crowd's attention.

I heard a loud crack, and then broken pieces of a paintball pistol slid diagonally across the hall floor toward their group. I glanced at Ethan in surprise. He stood with his fists clenched. A hulking football player stepped out of the group of pranksters, his dark features twisted in a scowl. "That was my gun, asshole!"

He'd started to cross the short distance between us, but a bleached-blonde girl stepped in front of him. Whispering something in his ear, she pointed further down the hall to the group of curious onlookers. Kurt's face turned beet red when he realized the girl was pointing at him. I couldn't believe it…*the girl* was Lila.

The football player's attention shot from Kurt to Ethan, wariness reflecting in his dark eyes. Grunting, he turned back toward his buddies, then paused to yell at the crowd watching, "What the hell are you looking at?"

"Mr. Brewer." Principal Wallum stepped out from behind a tall guy, addressing the running back in a stern tone. "My office. And bring that *gun* you're so fond of with you."

Everyone began to scatter the moment they heard Mr. Wallum's voice. Out of the corner of my eye, I watched Lila casually stroll to her locker, which happened to be five lockers down from mine. Before she opened the door, she glanced at Kurt walking past, eyeing the bruised hump on his broken nose. As she turned back to her locker, she caught me staring at her. A slight yellowish bruise traced her jawbone.

Even though I wasn't sure what to say, I felt the need to say something. "I—" but she cut me off with a quick jerk of her chin toward Kurt as he turned the corner then walked down another hall. Her gaze lingered on Ethan for a second before it slid back to me.

"Jay doesn't look any better," she said, her lips curving in a pleased smirk. "Consider us even."

Ethan's warmth radiated directly behind me. After Lila walked away, I glanced over my shoulder and whispered, "By lunchtime it'll be all over the school that *you* beat up Kurt and Jay." More fuel added to the rumors already circling about him. Could the guilt be slathered on any thicker?

His expression was as dark as it had been the day he'd saved me in the woods. "I don't care what people think about me as long as they leave you—"

When he paused, I quickly turned. He looked tense and had just put his hand on his forearm when I touched his shoulder. "Ethan?" Another terrifying image flared in my mind—this time a wrinkled, emaciated face with hundreds of razor sharp teeth. I swallowed a gasp. Even as the rational part of my brain said Ethan was the source, I shoved the logic and the fear away. He'd just protected me, saved me from harm. "Are—are you okay?"

"Yeah." He swallowed, lowering his hand to his side. "I just want people to leave you alone."

I searched Ethan's serious gaze, but I couldn't quite get the image I'd just seen out of my mind. The way he'd acted, shielding me when I'd tried to stop him from opening my locker, it was like...he knew. "How *did* you know about the paint gun?"

"I didn't know about—"

"Don't deny it," I shot back.

When he didn't respond, my heart began to pound and the concern I'd just shoved to the dark recesses of my mind began to glimmer. "You *knew,*" I insisted. The bell suddenly rang and I wanted to scream, *"Not now, you stupid bell!"*

Ethan turned and quickly grabbed a couple books from the haphazard stack in his locker.

"Ethan."

Pausing, he leaned close. His unique outdoorsy smell surrounded me as he spoke in a tense tone next to my ear, "Later. In study hall."

His comment put me on edge. "You're going to tell me, right?"

"Study hall." He backed away, his lips set in a grim line.

THE REST of the day moved like sap trickling down a tree. I could've sworn the clock's red second hand was stuck permanently *one second* before the end of every class. My thoughts spun. Beyond wondering *how* Ethan knew about the booby trap, I finally acknowledged the thoughts that had been simmering in the back of my mind. How did Ethan seem to know what I was thinking half the time? It was like he knew me better than I knew myself. The doubts about Ethan that I'd dismissed in the past, especially after I'd seen those freaky images when I'd touched him, rushed forward, along with a creepy, apprehensive feeling. *Was Ethan psychic? And what* did *those images have to do with him?*

I was so focused on my thoughts about Ethan that I hadn't given much thought to what had almost happened to me this morning, or the fact that Lainey's boyfriend had played a part in it. At least, not until I walked into study hall and saw her sitting with Jared.

Ethan's protectiveness made me reconsider my friendship with Lainey. She hadn't looked thrilled that Jared and his friends were responsible for "painting" me, yet she hadn't sought me out to apologize for them either. How had we drifted so far apart?

"Hey, Nara, you know this morning was just a joke, right? No hard feelings," Jared said as I started to pass them. He flashed me his classic, I'm-so-goodlooking-you'll-agree-with-anything-I-say smile.

Lainey's face was tense and pale. She looked like she wanted the floor to swallow her in one big gulp. Instead of anger, I felt sorry for her. I hoped she'd eventually figure out what a self-centered idiot Jared was.

I shrugged. "No biggie."

Beaming, Jared hooked his arm around Lainey's slumped shoulders. "See, Lane. She's cool."

"See you at practice, Lainey," I said, hoping she knew I didn't blame her. I was just sad our friendship was suffering.

While I waited for Ethan at an empty table in the corner, I opened my math book and was surprised to see a piece of folded notebook paper tucked inside the front cover. Pulling the paper out, I read the note my mother had written.

Inara,

I had a great time in Farmville. We should go on another trip. Maybe to Williamsburg? I hope you're happy with the new couch, since you spend more time on it than me. Ha! I wanted to let you know that I'm coming to your game this week. Aren't you glad?

Mom

Laying the paper down on the table, I smoothed the crease with my finger and then reread it three times, my heart swelling. Tracing my fingertips over my mother's intricately swirled writing, I marveled at her penmanship—mine had sharp points and thin lines, resembling a chicken on crack. The fluttery feeling in my chest made me lightheaded. After sending me hundreds of text messages over the past few years, Mom had no idea how much *this* handwritten note meant to me.

When I saw Ethan walk in, I folded my mom's note and slipped it back inside my book.

"Sorry I'm late." Ethan sat down in the chair beside me. "Mr. Markham kept me after to go over the stuff I missed in Chemistry the other day."

I waved my hand, my impatience hitting the red meter. "No detours. Spill."

A hint of a smile tugged on his lips. "Did you know your eyes are a much lighter green when you're excited or happy about something? I'll bet I can guess why."

Detoured already, but *this* should be interesting…and a good test to see if he really could read minds. I'd decided that *must* be his secret. No way he'd get this right. "Guess away."

"Your mom's coming to your soccer game."

My smile quavered. "Um, good guess."

Ethan glanced at my math book. "It's more about the note she wrote than your game, isn't it?"

A chill rippled through me. "How—how did you know about it?"

Setting his elbow on the table, Ethan tucked his knuckles under his chin. "I thought you wanted to know how I knew about the booby-trap in your locker."

"I did. I mean—I do." Unease tensed my muscles. "How did you know about both?"

"I could tell you that I saw them putting the paint gun in your locker." Ethan paused and raised a dark eyebrow. Faint remnants of red paint stained his fingers and wrist. His jacket still had the splatter pattern where the binder hadn't covered it. "And I could tell you that I saw you tucking a piece of paper back in your book from across the room."

"But that wouldn't explain how you knew the note was from my mom." I felt like I was trying to come up with the pieces to a riddle with only the answer as a clue.

"True."

I twirled my hand in a small circle to hurry him along. I wanted answers.

He shook his head. "I knew the answer, Nara."

It was one thing to play the mental game *Hey, the guy I really, really like is possibly psychic,* but another thing entirely to learn the truth. Several seconds passed before I responded. "As in you 'knew' these things ahead of time?"

"No, I *saw* them ahead of time." Ethan's gaze never wavered.

"What does that mean?" I whispered, my pulse thundering in my ears.

"How do you think I saw these things?"

He was so calm, while a maelstrom of emotions raged inside me. I was afraid to guess. My palms began to sweat and my voice cracked. "How did you know that my aunt lived in Barboursville?"

"I saw you drive there." He tapped his temple. "In here."

I eyed him skeptically, but couldn't get past the things he seemed to just "know". Finally, I blurted out. "So, you see things before they happen."

"Some things."

Excitement overrode my apprehension. I couldn't believe I'd met someone with a special ability, not quite like mine, but someone I could possibly share my secret with. Someone, who would understand.

I leaned closer. "How do your powers work?"

Ethan held my gaze. "I know that you made a necklace at your aunt's on Friday night, that you skipped burnt bacon for Starbucks on Saturday, and that you wanted the denim couch but your mom nixed your opinion and chose a tan color instead."

I was shocked and oddly excited by his pinpoint accuracy. "You can tell me what I did in the past?" I shook my head. "But I thought you saw things *before* they happened, like what happened with my locker today."

Ethan's expression turned serious. "I can only see what *you've* seen or will see."

My pulse was racing so fast, I barely got the words out, "How is that possible?"

"Because I have your dreams, Nara."

I couldn't blink, couldn't move. I should've known. Ethan had seemed incredibly intuitive whenever we were together, but now all the things that he'd seemed to "know" about me made total sense. Rage accompanied shock and embarrassment that he knew my secret. The accusation, *You're the reason my dreams have gone wonky!* scratched at the back of my throat, demanding release. "Why are you taking my dreams from me?" I finally managed in a low voice. It hurt to think he'd purposefully done it. "And how is that even possible?"

My emotions must've been written all over my face, because he leaned forward, his expression pleading for understanding. "It's not like that. You have to believe me, Nara. I'd never do anything to intentionally upset you."

Ethan's face didn't reflect triumph. It held intrigued interest, a desire for my understanding. My initial anger settled, even though I still felt a part of me was missing. "How did this happen?"

"Do you want to know what happens the rest of your day?" he asked in a calm voice.

I lifted an eyebrow. In my dream, the rest of my day went along normally. Of course, none of this stuff with Ethan had been in it. "You mean there's something *more* mind-blowing than learning you're seeing my dreams?"

He smirked and shook his head. "Nothing more eventful than that." Covering my hand, he slid his thumb rhythmically over mine. "Unless you count the end of the day—when you kiss me."

CHAPTER 12

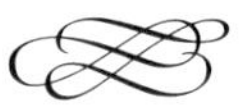

We kiss? *Why can he see himself in my dreams, yet I can't?*

We kiss!

Ethan's surprising comment played over and over in my head, beating away my doubts. My insides heated and curled inward like paper slowly burning along the edges. I was a steamy ball of nervous excitement. My gaze locked on his lips, which apparently was more obvious than I realized, because his gorgeous smile was back. It was almost predatory, the way his lips snared my rapt attention and kept me from acknowledging the hundreds of questions pinging in my head.

Cupping my chin, Ethan's smile faded. "Are you okay?"

When he traced his thumb along my jawline, swirls of steam shot everywhere at once. Clearing my throat, I pulled back to shake the fog out of my mind. "I—I'm fine." I glanced around nervously and saw several people watching us. "Tell me how this happened," I said in a hushed voice.

Ethan finally noticed the attention we'd drawn. His mouth set in a hard line. "Not here. Can you come to my house after practice?"

His house? My stomach fluttered. His brother was out of town. We'd be alone. "It'll probably be after six. I've got to go home and take a shower first. Where do you live?"

"Turtle Creek. First street on the left. Fifth house on the right."

A couple acres of farmland separated our neighborhoods. I could walk to his house. "Why didn't you tell me you lived so close?"

"You didn't ask."

My mind spun on an excuse to stay longer if I needed one. "You've got internet at home, right?"

When he nodded, I said, "Good. While I'm there, maybe we could research resources for our project. Like, I don't know, maybe the role superstition has played in wars? Does that sound okay to you?"

"That's fine," he said absently, his eyebrows drawing together. "You seem strangely calm."

Which was pretty amazing considering a full-blown freak-out episode was raging inside my head. *Why did this happen? What does Ethan think of me? He doesn't seem to be wigged out, but would he have even told me he was seeing my dreams if I hadn't confronted him? Why wouldn't he tell me?* I made a funny face, trying not to let my concerns show. "I'm fine."

"You're talking about homework for God's sake—" his gaze narrowed. "You *are* coming, right?"

I stared at him, unblinking. I didn't see any of this in my dream about today, but he'd seen us kiss, so obviously he saw more than me. "If you really see my dreams, you already know the answer to that."

"I'm not—" he paused, frustration reflecting in his eyes. "You've taken detours before."

My heart jerked. How would he know that? How long had he been seeing my dreams?

The bell rang, ending study hall and our conversation. I glared at the speaker. I was going to pound that bell with a sledgehammer.

~

TUCKING my hands in my jacket pockets, I lowered my head against the cool wind and set out for the woods down the street from my house. I could've driven, but I was curious to know just how close Ethan's house was to mine. Not to mention, I needed the exercise to calm my nerves before I got there.

There was still light outside when I'd entered the forest, but I hadn't considered the trees were mostly evergreens, their thick needles filtering out the last bit of daylight.

As I quick-walked, carefully picking my way over sticks, dry leaves and thick forest underbrush, shadows loomed and night animals began to croak, bleep and chatter. My pulse jumped at the flood of noises and my pace followed suit.

When dozens of wings flapped in unison, preceding a mass exodus of black birds taking to the night sky, I gasped. Thoughts of my scary dash through the woods and the near miss with Kurt and Jay rushed through my mind. Maybe I should've driven to Ethan's after all.

Heart racing, I began to run, pumping my arms and taking lungfuls of air to push me along. Once I was clear of the forest and halfway through the farmland's open pasture, I heard cows lowing in the distance. Their sounds were so unconcerned and normal, I slowed to a walk, feeling silly for panicking.

The scent of cow dung wafted my way, and I wrinkled my nose, paying closer attention where I stepped in the growing darkness. *Why didn't I think to bring a flashlight?* A drop of cold rain hit my scalp and then another pinged my cheek right before a third one landed in the part in my hair. By the time I'd pulled up my hood, hundreds of drops had quickly turned into a light rain shower. *Awww, come on!* I waved my fist at the dark clouds above and I dashed across the rest of the pasture, looking for Turtle Creek's main road.

The brief rain shower had stopped by the time I reached Ethan's house—a modest colonial blue two-story with a single car garage and a matching shed in the back. When I passed Ethan's car parked in the driveway, my hands were clenched at my sides. The idea of discussing my dreams with him made me tense. I wasn't sure if I was scared or excited. Maybe somewhere in between.

I raised my hand to knock on the door and paused, my mind racing. Moist wind battered the porch, pressing my wet zip-up jacket against me. I had no idea what was coming, yet

Ethan did. I wasn't sure how I felt about him knowing stuff about us that I didn't. As I stood there shivering, I couldn't help but think about all the kooky things I did in the privacy of my home, things Ethan had to have seen. Despite the cold, my face flushed with embarrassment.

Before I had a chance to knock, Ethan opened the door. The tension around his mouth instantly eased and he wrapped his fingers around my upheld hand. "I'm glad you came."

As soon as he touched me, all my balled-up worry vanished like morning mist burned off by the rising sun. "Um…hi."

"You walked?" he asked, pulling me inside.

I pushed the wet hood down to my shoulders and shivered. "This trip to your house wasn't in my dream, so I had no idea I'd get caught in the rain."

"You've gotta be freezing." Ethan stepped close and pulled at the zipper. As the zipper unwound, I held my breath, my mind wandering many miles down the road. Would I want more than a kiss from him?

Pulling off the wet material, he said, "I'll go put this in the dryer."

His sparsely decorated living room made me smile as I rubbed my sweater's sleeves to get warm. A dark leather couch and matching chair sat in front of a huge flat screen TV. Old wine barrels doubled as end tables on either side of the couch. Sports and music magazines littered the glass tabletop balanced on a gnarled tree-trunk base. Airplane photos and university campus sketches were the only decorations on the walls. It was *all* guy.

The mantle above the fireplace had two black-and-white photos. The first one was of two boys, around ten and five, holding fishing poles. One tiny fish dangled between their held up hands. Their feet were filthy, their clothes caked in mud, but huge victory grins were plastered on their faces.

I picked up the second picture frame. Ethan was older in this one, around eleven or twelve. He laughed as an older guy with short blond hair stood behind him, his arm wrapped around Ethan's neck. The guy was clearly enjoying the knucklenoogie he was inflicting on Ethan's head—as only an older brother would.

I saw some of Ethan's features in Samson's face, but their dark and light looks made them appear very different from each other.

"That's Samson's favorite."

Ethan's deep voice startled me. "Hey," I said, putting the photo back. "I wanted to see if you and your brother looked alike."

Ethan studied the picture. "We're pretty different. Samson's the responsible one."

He was standing so close, I had to lift my chin to meet his gaze. "I think you're responsible. You've saved me more than once."

A wry smile flashed. "It's much easier when I know what's going to happen, Nara."

"How long *have* you been seeing my dreams?"

"Since a couple weeks before you dreamed the school was going to be bombed."

Which meant, he had to know I was the one who'd called in the bombing tip.

I gripped his arm. "I'm sorry. I had no idea the police would think I meant you when I told them the bomber was an expelled student."

He shrugged, his biceps flexing underneath my fingers. "You were trying to do the right thing."

Heaving a sigh of relief, I dropped my hand. "How did all this happen?"

Ethan pulled me over to the couch. "Tell me about your gift first. It might help explain why."

Kicking off my shoes, I sat down and leaned against the couch's arm, facing Ethan. My hands shook as I set them on my knees, so I wrapped my arms around my bent legs, lacing my fingers tight. "It's kind of hard. I don't talk about…my dreams."

Ethan put his hand on my knee. "We need to trust each other, Nara."

He was right. He was seeing my dreams for a reason.

Blowing out a breath, I continued, "If you've been seeing my dreams, then you know me better than anyone else."

"You told your aunt you'd had this ability since you were seven."

I dug my fingers into each other, unsure what to say next.

"Your aunt seems great," Ethan prompted.

I smiled slightly. "I love Aunt Sage. She overwhelms me sometimes, but it's not the same as having your parents around and supporting you."

Ethan's hand slipped from my knee and he stared at a worn spot on his jeans. "I get that."

His issues seemed much deeper and sadder than my own. I plunged on, hoping he wouldn't start to think about his parents. "You already know that I see my entire day in my dreams. Well, at least until the day I called in the bomb threat. That whole day's dream was interrupted when I woke up. I've only had sporadic dreams since then."

When I finished speaking, something clicked in my mind. "Wait a minute. Did you ask me to study with you because you realized I hadn't seen my Trig test?"

He cut his gaze my way. "Partly."

I sat up straighter. "And offering to help me at soccer practice?"

"I watched you play, remember? I realized you were probably depending on your dreams, of *knowing* what would happen at practices and games, versus relying on your skills and instincts."

Crossing my arms, I sat back against the couch and frowned.

"You needed it," he insisted.

"I don't want to be someone's pity case."

Ethan looked surprised. "You think I did it because I felt sorry for you?"

My pulse elevated. "You didn't?"

"Nara, I did it for *you*." His blue eyes snapped, laser sharp. "Only for you."

"I'm sorry." I bit my lip, feeling stupid for not understanding how much he liked me.

"You have no idea how hard it was not to wale on those two jerks who'd offered you a ride that day." His hands were clenched into tight fists, his gaze burning holes in the wall. Fury and fear flitted across his features. "I had to watch them beat you, pummel your face, your body with their relentless pounding. They were merciless. Blood was everywhere and I felt every blow."

Unshed tears turned his blue eyes the color of midnight when he looked at me. Even as my stomach churned at the close call, I scooted close to him. "But they didn't. You stopped them."

He took a deep breath and his nostrils flared. "I almost didn't make it when they tried again."

"You're talking about the woods?"

"Yes. That's why I wasn't at school that day. Once I saw your dream, the next morning I went to my old school to find my friends and ask for their help. I didn't want to take a chance that I couldn't handle those jerks on my own."

Ethan had done everything he could to protect me. Gratitude, awe and affection swirled in my head. I couldn't decide which emotion was the strongest. Overwhelmed, I laid my head on his shoulder and whispered, "I—I don't know what to say. "

Ethan touched my jaw, his fingers warm and gentle. "Let me finish before you decide what you think about me…about us," he said softly.

About us? His comment echoed in my mind over and over. Why would he think I'd walk away? The possibility of a future together exhilarated me.

I sat up and tucked my legs underneath me. "Tell me how you're able to see my dreams."

Blowing out a breath, he raked his fingers through his hair. I'd never seen him so tense and uneasy. His hand dropped to his thigh, then quickly shoved across his jeans. "When I was thirteen, I started hearing voices and seeing images in my mind."

He paused and cut his gaze to me. I'd involuntarily raised

my eyebrows, but I wouldn't dare interrupt. Forcing my expression to settle, I waited for him to continue.

He stared at the wall again. "The voices were always angry and dark, the scenes negative and often horrific. I played my music louder, trying to blow them out of my mind. But they followed me in my sleep, too, where they'd morph into monsters doing unspeakable things—a full-on horror film. I'd wake up feeling nauseous from the blood, the gore and sheer destructiveness of my dreams."

"Didn't your parents try to help you?"

He glared at the wall. "For the next year and a half I was dragged from one shrink to the next to talk about my 'internal anger issues'. They pumped me with all kinds of drugs from bipolar to schizophrenic to sleeping pills. Nothing calmed the twisted, dark crap going on inside my head."

Torture and pain reflected in his eyes while he described his past. Every moment must've been terrifying and depressing. "What happened?" I asked evenly as my pulse raced.

His lips curled inward in a snarl of self-disgust. "I thought I was going stark raving mad. But a suggestion one of the psychiatrists recommended stuck with me, so I began to draw what I'd sometimes seen in my mind, but most often occurred in my dreams."

I was almost afraid to ask. "That drawing I saw of the horned demon-like creature in your notebook?"

"Is one of several hundred," he said with a heavy sigh. "Somehow sketching them helps me deal."

A cold trickle of unease skittered down my spine. "You're still experiencing all of it, aren't you?"

Ethan eyed me. "Still listening?"

I felt no threat rolling off him, despite the things he experienced. "Yes."

He looked relieved, but still grim. "The voices were always worse at school. I blew off classes and stopped attending soccer practices and games. I lost friends, acted out, got in trouble with the police."

"What'd your parents think?"

"They threatened to send me away if I didn't get myself

back to school, which as it turned out was a saving grace. I was miserably sitting in Science class, when the teacher started an open discussion on dreams. A few of my classmates described recurring nightmares they used to have but hadn't in a while. Their dreams sounded so familiar, and that's when I realized *I* was having their nightmares. I even recognized some of what they were describing as 'nightmares' to be actual facts in their real lives."

Tension drained out of me. "That must've been a relief to learn that you weren't losing your mind. Did you figure out why this was happening?"

"It took me a while to make the connection, but—" he paused and cupped his hand on my cheek. "What do you feel when I touch you?"

Soul-wrenching attraction. I put my hand over his and answered as truthfully as I dared. "Happiness. Whenever you're near I feel so good my worries just slip away."

Ethan didn't smile at my comment, instead he pulled away and my heart pitched at the loss of his physical connection. "That's what I finally figured out. It's like I'm a walking negative energy magnet. If I brush against or touch people, I'll soak up their bad thoughts, their horrible home life experiences, or in some cases, it's like I become the keeper of their inner demons, at least while I'm around."

"The keeper? So you don't take their negative aspects away completely?"

His bangs swept past his eyes with his quick headshake. "If I'm not around them for a while, usually it takes several days in a row, their negative energy leaves me and returns to them."

My mind warbled like an oversized bubble caught in the wind as I tried to wrap my thoughts around everything he was telling me. "What exactly do you mean by negative energy?"

"It's hard to explain." Standing, he shoved his hands deep into his pockets. He paced in front of the coffee table, his footfalls silent on the thick carpet. "It could be that the person's father beats him, or a girl's parents are dealing with an older sibling who's whacked out on drugs. Or something even more personal, like the person's suicidal thoughts. God, the list is endless." He sighed and stared at the ceiling. "Do you have any idea how hard it is not to brush against people in school?"

"No," I whispered, thinking it would be near impossible. Now I knew why he'd always kept to himself. "But you made friends with those guys from your last school."

He shrugged. "When I started school in Virginia, this time I had a plan. If I hung around with the rough guys, I'd get a rep and people would stay away from me. Then, I only had a few people's issues to deal with, not half the school population."

He turned his gaze on me. "But when you touched me, Nara, the random stuff I used to see and hear during the day disappeared. Now the images mostly just show up in my dreams." His expression shifted to a wry one. "At least now, the teachers don't think I'm always high on something."

Both times I'd seen those horrible images—he must've been seeing them too. "The first time you zoned and I touched you, an image flashed in front of me for a brief second, then it was gone. I thought I was going crazy."

His eyes widened. "You saw it?"

"Yeah."

Regret flitted across his face. "I didn't know you were seeing them." Spreading his hands wide, his lips tilted in a slight smile. "At least you haven't run out the door screaming yet."

That was one crazy confession. And I thought dreaming my next day was *different*. I gave a nervous laugh and ran shaky hands through my hair. Something had nagged at me since he'd revealed his secret. "So what's wrong with me?"

His brows disappeared behind his bangs. "You're asking a walking baggage-magnet what's wrong with *you*?"

My nerves wound tighter. "I've always thought I was a pretty stable person, but there's obviously *something* negative about me. Why else would you have taken my dreams?"

Rounding the coffee table, Ethan grabbed my hand and pulled me to my feet. I held my breath and waited to hear my fundamental flaw. "That's the thing, Nara. You make my nightmares bearable."

Clasping my shoulders in a firm grip, tension arced through him. "Through your dreams, I get to see your entire day, and as normal and as boring as you might feel they are...*you* are my peace, a bright light in all that darkness."

It also means 'a ray of light'. He'd said that he liked that meaning of my name best, and now I knew why. His words pulled at my heart. I felt oddly giddy that my dreams helped him, yet I was still confused. "But if negative energy or 'darkness' is what you attract and my dreams are light, why did they come to you, and why did my touching you push the images and voices you were experiencing during the day into your dreams?"

Ethan slid his hand into my hair, pushing it back from my face. "I don't know. We have some kind of connection, Nara. Remember I said that touching someone is how I take their negative energy?"

I nodded and my body tingled in anticipation.

"From the first day I saw you—that day we almost collided when you were kicking the soccer ball in the hall—that's the night I started seeing your dreams."

Ethan had looked so exhausted when he first came to our school. It made sense why he'd had dark circles back then. He didn't have any light to balance the darkness in his sleep...until we met. Was there such a thing as magnetic energy? Could two strong psychic fields bind together if they drew close enough to each other? I *had* almost run over him that day, less than an inch had separated our near collision. "My dreams have been flickering in and out lately," I admitted.

Sliding his hand down my jaw and along my neck, Ethan's fingers trembled slightly, his touch warming my skin. "You lost your dreams after my locker was moved next to yours. The day I touched you."

"I remember. You put your hand on mine to stop my locker door from hitting me," I whispered.

Lifting my chin, he bent close enough to kiss me. I resisted the urge to swipe my tongue across my lips to moisten them, but I couldn't help but inhale his appealing smell as I gripped his army jacket, my fingers crushing the canvas material. My arms ached to wrap around him and pull him close, but I was afraid he'd pull back. I didn't dare blink or move or breathe. I *wanted* this kiss, had fallen asleep many nights fantasizing, but no imaginings could hold a candle to the rich warmth and closeness of this unexpected reality.

Ethan's gaze lowered to my mouth. "If you ask me to stop touching you so your dreams will return, I will, Nara." His hand flexed on my neck and tension ebbed through him. "But not touching you would be the hardest thing I've ever had to do."

CHAPTER 13

Ethan's lips met mine in the barest of kisses, tentative, but full of intense promise. I pressed my lips to his, hoping to show him how much I wanted this. He unclasped my fingers from his jacket, then lowered my hands to his waist. When I leaned against him, his arm folded tight around me and a shudder rippled through him. I wanted to weep for his dark loneliness. I felt it reaching, yearning for light and affection. His fingers slid through my hair as his lips moved in a gentle, encouraging sweep against mine. Tenderness and elation radiated in his touch, making me gasp and dig my fingers into his jean loops.

"Please, Nara," he breathed against my mouth before pressing his lips against mine once more.

The building layers of Ethan's chaotic emotions washed over me in relentless waves, rushing against my cliff face of emotions until I crumbled and pushed back. I wasn't sure what he was asking for, but I gave into my own need to hold him close. Tears rolled down my cheeks as I slid my hands under his shirt and ran my fingers along his warm skin. The close contact felt right. I'd been kissed before by boys during movies, behind the school, at dances and parties, but none of those hasty kisses came close to Ethan's level of intimacy. This kiss went deeper, fueling our connection, feeding a need we'd both been missing. This journey was solid and real.

His kiss made me tremble as a delicious melting unfurled inside me. I smiled against his mouth, enjoying the sensation.

Warm hands framed my face and Ethan pressed closer, as if he needed to experience every part of me. I returned his deepening kiss with fervor, my body tingling and heart pounding out of control. Pushing my fingers into his thick hair, I reveled in the soft strands sliding against my skin and pulled him as close as I could. Now that I'd let down my defenses, I never wanted to let him go.

A beeping sound echoed briefly somewhere in the house. Ethan tensed and rested his forehead against mine. "Dryer's done."

I bit my lower lip, thrilled by the sound of our unsteady breathing in the quiet room. I had no idea that our physical connection would have such an amazing impact on us. It was like we were meant to meet, to be together. Now that I knew how much my dreams helped Ethan, I wasn't as worried about why they were no longer my own. At least that explained my sporadic dreams. Each time Ethan and I had been away from each other for several days, my dreams returned. I just wish I knew why he'd never shown up in my dreams.

Running my hands down his arms, I snagged our fingers together. I couldn't imagine not touching him either. Losing my dreams was a small price to pay for this kind of happiness, for both of us. I'd miss knowing how each day would unfold—and yeah, I'll admit to a twinge of jealousy and anxiety that he'd know what was coming when I didn't—but whenever I was with Ethan, I felt special and now *needed* in his life. Just like he was in mine. That was more powerful and immediate, overshadowing everything else.

My phone started ringing, *Alone Again*. Frustrated, I resisted the urge to shut it off and instead pulled my cell from my jean pocket. "Hey, Mom."

"I just wanted to let you know I'll be home in a half hour. I'm going to pick up dinner. What would you like tonight?"

"How about Thai?"

"Sounds good. Your usual?"

"Yep, see you in a little while. Oh, and Mom?"

"Hmmm?"

"Thanks for the note." Ethan ran his hand down my hair, his fingers curling around the ends. I caught his admiring gaze and my heart bloomed in my chest.

Mom cleared her throat. "I wasn't sure if you'd find it, since you're used to me texting. See you soon."

I hung up and grimaced. "Looks like I have less time than I thought. I'd hoped Mom would work late tonight. But before I head home, we should probably check out CVU's library database."

Ethan pulled me close and brushed his lips across mine. "Are you sure you want to do that with the little time we have left?"

"I—"

He kissed me again and my brain shut down. I leaned against his solid frame and pressed my lips against his with a mewl of happiness, and then the dryer beeped its reminder.

We both frowned and Ethan expelled a sigh. "Might as well get the research over with. I've bookmarked the page on Wars. There are a ton of books." Turning, he headed toward the hallway and waved for me to follow.

The moment I walked into Ethan's bedroom upstairs, I greedily surveyed the space, wanting to know everything about him. Oblivious to my ogling, Ethan sat down in a swivel rolling chair in front of a wood desk. While he opened his laptop, I checked out his room.

A huge soccer ball rug took up the center of the room, and the full-sized bed, with a natural wood headboard and footboard, sat against the opposite wall. Typical guy, I thought with a small smile as my gaze snagged on the bed's rumpled cream sheets and navy down comforter. A light brown fleece throw had fallen to the floor from the end of the bed. Lifting the throw, I'd intended to put it back on the bed, when a notebook fell out of the folds.

After I folded the cover and set it on the bed, I picked up the opened notebook and closed it without looking at the monstrous images.

When I glanced up, Ethan was watching me intently. "You should look at them," he said quietly before he returned to his computer and began to log in.

I stared at the spiral notebook in my hand, felt the images' weight, the mass conglomeration of other people's problems in graphic form, tingling my palm. Taking a deep breath, I opened the notepad. "Are these your most recent drawings?"

"If you look in the upper right corner of the page, you'll see a date."

I flipped to the latest images in the notebook, looking for the night I'd worn the crystal. I had to know if what I'd seen that night was straight from Ethan's nightmares.

My stomach roiled as I scanned through the familiar images: One page featured a leathery caveman-like creature with long canines, black piercing eyes and claws dripping with blood as he leaned across a gutted deer, holding a knife out to someone. Yet another showed a giant man with blackened teeth and a scarred, misshapen face beating a much smaller, younger version of himself with his oversized meaty hands. Another page with nothing but words and phrases; the bolder ones drew my eyes: *She's gone and it's all your fault. You're a waste of human space. You killed your mother, not the cancer*. Then finally, a page featuring the wild-eyed Minotaur snorting through his curled black snout, a slimy brown blob with thick arms and razor sharp teeth, and the mash-faced Pit Bull.

Every one of Ethan's drawings were of the same experiences I'd had. I turned the page, expecting it to be blank since that's all I'd seen in my dreams. Instead, I saw a beautiful drawing of me sitting in my mom's car, smiling. The sketch of Mom and me was just the soothing balm I needed to banish the horrific images from my mind. Now I understood.

Closing the notebook, I walked over to his side. "That was a great trip with my mom," I said as I set the notebook on the desk. "You captured my feelings well."

"I could tell you were happy."

Running my finger down the spiral ring, I wondered how

Ethan kept it together. I was nearly out of my mind when I woke up Saturday morning after an entire night of those awful nightmares. "The other night when I wore the crystal necklace, I had the most terrifying nightmares."

Ethan glanced my way. "I remember when you woke up you ran to the bathroom to throw up. They were that bad, huh —" He paused and then stared at my hand on the notebook. "Your nightmares…were they anything like my drawings?"

I dug my fingertip deep between the metal spiral. "They *were* your drawings."

He gripped my hand, pulling it away from the notebook. "I'm sorry, Nara. I only saw that you were upset by your dreams. I didn't know you'd seen *my* dreams, but I guess now you understand."

Nodding, I brushed his bangs out of his eyes and trailed my fingertips down his cheek. "How do you dream about such gruesome creatures, experience all those dark emotions and wake up unaffected by it? How do you *not* carry that around with you?"

Ethan clasped my hand and slid his fingers between mine. "I didn't handle it in the past the way I do today. Even now, sometimes I feel very old."

"What happened in the past?" I hoped he'd tell me. Ethan lowered his gaze and shook his head. I knew there was more, but whatever it was, he wasn't going to talk about it.

"With Samson's support." He lifted his eyes and I saw a painful memory slowly fading. "Believing in *me*, even when he didn't truly understand what I was going through every night —it helped me keep my mind open to possibilities." Rubbing his forearm, he continued, "Over time, I found ways to help myself."

Tugging on my hand, Ethan quickly wrapped his arm around my waist and pulled me onto his lap. "Enough about me. I have a question for you."

"Shoot."

He shook his head, bemused. "Why Latin? I've watched you translate stories and fables, articles, even the Catholic Mass you'd printed from the web, but I couldn't figure out the connection any of them have or why you're so fascinated."

I shrugged. "I'm just weird like that."

Ethan eyed me.

"Okay, fine. I chose Latin because even if I dream myself translating it, it won't be so easy for me to remember all the details, since Latin's not an easy language. In other words, I'll have to do some work, which means I get to enjoy the process of translating all over again."

Sympathy reflected in his gaze. "I enjoyed watching you so much, I hadn't thought about what it must be like for you to experience every single detail twice."

"Déjà vu and me…" I crossed my fingers. "We're like this," I said, hoping to lighten the mood.

Snorting, Ethan turned me around toward the computer and leaned his cheek against my shoulder. "You're running out of time, Sunshine. Let's go through this list and see if there are some books that might work for our project."

Sunshine? Well, he'd said I was his 'ray of light'. I smiled and started scrolling through the list. After cross-referencing books on Wars with books on Superstitions, we finally agreed on a dozen titles.

"I'll drive you home," Ethan said as we stood in his foyer twenty minutes later.

I slipped into my cotton jacket he held out for me. It was still warm from the dryer. "You don't have to drive me. I can walk— "

"You're not walking back by yourself." Ethan gripped my jacket and yanked me onto my toes for a long, bone-melting kiss.

Lifting his head, he lowered my feet back to the floor and searched my face, looking for…what…I wasn't certain. But now I understood the jumble of emotions I'd seen flickering through his eyes.

The low bass in his voice and the protective way he clenched my jacket, made me tingle in new places. I curled my fingers around his fist, totally attracted to his primal intensity. I didn't think he saw it in himself, but Ethan exuded an amazing self-awareness and confidence that drew me in. I was the lead filings to his magnetic inner strength.

I didn't know how I would've handled things if he hadn't been there to pick me up and force me to keep moving forward once I'd first lost my dreams. I could've spiraled down so fast. It was still a little scary walking around blind, but knowing Ethan had my back made all the difference.

When I got to school the next day, I waited by Ethan's locker. I was in the best mood. Mom and I had a great dinner last night, where we actually had a semi-normal conversation, and then I'd laid in bed thinking about Ethan. More Ethan. And even more Ethan. I loved that he wasn't the same as everyone else—that he wasn't totally normal. I'd never been happier to see his dark head weaving through the crowd as he walked down the hall. The deep blue fleece he had on brought out the blue in his eyes. All I wanted to do was wrap my arms around him and inhale his wonderful smell, but I held myself in check while he stowed his books and pulled out another set.

"How will today be?" I asked, excited by the intimacy of our shared secrets.

Ethan glanced toward the front of the school where morning light seeped through the windows. "Mostly sunny with a cloud here and there."

"I'm surrounded by comedians," I said in a dry tone. "What I meant was…is there anything I need to be concerned about?"

Sweeping his finger leisurely around the curve of my ear, he tucked a strand of hair behind it. "You'll just have to find out for yourself."

I pulled my books to my chest and lowered my voice, "Are you telling me you're not going to give me a heads-up on stuff?"

Dropping his hand, he leaned his shoulder against the locker. "Why would I do that? You can handle anything thrown your way."

He was dead serious. He wasn't going to tell me anything. "Why won't you tell me about *my* dreams?"

The corner of Ethan's mouth turned down and he slowly shook his head. "You're better off without them. You know I'm right."

My face grew hot and I curled my fingers tight around my books. "Who gave you the right to keep them from me?"

Ethan brushed his knuckles down my cheek. "You did."

His tender touch reminded me of our conversation yesterday. By allowing Ethan to touch me, I knew I'd continue to lose my dreams to him, but I didn't expect him not to share *anything* with me. That was so unfair. "Well, that's not what I intended. I wasn't expecting this."

A hurt look flashed across his face. "Any of it, Nara?"

He reached out to me again and I took a step back, pressing my lips together. I felt like he'd misled me by omission. Not to mention, playing on my emotions by making me want him to touch me. It was the perfect way to keep me in the dark. Literally.

The activity in the hall elevated around us as everyone poured in, jostling to their lockers.

Ethan's expression shut down. "It's not just because I know you can handle it, Nara. You can't *not* react to your dreams. Because you know what's ahead, you adapt, you avoid, you 'work around' and sometimes…you change things."

A prickly feeling started on the back of my neck, an inkling of something I didn't want to consider. "What are you saying?"

"You get involved in other people's lives. That's dangerous. I don't think you should interfere."

Don't interfere.

The words from my radio echoed in my head. Over and over. A shiver passed through me and I stilled.

"Do you understand what I'm staying?" he asked.

Could Ethan have been the one warning me all those times? He'd never said he had other powers, but he hadn't told me everything about his past last night, and he definitely didn't want me to use my powers for other people. My mind spun. He'd also called me on my cell right before I was going to help

Jody. He'd been in a chatty mood, too. Why *that* day? Why *then*?

"I—I've got class." Doubt and the timing of Ethan's appearance in my life pushed my foot back another step. As I bumped into a guy passing by, a sick feeling slowly spread through my stomach.

"Nara, what's wrong—" Frowning, Ethan reached for me, but I pulled back.

"I've gotta go," I said and took off down the hall.

The bell rang as I stumbled into the bathroom. I barely made it into the stall before I lost my breakfast. As another round of nausea roared through me, and I leaned over the toilet, puking my guts up, my whole body began to shake. Had Ethan gotten close to me for another reason? Did he take my dreams on purpose to make sure I didn't use my powers to help others? If I didn't know the future, then I couldn't get involved, could I? Is that why he never starred in my dreams, because he was here to stop me? Aunt Sage had said he was an "old soul" and his "power was off the charts". What did that mean? Question after question ricocheted through my mind. Questions I didn't have the answers to.

I squeezed my eyes shut and hot tears slid down my cheeks as I leaned against the metal stall. If any of that was true, I should fear Ethan, but fear wasn't what made me tremble all over. It was deep sadness and regret. He'd burrowed into my heart, knew me better than anyone. My entire world felt as if it was collapsing into a dark black hole.

The rest of the day I stayed away from my locker and took different halls than I usually would've to avoid running into Ethan. When I came out of the library after study hall, he was waiting for me.

"Talk to me," he said, falling into step beside me. He looked upset, but I wasn't buying it.

"Don't try to stop me anymore." I glanced away. "I'm not scared of you."

"Scared of me—what?"

I sped up my pace, my heart pounding. "Just don't."

"Nara," he called after me as I practically ran down the hall, tears burning in my eyes.

I was both relieved and sad when I didn't see Ethan at the end of the day. As I spun my locker combination, a part of me hoped he'd show up even though I'd blown him off earlier. I sighed and opened my locker. A piece of folded paper sat on top of my books. Someone must've slipped it through one of the slots at the top of my locker door. Tension knotted my shoulders as I unfolded the note.

Nara,

I'm sorry I upset you. The look on your face…it was what I was worried I'd see when I told you the truth about me. I don't want you to be afraid of me. I would never do anything to hurt you or scare you. I'm sorry. I don't want to lose you. Please talk to me.

Ethan

I read Ethan's note several more times that day, and as I lay in bed that night, uncertainty twinged and tears threatened. Was I wrong about him? Had I somehow twisted his comments and actions to coincide with the odd happenings that had been bombarding me since I'd first called in the bomb threat? I wanted to believe in him, but doubts and too many coincidences plagued me.

~

I MANAGED to avoid Ethan the entire next day, but by the time the day was over and I was heading home after practice, I knew one absolute truth—I was completely and utterly miserable. I wasn't miserable because I'd failed a pop quiz or because someone had tried to pull another prank on me. I wasn't miserable because I'd performed horribly at soccer practice or because I was sure to burn dinner tonight—okay, none of the other stuff *had* happened, and there was a fifty-fifty chance I *would* burn dinner now that my dreams were gone. Bleh. Like mother, like daughter. At least my odds were better.

I was miserable, because I missed Ethan.

Desperately.

I missed our conversations and the way we connected on many subjects. I missed the closeness I felt to him, like we were in our own intimate world. The last thing I wanted to do was go home to an empty house and wallow in my misery.

I'd just turned down my street, when my cell phone trilled. I quickly answered it, thinking it might be Ethan. "Hello?"

"Inara, my secretary just put through a call from Westminster." Mom sounded tense. My heart pounded and I slowed my car as I neared our house. I was afraid to ask, but I had to. "What's wrong with Gran?"

"She's missing. They called to find out if I knew where she might go."

Turning into the driveway, I started to push the garage door button, when I saw my bone-thin grand aunt squatting near our bushes in her black "fancy coat" (or so she'd call it). Wearing a look of deep concentration, she dumped a trowel-full of soil into a bucket beside her, then swirled the soil with her fingers. Relieved she was safe, I cut the engine. "Um, she's at our house. Digging."

"Thank God." Mom heaved a sigh. "Did you say, 'digging'?"

"Yeah, with a trowel."

"That's random. Does she look okay?"

"She looks fine, but she hasn't noticed I'm here yet."

"I'm glad she's okay. I'll call Westminster and tell them—"

"That I'll drop her off tomorrow morning before school," I insisted. Gran *never* left the retirement home. She was here for a reason. Not to mention, if she stayed, Mom couldn't avoid visiting with her. Win-win.

"I meant to tell you I have a dinner meeting. It'll be after ten before I get home," Mom said. "Think you'll be okay with Gran by yourself?"

How convenient, Mom. "Yeah, we're good. I'd better go stop Gran before she digs up our bushes."

I walked up our sidewalk and when I shifted my soccer bag and backpack to my other shoulder, Gran finally noticed me. "Hi, Inara."

"Hey, Gran. What are you doing?"

"You know all this already," she said matter-of-factly, going back to her digging.

I hadn't told her I'd lost my dreams to Ethan. "Remind me. Sometimes I'm fuzzy on the details."

She held up a handful of dirt full of squirming earthworms. "Clara says I need real worms in my plants." Dropping the dirt and worms into her bucket, she gave a grunt of satisfaction. "I'm gonna prove her wrong. Plants like sugar just as much as the rest of us. It's 'cause I don't get morning sunlight on my side of the building. That's what's killing my plants."

I glanced at the bucket, half-full with dirt and worms. "Westminster doesn't have dirt?"

Gran gave me an "are you nuts?" look. "Of course, they do!" Snapping a lid sporting air holes onto the bucket, she slowly stood, then brushed the dirt off her gnarled hands. "I was just biding my time until you got home. It's not like I have a key, you know."

"Why'd you come for a visit?"

Pulling a wad of used bingo sheets from her coat pocket, Gran's green eyes sparkled with mischief. "I need your help."

~

"I'M NOT GOING to help you cheat, Gran." I stood in the kitchen after my shower, watching her scuttle around, looking behind canisters and opening cabinets.

Yanking open the fridge, she leaned across the door, then pointed to the ten bingo sheets I'd spread out on the island. "It's not cheating. I won *all* those games." Huffing her frustration, she continued as she scanned the inside of the fridge, "Clara just called out bingo before I did."

"Gran..."

Holding up a bottle of soda, she said, "Here's the first part. Now where's the rum." An image of Gran, in her pink cardigan, crisp white shirt, khaki pants and orthopedic shoes, swilling back alcoholic drinks just didn't compute. Also, Mom would kill me if I let Gran get drunk. "Mom doesn't drink. Now, back to your problem..."

"She doesn't drink?" Gray eyebrows shot up. "Ever? What kind of a daughter did my sister raise?"

I grabbed up the sheets and waved them. "Gran, Bingo? The reason you're here?"

Setting the 2-liter on the island, Gran started to speak when the doorbell rang.

Since when did my house suddenly become Grand Central? Sighing, I walked over to the front door and opened it.

"Hey, Nara," Lainey said, holding a small bucket of…ice?

I was so surprised to see her, I simply said, "Um, hi. What's up?"

"I thought we could use some girl time." Shoving the bucket of ice into my hands, Lainey stepped inside, the latest chic cologne clinging to her zip-up sweater and skinny jeans. Noticing my Gran standing in the kitchen, she smiled and waved. "Hi, I'm Lainey, Nara's best friend."

Oh, really? You remembered? "This is my Gran," I said, gesturing to Gran as I walked into the kitchen. Though I was curious what made Lainey show up here—with a bucket of ice, of all things—I was more concerned with getting rid of the bingo cards. The last thing I wanted was for Gran to start talking about them again and accidentally reveal my secret to Lainey.

Setting the bucket of ice down, I quickly gathered up the cards and shoved them in a drawer in the island. "What kind of 'girl time' did you have in mind?"

"Did you bring any rum?" Gran asked Lainey, her gaze glued to the ice bucket.

Lainey laughed, holding up something silver. "No, but I brought a needle."

My eyes widened when I realized what the ice and needle were for. "Oh no. No way!" I said backing up, hands raised.

Lainey was already shaking her head as she pulled a bottle of rubbing alcohol from her purse. "You chickened out getting your ears pierced three different times at the mall, Nara. Now, it'll just be you, me, ice and a needle."

She planned to stick a needle in my ear lobe? And that I'd *let* her do it? "Thanks for the thought, Lainey, but—"

"I've always wanted to have pierced ears," Gran said, wistfully.

I shot her a "you're not helping" look.

"Stop being such a wuss, Nara." Lainey's disapproving expression brightened. "I even brought stainless steel earrings. I picked out a pair of 5 mm balls for you, since they go with everything. Those ears of yours will be pierced in no time."

I shook my head in fast jerks.

"Come on, Nara. It'll be a great bonding experience," she begged, which made me wonder again, what had made her want to rekindle our friendship.

"I don't see why you're putting up such a fuss, Nara," Gran said in a no-nonsense tone. "You already know if you get it done or not—"

"Okaaaaaaaay, I'll do it," I said loudly. I really didn't need Gran spilling the beans to Lainey.

"Yay!" Lainey did a little hop, then grabbed her purse and "instruments of torture" and made a bee-line for the hall bathroom.

Gran tottered after Lainey, saying excitedly, "I want to do an ear."

"Grab some paper towels." Lainey called from the hallway right before Gran disappeared into the bathroom behind her.

I started to reach for the roll, when I heard her finish, "They soak up the blood better than tissue."

"I can't believe I agreed to this craziness," I muttered, whisking the roll off the holder.

When I was six, I fell out of a tree and broke my left arm. In ninth grade, I sprained my right ankle playing soccer (even knowing ahead of time, it's hard to avoid an injury *and* remain focused on the game.). I saw stars both times. Truly. So when I say the idea of Lainey and Gran wearing maniacal grins and wielding ice and needles scared me far more than those two past experiences ever did, I'm *not* kidding.

My left ear, actually the entire left side of my face, from my cheek to my ear, was numb from the ice Lainey had applied for a good fifteen minutes. Still, my insides jerked as she closed in with that needle. At the last second, I pulled back. "Are you sure I won't feel it?"

Lainey rolled her eyes, then held the needle away and reached past my cheek with her free hand. "Did you feel that?"

"No, what'd you do?"

"I pinched your earlobe as hard as I could. You're ready," she said, coming at me with the needle again.

Grabbing her wrist, I glanced up at her. "This is a true test of friendship. I wouldn't trust just *anyone* to poke a hole in my head."

A faint smile tilted her lips, then she frowned in concentration. "Now be quiet and hold still."

I closed my eyes and held my breath as I felt a slight prick.

Her warm fingers brushed against my cold cheek and five seconds later, she announced, "All done."

"Really?" I swiveled on the wooden stool and glanced at my left ear in the mirror. It was red from the ice, but now a stainless steel ball the size of a BB decorated my earlobe (thankfully in the center). "I didn't feel a thing."

"Told you." Lainey looked proud.

As I held ice on my right earlobe, I was surprised Gran had been so quiet. Maybe she'd decided to just watch.

"My turn," Gran said, elbowing Lainey aside.

Grabbing up the needle, Gran turned to dip it in the alcohol we'd poured into the lid, but the needle dropped in the lid instead. She tried to fish it out, but the needle spun around like a confused compass. "Come here, you little pissant," she mumbled, digging her fingers into the alcohol.

My gaze jerked to Lainey, pleading, *Help me, please.*

She lifted her hands helplessly and mouthed, "What can I do?"

"Got it!" Gran bent toward me, her gnarled fingers clasping the needle at a strange angle. When her hand began to shake as she drew near and the needle between her fingers shifted even more, I panicked and blurted, "I just remembered where we have some rum."

Gran immediately straightened, a marionette yanked upright by rum's sweet lure. The needle slipped from her fingers. "Where?" she asked with bright eyes.

I watched the needle roll down the sink and right into the drain with an inward sigh of relief. "It's in the pantry, behind the big jug of vinegar."

Gran was already heading out of the bathroom, calling behind her, "Why would Elizabeth keep it there?"

"Rum cake," I automatically answered (well, Mom tried at least).

Lainey's hand was over her mouth, her shoulders shaking. Wiping tears of laughter from her eyes, she snickered in a low tone, "You just contributed to the delinquency of a...*major*." Then let out another peal of muffled laughter.

"I didn't want to end up with a nose piercing," I said in a low voice. "There's less than three shots left. She can't get drunk from that."

Sobering, Lainey rubbed her eyes to smooth her smudged eyeliner. "What's her fixation with rum, anyway?"

"The retirement home doesn't allow alcohol." Glancing at Lainey's purse, I asked, "Do you have another needle?"

"Yeah."

"Then sterilize it and let's get my other ear done before she comes back."

Several minutes later, while Lainey was putting the second earring in my ear, I asked, "Why'd you decide to come over?"

Lainey looked at me, then twisted the earring in its new hole. Stepping back to admire her work, she said, "It was my way of saying, 'I'm sorry I gave you a hard time about Jared'. We'd been having some random arguments, and I was feeling insecure when you called that day. As for the paint ball thing..." she paused and grimaced.

"I know you didn't agree with it," I said quietly.

Her brown gaze met mine, full of sincerity. "I didn't know they were going to do that. Guys prank each other all the time, but to prank a girl? I was pissed at Jared and told him to apologize to you."

Yeah, I remembered his half-hearted apology. "No harm done." I smiled to let her know we really were good. Touching my new earrings, I met her gaze in the mirror. "Thanks. I can't say the experience was totally stress free," I paused and jerked my head toward the kitchen, "but it'll be nice to wear small hoops when I want."

"Now you can wear pretty earrings when you dress up, like you did the other day." She bumped shoulders with me and smiled. "Though, I think that Ethan guy likes you just the way you are."

Her comment brought all my worries about Ethan back to the front of my mind. I'd been able to keep them at bay with Gran and Lainey as distractions. Before I could tell her Ethan and I weren't spending time together anymore, Lainey tugged on my arm.

"Let's go show your Gran your new studs and see if she's smashed yet."

CHAPTER 14

"I'm a cheap date," Gran giggled in my ear, then hiccupped.

Now she tells me. The scent of alcohol mixed with peppermint toothpaste tickled my nose while I helped her into our guest bedroom bed. "You just need to get some sleep, Gran. You'll feel better in the morning. I wasn't sure which would be worse: for Mom to think *I* drank the alcohol or for her to discover her aunt had gone to bed at eight because *she* had. My optimistic side hoped Mom wouldn't notice the rum was gone. After three failed attempts, I didn't think she'd try to make rum cake again.

Gran rolled to face me as I pulled the covers over her. "Come see me tomorrow at four-forty."

My gaze narrowed suspiciously. "Why exactly at four-forty?"

"So you can help me with bingo. If I end up with a winning card tomorrow, you can tell me two seconds before the last bingo number is called. That way, I can stamp and call bingo at the same time."

"Gran," I sighed.

She grasped my hand, her face flushed with frustration. "It's the only way I can beat Clara."

"That's what all this is about? Not winning the bingo prize, but beating Clara?"

"She only beats me by mere seconds, but she always rubs it in my face. It's so humiliating, this growing older and slower."

My heart ached for Gran. I touched her fluffy hair, then cupped her cheek. "I won't help you cheat, Gran, but I think I have an idea how I can help you."

Relief flitted across her lined face. "Thanks, Inara." Her eyes glistened with tears and she brushed them away. "Margaret always said alcohol made me weepy."

Her fingers tightened on my hand. "You're a lot like my little sister, Inara. I wish you could've known your grandmother."

Me too. Gran rarely brought up her sister…as if she missed her too much to talk about her. Guess Mom and Gran were more alike than they realized. "What was my grandmother like?"

"Pretty with strawberry blond hair. She was tall like you, but her eyes were blue." Gran sighed and rolled onto her back to stare at the ceiling. "Margaret had a big heart, but she also trusted her instincts. She could pick a bad apple off the vine in two seconds flat."

I smiled at the imagery of a cluster of apples growing on a vine.

Gran's green eyes shifted back to me, looking sleepy. "When she felt strongly about something or someone, Margaret never folded on her convictions. You're like that too."

"Thanks, Gran. Get some sleep and I'll take you back to Westminster in the morning."

Later that night, as I lay in bed, trying to fall asleep, all I could think about was Ethan. How much I missed his tender touch. Hot tears streaked down my temples into my hair. It reminded me of the time he'd wiped my tears away, comforting me while his concerned gaze searched my face.

Was I wrong about him? Had I messed up everything?

I clenched my fists, hating all the doubts I had. Whenever I tried to recall a sweet memory between us, another event I couldn't explain would pop into my mind, obliterating it. I hated that most of all.

Then something Gran said about her sister rolled through my mind: *When she felt strongly about something or someone, she never folded on her convictions. You're like that, too.* I did feel strongly about Ethan, and I really wanted to believe my first instincts about him had been right. But how?

I wracked my brain for a while, then sat up in bed when an idea came to me. Every time I'd received a warning not to interfere—the cold heaviness, the radio message, the foggy mirror and jammed bathroom door, even the message across the phone line at home—Ethan hadn't been present.

I wouldn't get my dreams back for a couple of days, but if he were with me the next time I used my powers to help someone, and he didn't try to intervene, then I'd believe him.

~

I SAT in my silent car absently sorting my shades in order of frame color as I watched a construction crew using bright orange plastic fencing to cordon off an area to the right of the school's main parking lot. For once, I'd gotten to school early after I'd dropped Gran and her bucket of wormy dirt off, then ran a quick errand.

I'd stopped by a flower shop (a different one) and ordered a dozen red roses (with cash this time). I'd given specific instructions for them to be delivered to: Cordelia Grant in Westminster's recreation room at 4:40 pm. I'd signed the card: *From your secret admirer,* all the while thinking, *I hope Clara chokes with curious jealousy*. I knew Gran would soak it up for all its worth.

As students began to move toward the school's entrance, I wished sending anonymous secret admirer flowers could also fix my problem. Jamming on my darkest pair of shades, I glanced at my car's clock. The last bell should've rung by now. Normally I'd be scrambling to get to class on time, but the idea of spending another whole day avoiding Ethan made my heart ache. I wanted to believe him.

If I stayed away from him for two more days, I should get

my dreams back. Then I could prove he wasn't responsible for trying to stop me, though I didn't want to think about the alternative behind the weird stuff I'd been going through either.

Normally I would've called Aunt Sage for advice. She'd always been a great sounding board in the past, but I wouldn't betray Ethan's confidence, even if I thought my aunt would understand. Knowing her, she'd probably agree with his "don't interfere" philosophy. Plus, she had given my dad my cell number, so I was reluctant to discuss anything with her right now. *God, I hope she hadn't told him about my dreams.*

Turning to the four text books I'd stacked in the passenger seat yesterday, I arranged them in order of which class was coming first, then slid the stack into my backpack. Like yesterday, I planned to avoid my locker and go straight to Homeroom. I glanced at the clock once more, then removed my keys from the ignition with a sigh.

A movement outside my window caught my eye. Ethan leaned against his passenger door. His hands were shoved deep into his jean pockets, black boots crossed at the ankles, his eyes locked on me. The brisk fall wind lifted the collar of his army jacket—amazingly paint-free—and ruffled his black hair. The impassive expression on his face gave nothing away.

My hand shook as I gripped the handle and pushed my door open. *Just two more days. Two. More. Days.* As I shut my door, I panicked, unsure what to say. Ethan's heavy stare weighed on me, but I couldn't look at him, so I focused on the school building straight ahead.

I'd only taken a couple steps toward the school when his voice brought me to a halt. "Not even a 'hello', Sunshine?"

His sweet nickname made my throat clog. Screw the two days. Gravel crunched under my shoe as I pivoted and dropped my backpack, stalking toward him. "All right. Here's the deal. Give me something and then we'll talk."

Ethan blinked. "What?"

I waved my hand impatiently. "Tell me something interesting about today. Not about me, but about someone else."

"Why?"

I could tell by his frown of disapproval "something"

happened in my dream. "Because no matter what it is you're not going to stop me. That's why."

Ethan stepped close and pulled off my glasses. He searched my face, looking for answers. "Why did you look so scared the other day? I'd never hurt you, Nara."

The crisp air circled around us, stirring dried leaves, gravel dust and the scent of fall fires. I closed my eyes for a second and clung to his promise. Sighing, I admitted part of the truth. "My dreams have been with me for a very long time. It's hard to let go."

"You know I'd never let anything happen to you."

He'd spoken with such intensity I desperately wanted to believe every word. I swallowed and tried not to let him see the turmoil I felt.

"I hope you believe me, and you'll listen to why I think I have your dreams."

His comment surprised me. "You said you saw my dreams *before* you touched me."

"But I didn't *take* your dreams until I touched you."

I'd forgotten that part. "Why did you take my dreams?" I asked with a heavy heart. Would he admit that he'd taken them on purpose?

He set my sunglasses in my hand, then folded my fingers around them. The brief brush of his skin against mine made me ache.

"It's the nature of my power, not a conscious thing, Nara. Maybe your dreams *are* your inner demon and that's why they came to me. You definitely have this need to get involved. Even now you're demanding to know something from last night's dream."

Not for the reason you think. Was he trying to make me feel wrong for using my ability to help others? My defensive hackles rose. "What about your powers? You see people's worst nightmares, their negative thoughts or their inner demons, as you put it. When you know someone's thinking about suicide, how can you *not* act?"

He sighed and raked his hand through his hair. "Most of the time I can't tell who has the issue. You've seen my drawings.

Do any of those creatures look like someone you've seen walking around at school?"

"I've seen you rescue a *dog*, Ethan."

Glancing away, he knew he'd been caught. "I haven't always stayed out of things."

The pained look in his eyes made me feel bad for making him recall the past. I started to speak, but he cut me off.

"She'd been raped and the guy who'd done it knew she was afraid to tell. Every day at school he tortured her; his snide remarks turned into groping hands. People thought she was easy, but I saw the marks on her wrists, new wounds near old ones. She'd started cutting." His voice hardened. "I decided to take care of the guy myself."

"Was he the one you beat up at your last school?"

Ethan looked surprised I'd guessed. "Yeah, that was the guy."

"See, *you* acted when you knew it was the right thing to do."

"I'll always watch out for you, Nara, but messing with others' lives like you do…it's dangerous. Let life around you happen as it was meant to. You and I, we might be different, but we should at least try to act like normal people."

He sounded so sincere, my heart wanted to believe him, even as my mind rebelled. "Will you do this one thing for me?"

Ethan's mouth set in a grim line, and just when I thought he'd say no, he said, "Sophia goes after Lainey during practice today, but instead of succeeding, she gets Lainey's elbow and a broken nose."

In order to prove Ethan's innocence, I was going to have to save *Sophia*? My mind screamed in rebellion, but it was the only way. "Can you be there when I talk to Sophia after school?"

"That's life, Nara."

I ignored the disapproval in his tone. I just wanted him *there*. "By the lockers."

"If you want." He put a hand on my shoulder, his face determined. "We *will* talk after."

"Uh, yeah, we should probably get to class now."

"You go first. I'll walk in a few minutes behind you."

Gathering my backpack, I raised an eyebrow. "Why aren't you coming?"

"It's probably best if we don't walk in late together, seeing how I'm such a bad influence and all," he said, hooking devil-horn fingers above his head.

"Fine. Keep your tarnished image," I snapped, irritated rather than amused by those devil horns. My stomach was in knots. I really, really wanted my first instincts about him to be right.

~

AFTER THE FINAL BELL RANG, I leaned against my locker and tracked Sophia as she flitted from one football player to the next, flirting her way toward her locker. When Jared and Lainey walked past holding hands, Sophia's entire attitude shifted. Her high laughter subsided and her wide eyes narrowed to jealous slits. Turning to her locker, she spun her combination with quick, jerky movements.

I ground my teeth, wishing there was another way to prove myself wrong.

"I'm here," Ethan's low voice sounded behind me.

Exhaling a tense breath, I dragged my tennis shoe's rubber sole down my pants leg to loosen the jean material—which currently clung to my socks as if magnetized. So annoying! After I did the same to the other leg, I squared my shoulders and nodded for him to follow me down the hall.

As I walked, static rode up my pants and hoodie, then filtered into my hair. Loose pieces of hair began to float around my head like gnats. I patted the strands down and casually leaned against the locker next to Sophia's. "Hey, Sophia."

Sophia glanced at Ethan standing behind me as she tugged her backpack onto her shoulder. Shutting her locker, she looked at me, her curly blonde hair bouncing with her movements. "What's up?"

"Nothing much. I just—" A frigid chill jolted through me at the same time something pushed against me, pinning my shoulder to the locker. Glancing angrily over my other shoulder at Ethan, I rasped, "Stop it, right now!"

"Stop what?" Confusion creased his brow. "Are you okay?" When he reached for my arm, electricity arced and he immediately jerked his hand back. "What the—"

"Can you two fight on your own time?" Sophia interrupted. "What do you want, Nara?"

Sophia's annoyed tone set me on edge. "I'm *here* about Lainey." As soon as I spoke forcefully, the pressure disappeared and I was able to breathe and move again. Pushing myself off the locker, I continued, "Going after her during practice is a bad idea."

Sophia's uneasy gaze pinged from me to Ethan. "What're you talking about?"

I snorted. "I saw you just now. You're so jealous of Lainey and Jared, your eyes are crossing."

She stared at me for a brief second, then flipped her hair over her shoulder. "You're the one who's jealous, but thanks for the heads up. I'll be sure to let Lainey know you plan to take her out on the field."

I wasn't usually a violent person, but it took all my willpower to keep my fist by my side and not yank a handful of her blonde curls. "Things will *not* go well for you if you try to hurt Lainey, Sophia."

"Are you threatening me?" She took a step back, glaring.

I shrugged. "Take it however you want."

"Stay away from me," Sophia said, then stomped off.

"That was just weird," Ethan commented quietly.

I turned to see him staring at his hand as he rubbed his fingers together. Even though I felt bad he'd gotten shocked, I was also giddy with relief. Ethan wasn't behind what had been happening. He'd seemed worried and concerned, but he hadn't tried to stop me. "Sorry about that," I said, grabbing his hand and rubbing the tips of his fingers with my palm. "I've been having major static issues lately." *Cheap dryer sheets.*

"That was more than just a little zap, Nara. It felt like I stuck my finger in a socket while standing in a puddle of icy water."

How odd. It just felt like a regular static shock to me. "You felt coldness too?"

"Yeah, I thought the air conditioner had turned on, but there aren't any vents in the locker hall." He clasped my hand, stopping my nervous rubbing. "What's going on? You looked really freaked out when you told me to stop. What did you think I was doing?"

"I thought you were trying to stop me from warning Sophia."

Confusion reflected in his eyes. "But I didn't touch you or say anything."

As I tried to think of the best way to explain, one of my teammates rushed past, cleats clacking on the hall floor. "Coach's in a mood, Nara. Don't be late."

I checked my watch. "I've got to change for practice. Can we talk afterward?"

Ethan looked frustrated. "I can't. I have to be at the shelter from four 'til close." He touched my cheek, his thumb sliding along my skin. "Just tell me *we're* okay. The rest can wait."

Ethan deserved an answer to my strange behavior the past couple of days. "We're okay. I'll come by the shelter later."

WHEN I WALKED INTO CVAS, Roscoe lifted his head from his lamb's wool bed beside Sally's desk. Sally glanced up from her paperwork and grinned. "Hi, Nara. Came straight from practice, I see. Ethan said you'd stop by. He's in the back getting a litter ready to go to a rescue group tomorrow."

"Thanks, Sally." I squatted to pat Roscoe, then headed back to the kennel area. My shoulders tightened with each step while I tried to figure out the best way to explain to Ethan what'd been going on with me. As I neared the kennel's main door, my soccer flops must've announced my arrival, because the dogs all started barking at once.

With animals, you gave love and you received love in return. The same wasn't always true with people. I smiled, seeing Ethan clearly now. I was pretty sure I understood why he preferred animals to people. They were a lot less complicated.

When I opened the door, Ethan was just starting to open a cage with three Sheltie puppies. "Great, you can help," he said, waving for me to come forward. The tension between my shoulders eased as I approached.

We were on even ground with the animals.

"How'd it go at practice?" Ethan pulled out a black and white male Sheltie puppy and set him in my hands.

"Sophia's nose remains unbroken." I sighed heavily and cradled the puppy's rear end, snuggling him close to wash away my disappointment.

"You and Lainey okay? Sophia didn't cause problems?" he asked, while scooping up the two tri-colored Shelties.

"Sophia's all bluff and bluster," I answered as the puppy licked my chin enthusiastically. It loved all that salty sweat from practice. I smiled at his sweet puppy breath.

"She seems the type." Ethan held the two female Shelties close and nodded for me to go ahead of him. "These pups are very attached, so I figured it's best to bathe them together."

Ethan and I didn't speak while we bathed the puppies. We just shared the shampoo and traded the sprayer as needed. The puppies whimpered when they first got wet, then wiggled and squirmed through the shampooing phase. By the time we moved to rinsing them off, they'd grown braver, playing with and making tiny yipping barks at the spraying water as it washed all the bubbles away. Every once in a while I caught Ethan smiling at them. It was nice to spend time together doing something we both enjoyed—an activity that didn't require any discussion about our abilities. Something…normal.

As Ethan began to towel dry the black and white puppy, he asked, "Why did you think I was trying to stop you from warning Sophia?"

I paused fluffing and buffing the first female puppy in order to pull the second puppy away from my sock. She'd decided it would make a great tug toy. When I was able to focus on drying the puppy again, I answered, "The cold sensation we both felt today, that wasn't new. Each time I've tried to prevent someone from getting hurt, I've felt this cool pressure bearing down on me. Right before I spoke to Sophia, it pinned me to the locker. Sometimes the sensation's accompanied by other freaky stuff." I met his expectant gaze. "When you refused to share my dreams with me and then said you thought it was best if I didn't interfere, I remembered you also tried to keep me on the phone the day I was trying to help Jody."

Ethan picked the puppy up and rubbed the towel gently around his eyes, then his gaze locked with mine. "You know I never intentionally absorbed your dreams, but I called you that day, because while I was working on the roof, I got a bad feeling, a worried vibe. I don't know...it's hard to explain, but since I'd had your dream, I knew you'd somehow get involved with Jody. I won't lie to you, Nara. I *do* think it's best to let nature take its course."

Now the other puppy decided the towel would make a good tug toy. Each time I rubbed her sister's fur, she tugged on the other end of the towel. I paused my buff/tug routine between the two pups. "Count yourself lucky I didn't let 'nature take its course' or that bomb in your locker *would've* gone off."

Ethan's rubbing hand stopped over the puppy's neck. "Er, good point."

"Anyway, that's not what sent me over the edge, making me believe you were the cause of the sensations I'd been experiencing."

"What did?"

I picked the puppy up and dried her sweet face. Setting her down, I gathered her sister and gave her face the same treatment. "Right after I rushed you off the phone so I could go talk to Jody, my car radio flipped around from station to station, saying, 'Don't Interfere' over and over. Don't you see...that's the same thing you'd said to me about getting involved: don't interfere."

Ethan stilled. "You thought *I* was behind the radio thing?"

"I don't believe that *now*. It occurred to me later that each time the weird stuff had happened before you weren't around.

When it happened again while you were with me today, *and* you felt it too, I knew you weren't causing it."

Realization dawned on his face. He didn't look happy. "*That's* why you wanted me there."

"It was the only way I could think to prove you weren't responsible for all the other weird stuff."

"Whoa." Ethan held his hands up, towel dangling from his fingers. "I'm confused. Slow down. What other weird stuff? And why did you think I was responsible?"

While I finished drying the two puppies, I told Ethan everything about the eerie supernatural events I'd experienced over the past few weeks. When I got to the part about the conversation I'd had with my aunt about him, his eyebrows shot up and his lips quirked in a smile. "Your aunt said I'm powerful and that I have an old soul?"

I threw a wet towel at him. "Don't get cocky. That was just another nail in your 'coffin of doom'. For all I knew, my aunt's gut feelings about you meant that you had telekinesis and could," I paused to tick off the list on my fingers: "prank call like a champ, fiddle with radios, fog mirrors, and block bathroom doors…all from God knew where."

"What about us, Nara? Did you really think I would scare you like that?"

Ethan was sitting on the floor and the puppies had abandoned me for his lap. All three were trying their best to climb up his body to get to his face. Ethan's big hands dwarfed their bodies, but he was so gentle with them. Seeing the hurt in his eyes and the puppies' complete trust in him made my chest feel as if it'd just been sawed in half.

"I'm sorry." I walked over to sit beside him. "I struggled with that, but I couldn't deny the fact that after I'd met you, my dreams started disappearing—which kept me from helping people at school who were getting hurt. Not to mention the fact that on the rare occasion that I had a dream, you were never in them."

Confusion etched his features. "That doesn't make any sense. I assumed *you* at least saw me in your dreams. All this time I'd been thinking that the reason I couldn't see myself was because *I* was dreaming *your* dreams, which, in a weird sort of way, kind of cancelled me out of your dream world."

I petted the black and white puppy, who'd moved over to settle in my lap. "You're never in them."

Ethan touched my chin and I met his gaze. "You knew I had your dreams because I touched you. But as far as why I'm not in them, honest to God, Nara, that's news to me. I have no idea why I'm not in them. I wish I were."

"After everything I've told you, you have to understand how I came to the conclusion I did." I hoped he heard the sincerity in my voice.

"I guess I can see how it all seemed, and for the record, I don't have telekinetic powers," he said with a snort.

Ethan had experienced some of the weirdness too, which meant there was no denying that my experiences were very *real*. A freaky kind of real. The black and white puppy began to suckle on my finger. I rubbed his soft head. "Who or…*what* do you think is doing this to me?" I whispered, trying not to let fear take over.

Picking the female puppies up, Ethan stood and waited until I did the same with the other pup. "This just proves what my gut has been telling me. Interfering is dangerous. All these strange things happened when you used your knowledge to try to help someone."

I followed Ethan out of the bathing area. "I don't understand. Why is this happening now?" Opening the cage, I set the puppy inside. "I've intervened in the past…well, okay not very often."

Ethan set the other pups in with their brother. After he shut the cage, he looked incredulous as he turned to me. "Not very often? Nara, that's *all* I've seen you do since I met you."

I shrugged and spread my hands wide. "When I was seven, I tried to help a girl and it backfired. Since then, I've mostly avoided getting involved with others, until the recent school bombing. It's not like I could just ignore *that* dream. But lately, so many things have been happening, I can't seem to stay uninvolved."

Ethan blue gaze searched mine. "Did you feel these odd sensations back when you tried to help that girl in the past?"

"No, they've only happened recently."

His lips set in a thin line. "Then something has changed. Do you remember when it happened the first time?"

"Yeah, it was when I called the police about the bomb."

"Hey, guys." Sally poked her head inside the kennel door. "All done?"

"Just about," I said.

"Great," she said with a nod. "If you could put the towels in the wash, I'll take care of the rest and close up the shelter for the night."

As I sprayed the dog fur and suds down the drain in the bathing area, Ethan cleaned up the towels. Holding the bundle in his hands, he paused, looking thoughtful. "What if all the weird stuff you've been experiencing was Nature trying to fix the imbalance you've created by acting on your powers?"

I grabbed the laundry bin and rolled it over to Ethan. "I don't understand how helping people is a bad thing."

He tossed the towels into the bin, then moved closer. "I know you have good intentions, Nara, but each time you've used your knowledge of the future to help someone, you've changed the natural course of their lives."

I shook my head slowly. "The stuff that's happened to me has felt eerie and purposeful, like it was trying to scare me into not doing anything." When my hands on the bin began to shake, Ethan slid his fingers down my ponytail and I met his gaze. "How is terrifying me in any way balanced or natural?"

Cupping the back of my neck, he pulled me close and murmured, "It's not."

CHAPTER 15

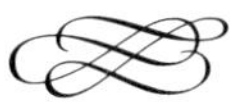

K*nowing the future was overrated,* I decided after several days of peaceful normalcy. It was nice to finally be able to walk into school on Wednesday without tense anticipation crawling along my spine. As I turned down the locker hall, I automatically moved out of the way of the "back brace" girl to give her space, when I almost ran into Kenny.

"Watch out! Coming through," he said as he led a blond guy by his elbow away from a locker.

The blond guy wore dark sunglasses and had medical gauze taped over his eyes underneath the shades. I glanced at Kenny. "What happened to him?"

"Jake's a dumbass."

"Eye doctor said I wore my contacts too long, called it fatigue syndrome or something." Jake shrugged. "I didn't though. I have no idea why my eyes got all messed up."

I couldn't stop staring at the gauze peeking beneath the shades. "Will you get your sight back?"

"Doc says I will after a few days." He grinned. "In the meantime, I'm soaking this 'teachers-taking-it-easy-on-me' shit up."

Kenny rolled his eyes. "Yeah, and now *I* get to 'help-a-student-out'."

He sounded so inconvenienced I couldn't help but snicker.

"Payback's a bit—" I paused when I saw Kristin open her locker to my left. The word *payback* echoed in my head over and over. Dread shot through me. "Where's your locker, Kenny?"

He pointed to the one next to Jake's. "Why?"

I scanned the set of lockers on either side of the hall, trying to remember. Jody's was two doors down. And the screaming guy from a couple weeks ago, Aaron, his locker was in this area somewhere. Wasn't there some guy who'd complained of vertigo? Alan something? I turned to see him opening a locker behind me. And I'd just passed the back brace girl leaving this area.

Kenny waved his hand in front of my face. "Why'd you ask about my locker?"

I mumbled, "No reason," even as my gaze darted across the blue doors, looking for Ethan's old locker. Some jerk had taped a drawing of an explosion on it, making it easy to spot. A sinking feeling hit my stomach. Ethan's old locker was in the center of all the injured students' lockers. Suddenly Lainey's comment from the day I'd called in the bombing rushed back in vivid clarity. *"Dad said that anyone within fifteen feet of that locker could've been hurt."*

I spent the next couple hours checking my watch and was so stressed waiting for Ethan outside his Chemistry class, that my palms had bloody half moons from my nails. The bell finally rang and as I waited for him, I rubbed my stinging palms on my jeans. I could barely contain myself when he finally appeared. "Let's go out for lunch."

His eyebrows shot up. "This isn't your lunch hour."

"I need to talk to you," I said in a low, urgent voice.

"What's wrong?"

I waved to the front of the school. "I'll tell you once we're alone."

As soon as Ethan's car rolled out of the school parking lot, he glanced my way. "You look worried."

"Remember when I said that the first time I felt the cold heaviness around me was when I called in the bombing?"

Ethan nodded.

"Well, you had the supernatural part right, but I don't think this is about Nature trying to maintain balance. I'm pretty sure it's more about keeping score."

His dark gaze cut my way. "That's doesn't sound good." Pulling into a neighborhood side street, he cut the engine, then turned to face me, his arm resting on the steering wheel. "What makes you think this?"

"Seeing Kenny in the hall this morning." I explained how seeing Kenny with the blinded guy, triggered a memory of the people I'd helped or seen, whose lockers were in that area of the locker hall. "Ethan, all the injured people in school lately? Their lockers fall into the section of lockers near where the bomb was found—your old locker."

Ethan frowned. "I agree with you about the pattern, but why do you think 'keeping score' is the cause?"

"Because of something you said to me last Friday. 'By interfering and trying to save people, you're changing the outcome of their lives'. I think the 'score keeper' is, well…I think it's fate somehow intervening. It all makes sense now *why* I started experiencing the eerie stuff when I did. Ever since I prevented the bomb from going off, a presence has been there." I shoved my hands through my hair, getting more and more worked up. "After that, whenever I saw someone get hurt in my dream and tried to prevent it, that chilling presence used all kinds of crazy scare tactics to prevent me from intervening. I—I think it was Fate, Ethan."

Ethan pulled my hand from my hair and rubbed his thumb along my palm. "That must've been what I felt the day I called right before you talked to Jody. Something felt off, like things were out of whack."

"I think Fate's trying to make sure all the people that I saved from the bomb get hurt anyway. If you had opened your locker that day, you would probably have been killed." I folded my fingers around his in a tight grip. "We have to stop Fate before it finds a way to make your intended fate reality."

Ethan shook his head. "We're not doing anything."

My eyes widened. "What? Why would you say that?"

"It's too dangerous. Plus, I don't think Fate will come after me."

I stared at him as if he'd sprouted horns. "That's crazy talk. Too many people from the same locker area have already gotten hurt. Why do think *you'll* get a free pass when no one else has?"

Ethan shrugged, unconcerned. "Like you said, I'm not in your dreams."

"That's your brilliant logic? Because you're not in my dreams?" I touched his face as panic set in. "You might not be in my dreams, but you're real. You're flesh and blood and you can be hurt or worse, killed. We can't ignore this."

His jaw hardened under my palm. "No, Nara. If what you say is true, that Fate is causing all this, then it has already zeroed in on you. Think how much your gift must piss it off. You have the ability to screw up *all* its carefully laid plans. The last thing you should do is openly challenge it. I don't want anything to happen to you."

Tears burned my eyes and my stomach roiled. In my mind's eye, I kept seeing Ethan in some horrible freak accident that tore him to shreds, just like the bomb would've done, had it gone off. More than anyone else, he had the most to lose. "Ethan, please!"

He traced his knuckles along my cheek. "Let it go, Nara."

"But—"

Ethan cupped my jaw with both hands, his gaze focused on mine. "We have other things we need to do."

The screeching fears in my head instantly shushed to mere whispers. I was surprised that he'd talked me down, but I suddenly felt less worried. "Like what?"

"Like heading over to the CVU's library to get research books for our History paper. Can you go after practice?"

At least we'd be together and I could keep an eye on him. "Yeah, can you pick me up around five-fifteen at my house?"

He started to speak when a loud rapping hammered on his window, startling us. An old woman in a floral housecoat stood scowling, her white hair bound in spongy pink curlers as she pointed her broom's handle toward the glass like a spear. "Find somewhere else to do the nasty or I'm calling the police."

As we drove away, Ethan shook his head and chuckled. "Do you feel dirty? Or is it just me?"

~

AT THE END of the day, I was pulling my backpack out of my locker, when Lainey brushed past, zipping down the hall at breakneck pace. She came to a sliding halt in front of a locker and spun the combination with swift precision. My heart ramped, hammering hard and fast and I suddenly felt light-headed. I'd forgotten that Lainey's locker was right next to Ethan's old locker. She'd been sharing Jared's for a while now.

I closed my locker, panic clawing my chest. Ethan wasn't the only one. Lainey was in danger too. Why had I listened to him about staying out of it? *Because he touched you on purpose to calm you down.* I had no idea he could be so sneaky.

This was all my fault and I needed to fix it. But without my dreams, I didn't know when something was going to happen. And now that Ethan knew about Fate, I was afraid he might not warn me. What I needed was the element of surprise, something Fate wouldn't be expecting from me. Then maybe it would leave Lainey and Ethan alone.

Lainey had just pulled her soccer bag out of the locker and was about to close the door. I couldn't stand by and wait for her to get hurt.

"Lainey," I called before she could walk away.

Tugging the bag's strap onto her shoulder, she waited for me to approach. "Hey, girl. How's your Gran?"

I smiled. "Chipper as ever. So, um, I'm doing this skit for the Central Virginia Animal Shelter. Can you be a stand-in for a sec?"

She shrugged. "Sure."

I surveyed the hall, floor and ceiling, then spoke in a clear voice, "I know you're here, lurking" Static popped in my jacket with my small movements. The sensation sent fear jolting through me, but I keep my face composed. "I want you to *back off*. No more accidents."

"Am I supposed to be responding?" Lainey stage-whispered, her gaze darting around furtively.

I shook my head. My back was so tense, a light breeze could've snapped my spine.

She gave me a "thumbs up". "Love the fierceness."

"Fierceness is required," I said, still scanning.

"Oh, I get it! 'No more accidents.' Your skit's about 'tough love' dog training, right?"

The frigid air had dissipated and my body began to relax. I laughed at her interpretation. "Uh, yeah, that's it. Thanks for being my guinea pig."

"Don't you mean thanks for being your 'dog'?" She smiled, then continued, "The only critique I have on your performance is: Turn those fierce eyes *on* the dog. You looked everywhere but at me."

I cleared my throat so I wouldn't laugh. "I'll keep that in mind. Thanks."

"No problem. You know I'd only let a *close* friend treat me like her bitch."

I smiled at the reminder that I'd said something similar to her. "See you at practice."

Exhaling a heavy breath, I waved after her and hoped my preemptive strike with Fate had worked.

~

AFTER PRACTICE, I checked voicemails when I got home and had a message from Gran.

"Inara." She sounded muffled and raspy, like she was talking into the phone with her hand over the mouthpiece so no one would hear. "You're brilliant! Clara has been hounding me, trying to find out who my secret admirer is." She snickered, then continued, "I even told her that's where I was, drinking it up and seeing my man. I feel like such a floozy. Haven't had this much fun in years! Well, I need to get ready for game night. Just wanted to say thank you. Come see me sooner than a few months, young lady." And with that final dig, she hung up.

Smiling fondly, I erased the message, then sat down to eat a small bowl of strawberry oatmeal. I'd just finished eating when I saw Ethan standing at my front door, raising his hand to knock.

I glanced at the microwave clock in confusion. It was almost five and I was still grubby from soccer practice. "You're early. What's up?" I said as I opened the door.

Stepping inside, he shoved his hands in his jacket pockets. "I thought we could get an earlier start."

His shoulders were stiff and the muscle in his jaw popped in and out. I knew that look. "Is everything okay?"

"Yeah. I just wanted to give you something." Ethan pulled his hand from his pocket, then slid a small pair of rimless sunglasses with light peach-colored lenses on my face. "Perfect," he said, nodding his approval.

"Thank you," I said quietly, touched by the gift.

A small smile lifted the corners of his lips and he slid his fingers down my hair. "Now you don't have to hide behind dark shades any more. At least not from me."

All I could do was stare. So maybe the sunglasses collection on my car dash looked a little over-the-top, but other girls bought shoes or purses. "I don't hide behind my glasses."

"Yeah, you do, because you *always* take your glasses off as soon as you get in your car."

I shrugged and his eyebrow shot up. "That's usually when most people put them on, Nara."

Oh, duh. When my powers first appeared in elementary school, I'd been worried that my gaze would give away the fact I knew stuff I shouldn't have known, at least not ahead of time. Sunglasses had been my answer. Over the years, my obsession faded, turning into a kind of hobby. I touched the edge of my new shades. "They're perfect. I love them."

Looking pleased, Ethan stepped close and dropped a kiss on my sweat-dried forehead. "No more secrets between us."

Guilt twisted my stomach. Ethan would flip if he knew about my experiment in the hall today. "Eww," I said, backing up. "I'm all gross."

"She tastes like chicken." He winked, then swiped his tongue hungrily across his lips.

Even though he was joking around, my heart fluttered. "Let me get a quick shower and then we'll go."

After my shower, I towel-dried my hair and had just slipped into a pair of worn jeans and a pullover sweater, when I heard my Irish music tape playing and the sound of wood tapping against wood, rapping to the beat in perfect rhythm.

Opening my bathroom door, I stared at Ethan in amazement.

When I was little I'd helped my father sand the intricately carved headboard he'd created for my bed frame. While the wooden headboard dried from the layers of stain he'd applied, he said to me, "As a reward for your help, I'll make anything you want next. Just name it." I'd clapped my hands and excitedly asked," Can you please make me a musical instrument?"

Dad's answer had been Jack-the-jolly-jigger.

"Since you can't read music, Jack here will be your instrument," Dad said as he held up the long stick with a wooden man attached on the end. Jack had jointed arms, legs and knees that swiveled, swung and bent with the slightest movement of the stick.

My dad sat in a chair with a long, thin piece of wood three inches wide underneath him. Holding Jack so his legs hovered on the end of the flexible "plank", Dad nodded to an old tape player he'd set on the table. "Turn the music on and I'll show you how Jack works."

I was doubtful, but pushed the play button. When the folk music began to play, Dad hit the board between his legs and as the wood vibrated and bounced, he lifted Jack up and down with the stick, making the ends of Jack's feet tap the board to the beat of the music.

Dad had made it look so easy. Which I found, it wasn't. I was little, but I was determined. After six months, I'd graduated to an Irish tape I'd found at a neighborhood garage sale. I'd hoped the Celtic drums would help me find the right beat so I could get the hang of Jack (instead of wanting to strangle the wooden jigger). But I never could get the right balance between tapping the board and lifting Jack's feet up and down.

I only remembered a couple pre-Dad-leaving events with my father. Helping him sand the headboard was one and Jack-the-jolly-jigger was the other. I hadn't tried to play Jack and the old tape in years. Yet, Ethan sat there on my desk chair, making

Jack tap out difficult steps on the bouncing board in perfect cadence to the Irish music.

"I can't believe you're making Jack dance a jig," I finally said.

Glancing up, Ethan smiled. "I hope you don't mind. This is great. I've never seen one of these before."

Never seen one? How could he play it so easily then? Trying not to feel totally inept, I clasped my comb tight and walked into the room, confessing, "I've never been able to get him to dance like that."

Ethan tapped the board a couple times and Jack's loose legs clicked out a beat. "It kind of drew my attention so I picked it up. Once I started messing and playing with ways to turn it, make it jump and such, the rest came to me. It's not that hard to learn. Want me to show you?"

"Yeah," I said, swallowing my pride that he'd figured out in mere minutes what I never could.

Ethan hopped up and held the board for me to sit on it. Once I was settled in the chair, he knelt beside me and said, "You hit the board and I'll hold the guy."

While the music played on, I tapped and Ethan made Jack dance. I watched him flick his wrist and tried to track how he moved the wooden man.

When a new song started, Ethan handed me the stick. "Your turn. I'll tap the board and you hold Jack."

Nodding, I took the stick and tried to mimic Ethan's earlier movements as he tapped the board. I did better than I had in the past, but nowhere near the smooth sounds Ethan had tapped out.

"It's all about timing," Ethan said, reaching for my stick hand.

His hand was warm and my heart ramped when his fingers folded completely around mine. I loved being close to him like this, sharing something fun. "Watch. It's like this," he said in a patient voice.

After several more tries, with Ethan guiding my hand and tapping the board, I was able to make Jack dance to the beat. Laughing as Jack's arms spun and he kicked up a fun jig, I said,

"You have no idea how many times I've tried to make this stupid toy dance."

The tape ended and silence filled the room. Ethan's blue eyes locked with mine. "Well, now you can. Whenever you want."

I smiled. "Thanks for the pointers."

Once I'd moved Jack, the board, and my dad's old tape recorder back against the wall, Ethan asked, "When am I going to meet your mom?"

When I turned, he was sitting on my bed, holding my hot pink throw pillow (the only project I'd finished, since I could complete it in *one* day). "Maybe you'll get lucky and she'll come home early one day." Whoa, that had sounded more sarcastic than I'd meant. Clearing my throat, I grabbed my wide-toothed comb from my desktop. "I'd like to meet Samson, too," I said as I sat down beside him, then ran the comb through my damp hair.

"He'd like you." Tossing the pillow, Ethan tugged the comb from my hand and twirled his finger in a circle, telling me to turn around.

Facing away from him, I leaned on my hands and tilted my head back, closing my eyes as he combed the tangles from my hair. "That feels so good," I sighed, enjoying every single stroke. "I could sit here all day."

Ethan's fingers replaced the comb, making me tingle all over. I hmm'd my approval, loving the intimacy of his fingers sliding through my hair instead of the hard plastic.

When his lips pressed against the small scar near my hairline, my heart leapt and every muscle in my body tensed. My eyes flew open and I stared at him upside down as he peered down at me.

"Did you get this scar playing soccer?" he asked, his hands cupping my face.

I'd always been a little self-conscious about the scar, but when Ethan asked, I only heard curiosity, not disgust. "I don't remember really. I was little when it happened."

His thumbs stroked my cheekbones as he kissed my scar again, and then pressed his lips to the space between my eyes before kissing the tip of my nose. Every touch, every movement was slow, tender…reverent. My heart raced when his warm lips met mine, his plump lower lip pulling gently on my upper one.

My fingers crushed the bedspread as I pushed on the bed, kissing him back. When he slid his mouth to my jaw, I quickly turned and faced him, wrapping my arms around his broad shoulders. Ethan grasped my waist and tugged me close, murmuring my name.

As his lips pressed against mine, every part of me centered on him. I slid my hand across his jaw, enjoying the sensation of his five-o-clock scruff scratching my palms as he lowered us to the bed. I dug my fingers into his neck, pulling him close. Ethan pressed against my mouth, rolling me underneath him with a swift fierceness that made every nerve ending under my skin jump and tingle. The electric feeling had nothing to do with the unending static that permeated my sheets and covers.

"You even taste like sunshine." Static popped as he nipped at my bottom lip. Ethan jumped and when I started to apologize, he pressed his lips to mine once more. This kiss was harder and edged with a rough intensity.

Blood pumped through my veins. I savored the feel of his chest and weight crushing me, the slide of his hand along the curve of my butt. When his grip on my thigh tightened and he pulled my leg around his hip, locking us together perfectly, excitement thrummed through me.

Ethan paused, his body tensing. "Did you hear the garage door?"

I glanced at my clock. Five-twenty-five glowed back at me. "Crap. Of all times…that's my mom." I jumped up and straightened my sweater. "A couple times a month she leaves early to do grocery shopping." Waving him on, I said, "Go wait in the living room. I'll be right out."

As I finger-combed my messy hair, I heard the rumble of voices in the kitchen. My lips looked slightly swollen and my cheeks were rosier than normal, so I quickly brushed on some powder and dabbed on lip gloss. Hopefully the makeup would explain my perky look.

I paused in the kitchen doorway when I saw Ethan helping

Mom with the grocery bags from the garage. "Hi, Mom, I see you met Ethan."

Mom set two bags on the counter and glanced at Ethan, who was carrying a couple bags. "Yes, I did. He says you two are working on a History paper together."

"I really hope you got some more dryer sheets. The last ones you bought were awful." I grabbed one of the bags from Ethan. "Yeah, we're doing a paper on Superstitions and War and plan to check out CVU's library for resource material."

Mom heaved a sigh. "I guess I'll just save you leftovers."

I paused pulling out the new box of dryer sheets. "You were going to *cook*?"

She cast an embarrassed glance toward Ethan. "My cooking's not that bad, Inara."

"I meant…you usually bring dinner home or order out. Were you going to make spaghetti?"

"Yes."

I glanced at Ethan, silently seeking his understanding.

When he nodded, I smiled. "Then Ethan and I will make the salad. We'll head to the library later."

After dinner, while Ethan was in the bathroom, Mom took the pan I'd just dried and put it away. Turning, she held her hand out for the cookie sheet I was almost done drying and said in a casual tone, "That's an interesting tattoo your friend has."

Nothing with my mom was casual, yet I was surprised she'd seen Ethan's tattoo. Then I remembered he'd pushed up his sleeves to help wash the dishes. I couldn't believe I hadn't looked while I had a chance. He'd kept his sleeves down at the shelter—we all did—to protect against scratches. "What tattoo?" I said innocently, handing her the cookie sheet.

Mom visibly relaxed. "You haven't seen it?" She slid the pan into the cupboard and glanced my way. "He has a dragon tattoo on his arm. I'm not much for body art, but that one was tastefully done with the dark outline and muted coloring. I just hope he doesn't have them all over his body."

Was she fishing about my sex life by asking about the tattoo? Mom never asked direct questions about personal stuff.

I stiffened, resenting it. It's not like she was around enough to know one way or the other. Regardless, I was glad I was already on the pill to regulate my period. That way she wouldn't do something embarrassing like make a doctor appointment for me with the excuse it was time for my annual exam. "A dragon tattoo, huh? That's kind of interesting."

We heard Ethan coming back down the hall and she leaned close, whispering, "I like him. He seems like a nice boy."

Her approval made me happy and my earlier resentment faded. I beamed as I swiped the towel inside the salad bowl. "He's great. I'm glad you like him."

Clasping the wooden bowl I handed her, she murmured, "Just don't let him break your heart."

CHAPTER 16

"That makes six," I said, tucking the thick history book into my backpack.

As I started to heave my nearly full backpack onto my shoulder, Ethan grasped the strap and took it from me, hoisting it onto his shoulder instead. "Six is probably enough."

"Oh, no. You insisted on looking up all twelve. We've gone through ten. Might as well check out the last two."

"We started later than we'd planned." Ethan shrugged. "I think a half dozen will do it."

"Going home to an empty house is how you want to spend the rest of your night?"

"We can always go back to my house and start taking notes on the books we have."

The longer we'd stayed at the library, the more on edge Ethan seemed. I squinted at him. "You don't like libraries much, do you?"

Leaning close, he kissed my nose. "We're not alone here."

"Shhhhh." An older man glared at us from a side table.

Ethan's comment made me tingle all the way to my toes, but I felt we needed at least one more resource since our subject was so unusual. Snickering, I tugged him along behind me as I headed for the elevator. "Come on. We'll just go up the stack to the periodical room, check it out, and then we'll leave."

The stack elevator moved so slowly we could've taken the stairs and gotten there faster. It was stuffy and small, holding four people max. I breathed through my nose, taking in as much air as possible as the elevator squeaked and moaned its way up to the eighth floor. Housing old resource material that was rarely used, the stacks felt like a separate world that was cut off from the main library.

The lights popped on the moment we stepped into a room no larger than twenty by twenty. Tall shelving featured bound periodicals that dated back f-o-r-e-v-e-r.

Our shoes slid across the dust on the hard floor. "Guess the eighth floor's rarely used, huh?" I said in a whisper, not at all sure *why* I was whispering. No librarians were up here to tell us to keep our voices down. The place was a tomb. The room was so packed that the shelves started two feet out from the elevator, creating the same claustrophobic feeling I'd experienced on the way up.

Ethan pulled the piece of paper with the info we needed from his back pocket. Glancing up, he said, "We need to check out 'open aisle', shelf three for the article we're looking for."

I started forward, but Ethan quickly wrapped his arm around my waist and walked us around the stack.

I loved being close to him, but I figured we'd find what we were looking for faster if we split up. I started to step away, but he grasped my hand in a tight hold and frowned. "Stay close."

The florescent lights above us buzzed as I glanced back at him, surprised by the sharpness in his comment. "Um, sure."

Pointing to a sign taped on a tall bookshelf that sat halfway down the main open aisle—duh—I said, "Here it is," and quickly squatted to knee-level to find shelf number three. I had to tug several times to pull the extra tall, three-inch black binder out.

When Ethan stepped beside me, but didn't comment on my battle to free the binder, I looked up, expecting to see amusement on his face. Instead, he was standing with his hand on the edge of a square metal bin sitting three shelves above me. "What are you doing?"

Shoving the bin until it clanked against the shelving's metal back, he kept his hand on the edge of the shelf. "You were tugging so hard, the bookcase shook. I wanted to make sure the bin didn't fall."

My gaze shot to the bin with its sharp edges and pointy corners. I winced, thinking how much that would've hurt. "Thanks for paying attention..." I trailed off when a creak behind the bin drew my attention. Through the bookcase's open back, I saw the bookcase behind it tilting forward, bins and binders tumbling out.

Clutching the binder, I gasped, "Watch out! Another bookshelf's falling—"

I heard Ethan yelling and my brain said *move*, but my body was locked in place as a vivid childhood memory—of a towering dark bookcase packed with books leaning toward me —slammed into my mind.

I held onto a lower shelf and stood on my toes, trying to reach a toy my mom had purposefully placed out of my reach on the tall bookcase—my punishment for banging it on the brand new coffee table. When the bookcase began to tilt and books began to shower down around me, I screamed but was so scared I couldn't move. A man's voice called my name and I glanced up in time to see a wooden globe bookend slide off the edge of the shelf, heading straight for me.

Pain shot through my back and chest, yanking me back to the present. Ethan laid on top of me. We were pinned to the floor under the weight of two heavy bookcases, the thick binder wedged between us.

I coughed and gasped, trying to recover from having the wind knocked out of me.

"Are you okay?" Ethan grunted.

I tried to inhale. "Can't breathe."

He'd put one arm around my head to protect me from the falling periodical binders and his other arm was behind his own head. "Me either," he croaked, then grunted as he worked to free his arm trapped by the heavy bookcase.

Once his arm was free, he pushed a binder out of the way, then flattened his hands on the floor on either side of me. "As soon as I say, 'Go', slide out from under me and get clear of the shelving. Got it?"

I was so lightheaded all I could do was nod.

Setting his jaw, Ethan pressed his shoulders against the shelving at the same time he pushed his hands against the floor. The shelving creaked as Ethan's improvised push-up lifted it a couple inches off of us. "Now," he gritted out.

My chest ached, but I slid myself backward along the floor as fast as I could.

The moment my feet were free, Ethan's arms collapsed, sending him and the heavy metal shelves back to the floor.

"Ethan!"

Scrambling to my feet, I grabbed the top of the bookshelf, then pulled upward, using every muscle in my body.

When the bookcase began to lift, I heard Ethan take a gasp of breath. "Just a little more."

But the weight of the second shelf was too much. "It's too heavy I can't move it any more!"

Ethan grunted and my fingers began to ache as I frantically looked around for something to take some of the weight. Against a far wall, I saw a low stepstool sitting next to a rolling book cart. "I have to put it back down for a sec. I think I can use that stool for leverage."

As soon as I lowered the shelf down, I ran to get the step stool. Setting it near the lowest part of the shelf, I said, "When I lift, pull the stool under the shelf. Got it?"

"Hurry," he wheezed.

Grabbing the edge of the shelf again, I lifted it as high as I could, then said, "Now!"

The stool slid, jamming under the metal shelving's edge.

As some of the weight shifted off my hands, I bent my knees lower and strained harder, lifting the shelf another inch.

Ethan crawled out, sucking in lungfuls of air.

Releasing the shelving, I moved to his side. For a couple of seconds we stared in silence at the two bookcases and the mess on the floor underneath it.

"What happened?" I finally spoke.

Pushing my backpack off his shoulders, Ethan rubbed the back of his neck. He looked at me, concern in his gaze. "Are you okay?"

"Yeah. Are you?"

"I'm good," he said and lowered his hand to his side.

A streak of blood was smeared across his palm. "You're hurt," I said, turning his shoulder to see.

Something, probably one of the binders, had nicked the back of his neck. "I'm fine," he said, pushing his collar against the cut to stop the bleeding.

Still reeling, I stared at the mess and exhaled quickly. My back ached a little. "Did you tackle me?"

Grimacing, he stared at the bashed in metal bin poking up through the open backside of the bookshelf, magazines scattered all around it. "Sorry. That bin would've fallen on you first if I hadn't pushed you out of the way. Why didn't you move? It's like you were in a trance or something."

My hand shook as I touched the old scar along my hairline. "I—it was just like…" I met his gaze. "I remember how I got my scar now." Squinting, I tried to recall the details. "Something similar happened when I was a little girl, except it was a huge wooden bookcase that fell and a bookend came crashing down on me."

As I spoke, past images flashed in my mind: *My dad's vivid green eyes, wide with panic. He's dashing toward me, yelling, "Nari, look out!" We roll together on the floor as the bookshelf hit the floor with a loud boom. Another scene flashes. He's dabbing my head wound. I'm trying not to look at the blood on the tissue, because it makes my stomach woozy. Instead, I focus on my dad's stricken expression. He gently pushes the wound on my forehead together and applies a butterfly bandage, whispering, "I bolted it to the wall. This wasn't supposed to happen."*

Ethan gathered me close, pulling me back to the present. Kissing my scar, he murmured, "This shouldn't have happened."

I jerked back. His comment was so similar to my dad's. Not to mention the double coincidence—that both situations involved falling bookcases. "Wha—what'd you just say?"

He pressed his lips together. "I fell asleep while I was studying and dreamed about the rest of your day after school. Except in this dream, a metal bookshelf fell on you when you tugged on a binder. That's why I've been tense since we got to the library. I knew magazines were bound in binders. I didn't want to come up here."

I gaped. "So, none of this was in your dream of my entire day last night? Why didn't you tell me?"

"No, it wasn't in my dream last night. And I didn't tell you because I didn't want to freak you out. I knew what was going to go down, so I just made sure the bookshelf never had a chance to rock like it did in my dream. I held onto it while you pulled."

My gaze slid to the bookshelves now on the floor, their contents scattered everywhere—like my brains could've been if Ethan hadn't thrown himself on top of me. The tiny hairs on my arms started to rise.

"I'm sorry, Nara. I should've told you."

"Yes, you should have."

"This was all my fault."

"It was an accident." I pointed to the other bookshelf where the metal side was bent and warped. "The binders' weight must've been too much for it. Maybe when you righted the bookshelf to keep it from falling, the jarring on the floor caused this one to finally collapse."

Ethan didn't say anything. He seemed quiet, pensive.

With swift movements, I pulled the rolling book cart near the fallen bookshelf, then began gathering binders though the bookshelf's open back and putting them on the cart. I knew he felt responsible and I didn't want him to feel bad. "I'm so thankful you took a nap," I said in an upbeat tone as I stopped to shove the one binder we needed into my backpack.

When I turned back to cleaning up, I tried not to show how truly shaken I was by the fact his "night" dream—which should've been about my entire day—hadn't included the bookshelf falling. Why?

"The library will take care of this, Nara," Ethan finally said.

I ignored him, completely focused on organizing the periodicals in front of me. Frowning at the binders I'd placed on the cart in haphazard abandon, I realized they were totally out of order. I began to reorder them in numerical order at a rapid pace, jerking books out, sliding books over, moving the correct ones into place. "This is such a mess. We can't leave it like this."

"Nara."

I started to grab another set of periodicals from the floor, frantic to put every single binder in the right numerical order, but Ethan gripped my shoulders and pulled me against his chest, holding me tight. "It's okay."

Taking a deep breath, I pressed my face to his neck. "We both could've been really hurt."

He stroked my hair. "We'll be bruised and sore tomorrow, but we're fine. And you're right. All those thick resource books in your backpack came in handy. They saved my spine from being crushed."

I gripped his jacket. "My dreams have *never* been wrong, Ethan. Why didn't you see the other bookshelf falling in your dreams last night?"

He turned serious. "I dreamed about the bookshelf this afternoon, remember? Your dreams are still right. But I prevented it from falling. Maybe you're right and I caused the chain reaction with the other bookshelf like you said. But what I'm wondering is what happened today that caused a change in 'your future' from what I saw last night?"

As I shook my head, the one thing I'd done that would've been out-of-the-norm from my regular day came to me. I'd told Fate to back off.

An hour later, Ethan pulled into my driveway. The head librarian had freaked when he found out that the bookcases had fallen on us. I was sure it was because the timid man was terrified our families would sue. Ethan cut the engine and hooked his wrist on the steering wheel, thrumming his fingers on the dashboard. "What could possibly have changed your future...well, other than you? And since you didn't know your dream from last night, you couldn't have consciously changed anything."

He stared at me and I resisted the urge to fidget under his steady gaze. I wasn't ready to admit I might've caused the change in my future by pissing Fate off. It could just as easily have been a fluke.

I shrugged. "A random glitch maybe?"

He frowned. "I don't buy it."

I rubbed my temples. My head hurt from worrying that I might have caused this. "It's weird, I agree, but I've never dreamed my day twice, so who knows." Leaning over, I kissed his clenched jaw. "We can go over everything you remember from the two dreams in detail tomorrow in study hall." Grabbing my backpack, I started to get out of his car, then paused. "No more holding back on the big stuff to save me from worrying. Deal?" *And, just in case, I'll try not to go around challenging Fate any more.*

Hard lines settled on his face. "You'll have every detail."

~

I WALKED into school feeling like a zombie. I'd had a terrible night's sleep. In the wee hours, a thought occurred to me that alleviated some of my guilt, but the realization set off a bout of new concerns. Ethan had gotten hurt too. What if *I* wasn't the target?

I didn't want to explain my theory about last night to Ethan in the morning, so I avoided running into him until study hall. When I arrived in study hall and Ethan wasn't there yet, I immediately tensed with worry.

Once Ethan finally walked in five minutes after the bell rang, I exhaled a sigh of relief. As soon as he sat down, I started talking at a rapid pace. "I don't think last night was about me. I think it was about you—" but I stopped when I saw his bruised jaw.

"Ohmigod, what happened?" His lip was slightly swollen with a split near the corner. I started to touch his face, but he winced and pulled back.

"It's nothing to worry about."

"Nothing to worry—" Fisting my hand on the table, I hissed in a low tone, "How did that happen?"

Ethan's dark gaze drilled into mine. "I want to talk about *you*, about my dream last night, Nara. Forget about this." He waved, dismissing his bruised face. "You need to listen, okay?"

I couldn't stop staring at the split on his lip. It was crusted over, as if he'd gotten the wound hours ago, probably even last night. Did that happen after he dropped me off?

"You with me?" Ethan's voice was gruff.

Swallowing my apprehension, I nodded.

He touched my jaw lightly. "When the last bell rings, wait for me at the main door. Don't walk out to your car by yourself."

"What happens?"

The worry brackets were back, digging creases around his mouth. "There's an accident in the parking lot."

Loud buzzing sounded in my ears. "What?" I squeaked.

Determination darkened his eyes. "I won't let anything happen to you."

"I thought you didn't believe in changing the natural course," I said, tears burning.

"This feels wrong."

Banked fury reflected in his eyes. "How bad is it?"

Ethan shook his head. "I was so freaked out, I woke up." Curling his lips inward, he continued with a determined snarl, "Nothing will happen to you."

My lips trembled at the tension vibrating in Ethan. My theory that the bookshelf falling had been meant for Ethan and not me had just been blown out of the water. Or, maybe not. Maybe it was *just* like last night. "Do you—" I started to ask if he got hurt too, then remembered he never stars in my dreams. "You could get hurt, too, Ethan. Last night and now this." I rubbed my temples, feeling another headache coming on. "It's too much." If Fate was after me or Ethan, either way, I'd failed. "This is all my fault."

Ethan's expression shifted to firm resolve. "It'll be fine. You'll stay by my side and away from the area where it happens."

"You don't understand. I think I caused this."

He tensed. "What do you mean, you caused this?"

"Last night you asked what changed in my day that could've changed my future. I didn't want to believe I was the cause of the bookshelf falling, but after your dream last night, I think maybe I was."

His brows drew together. "How?"

"Yesterday, when I saw that Lainey's locker happened to be right next to your old one, I realized she was on Fate's hit list as well. I couldn't let Fate hurt either one of you. I couldn't."

"You challenged it?" Ethan closed his eyes and slowly released a breath. When he focused on me once more, his eyes were so dark they looked black. "I want you to do exactly what I say, no deviations."

"Is this accident something we can call the police about? Stop it before it happens?"

"No changes, Nara. It's better if I know the order of things, but if we start changing other aspects, then I won't know *that* future. Last night freaked me out. I won't take that kind of risk with your safety."

"Do other people get hurt?" I was almost afraid to hear the answer.

Ethan didn't respond.

"Ethan." Guilt and fear battled inside me. All I could think about was Sadie and now all those people in the locker hall. *All. My. Fault*. I couldn't let the idea that, by saving myself today, others would pay the price. "If I'm not where I'm supposed to be, will someone else get hurt? I have to know."

"No one else gets hurt." Clasping my shoulders, his fingers dug deep. "Do you trust me?"

Trusting Ethan was the only instinct I was absolutely certain about. "Yes," I said, gulping back the burning sensation that had started to creep up my throat.

~

WHILE STUDENTS POURED out of the school, I leaned against the wall, waiting for Ethan. Pulling out my cell phone, I knew I'd be too emotional to say anything, so I sent two text messages. The first one was to my mom.

I love you. I'm glad you're coming to my game. The last sentence was my way of believing in Ethan, even though my chest ached with worry.

I thought of calling my Gran, but the last thing I wanted to do was worry her. I sent the second text to my aunt.

Just wanted to tell you that I love you.

After I hit send, I stared at the last text message my dad had sent me. I hadn't opened it, nor had I deleted it. My mind warred with my heart. The look on his face when he'd rushed toward me, full of panic and fear as the bookcase had started to tumble over, flashed in my mind once more. I tried to open the text and the same garbled letters and numbers appeared. Closing the text, I opened it once more.

Please text me, Nari.

"Why did you leave us?" I whispered.

"Hey, Nara."

Lainey stood in front of me. "Hey." Turning my cell off, I dropped it in my backpack.

"How's the skit going?"

If I didn't make it today, I hoped Lainey stayed safe. She'd made me laugh yesterday. I missed spending "girl time" with her. "Um, it's a work in progress."

Ethan stood behind Lainey and I glanced at him, then at Lainey, saying, "Ethan, this is Lainey. Lainey, Ethan."

Lainey openly stared at his face. "What happened to you?"

He shrugged. "Just helping a friend out."

The swelling had faded, but Ethan's comment made me wonder what kind of *friend* got him popped in the jaw and lip. Then again, he'd taken the brunt of two metal bookcases for me last night.

Shaking her head, a bemused smile curved Lainey's lips. "You coming to the game tonight, Ethan?"

Ethan moved to lean on the wall beside me. Bending his knee, he flattened his boot against the wall. "Wouldn't miss it."

"I've seen you two in study hall." Lainey glanced back and forth between us. "You're totally into Nara, aren't you?"

"Lainey!" My face raged with heat.

"You could say that."

The conviction in Ethan's voice made my heart melt. Too

emotional to keep staring at him, I looked away as Jared walked up and hooked his arm around Lainey's neck. "Come on, Lane. I've got practice in a few."

Lainey laughed and backed away, waving. "See you at the game, Nara."

While a few people still lingered in the atrium talking among themselves, Ethan reached down to clasp my hand. "You ready?"

I felt giddy when his fingers folded tight around mine, my fear temporarily eclipsed. It was the first time Ethan had purposefully taken my hand in view of everyone since that day in the assembly. Sure he'd touched my face, brushed his fingers against my hair and stuff, but it never lasted very long and I always missed his warmth when he moved away.

I exhaled a steadying breath. "Yeah, let's go."

My chest felt like it was caving inward when we walked outside into the cool afternoon air. "What doesn't make sense is why Fate would try to attack me. It knows I can see my future and avoid getting hurt." I lifted our locked hands. "Well, at least I can through you."

Ethan's hold tightened. "It has tried to scare you before. Now it's making it personal and deadly."

A raven sat on one of the school's tall light posts, cawing away. I shivered. It was like the bird was calling for my death. "What happened in the dream?"

Ethan veered to the left side of the parking lot and stepped up on the sidewalk. Most people ignored the sidewalks, preferring to walk the line of parked cars in the lot to get to their vehicles. Nodding to the right side of the lot, he said, "You were walking along that side of the lot on the sidewalk.

The one day I followed the school rules and used the sidewalk, I bought it. Fate truly hated me. Two guys, hopping the bright orange plastic netting that blocked off the construction area near the sidewalk, drew my attention. One of them climbed into the huge construction vehicle. "Don't tell me those two cause the accident?"

His fingers tightened around mine. "Okay, I won't tell you."

"Ethan!"

"The jerkoffs turn on the tractor and—" Ethan paused, staring at the pyramid of metal piping stacked near the equipment.

The construction vehicle had started up. The guys pumped their fists, whooping and hollering at their success. Idiots. I glanced at the bird, surprised it was still on its perch with all the racket going on down below. I couldn't hear his gronking over the construction vehicle's engine, but its black beak was wide open.

Ethan nodded toward the vehicle's claw. "They pull a lever that makes that claw swing around and knock into the stack of pipes. The pipes tumble outside the netting and roll toward the parking lot. You tried to get out of the way, but one of the pipes slammed into you."

I gripped his arm. "No one else is hit? The pipes don't go into the parking lot?"

He shook his head and just like he described, the claw swung swiftly around, ramming into the stack. Four large dark pipes rapidly tumbled over the netting, rolling one after the other. I winced at the reverberating throooong of heavy pipes bouncing off each other. Someone screamed, "Lookout!" and a couple of people dove out of the way. Everyone else gawked as the pipes came to a stacked-up slamming halt against the low cement girder supporting the heavy light post.

Swooping ink-black wings drew my attention and I looked up, then screamed, "The light!"

Ethan yanked my arm and dove, rolling us both. He landed on the cement first, taking the hardest hit before the momentum turned us over a couple times until we came to a painful, jerking halt. A second later, the six-inch wide light post fell across the parking lot, landing with a heavy thud just a few feet away—exactly where I'd been standing.

Ethan's hand cradled the back of my head and we both panted as we stared at each other in shock. "Are you okay?" he asked.

My right arm ached, but I didn't think it was broken. "I think so." No one else appeared to have been hurt, but people were screaming and yelling. They sounded like they were talking through a tunnel from far away.

Moving quickly, Ethan stood and pulled me to my feet. He grabbed my backpack and his books. When someone said, "Shouldn't the school nurse check you out?" Ethan didn't stop. Instead, he tugged me straight to his car and unlocked the passenger door.

I was so shaken, I slid into the seat without a word and automatically snapped the seatbelt around me. Closing my eyes, I welcomed the comforting smell of pine and Ethan.

I don't remember the ride, just the feel of Ethan opening the door, lifting me out of the car and carrying me inside his house. Soft leather surrounded us as he sat down on the sofa with me still in his arms and gathered me close. I shivered, clinging to his tense frame like he was my lifeline. In many ways, he was.

Ethan's hand trembled as he stroked my hair. Pressing his lips to my temple, his heart pounded against my arm. "You're safe," he said in a shaky whisper.

After a while, my shivers finally passed and I started to slide off his lap, but he clasped me close, his voice a husky rasp, "I'd lose it if something happened to you, Nara."

The wrecked emotion in his voice surprised and worried me. "Ethan—

Sliding his hand along my jean-covered thigh, he flashed an embarrassed half-smile. "Sorry. Didn't mean to hang that on you."

His gaze looked vulnerable, making my heart twist. I told myself that adrenaline drove his words, but I loved hearing the emotion behind them. Smiling, I shook my head. "Don't you dare take it back."

His hand tightened on my leg. "Not a chance. God, that was too close..."

The angst in his voice reminded me of that day in study hall when he wasn't ready to let go of my hand. I was glad he seemed to need me as much as I did him. "You saved me. Again," I said, laying my head on his shoulder and snuggling closer.

"I had help. How did you know about the light post?"

"That part wasn't in your dream?"

His chin touched my forehead and then moved away as he shook his head.

"I didn't." My laugh sounded flat. "The raven flying away from the top of the post caused me to look up."

Ethan rested his chin on my head. "A raven, huh?"

"When we first walked out of school, he was sitting on that light post cawing. I remember thinking the bird was making all that noise, like he was announcing my impending death. How morbid is that?"

His arms tightened around me and his voice turned hard. "You're not going to die."

I glanced at him with a half smile. "Maybe he was cussing you out for making him wait for his afternoon kibble."

Ethan's chuckle turned into a pained hiss. "You're hurt." I immediately sat up and tried to see where he was wounded.

He shrugged, then gritted out, "I'm fine."

"No, you're not." Before he could stop me, I slid off his lap and grasped his shoulder. Pushing it forward, I saw blood starting to ooze through his fleece along his left shoulder blade. "You're bleeding!" I jumped up. "Where's your first aid kit?"

"I'll be okay." Ethan tried to grasp my hand.

"Where, Ethan?"

He pointed toward the hall. "In the bathroom closet on the top shelf."

Two seconds later I was back. Opening the small plastic box on the coffee table, I said, "Take off your shirt."

When he winced as he pulled his shirt and fleece off, I gulped at the nasty, oozing scrape and grabbed a disinfectant wipe. "This is going to hurt."

"No more than landing on it did," he grunted.

"I'm sorry," I mumbled as I tore the foil package then dabbed antiseptic on the angry wound the size of a racquetball.

Ethan grabbed my wrist and stopped my movements, his blue gaze sharp and intense. "All that matters is that you're safe."

When he turned away and lowered his hand back down to his thigh, I continued dabbing at his wound, even as my gaze strayed to the dragon tattoo that took up half his left forearm. My mom was right, the intricate black outlined design and muted color was striking.

The dragon's tail whipped around the corded muscles in Ethan's forearm before swinging back up and around the top of his forearm, where the end of the tail touched the dragon's chin. Instead of flames flowing from the dragon's open mouth, a flame-like design fanned out from the dragon's muscular shoulder and powerful back leg. Several different symbols were embedded in the flames' tips.

My gaze ate up every inch of Ethan's broad, sleekly-muscled back, straying to the six-inch long feather tattoo that pointed diagonally down his other shoulder blade. I thought it was interesting that he'd left the feather tattoo a mere black outline, yet he had the dragon tattoo shaded and shadowed with various grays, giving it depth. Either way, the tattoos were hot and intriguing.

As I smeared an antibiotic ointment across his wound, I said, "I like the design of your dragon tattoo. Does the dragon mean something important to you?"

Ethan's back muscles tensed until I lifted my ointment-coated finger from his wound. "It gives me peace of mind."

Laying a sterile gauze pad gently over his wound, I applied medical tape to hold it in place. "Peace of mind?"

"Yeah." He pulled me back into his lap and took my hand, sliding my fingers across the ink on his arm. "You asked me how I dealt with all the negative stuff I see. This is one of the ways I do that. To some, the dragon is a symbol of protection."

I gripped his arm, my heart thumping. "Protection?"

He gave a crooked smile. "You've seen the monsters I've drawn and experienced my dreams yourself. I think those creatures are mostly my mind manifesting images to interpret the crap I'm experiencing, but sometimes what I feel and see in my dreams is more than darkness and negativity. It's pure evil, Nara."

I shivered, remembering how awful his dreams felt, how sick to my stomach I'd been when I awoke. I could only imagine the different kinds of "negativity" he'd had to face over the years. Now I knew why I'd seen him grip his forearm each time he'd seen the creatures during the day. "Is the feather also a symbol of protection?"

He dropped his gaze to the dragon. "Dragons have scales, not feathers. Those are flames."

"I know those are flames. I was referring to your feather tattoo."

His forehead creased. "I don't have a feather tattoo."

Laughing, I clamped my hand on his right shoulder and thrummed my fingers on his skin. "The one on your shoulder blade, silly."

Realization flickered on his face. "The only thing on my shoulder is probably an irritated rash. A while back my shoulder was itching and burning, so I got up and slapped some cortisone on it." He grimaced. "I guess it didn't help, and now it looks like a feathery rash."

I shook my head, feeling my stomach tense. "It's a feather in black ink."

Frowning, Ethan clasped my waist, then set me on the couch. When he stood and headed for the bathroom, I followed.

He turned and leaned against the sink, his back to the mirror. As he reached over his shoulder to rub the feather with the tips of his fingers, I snickered. "I know it's on your back and all, but surely you didn't forget you had that tattoo."

His blue gaze snapped to mine in the mirror, his jaw working. "I didn't get this inked, Nara."

I smirked and leaned against the doorjamb, arms folded. "You mean you don't *remember* getting it. You must've *really* been smashed that night."

He turned to look at me. "With all the stuff I have to deal with, the last thing I need is to add alcohol or drugs to the mix. I don't do either."

Disbelief replaced my amusement as I stared at the feather in the mirror. His biceps flexed as he folded his arms and leaned against the pedestal sink, looking angry and shaken.

"What—what about sleepwalking?" I was grasping at straws, but there had to be a logical explanation.

He looked skeptical. I shrugged. "I've read stories about

people who sleepwalk, some who've even driven and done other crazy things while sleeping and they never remembered doing it…" I trailed off.

"Even if that were possible and I somehow ignored the pain as it healed," exasperation hardened his tone, "a feather means *nothing* to me symbolically, Nara. I would never have chosen it for a tattoo. I should've turned on the light that night I put on that cortisone. I never even looked."

Like that would've made a difference. He didn't even know how it got there. I could tell he was confused and growing more agitated by the minute. I didn't have an answer either, but it wasn't like he and I were "normal" people anyway. At least the tattoo wasn't hurting him. Right now he needed someone to talk him down. Stepping close, I leaned against his tense body and slid my fingers down his shoulder, running my hand over the feather. "Wherever it came from, it's a beautiful tattoo."

Wrapping his arm around me, he crushed his fingers in my hair and pressed my head to the crook of his neck. "Thanks for trying," he said as he exhaled a harsh breath.

His chest felt hard and warm. While his pulse beat a rapid pace along my cheekbone, I wracked my brain, trying to come up with a positive spin. "Feathers can have some cool meanings like…I know *Free Bird*," I said. He chuckled softly at the old song reference and his stiff frame relaxed a little.

Burying his nose in my hair, he murmured, "Keep shining that light, Sunshine."

CHAPTER 17

"Thank God you're all right. I just heard about what happened in the parking lot," Lainey said as she sat down beside me on the bench.

I adjusted my sock over my shin guard. "Yeah, it was a close call, but I'm fine."

Nodding to the bleachers, Lainey rolled a soccer ball under her cleat. "Your mom *and* aunt are here? What gives?"

Mom and Aunt Sage? I glanced up from tying my shoelaces to see Ethan sitting down beside Mom. "I have no idea. It's like a miracle or something," I mumbled, wondering why they'd both showed up for this game.

When Ethan spoke to Aunt Sage, who sat next to Mom, I couldn't get over how mouthwatering he looked in black. Before he'd driven me to my car earlier, he'd pulled on a black fleece jacket over a gray vintage t-shirt.

Lainey snickered, eyeing Mom and Aunt Sage. "Yeah, since they're both here, maybe you should buy a lottery ticket."

My luck had been pretty crappy the past couple of days. No thanks to Fate. But seeing my mom and aunt in the crowd made me feel so good that optimism began to surge through me. I wasn't going to let Fate freak me out. I didn't believe it was my time to die. "Not old enough for lottery tickets, but I'll bet you that *no* balls will get past me tonight."

A competitive glint sparked in Laniey's eyes as she held up her hand. "Nothing would make me happier than to shut this team down on their own turf."

I slapped her hand, sealing the deal. "What're the terms?"

She looked thoughtful. "If even one ball gets past, then you have to come to Jared's party next week…and bring Ethan."

Ugh. The last thing I wanted to do was force Ethan to attend a crowded house full of drunk-assed people. They'd all be bumping and stumbling into him, sending God only knew *what* kind of negative vibes his way. But I was feeling reckless and daring after everything that had happened. I needed to exert aggressive energy and celebrate being alive, because *that* was my destiny. I wanted to fight, to prove that I could cause a positive outcome and end today on an upswing. "It's a deal. But if I win the bet, then you're gonna help me convince Coach you're a much better backup goalie than Sophia."

"Uh, but—"

I gave her a "you'd better" look.

"Fine." Lainey released a heavy sigh. She knew I was right. Sophia was a horrible goalkeeper.

Waving to my family and Ethan, I pulled my ponytail tighter, then jumped off the bench, tugging Lainey to her feet. "Let's shut out Albemarle."

~

WHEN THE GAME WAS OVER, Lainey ran toward me full-throttle, tackling without warning. Landing hard on the ground, we rolled inside the goal, and she sat up, pumping her fist in the air, screaming, "Goal!"

I wheezed. "You're a nut. That doesn't count."

She punched my arm, then put her sweat-streaked face near mine. "I can't freakin' believe you did it. You didn't let the toughest team score. Not once."

"Don't forget our deal."

Her enthusiasm dipped a little. "Oh, yeah. I guess I'll have to talk to Coach." Eyes lighting with hope, she asked, "But you're still gonna come to Jared's party, right?"

I was surprised she was so insistent. I had no idea how Ethan would feel about going to a party. "I'll try."

Grinning, she scrambled to her feet. "Great. Then you can introduce Ethan around."

I squinted at her. "Why are you suddenly pro-Ethan?"

Lainey waved to my mom, Aunt Sage and Ethan as they walked toward the field. Looking at me, she shrugged. "There might be rumors about him, but he seems to be into you." Pulling me to my feet, she added, "Plus, I miss hanging with my friend."

"Lainey," Jared called from the metal bleachers. "Great win, baby!" he continued in a stadium-loud yell, pumping his fist in the air before turning to wrestle with a couple of his football buddies.

Lainey's cheeks turned bright red. "He's such a *guy* sometimes. See you on Monday," she called out as she ran off toward the bleachers.

Monday? Then I remembered. Friday was a teacher workday.

"That was a great game." Mom's eyes were bright with pride.

"Thanks. I'm glad you came." Turning to Aunt Sage, I raised my eyebrows. "And it's great to see you here. I'm shocked, but thrilled."

Aunt Sage grinned and spread her arms wide, her bangles making a pleasant tinkling sound. "It's true that I don't like watching sports, but well, after receiving your text, I just had to come see my favorite niece." Pulling me into a tight hug, she whispered, "Have your dreams returned?"

"No dreams, but I'm good," I responded in a whisper—which was true since Ethan had my back against Fate—then I quickly tugged away, saying in a normal voice, "Your clothes. I'm all sweaty."

Aunt Sage laughed. "But that's hard-earned sweat and I thoroughly enjoyed watching you play, sweetie."

"You were on fire." Ethan's gaze locked with mine. I saw the question in his eyes. *How'd you pull off a total shutout?*

"I was determined to make my own luck," I told him. After

tonight's game, I felt invincible. Like I'd just shown Fate I wasn't scared and at the same time had squashed the fear that had gripped me earlier today.

Mom and Aunt Sage laughed, and it felt good to see them smiling at each other. They never did anything together socially. I was the only reason they interacted at all. They were two very different people, but I was pretty sure that before my dad left they used to get along. At least I knew Aunt Sage had attended events with my parents and me in the past. In old family photos, we were all at a fair, at the zoo, at the park, at the pool, Thanksgiving, Christmas, my birthday parties. She was always there. Now, I celebrated birthdays and holidays with my aunt separately.

"Do you want me to wait around until you're all packed up?" Mom asked.

Her question threw me off. She was being *very* attentive. Way more than usual. "Thanks, but I'm good. See you at home."

"I'll walk Nara to her car, Mrs. Collins," Ethan said.

"Elizabeth, if you want, I'll drop you off at your car. I saw it parked in front of the school," Aunt Sage said to Mom. Before they turned toward the parking lot, my aunt smiled at us. "It was nice to see you, Ethan. I'll call you this weekend, Inara."

Once my family was out of earshot, I said, "Seeing them both here felt like I'd jumped into an alternate reality."

An incredulous look crossed Ethan's face. "Fate trying to scare you to death doesn't already feel like an alternate reality?"

I tensed as a touch of anxiety started to bleed into my euphoric mood. "But see, that's even more of a reason to celebrate tonight ending on a good note. Not to mention, Mom *and* Aunt Sage came to my game. That's a good sign. Do you have any idea the odds against them coming at all, let alone at the same time?"

Ethan's brows pushed downward. "Your aunt said something about you texting her."

His comment jogged my memory. "I can't believe I forgot. Before we went out to the parking lot after school, in case, well...things didn't work out, I sent my mom and my aunt an 'I love you' text. Which explains Aunt Sage breaking her 'no sports, ever' rule for this game *and* my mom's strange hovering." Still, I smiled. Mom and Sage had laughed together, something I hadn't seen in a long time.

Ethan's expression turned dark as he shoved his hands in his jean pockets. "My parents wouldn't respond if I sent them a text message like that. They'd assume I was just saying that because I was in some kind of scrape and needed them to get me out of it."

"Don't they know that you've gotten your act together?"

His lips thinned. "Samson wanted to tell them, but I told him to forget it. They haven't called or asked about me. Instead they just send 'we're thinking about you' cards for Christmas and my birthday."

Ethan must feel completely abandoned. Tugging his hand out of his pocket, I clasped it, giving him my warmth. "You've never told me your birthday. When is it?"

His fingers curled around mine, his eyes softening. "It was October 24th. And yours is coming in December, right?"

He must've seen where my mom had circled the date on the calendar on the fridge. "Yep, you really are observant." I was disappointed that he'd already had his birthday. I wanted an excuse to celebrate 'him'. "There's this nasty rumor floating around that seventeen is the magical age of responsibility."

"Yeah, I heard it, too. Something about becoming a responsible adult from one day to the next."

I studied him curiously. "Do you feel like a responsible adult now?"

Glancing away, he murmured, "Sometimes I feel so over stuff, like an old geezer." His gaze snapped back to me, wry amusement dancing in the blue depths. "As for being a responsible adult…" he shook his head and blew a purple bubble with a loud pop.

As we walked to my car, Ethan grew quiet and thoughtful, as if he were wrestling with something. "My brother called last night. He's coming back early and wants to use the long weekend to hike and camp in the mountains before it gets too cold. We're leaving early tomorrow morning. Samson will have his cell. I promise if I see anything in my dreams, I'll call you."

"Don't worry about me, Ethan."

We stopped next to my car and I could feel the tension radiating off him. "I don't want to leave you right now. Especially after what's happened."

Even though I was disappointed that I wouldn't get to see Ethan this weekend, I didn't want him to spend his time in the mountains worrying about me. I smiled reassuringly. "I'll just be hanging at home with my mom. I'll be fine. You and your brother have a great time…and be careful." A part of me still worried I wasn't successful and Fate would go after Ethan and Lainey. "I'll miss—"

Ethan leaned close and kissed me. He made me feel so special, I didn't care that I was all sweaty. When my breathing ramped and my heart felt like it might explode, he raked his teeth gently across my lower lip, leaving a tingling trail along the plump skin as he pulled back. "I'll miss you, too."

Tucking loose strands of hair behind my ear, his intense gaze tracked my face. "I lo—" He paused, then said, "You mean a lot to me, Nara." Don't go anywhere alone. Promise you'll stay safe while I'm gone, okay?"

The sweet flavor of Ethan's bubble gum lingered on my tongue, and my lower lip still felt his warmth. I was pretty sure he'd almost told me that he loved me, and even though my heart had slammed against my chest at the thought, all I could do was nod mutely.

My throat ached as he walked to his car. If he'd said, "I love you", the words would've locked in my throat. I wouldn't have been able to say it back. Sliding into my car, I choked back a sad laugh. I couldn't even tell my own mother, aunt or Gran that I loved them either. I'd avoided Gran and texted Mom and Sage instead. *You're such a whack job, Nara.*

Whether he said it first or not, when Ethan got back, somehow I'd find a way to tell him how I felt about him.

~

"Inara, come in, sweetie. What a wonderful surprise for my Sunday afternoon." Aunt Sage opened her door wider and yanked me into a tight hug. "I'm so glad you came. I've been thinking about you."

I pulled back in surprise. "You have?"

Aunt Sage lifted the necklace lying against her chest. "Look, I'm taking lessons from my niece."

She'd created a feather design around a long amethyst crystal. Hers was much better than mine, more intricate and with an artsy, whimsical flair. "You're so talented," I said. "Look at that detail. Your design should sell really well."

"I already have several orders. Can you believe it? I'm calling it the *Inara Designs Collection.*"

I was stunned. "You named the new collection after me?"

Pride filled her face. "Don't look so surprised. You designed it. You deserve the credit."

Snorting, I pointed to the necklace. "I didn't design *that*. You did."

"Ah, but you were the inspiration," she said with a wink. "And that's all that matters."

I shook my head, knowing I wasn't going to talk her out of changing the name. When my aunt set her mind to something, it was pretty much a done deal. "Speaking of inspiration." I nodded to the necklace. "That's one of the reasons I'm here. I've done some research on the net, but could I look through your books for other symbolic meanings for the feather."

Her hazel eyes sparkled. "We must be on the same wavelength. While I was designing feather jewelry, you were digging into the symbolism. You're more than welcome to use my books. I'd love to see what you come up with. I could use an 'info' card to put in with the *Inara* pieces when I ship them off to customers. They love that extra touch, you know."

"Will do," I said, slipping out of my jacket.

"Well, I'll leave you to it. Oh..." she said, turning back from the hallway that led to her studio. "You'll stay for dinner, right?"

She knew how much I loved home-cooked meals. "Wouldn't miss it."

Aunt Sage began to hum as she walked through the door to her studio. When I heard her "work" music start up, I stared at the books on the shelves and pulled the first one out. Might as well start from the top and work my way down.

Three hours later, I was sprawled out on my stomach on the floor, taking notes on a notepad as I read passages from a book. All the dogs in the house were curled up against some part of me when Aunt Sage walked out of the kitchen. "Dinner will be ready in—awww, don't move. I've got to get my camera."

When she came back a few seconds later and snapped a shot, I snickered. "I'm sure that was a great picture of my butt."

She scrunched her nose and turned off the digital camera. "I was taking a picture of the dogs. Your cute butt just happened to be in it."

"Even *I* rank lower than you." I sighed dramatically to Bo, who'd jumped up and was shoving his cold wet nose in my face, demanding attention.

"*They* get food from a bag. You get homemade meals. Dinner will be ready in fifteen."

After she retreated into the kitchen, I organized all my notes, then put the books I'd pulled out back on the shelves. I had no idea my aunt's interest in all things paranormal or New-Agey was so varied. From dictionaries, to books on government psychic programs, to mind-reading techniques, to crystal healing, to historical books on the Salem witch trials, to books on spells and herbs and aromatherapy. Her eclectic collection gave me plenty sources to glean a few tidbits on feathers, including beliefs, symbolic meanings and their uses in rituals and ceremonies.

Armed with what I'd learned, I could be more specific in my searches on the net and maybe come up with some information that might help Ethan feel better about his feather tattoo. How he got the tattoo might forever remain a mystery, but I wanted to help him come to terms with it.

"Did you find some additional information?" Aunt Sage asked as she set a plate with a delicious smelling twice-baked potato in front of me.

"I found some interesting symbolism I didn't know about."

I slid a piece of paper across the table toward her. "I compiled a list for you so you can create a 'did you know' facts insert for your customers."

Did you know…some fun feather facts

** The eagle feather is used in some Indian ceremonies to communicate with the Spirit for celestial wisdom.*

** Some consider the feather to represent the power of air and wind.*

** Feathers are believed to symbolize higher thoughts, enlightenment and even spiritual ascension to a new plane.*

** The Celtic believe the feather represents knowledge of the celestial realm.*

After she scanned the paper, Aunt Sage looked thoughtful. "There are so many intriguing angles, aren't there? Thank you for the fact sheet. You truly deserve all the credit for this new jewelry line."

"Feels like cheating somehow," I snickered before taking a bite of my potato.

Aunt Sage smiled. "My tarot reading this morning said today would be fruitful. I'd say fifty orders for Inara pieces counts."

"Fifty? Wow, that's great. Who knew adding feathers could make such a difference. Oh, another thing I learned, did you know that birds have also been used for divination? Ravens were mentioned specifically in one of your books."

My aunt slid her fork into her own potato. "I remember reading something about ravens being kept at the Tower of London."

"Yep, I read that excerpt. It had to do with a long ago superstition that has continued into modern times. The whole Tower of London thing was interesting. I'm going to include that information in a History project Ethan and I are working on."

My aunt smiled. "I can see why you like Ethan."

I picked up my glass. "He's amazing. I'm glad you like him."

"Have you told him about your gift?" she asked before chewing a bite of salad.

I choked on the water. The hard lump rolled painfully down my throat and into my chest. "Um, well, there's not really much to tell since I don't dream any more."

"Ah, I see." She balanced the fork on the tip of her finger. "Do you think he would understand if you told him?"

The last thing I wanted to do was accidentally betray Ethan's confidence. Shrugging, I grasped onto the first thing that popped into my mind for a change of subject. "Hey, I've been meaning to tell you." I touched the scar along my hairline. "I remembered how I got this."

Aunt Sage's fork clattered to her plate, splattering salad dressing everywhere. "Damn," she muttered and jumped up to grab a dishtowel. As she wiped the tiles on the table, she asked, "What did you remember?"

Once I relayed the images that had flashed through my mind in the library, I frowned. "I remember the fear in Dad's eyes and his shaking hands as he cleaned and bandaged my wound, but I thought something he'd whispered to himself was kind of odd. He'd said, "I bolted it to the wall. This wasn't supposed to happen."

When my aunt's hand stopped mid-wipe, I continued, "It wasn't so much *what* he said, Aunt Sage, but the look in his eyes. It was almost, well…as if he'd *expected* the bookcase to fall over on me."

Slowly lowering herself back to her chair, Aunt Sage suddenly looked very tired. "You've always had a knack for reading people, Inara. Your dad *had* expected the bookcase to fall on you and yes, that's why he bolted it."

I gripped my fork tight. "He knew that would happen?"

Aunt Sage blew a wayward red curl out of her face. "You inherited your abilities from him."

A flush of heat swept over me, followed swiftly by anger. Why had no one ever told me? "Has Mom been lying to me all these years, too?" I said in a steely voice.

"No, honey. Your mom never knew. She still doesn't." She tried to put her hand on mine, but I jerked back. Sighing, she continued. "I wanted to tell you, but your father insisted that you might not develop his abilities. He hoped that you wouldn't."

"Why wouldn't he want me to have them?"

Tears rimmed her eyes, spilling down her cheeks. "Because you're just like him and having the ability to see ahead can be dangerous. You'll be tempted to intercede on behalf of others. The older you get, the more responsible you'll feel. Do *not* intervene, Inara." Her gaze pleaded with me, and I instantly thought of Jody and Kristin and all the other people in the locker hall who'd been injured. Were they paying for my involvement? If I'd done nothing, the bombing would've been worse! Aunt Sage's next comment yanked me out of my chaotic thoughts. "Your father paid dearly for that. The highest price."

I slammed my fork down. "He left us! I don't care one bit for whatever price he paid."

Sage swiped her tears away. "He tried to contact you once I told him you had his abilities, but had recently lost your dreams. Since your dreams never returned, he was relieved and decided it was best not to tell you that you'd inherited his ability—to let it all fade away."

Ethan has my dreams, I wanted to scream, but I was too angry that I'd been kept in the dark all my life. She'd let me tell her about my dreams the other day, while pretending ignorance. I curled my lip in annoyance. "Even though he walked out, he's trying to be my parent, like he knows what's best for me."

"Inara, I know you're hurt and I'm sorry. Your father is doing what's right for you. He'd be furious that I even said anything, but I thought you deserved the truth."

What's right for me? I didn't want to hear any more. I stood up quickly, the chair scraping behind me. "Don't worry about it. Like you said, '*I* no longer have my dreams'."

I stalked out of the kitchen and scooped up my jacket and keys.

"Inara, please stay and eat." Aunt Sage stood in the kitchen doorway. "I'm sorry I upset you. I don't want you to drive home all worked up. I wish I'd—" she paused, opening and closing her hands by her sides.

"What?" I grabbed up the notes I'd taken. "You wish you'd told me the truth when I *first* mentioned my powers?" Her hurt expression told me how bratty I sounded. I exhaled a breath of guilt. I was being unfair to her. Secrets aside, my aunt had always been there for me. My dad was behind this. Hurting me all over again. "You did the right thing for me by telling me the truth. If Mom doesn't know about Dad, it sounds like he's always kept secrets from those he *supposedly* loved." Opening the door, I said, "As far as I'm concerned, he can keep his secrets."

"He was only trying to…Inara," she called after me.

Warm tears slipped down my cheeks and I angrily brushed them away as I walked to my car. I was glad it was dark so my aunt couldn't see my damp face when I turned toward the porch. "Tell him *never* to contact us again. He didn't see Mom fall apart when he tried to call our house a few weeks ago."

Aunt Sage looked stunned. "He talked to Elizabeth?"

"No, I made sure he never got through. After I saw Mom's reaction to his call in my dream, I blocked all unsolicited calls."

I straightened my spine. "I want him to stay out of our lives. He gave up his right to speak to me—to us—the day he bailed."

CHAPTER 18

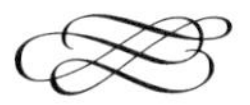

On my way home, I stopped by the grocery store's video rental kiosk to give my puffy, red eyes a chance to clear. I rented a romantic comedy—an older one I hadn't seen. Mom never watched movies with me, so I knew that'd be a good excuse to go straight to my room and watch it on my laptop. As I drove home, sadness made my chest ache. I felt like I'd lost my aunt—the one person I ran to when I needed a shoulder to lean on. Why couldn't I have that with my mom? Pulling into the driveway, I glanced at the video and desperately wished Mom and I had a family movie night. It sounded so cliché, but I couldn't think of a nicer cheesy tradition.

When I walked in, Mom lowered the newspaper and waved from the couch. I started up the stairs, already wondering where my headphones were, when I decided it couldn't hurt to ask. "I—uh, rented a movie. Would you like to watch it with me?"

Mom closed the paper. "Sure, as long as it's not one of those slasher movies."

Surprised she agreed, I laughed and said, "No worries there," then walked over to the DVD player to slip in the movie.

Pushing the Play button, I sat beside my mom and waited for the movie to start. When English subtitles came up and the actors began speaking in Spanish, I jumped up, saying, "I forgot this movie is subtitled. It has an English version too."

As I hunted around for the remote, Mom stared at the screen. "I really could use some Spanish lessons. Several of our sites have Spanish speaking employees."

Finding the remote in the end table drawer, I met her thoughtful gaze. "Mr. Dixon teaches outside classes. I'll bet you could get him to tutor you."

Mom shook her head. "This would be business-type conversations, finances and such, Inara. Not, 'I'd like two beers, please.'"

I rolled my eyes. "I know that. Mr. Dixon mentioned that he sometimes teaches Business Spanish at the community college."

She looked thoughtful. "That's something to consider."

Clicking the menu, I changed the settings to English and sat down beside her. "Let me know and I'll get you his info." I couldn't help but feel hopeful. Mr. Dixon had thanked me for bringing my mom to the dinner. Twice. Then he'd casually suggested making it a quarterly event. Of course, the class shot that idea down faster than a row of carnival ducks.

Mom pointed to the remote. "Hit Play. I'm ready to watch."

By the end of the movie, the boy got the girl (like Ethan and me), and the girl and her mother had worked through their strained, screwball relationship, making me wish life could fully imitate art.

I'd taken the DVD out and put it away, when I decided I had nothing to lose. Walking behind the sofa, I dropped a quick kiss on my mom's cheek and then immediately jogged up the stairs, calling behind me, "Night, Mom. Thanks for watching the movie with me."

"Night," I heard her say in a soft voice. Peeking through the banister railings, I was surprised to see tears glistening in her eyes, and she was touching her cheek where I'd kissed her.

Why hadn't I tried that years ago? Feeling elated, I tiptoed the rest of the way to my room.

As soon as I got to my room, I pulled out my cell phone and erased the second text message from my dad, then shredded the piece of paper where I'd written the phone number down from my dream. We had a chance to move forward. I wasn't letting Dad mess Mom and me up. Not now. Not ever.

~

WHERE WAS ETHAN? I was so disappointed when I didn't see him at his locker on Monday morning. I really wanted to talk to him about my dad. Was he as surprised as I was? Since Ethan would've dreamed my entire Sunday while camping, he would know exactly what was said between my aunt and me.

The school day dragged. During each class period, I literally hung on the edge of my chair, ready to pounce the moment the bell rang. I'd seen Ethan ahead of me in the hall a couple of times, but he must've not seen me or he would've slowed down and waited.

By the time fourth period was almost over, I was wound so tight, Mrs. Bose stopped in the middle of her lecture and asked in a snotty voice, "Do you have somewhere more important to be, Miss Collins?" I'd never been very good at subtlety.

When I saw Ethan tossing books into his locker and then grabbing another set, I leaned against my locker and tried to act casual, despite the bundle of nerves squirming in my stomach. "How was the camping trip?"

Ethan's eyes were bluer than usual against his darkly tanned face. The few days' scuff on his jaw only made him even more drool-worthy. God, he had no idea how incredibly good-looking he was.

"Hey." He grinned and for a second I wondered if he'd read my mind, but then sympathy flickered through his eyes. "That was a rough day with your aunt, huh?"

I hugged my books to my chest. "You saw my reaction."

He shut his locker. "Yeah, I did. I've gotta go, but we can talk about it in study hall if you want."

I swallowed the tight knot in my throat. "I do."

Ethan raised his fingers toward my hair and the bell rang. Dropping his hand, he looked regretful. "See you later."

I watched him stroll down the hall and my chest tightened with sudden concern. His split lip had healed, but I noticed the shadows under his eyes and tension around his mouth before he'd walked away. What was wrong?

~

ETHAN WAS SITTING in our spot in the far right corner when I walked in study hall. I set my books on the table and moved my chair closer to his. "You're early today."

Sliding his chair back, he folded his hands behind his head and stretched his legs out underneath the table. "Mr. Walker asked me to drop something off at the office, so I got to leave class before the bell."

He really did look tired. "Did you stay up late every night during your camping trip?"

"No, we went to bed early. My brother likes to hike until he's dead tired. We logged eight-mile hikes each day, then camped. Of course, each morning he got me up at the crack of dawn to start the torture all over again." Ethan snorted, then winced as he bent his knees.

"A bit sore?" I teased, reaching out to touch his thigh.

He immediately sat up and his leg shifted out of my reach. "I'll live. Let's talk about Sunday."

I furrowed my brow, uncertain if I'd just imagined that he'd sat up to purposefully pull away from me or if I was being paranoid. "That wasn't a fun scene."

Setting his elbows on the table, Ethan steepled his fingers and pressed them against his mouth. "I know it bothers you that you're just now finding out about your dad, but look at it this way, Nara, it's got to feel good to know you're not alone."

"I don't feel alone," I said and then it hit me where he was coming from. "And you shouldn't either. We have each other—" I started to touch his hand, but he quickly moved it under the table. My stomach dropped. "Why do you keep pulling away from me? I'm *not* imagining it."

Ethan blew out a breath. "Being up in the mountains gave me time to think about everything. Since things kept happening that I couldn't predict from your dreams, I think it's best if you get your dreams back."

A heavy weight thumped against my chest. "Are—are you saying you don't want to see me any more?"

His jaw clenched and his hand fisted on the table. "No, Nara. I just think it's best if two of us are seeing your dreams. If we spend time together, I'll still share your dreams like I did before, but..." His gaze skimmed my hair, my face, then lingered on my lips, before he finished," I can't touch you any more."

You're having your first real nightmare. Wake up! Wake up! I dug my short fingernails into my palms. The pain came, radiating up my arms, but nothing changed. Ethan was still staring at me with his steely, determined gaze. "I don't—" I choked and blinked to hold back tears. "I don't know—"

"Nara..." Sadness reflected in his eyes. He started to lift his hand toward my face, but curled his fingers inward and set a tight fist on the table. "I don't like it either, but I'd never forgive myself if something happened to you because I'd stolen your dreams."

There had to be another way. I couldn't imagine spending time with Ethan and not being able to touch him. Ever. Again. "Maybe *I* need a dragon tattoo."

Amusement flickered, but he shook his head. "You've been given your powers for a reason," he said quietly.

"I inherited them," I said in a flat tone. "And what about your powers? Do you believe you have them for a reason?"

His expression hardened. "That's not fair. This isn't a gift. It's a curse," he said through gritted teeth.

"I'm sorry," I murmured, instinctively reaching for him. Catching myself, I jerked my hand back, then grabbed my books and stood. I needed to get out of there before I started to cry. "I have to do some research in the library," I said, then turned and walked out.

I found an empty seat in the back corner of the library and sat there rubbing my temples so I wouldn't cry. After all we'd been through, I couldn't believe what Ethan had just done. Didn't he know it broke my heart? I pictured the sadness in his eyes and hunched my shoulders, letting the tears fall. He was right.

He has an inner strength that's amazing to see in someone so young. Aunt Sage's comment about Ethan floated through my mind. He always tried to do what was right by me, regardless of his own feelings. Why was that fact so easy to forget?

Because you'd wanted to work up the courage to tell him how you feel about him and now you're scared you lost your chance.

~

AT THE END of the day, I was so relieved to see Ethan leaning against my car, my eyes instantly misted. The determined set of his jaw told me he hadn't given up on me. I loved him even more for his belief in us. I'd worn the peach sunglasses he'd given me, hoping he'd know we were all right. I blinked away the moisture and dug into my backpack as I approached.

Stopping a couple feet away, my hand shook as I held the folded piece of paper out to him. "You probably saw all the research I did on the meaning of feathers, but I thought you might like the information compiled in one place." I gave a tentative smile when Ethan took the paper and unfolded it.

"Thanks for doing this," he said quietly. Scanning the contents, his brow creased and he pointed to a website address I'd added at the end. "What's this? This website wasn't something I remember you finding in your aunt's books."

"I thought you saw my *entire* day," I said with a smug half-smile.

"I usually do, except when my brother interrupts my normal sleep pattern to 'get an early start on the day'."

I was pleased to share something new with him. "I found an old posting from a couple years ago on a message board, asking about the significance of a feather tattoo on a shoulder blade." I shrugged. "Though this person's wasn't exactly the same as yours, since they mentioned a fully inked feather, not just the outline of one."

The paper crumpled in his hand. "You mean like this?" Jerking his jacket and shirt down, he turned so I could see his shoulder.

I gasped and my stomach bottomed out. The feather was

now completely filled in, except for an area along the middle. There, purple and green colors merged together, like the shimmer of light reflecting on an otherwise pitch-black feather.

"I don't understand. How—how'd this happen? You were in the mountains with your brother, right?"

He folded the piece of paper and shoved it in his jeans' pocket. Jaw clenched, he stared at the mostly empty parking lot. "When I left for the mountains, it wasn't filled in," he paused, his blue eyes sharpening. "I have no idea how this happened, but I'm going to find out."

Worry tightened my chest. "Have you told your brother about the feather?"

His focus snapped back to me. "Other than you, Samson's the only one who's on my side. The difference is, he doesn't really get what's going on with me. You do, Nara. Do you really think he'd understand a tattoo appearing from nowhere and then, in a matter of a few days, filling itself in?"

"Show it to him and explain. He's your brother, Ethan," I said in an upbeat tone. Ethan's stubborn look dashed my hope that he would tell his brother anything.

The creases were back, making deep grooves around his mouth. "Telling Samson might put him over the edge. I need his support. I can't lose that."

I wanted to wrap my arms around him and hold him close, but I knew he wouldn't let me. "What are you going to do?"

"More research."

Research didn't sound so bad. "I've scoured the net, but let me know if you find anything." I stared at him, still a bit worried. "Are you…okay? About the feather, I mean?"

"I *have* to be okay with it."

"Does it hurt at all?"

"Only where I scrubbed my skin trying to get rid of it." He gave a grim look. "It's there to stay."

With a sigh, I turned and opened my trunk. As I retrieved my soccer bag for practice, Ethan said, "I've been thinking about something your aunt said about your dad."

Tugging the soccer bag onto my shoulder, I slammed my

trunk harder than I'd meant to. "I don't want to talk about him."

"Just listen."

I faced him, arms crossed. "Fine."

Ethan ran his hand through his hair. "While I was laying there staring at the stars, something your aunt said kept bothering me. She said your father only tried to contact you once he'd learned you had his powers and had lost them, right?"

I nodded.

"Remember, I'd been seeing your dreams for a while before we officially met."

Where was he going with this? "And?"

Ethan rubbed the back of his neck, looking puzzled. "If your aunt was telling the truth, then why did your father try to call your house that day a few weeks ago? That was *before* you told your aunt you had the ability to see your future through your dreams."

I opened my mouth, then closed it, because I didn't have an answer. "Now that I think about it, Aunt Sage had seemed surprised to learn my dad would've called our house if I hadn't blocked his call."

"Do you remember what he said to your mother in your dream?"

"I only heard Mom's responses." I closed my eyes, trying to remember. "She said, 'Inara's here. She's fine.' And then she paused and said, 'She's perfectly safe'. I assumed that he called to ask about me once he'd seen the bomb threat on the news."

"Yeah, that would've been the day after you called in the school bombing."

I gripped my soccer bag's strap. "So what's bothering you?"

Instead of answering, Ethan asked another question. "When you dream your entire day, how do you see it? Do you see yourself like you're starring in a movie?"

I'd never thought about *how* I saw my dreams. "No, it's not like that. I see everything from my point-of-view. I don't see myself. Do you see something different?"

"Yeah, it's like I'm watching a movie and you're starring in it."

I had no idea Ethan was seeing my dreams from another perspective. "What does that have to do with my dad?"

"Because I heard what your dad said to your mom, Nara. He said, 'Elizabeth, I know I'm the last person you want to hear from. Inara is *special* and her safety's of the utmost importance. Can I please speak to her?' Maybe he was calling because he wondered if you'd been the one to call it in."

My pulse whooshed in my ears. "You think my dad knew that I called the bombing in because of my dreams?"

Ethan shoved his hands in his pockets. "I don't know for sure, but putting what he said together with the timing of his call—right after the bombing incident was averted at school—and then the fact your aunt said he'd paid the highest price for interfering, it just got me wondering." His blue eyes focused on me. "Maybe you should talk to him. Find out all you can about your powers."

Setting my lips in a firm line, I shook my head. "I've dealt with this 'gift' for a while now. When my dad left us, my mom nearly lost it. I won't go there again, Ethan. I won't put her through seeing or hearing from him, just because I'm curious about my powers."

"I would kill to have someone to talk to about my power, to know I wasn't the only one—" he started to say, then cut himself off, sighing heavily. "Whether you like it or not, you have your dad's ability. Your aunt and your dad don't know that your dreams never really disappeared. With the warnings your aunt mentioned 'to respect your power and not intervene' and your recent run-ins with Fate, you have to be wondering what price your dad paid."

CHAPTER 19

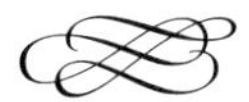

What price *had* my dad paid?

The question had echoed in my mind ever since I learned we shared the same ability. But my desire for answers didn't override my worry of how my dad's sudden reappearance would affect Mom and me…except for one burning question.

What if my dad had dealt with Fate before?

Had my dad prevented a disaster, only to watch people get hurt anyway, like I'd experienced with people at school?

The nagging "need to know" had me picking up my cell phone several times to call my aunt and ask for my dad's info, but I'd always put it back down. Resentment and curiosity fought major battles in my brain, making my thoughts a mish-mash of contradictions.

I hated my dad for what his leaving did to my mom and me, but a part of me really wanted to know more about my powers—why we had them and what to expect as I grew older. And yeah, the insecure part of me wanted to confront him and demand, "Why did you leave us? How could you leave me?" But then I pictured my mom falling apart and worry for her stamped out all the "pro-reunion" voices in my head.

It was hard enough to see Ethan at school and talk with him in study hall. Spending any time alone together without being able to touch would've killed me, so I suggested we finish up our History project via email. It hurt that he agreed, but it was for the best.

Wednesday morning, the sunlight slipped sleepily into my room, its rays warm and inviting. My eyes slowly opened and as my brain engaged, a floodgate of emotions rushed forward. I was tired again. My dreams had returned, but I didn't feel whole or happy. Instead, sadness and regret engulfed me. Tears fell hard and fast, while deep, heart-wrenching loss clogged my throat. I wasn't crying because of my dreams. I was crying, because dreaming about my future again meant that my special connection with Ethan had diminished…and would never return.

I was all put back together, but had never felt more torn apart.

Mom had left on business the night before, and as I dragged myself through my morning routine of getting ready for school, the silent house felt quiet and echo-y, making me feel especially alone.

I kept to myself the entire day at school and even spent study hall in the library. I knew I was moping and feeling sorry for myself, which meant I was probably punishing Ethan in the process, but I couldn't help how I felt. Ethan didn't complain, though I saw the resigned understanding in his eyes when he walked me out to my car after school.

"You got your dreams back last night, didn't you?" he asked when we stopped beside my car.

The wind swirled his black hair around his face, making me jealous. I wanted to feel the thick mop twist and curl around my fingers. "Yeah," I said, peering up at him through my peach shades. They were the only ones I wore now.

Ethan hunched his shoulders to ward off the chill air, his army jacket bunching around his chin. "You coming back to study hall tomorrow?"

His blue gaze held more than a question. It reflected the need I felt deep inside, the same knocked-in-the-gut pain I'd experienced this morning when I realized I had my dreams back. "You still see my dreams, don't you?"

When he nodded, I exhaled a sigh of relief. "That's good. What about the visions and voices? Are they coming back during the day?"

He shrugged. "Nothing I can't handle."

My heart twisted. I wanted to touch him, to take away his pain and lessen my own.

Awkward silence passed between us, then he took a couple steps back so I could open my car door. "I guess you need to head home now."

There was so much I wanted to say to him. "Ethan, this is just so hard—"

He suddenly stepped so close that I tensed, even as my insides skittered in excitement. "I want to touch you, Nara, but I can't," he said in a low, tortured tone. "I want to kiss you, but I can't. All I can do is watch you from a distance and it's killing me." His gaze searched the planes of my face before he stepped back again. "I'll see you at your game."

I didn't think it was possible to fall even more deeply in love with him, but my emotions shredded in the wind whipping around us. "I miss you, too," I said in a strangled voice, then opened my car door. Before I closed it, Ethan asked, "When are you going to contact your dad?"

"I can't. I deleted all his text messages."

He frowned. "That's a cop out."

"It's the truth."

"You can call your aunt anytime for his information, Nara. Hide it from your mom if you think that's best, but I think you should contact him."

Shutting the door, I drove off, wishing I wasn't such a chicken and that Ethan's opinion didn't matter so much.

THE NEXT DAY, I waited by Ethan's locker first thing in the morning, my nerves wound tight. My heart jumped when I saw Lainey and Jared walking hand-in-hand down the hall.

She stopped beside me, her eyes shining with excitement. "You're coming to Jared's party tonight, right?"

Jared flashed a big smile. "Yeah, come on, Nara. I want to celebrate my girl's win last night."

I swallowed the hard lump in my throat. While Jared turned to high-five with one of the football players, Lainey clasped my hand and squeezed. "Bring Ethan. Coming to a party might help loosen him up some."

"I'll try."

"Great." As Jared dragged her away, she waved. "See you later."

"Not a good idea," Ethan said near my ear, making me jump.

I turned to him, eyes pleading. "I know this party will probably give you a whole slew of new nightmares, but can you please go with me?"

Ethan's jaw tensed. "You're not going to warn her about him, are you?"

"It wouldn't do any good. She needs to see for herself this time."

"What about the other?"

I heard the tension in his voice. "Even if I hadn't dreamed it, I would never have let her drive drunk."

When Ethan leaned back against his locker, a look of disapproval on his face, I folded my arms across my chest. "What? You expect me to stand by and do nothing?" My voice rose slightly as anxiety clawed at my throat. "I would've taken her keys anyway, like a good friend should."

"You *did* take her keys."

"Her sneaking out of the bathroom and snitching the keys from the shelf where I'd set them wasn't what I expected."

"Exactly. You tried."

"We might not know how bad the accident is, but we *know* she has one. I'll just drive her home myself."

He slowly shook his head, his jaw set. "Maybe…it was meant to be, Nara."

"Ethan" I was in a panic. He had to help me help Lainey. I'd thought I'd been successful in making Fate back off, but it was continuing the pattern. I couldn't *not* act.

"You've challenged Fate, Nara. I'm worried what it'll do if you go through with this."

"I'm going," I said in a tight voice.

Ethan raked his hands down his face. "I don't want you going alone. I'll come."

"Thank you." I was so relieved he was coming. "I'll drive since this is my idea. I'll pick you up on the way."

~

TUGGING my black coat tight around my dark blue cable knit sweater, I ran sweat-soaked palms down the front of my jeans and knocked on Ethan's door. I was glad I'd worn my hair down and added some eyeliner on top of my mascara. I was suddenly nervous to meet Samson.

The door swung open and a tall blond guy stood in the doorway. "Hi, I'm Nara," I said a little too brightly.

Samson might look young, but the set of his shoulders and the way he assessed me—a quick, parental sweep of his eyes—made him appear much older. He thumbed behind him with a smile. "Ethan's upstairs. Come in."

As I stepped into the foyer, Samson stuck out his hand. "I'm Samson, by the way, and don't believe anything Ethan has told you about me."

I relaxed a little and shook his hand, noting how different his bright blue eyes were from Ethan's dark blue ones. "It's nice to meet you, Samson…and it's all been good, I promise."

"Somehow I doubt it's *all* been good." Samson glanced at Ethan, who'd walked into the room.

"Hey, Nara."

I read the tension in Ethan's face, but didn't want to discuss tonight in front of his brother. "Ready to head to the library?"

"Right." Ethan tugged into a thick heather gray fleece he pulled off the back of the couch.

Broader and thicker than Ethan, Samson clapped his brother on the shoulder with a knowing grin. "Library…riiight. Don't stay out too late, kids."

"Kids?" Ethan rolled his eyes. "You're only a few years older than me."

"And a heck of a lot wiser." Samson glanced at me. "Then again, I didn't have a girlfriend like Nara in high school, so you must be doing something right."

Heat shot to my cheeks and Ethan stepped to open the door. "Let's go before he starts telling embarrassing stories."

Samson's laughter followed us out the door as Ethan pulled the door closed. "And now you've met my brother."

The ride over to Jared's was tense and quiet. When we got there, I'd just cut the engine and started to get out of the car, when Ethan spoke, "Nara, after the experiences in the library and the parking lot, I'm worried Fate might've changed tactics."

I paused, my fingers tightening on the door handle. "What do you mean?"

He shook his head, his face rigid. "Something just doesn't feel right."

The party was in full swing, muffled music thumping. I glanced at the huge five-thousand-square foot house, tension building inside me. "I have to do this. I couldn't live with myself if I didn't try to save Lainey."

He gave a resigned sigh. "I know. Let's go."

As we walked up the driveway from the road, Ethan commented, "I'm surprised his parents allow him to have a party during the week, especially with a game coming up tomorrow night."

Cool wind blew right through my sweater, making me wish I hadn't ditched my coat. "Jared's parents are big partiers. Supposedly they start partying on Thursday night and go through Saturday. I guarantee they aren't even here."

Standing on the porch, I skimmed Ethan's edgy stance. "You going to be okay with all these people?"

"I'll be fine," he said in a clipped tone.

"Thanks for coming." I hoped he knew I was sincere. The porch light's glow shrouded his face in darkness, but I could tell he was studying my face.

He stepped close. "She'd better appreciate your friendship."

I took a deep breath and pushed the door open.

Cups of beer were shoved in our hands the moment we walked in the door. Lainey squealed our names and ran over, babbling, "More friends." I could tell she was already tipsy.

"You *have* to meet everyone, Ethan," she insisted. Grabbing Ethan's arm, she dragged him to the basement where most of the partiers were.

Wincing, I thought of all the people he would brush against tonight. I hoped he could handle all the dark energy that would flow his way.

Several of my teammates were in the kitchen playing flip cup with a half dozen football players. I leaned against the doorjamb and watched Sophia flip her lipstick-stained cup with ease. She might be drinking, but she was more sober than Lainey. My gaze narrowed. Definitely in control and fully aware what she was doing…which was currently leaning down so Jared, who was across from her, got a full view of her good-sized breasts, nicely framed by her V-neck shirt.

I'd never wanted to rip someone's hair out as much as I did at that moment, but I promised myself I would let certain events unfold naturally for Lainey's own good.

Jared grabbed a grape from the table behind him and tossed it across the flip cup table and into Sophia's shirt. The guys went wild with hoots and catcalls. I walked out. I might not plan to get involved, but I wasn't going to watch it progress downhill either.

Dumping my beer in a nearby potted plant, I passed through a cloud of pot smoke floating from the bathroom area. In the living room, Miranda was sandwiched between two wrestlers on the couch. All three held cigarettes and were apparently competing for the biggest smoke ring. Ignoring them, I headed downstairs.

The music's bass thumped even louder in the basement, and a whole group of people danced drunkenly on one side of the big room, while several guys were playing a serious game of foosball on the other side. Two sophomore boys from the JV football team manned the bar in the middle, pumping the keg and handing out beer to the juniors and seniors like it was water.

True to her word, Lainey was introducing Ethan around. Walking up to them, I said, "I'll take over so you can have fun, Lainey."

"Okaaaay, great. Be right back," Lainey slurred slightly before she grabbed another cup of beer, then ran upstairs.

Standing near the group of people dancing, I glanced down at Ethan's cup, saw the beer was half gone and raised my eyebrow. "I thought you didn't drink?"

Ethan set the cup down on a side table and pointed to an alcove between the stairs and the bathroom. Following him, we ducked into the shadows underneath the stairs. I was surprised how much the small space blocked out a lot of the noise.

"I'm going to pay for this for a month."

He sounded so disgruntled, I grimaced. "I'm sorry."

Placing his arm on the angled wall above my head, Ethan moved close, forcing me to step back. He bent down and inhaled near my hair. "That's nothing compared to the torture of not being able to touch you."

My heart pounded at his closeness. In my dream, I was at the party by myself. Lifting my chin, I greedily inhaled his clean scent. I'd missed his amazing smell. Pent-up emotions arced between us.

When I turned my head at the same time he did and our lips almost met, I sighed away yearnings and tried to break the tension. "It really bothers me that you're not in my dreams. I'm scared Fate will go after you next and we won't have any warning."

Ethan leaned back. "I have no idea why I'm not in your dreams. It's been driving me crazy, but not because I fear Fate." Desperate sadness reflected in his gaze. "It's like I don't exist in your life, Nara. At least not in your future. That terrifies me."

The near panic in his voice ripped my heart open. "You're very much a part of my life." I reached for him, then caught myself, curling my fingers into a fist. Lowering my hand back to my side, I whispered fiercely, "You are my future, Ethan."

Ethan started to speak when a loud scream sounded above us, followed by thundering footsteps.

"Oh, God, Lainey!" I'd been so wrapped up in Ethan, I'd almost forgotten about my friend. Ducking underneath his arm, I ran up the stairs and pushed past people doing the same, except they wanted to *see* the fight, not stop it.

"You cheating bastard!" Lainey screamed. One of the football players held her back from Jared as the jerk quickly tucked his shirt back in his jeans and said, "Lane, let's talk about this, babe."

Sophia tried to slip out of the bathroom behind Jared, but Lainey broke free and yanked the girl around. She slapped her hard across the face before the guy snagged her arms again. "Back-stabbing slut!" Lainey screeched.

The moment she saw me, Lainey broke into tears and the guy let her go. I wrapped my arm around her shaking shoulders and led her away from the bathroom, where she'd apparently walked in on Jared and Sophia making out.

As I sat Lainey down on the sofa to talk, Ethan shooed the crowd, saying, "The party's downstairs. Not up here."

I appreciated his effort to give us some privacy and couldn't help but smirk when he stepped in front of Jared and said, "Dude, you're *not* who Lainey needs to see right now. You look like you lost a fight with a tube of lipstick."

Lainey was sobbing, her face pressed in her hands. I stroked her hair. "I'm so sorry, Lainey."

Turning her puffy-eyed, mascara-streaked face up, she hiccupped. "I—I wish I had lis—listened to you about her."

"Don't worry about that. Would you like me to take you home?"

She shook her head in fast, furious jerks. "I need to tell Jared what a complete ass he is."

I pursed my lips. "I think he knows that. And so does everyone here."

Her eyes widened. "Everyone knows..." she said slowly, then burst into tears once more.

"That's not what I meant. Let me take you home," I repeated gently.

"No." She dug for her keys, pulling them from her pocket. "I can't face *anyone* right now." Standing up too fast, she stumbled forward, mumbling, "I'll drive myself home."

Before she took another step, I was by her side. "Lainey." The moment I grabbed her arm, a prickly, electrical current zipped through me, followed by a thick heavy sensation in the air. It felt as if someone had just thrown an ice-cold blanket over me.

"I need to go," Lainey said, resisting my hold.

"You're not leav—" My lungs started to seize, cutting off my words. I coughed hard a couple times to expel the icy dampness spreading through my chest. As Lainey tugged against my hand, I straightened my spine and shook my head to release the pressure that pushed on either side of my skull. No matter what, I wouldn't let Lainey drive. "I won't stop," I rasped.

The crushing sensation began to ease and I tightened my hold on Lainey.

"Are you okay?" Ethan's concerned gaze searched mine. It had all happened in milliseconds, but I nodded, appreciating his presence more than he would ever know. Taking a deep breath, I pried the keys from Lainey's fingers. "You're too drunk to drive. Get your stuff and I'll drive you home."

Lainey let out a heavy sigh and her shoulders slumped as she walked over to the hall closet. While she shoved her arms in her coat, Ethan whispered in my ear, "I felt the cold and a charge in the air. The entire atmosphere around you changed, like a drop in barometric pressure."

"You felt all of it?" I started to ask, but had to immediately move toward Lainey the moment I saw Jared come up the stairs from the basement.

Lainey had started screaming at Jared and I tucked my hand around her elbow. "Come on, Lainey. You're too upset. Save it for later." I looked at Ethan for help when she tried to shrug my hand off her arm.

Stepping beside us, Ethan wrapped his arm around Lainey's shoulders. "Let us take you home," he said in a calm voice, then escorted her into the cool night air, shutting the door behind them.

"It's probably best if she goes home and sleeps it off." Jared appeared a bit paler now that he'd scrubbed off the lipstick smears.

I glared at him. "You're not getting off that easy. I just want her to have a clear head when she tells you what a total self-serving jerk you are."

He actually looked upset. "Can you talk to her? It was a mistake. Sophia came on to me."

"You had a choice and you made it. Now you'll have to deal with the fallout," I said, then shut the door behind me.

CHAPTER 20

Ethan and Lainey were waiting by her car when I walked out of the house. Tossing my keys to Ethan, I said, "Can you follow us in my car?"

As he headed down the driveway, I looked at Lainey. "Come on, hon. Let's get you home."

Lainey crawled into the passenger seat and immediately slumped down in it. Leaning over, I snapped her seatbelt around her and pushed her hair out of her face. She was still pretty drunk. Her dad would be furious if he saw her like this. "Is there a way I can sneak you into your house without your parents seeing?"

Lainey waved her hand, sounding sullen. "They went out on a date tonight. All wine and roses for them, while I get shit on. How freaking unfair is that?"

"They're out?"

"Yes."

Relieved, I turned to back out of the driveway.

"Why couldn't he be like Ethan?" Lainey lamented in a half slur as I turned out of Jared's neighborhood.

I glanced at her in surprise. "You want Jared to be like Ethan?"

She wiped her eyes with her coat sleeve. "Ethan treats you

right. He might seem kind of strange, but his heart's in the right place."

"I didn't think you knew Ethan all that well," I said, flicking on the blinker before taking a left onto the main road.

"Did you know Ethan tried to save some kid in his neighborhood from being beaten by his dad?"

I turned wide eyes her way. "No. How do you know about it?"

"My dad told me Ethan called the police station to report the dude and now the kid's in foster care."

That must've been where the split lip and bruised jaw came from. "Ethan's a good person. He just doesn't always share that with everyone."

When I stopped in her driveway and pushed the garage door button on her sun visor, Ethan pulled in behind us. Lainey unsnapped her seatbelt and wailed, "I've made a mess of things, haven't I?"

Grasping her shoulders, I turned her toward me. "This wasn't your fault, Lainey. Sophia's finally showing her true colors and Jared only cares about Jared. I guess tonight you finally saw that for yourself."

"I thought he loved me." Tears welled once more and she began to cry again in deep, heart-wrenching moans. "I should…should've broken it off with him tonight," she bawled.

"Wait until tomorrow, then he'll know it's not just drunken anger talking." I rubbed her back, feeling so bad for how much she was hurting. After she calmed down, I walked her into her quiet house and up the stairs to her bedroom.

Lainey shrugged out of her coat and flopped onto her bed, throwing her arm over her eyes. I tugged off her shoes and sat down beside her. "Get some sleep and we'll talk tomorrow, okay?"

Lainey sniffed behind her arm.

When I turned to leave, she said, "Nara?"

"Yeah?" She'd lowered her arm to look at me.

"Thanks for being my friend. I know I haven't made it easy for you lately."

I smiled. "Friends look out for each other. I'll come by in the morning to bring your keys."

Her trembling smile faltered. "You can leave my keys."

No way. I'd learned my lesson in my dream last night. I shook my head, but kept my expression upbeat. "I'll be here bright and early. Your parents won't know. Don't worry."

Closing her bedroom door, I headed downstairs.

Ethan had moved to the passenger side of my car by the time I locked Lainey's front door and tucked her keys away in my jeans pocket. I hopped in my car quickly, thankful he'd started the engine and cranked up the heat.

When I put the car in reverse, he asked, "Think she'll be okay?"

"Eventually. Right now she's really hurt." I drove off, pressing harder on the gas than I'd intended. "It probably would've been better if I'd prevented her from seeing them together in the first place."

Ethan shrugged. "Maybe after hooking up with Sophia, Jared never would have cheated again. Who knows? The point is, now Lainey knows the facts and can decide if she wants to continue dating him."

I sighed. "I know. You're right."

After several seconds of silence, Ethan said, "I've been so tense about this, I haven't eaten. Let's get some food. I'm starving."

"There's that new pizza place with the high-backed booths on the downtown mall."

He grinned. "Sounds great."

Forty minutes later, we were sitting across from each other, munching on the best California style pizza I'd ever tasted.

"I've died and gone to heaven," Ethan said, taking another bite.

"I don't see how you can taste anything through the thick layer of hot pepper you just shook on that slice."

"Adding spice makes the flavors explode."

Picking up another piece of pizza, I laughed. "I have this mental image of *flames* coming out of your mouth." I pointed my piece of pizza at him and gave him a skeptical look. "So, you've *never* seen yourself in my dreams, huh?"

Ethan shook his head, then took another bite.

"How do you explain when you first told me you had my dreams, you said, and I quote, 'Unless you count the end of the day—when we kiss.'"

"That's because it was *my* dream," he said with a look that could melt an iceberg.

Laughing, I threw my napkin at him.

After we'd staved off the hunger pains and were just picking at our pizza, Ethan looked contemplative. "About tonight. I'm glad things worked out with Lainey, but I keep thinking about the library and the accident in the parking lot. I'd dreamed your future, Nara. You said that your dreams had never been wrong, yet both those days felt skewed to me. Not just because I was determined to keep you safe, but truly off-kilter, almost like balance had shifted."

"What do you mean 'balance'?"

His brow furrowed. "The balance in Nature I mentioned to you before. I don't know how, but I can sense a misalignment. When the air charged and the pressure changed tonight, I felt that all the way to my bones."

"Welcome to my world. It's been like that since the day I called in the bombing."

"I knew you felt cold pressure, but the electric current…has that always been there, too?"

"Unfortunately." I started to push my hair over my shoulder, but the crackling static of my hair dragging across my sweater caused me to pause mid-swipe. I gaped at Ethan. "I can't believe it. All this time I thought my crazy static issue was due to the fall weather and cheap dryer sheets, yet even the more expensive brands didn't work. But what you're asking made me think it might've been Fate's constant presence."

"Like it's stalking you." Ethan said in a low tone, balling his hands into fists.

Witchy Woman started playing on my cell. I sighed. "She's checking on me since Mom's out of town." I slid my phone open. "Hey, Aunt Sage."

"Inara, I'm so glad you're okay."

My aunt sounded worried. I pressed the phone to my ear. "Why wouldn't I be okay?"

"There was a news flash just now about a car accident involving a student from your school."

I glanced at Ethan and my heart started to pound. "I'm fine, Aunt Sage, but thanks for telling me. I'll find out who it was tomorrow."

"I got concerned when you didn't answer the house phone. That's why I called your cell."

"Ethan and I are out having pizza. I'll be heading home soon."

"Okay, sweetie. Drive safe and call me tomorrow."

"What's wrong?" Ethan asked as I immediately dialed Lainey's cell.

When her cell went to voicemail, I tensed. Hanging up, I dialed her parents' house. My hand began to tremble when the phone rang and rang. "Someone from our school's been in a car accident."

"It's not Lainey, Nara."

"We don't know *anything* about the rest of her night since I altered its course," I said, punching the End button.

"You kept Lainey's keys, right?"

Her keys were currently digging into my thigh in my jean pocket. Nodding, I slid my phone closed and relaxed.

When my phone began to ring again, I jumped, then glanced at the Caller ID. It was Miranda. She never called me. My chest ached as I answered. "Hey, Miranda."

"Nara, ohmigod! Did you hear? Lainey's been in a car accident."

I'D JUST WALKED into the Emergency Room entrance when Lainey's dad jumped up from his chair and rushed over to us, his round face an angry, mottled mass of bulging veins. "You're supposed to be her friend, Nara. How could you let her drive?"

I shrank under her father's tirade, tears trickling down my cheeks. "I'm so sorry, Mr. O'Neal."

Lainey's petite mom was by her husband's side, tugging on his thick arm, her brown eyes sad, but apologetic. "Joe, Nara didn't make Lainey drink and drive."

Mr. O'Neal raked his hand though his graying short hair. "Still, she's her friend."

Ethan stepped in front of me. "You've got it wrong, sir. I followed Nara in her car when she drove your daughter home over an hour ago. She made sure Lainey got home safely."

"Who are you?" Mr. O'Neal lost some of his bluster as he scowled at Ethan.

"Ethan Harris. A friend of Nara and Lainey's."

While fleeting recognition, then grudging respect cycled through Lainey's dad's face, Mrs. O'Neal put a trembling hand over her lips and focused on me. "You drove her home?"

I pulled Lainey's keys out of my pocket, then set them in her mother's hand. "She must've used a spare key to drive herself back to Jared's after I left her. I wish...I wish I'd stayed with her now."

Mr. O'Neal put his thick hand on my shoulder. "Julia's right. It's not your fault, Nara. I apologize for coming down on you. That's just my baby girl in there, ya know?" he said, his eyes turning red.

As Mrs. O'Neal walked her husband back over to the waiting room area, I followed them. "How bad is it?"

Mrs. O'Neal shook her head, a piece of her strawberry blond hair falling from the clip holding the rest back. "We don't know. She was unconscious when they brought her in."

Unconscious! I felt the color drain from my face. *Please don't let Lainey die.*

"Maybe we should go sit down," Ethan suggested evenly.

Forty minutes later, a doctor in a white coat came breezing out of the clinic double doors, his gaze scanning the waiting room crowd. "Mr. and Mrs. O'Neal?"

Lainey's dad approached the doctor. "How is she?"

As we all stepped into place behind Mr. O'Neal, the dark-haired doctor flipped through the chart, then met Lainey's parents' expectant gazes. "Your daughter has a few contusions and her internal organs are fine, but she still hasn't woken yet."

"What does that mean?" Mr. O'Neal asked, sounding gruff and incredulous.

"We'll be running a few more tests and I'll fill you in as often as I can."

Once the doctor walked away, we all sank to our seats, lost in our own worries. After a half hour of waiting, Mrs. O'Neal turned to me. "Thank you for coming, Nara, but you've got school in the morning, so you should go home and get some sleep. We'll give you an update on Lainey's progress tomorrow."

Waves of guilt hammered at my chest, but I managed to rasp, "Please call me as soon as you know something."

The ride home from the hospital was a blur. My head throbbed by the time Ethan pulled into my driveway and pressed the button for the garage door.

"Wait. I have to drive you home."

"I'll walk home."

"It's almost midnight. I'll take you home."

Ethan climbed out of the car and closed the door, leaving me no choice but to follow.

Closing the garage door, he used the only other key on my keychain to unlock the house. "I want to make sure you get inside safely, especially since you're staying here by yourself."

I was too tired and emotionally beat to argue, so I followed him inside. Ethan led the way through the kitchen and I walked with him to the foyer. Gazing into his face, which was only partially lit from the light in the kitchen, I said, "Thank you for being there tonight. I know you wished I'd stayed out of it. Maybe you were right."

He started to speak, but I put my hand up, my chest tightening with emotion. "I don't want to argue. Not tonight."

Ethan watched my hand shaking like a leaf, his expression full of frustration. "I can't stand to watch you blame yourself for this."

"It might be nice to know my future..." I started to say. My lips trembled and my gaze pleaded for him to understand. "But I need you more right now—"

Before I could finish, Ethan grabbed my hand and gathered me into his warm embrace.

"You did everything you could," he whispered into my hair.

I sank into his warmth and reveled in his strong arms holding me close, bands of steel keeping me from falling. I'd missed his touch so much. "I can't help how I feel," I wept against his neck. "It all seems so fruitless now. Like Fate made sure it had the last say-so with Lainey."

Ethan grasped my face and made me look at him. "You made a difference, Nara. If Lainey had driven home from the party when she'd wanted to, at that hour the traffic was much heavier. She could've been killed and other people could've been hurt."

"What if she doesn't wake up, Ethan? That's worse than death."

His grip tightened around me. "Lainey will wake up."

I tried to smile, but failed miserably. "Maybe I should call *you* Sunshine for trying to cheer me up."

Ethan rolled his eyes, then kissed my forehead.

Sniffing back tears, I closed my eyes and inhaled his wonderful smell. He was trying to make me feel better. *Now would be a good time to tell him you love him,* but the words jammed in my throat. They just wouldn't come. So, I stood on my toes and kissed him.

Ethan's arms tightened around my waist and his lips pressed against mine for a long simmering second, then he quickly stepped back and exhaled. "I need to get home before my brother thinks *now* might be a good time to start enforcing a curfew."

"Are you sure you don't want me to drive you—"

Ethan dropped another quick kiss on my lips, then opened the front door behind him. Before he stepped outside, he said, "This imbalance thing really bothers me. I think you should call your dad."

When I slowly nodded my agreement, he pointed to the

deadbolt. "Lock this behind me." Then he was gone, leaving me leaning against the door and missing him already.

Twenty minutes later, I stepped into the shower and scrubbed myself clean, hoping the warm water would help me relax enough to fall asleep. Soaping my hair, I dunked my head under the spray until the suds were gone, then held my hands under the hot water for several minutes, waiting for my tense muscles to loosen.

All I could think about was Lainey lying unconscious in a hospital bed. Closing my eyes briefly, I sent a silent prayer for her full recovery. *Please let someone hear it.* I watched the water trickle through my fingers, but I barely felt it. I was numb all over. And angry. Angry at Fate. *It's not fair.* "She'd better wake up," I hissed into the steam.

Cold air brushed my exposed shoulders, making my skin pebble. Gasping, I glanced behind me, my heart knocking against my chest. Nothing but tufts of steam swirled in the empty space. It's just your imagination, I told myself. As I turned to push my chilled shoulder under the warm water, something shoved me from behind. I slammed against the tile and pain exploded across my face.

Gripping my bloody nose, I moaned as I jammed my back against the cold tile and slid into the corner to better protect myself from the unseen force that'd attacked me. I stood there, shivering, while water sluiced crimson blood down my wrist, streaking it to a lighter red along my bare skin until it turned pink at my feet. I'd never felt more vulnerable…and it knew it. "Screw you!" I tried to scream, but the words came out in a hoarse rasp.

Movement along the bottom of the glass door drew my attention. A vertical line had formed at the base of the door, like an invisible finger was sliding through the fog. My legs wobbled, threatening to collapse as I followed its slow, meandering path upward. The line pointed to a message that had already been written on the glass.

You can't save them all.

Shutting the water off with a shaky hand, I drew on the fear, anxiety and determination to protect the ones I loved. "Watch me," I said in a surprisingly steady voice, which gave me the confidence to continue, "Go. Away."

Instantly the room felt bigger, the air lighter. Exhaling a sharp breath, I grabbed the towel from the top of the shower door and wrapped its flimsy protection around myself. Chanting *Laniey'll wake up and Ethan will stay safe* over and over in my head, I swiped my hand across the glass in furious, determined swipes, rubbing away Fate's presence.

CHAPTER 21

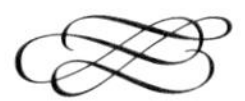

The next morning, a booming clap of thunder and flash of lightning jerked me from a restless sleep. My heart pounded as I sat up in bed. Normally daylight would be glimmering in by now, but the storm clouds kept the sky dark and gloomy.

The phone rang and I quickly picked it up. "Hello?"

"Good morning," Mom said at the same time thunder rumbled, followed by a zap of lightning. The phone's reception buzzed in and out. "What was that?"

Mom always got up with the roosters. I blinked hard, trying to wake up. After my scary run in with Fate, I hadn't been able to fall asleep last night, but among worrying for Lainey and Ethan, I must've finally dozed for a couple hours. "It's storming here. How's Texas?"

"Warm. I despise doing audits."

I rubbed the achy tiredness from my eyes. "I thought you lived and breathed numbers."

"*Other* numbers. Audits give me a migraine. Maybe I will call your Mr. Dixon."

"You're serious about learning Spanish?"

"It could be helpful to know the gist of what's being said around me while I'm auditing."

"I'll get you his contact information," I said on a big yawn. I wished I could feel excited that my match-making plan was in motion, but all I could think about was Lainey lying unconscious in the hospital and Fate lurking.

"Sounds good. It's a good thing I called. From the amount of yawns I'm hearing, your alarm clock wouldn't have woken you. Everything going okay there?"

I considered telling her about Lainey's accident, but I didn't want her to worry. I'd tell her when she got back. "Mmm-hmm." The phone buzzed in and out again.

"Whew, I heard that pop, Inara. That's a bad storm. I won't keep you on the phone. I just wanted to remind you I'll be home around noon tomorrow."

"Okay, have a safe trip back."

"Inara? Let's plan to go to Williamsburg soon. Have some *us* time. Maybe do some early Christmas shopping? What do you think?"

Warmth spread through me, briefly overshadowing my concern over Lainey and worry for Ethan's safety. It felt good to finally press Play and move forward. "Sounds great, Mom. See you tomorrow."

~

ONCE I PULLED into a space in the school parking lot, I called Aunt Sage.

"Morning, Inara. You don't usually call so early. Is everything okay?"

I tried to keep my voice even. "My friend Lainey was in the car accident last night."

"Oh, no! Is she all right?"

"She hasn't woken up yet." My voice shook. "I'm so scared she won't."

"I'm so sorry, sweetie. Hopefully she'll wake up soon."

"Aunt Sage."

"Yes?"

"What price did my dad pay?" When she didn't answer right away, my chest started to squeeze. Long pauses were never a good sign. "Did you hear me?"

"Why are you asking?"

I gulped back a sob. "I tried to stop it, but I couldn't. I even drove Lainey home. Since I'd changed what was supposed to happen last night, everything beyond that moment for her had changed. I had no idea she'd leave her house and drive back to the party."

"Slow down, take a breath, and tell me what happened. You said you tried to stop something from happening. Did you get your dreams back?"

"Yes, I got my dreams back. I dreamed Lainey got into a car accident when she left the party last night."

"And you tried to stop her from driving. Was she drinking?"

I wasn't mentioning that she'd been drinking. "She—she was upset with her boyfriend, who turned out to be a cheating jerk, so I drove her home. I tried to help her, Aunt Sage."

"Inara, I know you were just being her friend, but you also acted on precognizant knowledge. Changing the natural course can sometimes have consequences."

I wiped the tears from my face and sniffed to calm down. "Is that what you meant when you said Dad paid for interfering? Did he try to help but it didn't make a difference? What price did he pay, Aunt Sage?"

"He paid by losing something precious."

She sounded so sad, worry gripped me. "What did he lose?"

"He—he'll want to tell you himself. I'll let him know that you have your dreams back. That should be enough for him to contact you."

"Aunt Sage." I couldn't believe she wouldn't tell me. I wanted her to help me connect with my dad. After last night, I needed to learn everything I could about my powers, but I wanted some answers now.

"I made a vow, Inara. I promised my brother."

"What did he lose?" I said in a higher pitch.

"He lost you and your mother," she said quietly.

"He *left* us!" I screeched, my fingers forming claws around my cell.

"I've said too much." Sage's tone turned brisk. "He *will* contact you, even if I have to threaten him to make it happen."

"Aunt Sage."

"I'll get back to you soon. And no more interfering, please."

Before I could say another word, she hung up.

"Damn it!" I'd just tossed my cell phone into the passenger seat when someone knocked on my window. Jumping, I pressed my hand against my pounding heart.

"You coming?" Ethan stood outside my car, the stormy wind blowing his hair in every direction. "The first bell rang already," he said through the glass.

Glancing quickly in the mirror, I was glad to see the makeup I'd used to cover the bruise on my nose held up in morning light. I grabbed my cell, then shoved it in my backpack before climbing out of the car.

"Did the storm wake you early this morning, too?" Ethan asked.

"Yeah." We were almost to the main door when Ethan said, "You want to talk about it?"

I tensed, wondering if he was referring to Fate's visit last night, but then I realized he hadn't seen that in my dream or he would've warned me. "I can't believe my aunt won't tell me the price my dad paid for interfering. Now I have to wait for him to call me about it."

He stopped and shifted his books from one hand to the other. "You're still blaming yourself for what happened with Lainey, aren't you?"

Halting, I stared at him, then bit my lip to keep it from trembling. I wanted to tell him about Fate, but I knew he'd be upset. Before we walked into school, I had to say something to let him know Fate had gone beyond lurking, so I said, "Please be extra careful, okay?"

Ethan held my gaze for a couple seconds, then nodded and headed off to class.

THE MOMENT I leaned into Lainey's hospital room, the medicinal smells instantly made me think of death. Shoving my nose into the bouquet of flowers in my hand, I knocked lightly to let Mrs. O'Neal know I was there.

"Nara." She waved me in from her chair near the bed. As I set the flowers on a nearby table, she glanced at her daughter. "She looks so peaceful, doesn't she?"

An IV was taped to Lainey's wrist and a blood pressure cuff was wrapped around her arm, but beyond the scrape and bruise on her forehead and a few more bruises on her arms, she looked like she was sleeping and would wake up any moment. My heart thumped and I felt light-headed, but managed a nod. "What did the doctors say?" I asked in a strangled whisper.

"There's no change in her condition." Lainey's mom ran her hand across her forehead. She looked like she hadn't slept in three days. "And there's no need to whisper, hon. The doctors want us to talk to Lainey. They said it might help her recover."

"Oh, okay," I said in a crackly voice.

Standing, she arched her back and then stretched her arms. "Would you mind sitting with Lainey while I go talk to the nurses? Her father's getting us lunch and I don't want to leave her alone."

I bobbed my head and waited until Mrs. O'Neal left to sit in the chair she'd vacated. Clasping Lainey's cool fingers, I pressed my warm ones against hers. "Can you hear me, Lainey?"

Her hand remained limp. Guilt roared through me in flashes of hot and cold. "I'm so sorry. I tried, Lainey. I tried to stop it, but I couldn't."

Turning her hand over, I ran my thumb across her open palm, wishing she could hear me and know how much I wanted her to get better. "You're probably wondering what I'm talking about, huh?"

A hollow laugh escaped as a hot tear rolled down my cheek. I brushed it away and squeezed her fingers. "I dreamed about your accident and I tried to stop it. You have no idea how frustrating it is to have this ability to see the future and still not be able to help you."

Sniffling, I tightened my hand on hers, my voice turning

stern. "You need to wake up, Lainey. How are you going to tell Jared off if you're laying in bed, taking a long nap?"

Lainey's fingers jumped against mine, making me gasp. When I looked up, her eyes were sliding back and forth under her eyelids, like she was dreaming. "Did you hear me?" I whispered.

Mr. and Mrs. O'Neal walked in carrying their lunch. "Hey, Nara," Mr. O'Neal said. His overnight beard shined gray against his tan chin and his voice sounded like ground-up glass.

I stood, still holding Lainey's hand. "I—I'm not certain, but I just thought I felt Lainey's fingers move."

"Really?" they said in unison. Hope filled her parents' faces. As Mrs. O'Neal rushed to Lainey's side, Mr. O'Neal dashed out of the room, calling for a nurse.

Trying not to get my own hopes up, I laid Lainey's hand back on the bed and kept my voice calm and even. "I need to get back to school. My lunch hour's almost over, but please let me know if anything changes, Mrs. O'Neal."

Reaching for her daughter's other hand, tears brimmed Julia's eyes. "I promise I'll call as soon as there's any change."

~

LATER THAT DAY, I was in the library searching the online catalogue of Biology texts when my phone began to vibrate. Glancing up to make sure the librarian wasn't around, I answered my cell with a quick whisper, "Hello?"

"Nara, it's Julia. I just wanted to let you know Lainey woke up twenty minutes ago."

"Oh, thank God! I'm so glad," I squealed, then instantly lowered my voice. "How's she feeling?"

Julia sniffed back tears. "She's pretty banged up and tired. The doctors are checking her vitals now. They want her to rest tonight. No more visitors, but please come see her tomorrow. Can you let her other friends know the good news for me?"

"I will, Mrs. O'Neal. Thank you for calling."

I was in such a good mood that I had a hard time concentrating the rest of study hall. I was just about ready to log out when someone set a chair beside me. As Ethan sat down, I beamed. "Lainey woke up an hour ago."

Relief flitted across his face. "I'm glad she's going to be okay." We sat in silence for a couple of seconds before his expression turned serious. "I wanted to talk to you about Fate, about you challenging it."

Tensing, I exited out of the list of Biology books I'd been searching. "I know you didn't think it was a good idea—" *What would he say about last night?*

"No, that's not it. I think that might be exactly what you need to do."

I stared at him, wide-eyed. "You want me to challenge Fate? You said it was dangerous."

He blew out a harsh breath. "I thought about this all last night. In the library and again in the parking lot, I think Fate was trying to make you pay for getting involved. I don't think it was trying to scare you, Nara. I think it was trying to take you out."

Terror shot through me. *Fate had gotten personally physical last night at a time when I'd felt the most exposed, but was it really trying to kill me?* "But we talked about this. Since I know my future, I would've known what Fate was going to do and I would've avoided the situation."

"I agreed with that idea at first, but the sense of wrongness I've felt has stayed with me, and then after I felt it again last night at Jared's and it still didn't go away, I considered what's happened recently in a whole new light. I think all of this ties into the fact I'm not in your dreams."

Intrigued, I turned to fully face him. "You figured out why you're not in my dreams?"

"Not that part, but just hear me out. In the past, you had your dreams and therefore you knew your future. With me in your life, you've lost your dreams."

"But you've told me the important stuff, so I didn't really lose them."

"I've been thinking about that." He rubbed his jaw. "Neither one of us have seen me in your dreams, which is about *your* future. What if Fate is aware that you don't have your dreams any longer? That'd be a pretty big deal. Without your dreams, Fate would assume you wouldn't be able to protect yourself against "future" stuff that would happen to you."

Like what happened to me last night. I was totally surprised by Fate's attack.

Ethan continued, breaking into my train of thought. "But since you can't see me in your dreams, maybe Fate can't see me either."

"That's an interesting theory," I said, my head spinning.

Ethan slid his palms across his jeans. "If that's true, then Fate would have no way of knowing that I would've been there to help you when things were 'predicted' in your dreams—things *you* couldn't have anticipated because you didn't dream anymore. Like when the bookshelf in the library almost fell on you. I stopped it because I knew your future."

"And right after that the bookshelf fell on us anyway," I whispered.

"Which had no reason to fall since I was holding it," he said in a hard tone.

"But that was because the one behind it fell—" I started to say, but stopped at the "ah, now you see where this is going" look on his face. Feeling lightheaded, I continued, "I—I was supposed to be hit by those runaway pipes."

Ethan looked solemn. "Since the accident woke me up, I didn't know how bad you were hurt by the pipes, but I'd seen your future and made sure you were on the other side of the parking lot."

"Where the light pole would've fallen on me if I hadn't glanced at the raven flying away from it." Everything he said made total sense. My stomach suddenly felt as if lead had been poured straight into it. "You think Fate's never going to stop coming after me."

"You told it last night at Jared's that *you* weren't going to stop, remember?"

I was referring to stopping Lainey's car accident when I'd said that, but by blatantly challenging Fate a few hours later, I'd meant "everyone" then. I didn't regret it though. Fate was bullying me, and I was fighting for Ethan, Lainey and anyone else Fate went after.

Ethan looked grim and worried. "I don't think Fate will stop until you *make* it stop, Nara."

Was last night in the shower a stronger warning? Could Fate have thrown me hard enough to kill me? Panic set in and I spread my trembling hands wide. "I couldn't stop it before. Maybe this *is* my Fate."

A determined look settled on Ethan's face. "That's the whole point. All of this feels unbalanced to me. I think Fate is messing with your destiny. It shouldn't be able to alter your timeline. I think you can make Fate stop if your will is strong enough."

"But how do I do that?" I felt powerless last night. Totally at Fate's invisible mercy.

Ethan leaned forward and set his elbows on his knees. Steepling his fingers, he pressed them against his lips.

"How do I fight something I can't see?" I finished in a helpless whisper.

Ethan lifted his head, eyes alight. "That's it!"

"What? You have an idea?"

"Maybe. I have to check something first. You're safe today. I didn't see anything in your dreams. Can you meet me at your house?"

I was more worried about him. "You're going straight home until then?"

When he nodded, my tension lessened a little. "I'll come home right after practice," I said, feeling excitement build at the idea of spending some time alone with him.

"Get back to your research." Standing, Ethan slid the chair back under the table.

"You're leaving me all tied in curious knots. I'm so not getting anything done now."

Ethan ran his hand from the top of my head to the ends of my hair, then spoke in a calming voice next to my ear. "Feel better?"

As I watched him leave, I was curious what he planned to "check" but the fear was gone. Not only had he settled my seesawing emotions, but his touch had left me tingling all over.

His power to sweep my worries away still amazed me, but Ethan had his own special ability to affect me that had *nothing* to do with him being a negative energy magnet.

~

SOCCER PRACTICE WAS MORE interesting than usual. Miranda was the only one who spoke to Sophia the entire time. Everyone else took their annoyance out on her like they'd done to me not so long ago. Even Coach rode her incessantly, though he couldn't possibly have known about Sophia and Jared hooking up at the party. Maybe there was something to that whole "what comes around, goes around" theory.

An hour into practice, Sophia was near tears. I almost felt sorry for her, until I caught her glaring at me. I glared back, then kicked the ball hard in her direction. The wind hadn't let up all day and it seemed to increase the ball's speed. Sophia had to dive to keep from being pegged in the face. I couldn't help but snicker.

The windy gusts had been a problem all practice, but we'd soldiered on, doing our best to compensate for its effect on our accuracy with passes and shots on goal.

With twenty minutes left in practice, I was surprised when Coach said, "I'm cutting practice short. I know Lainey can't have visitors today, but if anyone wants to go get flowers and a card, head on out. Who wants to volunteer to collect the gear?"

"I will," Renee said.

"Me, too," I raised my hand, since I wouldn't be staying alone. "I'll put the gear in my trunk until next practice."

The rest of the team collectively called out, "Thanks, Coach," then immediately ran over to gather their bags.

After everyone took off for their cars, Renee started picking up cones on one side of the field and I headed for the other side. Orange practice cones littered the field, blowing around the open space at the wind's whim.

We were almost done when Renee's boyfriend drove up and honked his horn.

Renee looked sheepish. "Would you mind finishing up?"

Tension welled inside me, but I couldn't live my life in fear. "It'll only take me a couple more minutes." I waved her on, and then spent the next five minutes chasing down the last couple of tumbling cones and rolling balls.

The field lights popped on as I grabbed the net bag. Dragging it over to the goal where Renee and I had dumped all the gear, I began to fill it with the cones and soccer balls.

When the buffeting wind spun the net bag around, I grumbled and untwisted it. Shoving the cones in, I grabbed a couple of balls and had just dropped them into the mesh, when a bird's loud cawing drew my attention.

The sound came from the top of one of the soccer field lights. Squinting, all I could see was the bright light as I called out over the wind, "What is it with you birds and light posts?"

No sooner had the words left my mouth, then the bird swooped down straight toward me. Ducking to avoid being pegged in the head, I immediately turned and called out, "No, you crazy bird!" It was going to get caught in the goal's netting.

At the last second, the bird folded its wings and shot through one of the openings, clearing the net. Breathing a sigh of relief, my gaze snapped to the goal's base. It was rocking with the wind.

Heart racing, I glanced to the metal tie downs that normally held it in place. Both sets of ties had uprooted from the moist ground and were covered in grass and mud.

At that moment, a huge gust of wind whipped across the practice field, wrapping the net bag around my ankles and sending the metal goal over, heading straight for me.

I tried to dive to clear the goal area, but my cleats caught in the sports bag, sending me tumbling instead. I knew the goal could crush my spine, so I rolled at the last minute and caught the metal post with my hands to keep it from slamming onto my chest.

The jolt jarred my arms all the way up to my shoulders, but I held the metal pole as long as I could before my muscles began to shake under the weight. Panting, I lowered my elbows to the ground. Wind howled around me as I tried to think of a way to squirm out from underneath it. A rumble of thunder rolled, followed by streaks of lightning veining across the dark sky. Great, another storm's coming and I was trapped holding a huge lightning rod. "This is just freakin' fantastic," I muttered.

The air turned cooler with the impending storm and my breath began to mist in front of me. My gaze landed on the bag of balls a few inches from my foot and an idea formed. If I could somehow reach the bag without losing my grip on the pole, then maybe I could bend my leg and push some of the balls under the pole, creating a temporary wedge so I could slide out from under the goal.

I was surprised when a raven landed on the bag of balls. His feathers ruffled in the wind and he didn't make his usual gronking sound. Instead, he just stared, turning his head this way and that, as if he were surveying the area around us.

"What do you want?" I snapped, feeling cranky as the cold, wet ground seeped all the way to my bones. "This is all your fault."

He hopped off and pecked at the netting, then tilted his shiny dark head and made a low tok-tok noise. Rain started to fall in random fat drops and a cold chill rocked through me. My wrists and forearms began to ache and as I turned my head and groaned, I saw that the bird had inadvertently moved the netting closer to my shoe. Maybe if I talked to him some more, he'd play with the bag again.

"I guess you helped by flying toward the goal." The bird bobbed his head, then fluffed his feathers. I grimaced that my plan wasn't working. "Think you could grab—" I started to say, when the bird pecked at the bag once more. "That's it…closer to my shoe." This time, he flapped his wings and lifted the bag's string, dragging the netting over the top of my shoe before taking flight.

"Smart bird!" I said and immediately tried to bend my leg to the side, but the rain and my movements made the pole slip in my hands. I grimaced in pain as I rearranged my grip on it once more.

Making sure that I had the pole secured in my hands, I tried to pull the bag toward me once more, but I must've strained too hard because my elbows began to slip in the dewy grass.

No, no, no, no! I mentally screamed as the heavy goal began to slowly inch its way to my chest. My fingers clawed and my palms scraped against the painted metal, but at this new angle I couldn't regain my grip.

Terror rippled through me and I let out a yell as the full weight of the goal pressed on my chest. Heavy. So heavy. *Why did it feel heavier now than it did when I was holding it?* I wondered hazily as my ability to breathe was slowly pushed out of my lungs.

Spots floated in front of me and I thought, *I'm going to die.* Mom, Aunt Sage and Gran's faces appeared in my mind next. *You meant the world to me. I love you all.*

My vision grew fuzzy and I gasped one last raspy breath as Ethan's face, so intense as he started to say, "I lo—" flitted through my mind. *I'm sorry I never told you how much I loved you, Ethan.*

CHAPTER 22

My vision cleared as the soccer goal slammed against the ground. The jarring was so hard I was surprised I didn't feel the vibrations under my feet.

"Nara!" Ethan called above the shrieking wind, drawing my attention.

Ethan saved me? Why didn't I remember him helping me stand up? I turned to smile at him, but Ethan was on his knees bending over someone. Running to his side, I fell to my knees to see who else was hurt. I froze when I saw my own face, my green eyes staring sightlessly at the lightning-streaked sky.

"Nara." Ethan looked frantic. He pressed his fingers to my throat, then leaned down to listen to my chest. Rocking back on his heels, he shoved his hands through his hair and anguish rolled across his features. "No, Nara! God, no!"

"Ethan," I called out, but he flattened his palms against my chest and pumped, counting. When he moved to pinch my nose and then breathe into my mouth, I waved my hands to get his attention. "Ethan, I'm right here."

He kept going. While he pushed on my chest again, fear and anger filled his face. "Don't you die on me."

"I'm here!" I screamed, but he didn't hear me. That's when I realized that I saw the wind buffeting his hair and his fleece, but I didn't feel a thing.

I glanced down at myself and sat back on my heels, curling my hands into fists. I could see through my fists to my thighs underneath. I really was gone.

Jerking my gaze back to Ethan, I started to get up and move closer to him, when the sound of hundreds of birds' flapping wings and loud cawing rose above the wind.

A bald man, shrouded in a flowing cloak and outlined by a violet blue glow, moved toward us across the soccer field in an unhurried, otherworldly glide. The birds heralded his approach, surrounding the figure completely. Though they never came in contact or prevented the person's movement, they dove and swirled all around his frame, creating a kind of sketchy outline.

His eerie presence carried a sense of finality that sent a chill rippling through me. *This,* I felt, just as sure as if someone had dumped a cup of ice water down my back. The closer it got, the weaker I felt. Jumping up, I moved to Ethan's other side. Putting more distance between myself and the unknown man, I instantly felt more like myself again.

"Do you see him?" I called over the wind to Ethan, but he wasn't looking directly at the person. He was squinting at the birds, as if he were trying to figure out what they were doing.

I realized Ethan couldn't see what I did. The figure wasn't something he was supposed to see, because it was coming for me.

Death.

I tried to grab Ethan's arm, to shake him and tell him what the birds were trying to show him, but my fingers went right through his bicep.

Somehow Ethan must've figured it out, because formidable fury filled his face. My scalp tingled as energy surged in the stormy air stirring around us. "You can't have her," Ethan gritted out as he shoved his hands, palms-outward, toward the birds and figure.

The pocket of energy rushed away from us at the same time the birds and man flew backward, tumbleweeds at its mercy. I blinked, both amazed and thankful for what he'd done. *How had he done that?* I wondered, but Ethan was speaking to my unconscious self once more.

"You can't be gone," he said as he began to pump my chest again. The figure had recovered and was moving toward us again at a fast, angry clip.

Tears streaked Ethan's cheeks as he tilted my head and prepared to blow air into my lungs once more. "Don't leave me," he said desperately. "I love you!" Raw emotion carried on his words as he pressed his lips to mine.

I coughed and blinked until my blurry vision finally focused.

Ethan was leaning over me. "Nara? Thank God!" He touched my cheek, elation and relief filling his gaze. "Can you hear me? Say something. How do you feel?"

My chest ached and my throat felt scratchy, but I cupped my hand over his and rasped, "Thank you."

Kissing my forehead, Ethan gently scooped me into his arms. "We need to take you to the hospital. Have you checked out to make sure you're okay."

I pressed close to his warm fleece and shook my head. "I want to go home." I didn't want strangers poking and prodding me for hours in a strange hospital bed. I just wanted Ethan.

"Nara."

"Please, Ethan," I said, making sure my voice sounded strong.

Ethan sighed and started walking toward the parking lot at a brisk pace. "I got worried while I was waiting at your house," he said, glancing down at me.

Cool air blew around us, making me shiver. "The wind kn—knocked the go—goal on me. I could only ho—hold it up for so long." The cold was starting to get to me and I couldn't keep my teeth from chattering.

When he started to bypass the bench, I said, "My so—soccer bag."

Ethan tightened his hold on me. "You're freezing. I'll put you in my car first and then get your bag and the soccer equipment."

"I ca—can't leave my car here overnight. It might get stripped for parts if I do that."

He frowned. "Are you sure you're okay to drive?"

I felt a little weak, but it wasn't very far. "Yeah, I can handle driving two miles."

"This insanity will stop," he said through gritted teeth, his breath expelling in frosty plumes as he stopped to let me grab my soccer bag.

The rain started coming down the moment he set me next to my car. Ignoring the mud and grass caking my body, I slipped inside and popped my trunk, thankful for the towel I'd thought to lay across my seat before practice started.

After Ethan had stowed my bag in the trunk, I rolled the window down halfway so I could hear him over the wind. "I'm going back to get the rest of the equipment and then I'll meet you at your house."

Nodding, I blinked against the rain pinging my face with frigid droplets. There was so much I wanted to say to him, but right now wasn't the time. "I'll see you in a few minutes."

"I'll be right behind you. This ends tonight." He tapped my window, telling me to roll it up.

After Ethan's parting comment, I really wanted to hear what he had to say about my close call tonight. Had he figured out a way to help me with Fate? Ethan had been right. Fate had every intention of killing me, which it would've accomplished, if Ethan hadn't shown up when he did.

I ached all over and had never been so glad to see my driveway. Once I started my dirty clothes in the washing machine, I immediately headed for a hot shower.

Twenty minutes later, dried hair swept up into a ponytail, I came out of my bathroom, tugging a long-sleeved heather green t-shirt down over a tank top and jeans. My chest didn't hurt as much after my shower, but I had a feeling I would be sore for a while.

Opening the front door, I used my foot to block it from being blown by the gusting wind and peered through the pouring rain. Ethan sat in my driveway, playing drums on his steering wheel. Bet he was listening to that new band we both liked *Cracking Knuckles*. I waved him in.

By the time he came through the front door, his fleece was completely soaked. Beckoning him to follow, I walked through the living room and into the hall, saying over my shoulder, "Take off your wet stuff and we'll stick them in the dryer."

When he set a notebook on the rumbling washing machine, and then tossed his fleece and t-shirt into the dryer, my stomach fluttered. Shutting the door, I turned the machine on low and stretched to reach for a clean hand towel on the rack above my head.

Ethan's warmth covered my entire backside as he leaned against me and grabbed the towel. "How are you feeling?" he asked, handing me the towel and then moving back.

I didn't want him to treat me like I was going to shatter. "I feel much better now that I've had a shower." Swallowing the giddiness that had surfaced when he pressed against me, I turned and stepped toward him to spread the towel over his head. "You're soaked," I said, scrubbing at his wet hair.

"I've never been more scared in my life," Ethan murmured as he gripped my hips and pulled me close. Sliding his nose along my cheek and into my hair, he inhaled deeply, "Mmm, I love the way you smell. Like sun-warmed air after a spring rain."

His sweet comment made my nerves jump and my stomach tense with excitement. Abandoning the hair drying, I tossed the towel on top of the machine behind me, then wrapped my arms around his neck. "Is 'too good to describe' a smell?" I asked, snuggling into his warmth.

Ethan pressed his lips to my forehead, murmuring, "I thought I'd seen your entire practice before the storm woke me."

I pressed my face against his jaw. "It's okay. I'm fine."

His arms tightened around me. "No, it's not. I knew you were coming here straight after practice was over, so I didn't worry, but then I got another vibe. I'm sorry that I didn't get there a few minutes earlier."

He sounded so upset I pressed my hands to his face. "If it weren't for you, I'd be dead. Don't apologize to me."

"That was beyond too close, Nara." He looked tortured as he searched my face. "I don't know what I'd have done if you hadn't started breathing again."

My chest squeezed at the very real reminder of my brush with death. "What happened?" I asked, setting my hands on his shoulders.

He blew out a sharp breath. "When I got there you were unconscious. After I moved the goal, I realized you weren't breathing. I only had minutes to get your heart going again, so I immediately started CPR." He hesitated for a second, then continued, "It took several tries, but finally you started breathing on your own."

I shook my head in amazement. "The last thing I remember before I blacked out was how hard it was to breathe." I pressed a kiss to his jaw. "Thank you again for saving me."

Ethan squeezed my waist, his voice rasping in my ear. "Don't scare me like that again."

"Did anything else happen?" I hoped he'd tell me how he managed to fight off Death.

"I didn't feel Fate, if that's what you're asking." His gaze narrowed. "But I'm sure he was skulking around somewhere. I think I might've figured out a way to stop him."

Ethan didn't say a word about what I'd seen while I was dead. *Had I dreamed seeing Death coming for me*? *Did dying somehow allow me to have a normal—read: crazy, out there—dream, since I no longer had a future to dream about*?

Ethan was right. Fate was my biggest problem right now. "If it weren't for that raven swooping down in front of me, I never would've turned and seen the goal falling toward me."

"Animals can sense a disturbance in Nature. The bird was probably trying to warn you." he paused, then asked, "Did you ever hear from your dad?"

"I don't know." Walking into the kitchen, I retrieved my phone from my backpack's inside pocket. There weren't any messages. "Not yet."

Ethan had followed me and I glanced at the notebook he'd tucked in his hand. "Why did you bring your drawings?"

He gestured toward the couch. "Let's sit."

Setting my cell phone on the island, I winced at the dull ache in my chest, then walked with him over to the sofa. "How's the wound on your shoulder?" I asked.

"All healed." He turned so I could see. His wound was just a faint pink circle now. I gingerly touched the new skin, then slid my hand across his shoulder to the feather, running my fingers over the tattoo. When he shuddered, I said, "It's a shame you can't see this feather up close. It's so real looking I feel like I could pluck it right off your back."

I rose up on my toes and pressed my lips to his skin. I wanted to show him I thought his tattoo was beautiful and not something that freaked me out.

Exhaling a shaky breath, Ethan turned and sat down quickly on the couch. "Let's talk before you distract me even more."

I loved the fact I could distract him so easily, but forced myself to focus as I sat beside him.

When Ethan opened his notebook, I tried not to look at the graphic images as he flipped through them, but my gaze was drawn, despite my squeamish stomach. Ethan blew past a picture he'd drawn of me slipping the telephone into the end table drawer, then turned to a page he'd dog-eared.

"What do you see?" he asked, placing the notebook in my lap.

I studied the drawing of me standing near the payphone at Walmart. Ethan's artistic skills were truly awe-inspiring. The art leapt off the page. "You should enroll in college art classes. Your talent is truly amazing."

His lips crooked as if pleased, but he clasped my chin and turned my attention back to the page. "What do you *see*, Nara?"

Thunder boomed as I scanned the picture once more. "I'm dressed in winter clothes and standing next to a payphone. The building, streetlights and shadows are in the background. I look very tense and worried, which I was."

Ethan quickly flipped to another page he'd marked. "And here?"

I studied the second drawing. "I'm on the phone. I have an anxious look on my face as I glance over my shoulder."

"What else?" Lightning flashed through the room, highlighting his expectant expression.

I furrowed my brow. "There's a dark sense of tension in this picture, though I don't know why I feel that way."

Ethan turned to another page. "This is you talking to Jody outside her car. What do you see?"

I studied myself. "I'm fisting my hands. I look anxious. Tension is all over my face and in the way I'm standing. It wasn't as dark outside as you've drawn it though."

Rain pummeled the front door while Ethan turned to yet another page. It was the scene from the hall when I'd tried to warn Sophia. "Whoa," I said, an eerie shiver passing through me. Blinking at the image, I pointed to the paper. "Why is there a dark shadow all around me? It was the middle of the day."

"Exactly. That dark shadow is in every one of these pictures." As Ethan flipped through all the pictures once more, I saw what he was talking about.

My gaze locked with his. "I've never seen any shadows when these events happened. And how is it that you saw them? Except for the event with Sophia, none of these were *from* my dreams, but real-life outcomes *I* initiated after my dreams."

"Remember I told you that I used to see flashes of images in my mind whenever I touched people. Each of these scenes were outside of the 'dream' I'd had about your normal day. I figured they might have something to do with your negative vibes—the reason I'd taken your dreams in the first place—so each time a scene came to me outside of your dreams, I drew them."

Ethan flipped to a few more drawings: the one of me riding in the car to Farmville with my mom, another of me laying on the floor at Aunt Sage's, surrounded by the dogs and the next one of me diving for a ball in goal during practice.

"There aren't any shadows in these pictures, Nara. They've only shown up in the scenes where you were trying to change the outcome of something you'd dreamed."

Rumbling thunder shook the house and the lights flickered. My pulse accelerated and I reflexively dug my nails deep into my palm. "You think the shadows are Fate, don't you? I noticed you called it 'him'."

Ethan nodded. "After I made the connection to the shadows in my drawings, *it* became a *him*."

"But I can't see him, so how do I stop Fate?"

Ethan threaded his warm fingers with mine. "I have an idea how you might be able to see Fate. I don't know if it'll work, but I think it's worth trying if you'll trust me."

I wasn't ready to face Fate as a physical entity. He was ominous enough as an unseen presence. But I folded my fingers around Ethan's, feeling more confident. "I trust you."

Running his finger in a gentle caress along the bend of my thumb, Ethan searched my face. "Do you trust me enough to sleep with me?"

CHAPTER 23

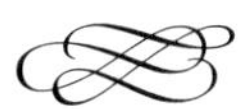

"What?" I stood and gulped my excitement and apprehension, even as my hand remained locked with his.

Ethan followed me, folding his hand tighter around mine. A burst of heat shot across my cheeks, and I involuntarily swept my gaze along his bare chest and defined abs. The dragon tattoo only enhanced his earthiness and dark mysterious edges. Without even trying, he was devastatingly beautiful and dangerously seductive. Warmth flowed like melted chocolate sliding through my veins, its rich thickness slowing my ability to think. "Well, I—"

His lips twitched in amusement, even as his blue eyes sparked. "I meant *sleep* with me. Like, literally."

"Oh." I released the breath I'd been holding and felt a brief stab of disappointment. Loosening my tight grip on his hand, I squinted in confusion. "I'm not sure how that will help—"

Before I could finish, he pulled me close and spoke in a velvet purr in my ear, "Loved your reaction though."

I pressed my hot face to his jaw and felt him smile.

Kissing my forehead, he pulled back, his expression serious once more. "Back to my idea. I think the crystal your aunt gave you is what allowed you to see my dreams. If you wear the necklace and fall asleep while I'm holding you, maybe you'll be able to see your own dreams through my eyes. In other words, you might be able to see the shadows I've been seeing."

I shuddered at the idea of wearing the crystal necklace again, but his idea was worth trying. "If this works, how does this help me face Fate?"

Ethan's eyes held warmth and encouragement. "The shadow seems to show himself when you're interfering in the natural course. You'll just have to try to change someone else's Fate."

I frowned. "But I've never consciously tried to manipulate something within my dream, since my dream is just a preview of my next day. I'm just going through my day."

"Hmmm." He gnawed his bottom lip for a second, thinking. "I still think you can make this work, mainly because you'll be watching yourself go through your daily routine."

"You think I'll see myself like you do?"

"That's the hope. That picture I drew of you hiding the phone in the end table drawer? That was the night your dad was supposed to call. Even though you'd already prevented him from calling by contacting the phone company, you hid the phone in the drawer. Were you trying to make sure?"

"Exactly. I wasn't taking any chances."

"Did you notice the slight shadow in the background behind you?"

"No. Was Fate there?"

"He was, but just barely. If you can do something like that in your dream tonight, you might be able to get him to show himself, however faint he may be. And then you can confront him."

I scowled doubtfully and Ethan squeezed my hands. "Don't you think it's worth a try?"

"I'm scared."

He pulled me close and his chest felt so warm. "I'll be with you, holding you tight. I promise I won't let anything happen to you."

I marveled that he cared enough to come up with a plan to help me. "I'm so lucky I met you."

He kissed the tip of my nose. "I'm the lucky one."

"Then if we're going to sleep, we may as well be comfortable." Taking a step back, I pulled my long-sleeved t-shirt off. Static electricity crackled as the shirt dragged against the white spaghetti-strapped tank top I'd left on.

Ethan waited for me to shut off the kitchen light before he followed me upstairs to my room.

Thunder rolled, followed by lightning strobes as we entered my room. Crawling across my bed, I turned on the tiny lamp on my nightstand and retrieved the crystal necklace from my jewelry box.

Ethan kicked off his shoes and took the necklace. Sitting beside me, he slid the chain over my head. When he tugged my comforter and sheets back and bolts of static flashed, Ethan's hand fisted on the bedding. He didn't say a word, but I couldn't miss the protective anger in his eyes as he pulled me down beside him. For several seconds, we laid side-by-side, staring up at the ceiling. Then he hooked his arm around my waist and gathered me against him, spooning my back to his chest.

Snuggling close to his warmth, I listened to the storm raging outside. Lightning lit up the entire room, highlighting the dragon tattoo on his forearm. I stared at the symbols inside the flames' tips. There was an Egyptian Ankh, a Native American medicine wheel, a Celtic cross, a rising phoenix, the Hindu Om symbol. On and on they continued.

I slowly ran my finger across his tattoo. "What do all the symbols mean?"

He brought my fingers to his mouth, kissing each knuckle. "They're for protection, just like the dragon is a symbol of protection."

"But why all the different ones?"

Ethan tugged on the elastic band in my hair, freeing my ponytail. "I've come in contact with people with different religious beliefs," he said as he slid his fingers through my hair. Lifting the tips to his nose, he inhaled. "Their issues are entwined with their cultural and religious beliefs, so I do what I can to protect myself."

I hadn't thought about the religious perspective as it pertained to the darkness he saw, but it made sense that he would experience different kinds of "negative energy" based on the sender's belief system. Lacing my hand with his, I lifted our linked hands and kissed the dragon on his forearm. "I'm in awe that you figured out how to protect yourself."

"Not in every way," he murmured, sounding frustrated. Was he thinking about the feather tattoo?

Thunder crashed as I glanced over my shoulder. "Did you find anything on the web about your feather tattoo?"

Lightning illuminated his blue eyes a split second before the power failed, sending the room into total darkness. "Nothing new," he said right before his lips touched mine.

Caught by surprise, I gasped, then pressed my lips to his and flattened my palm against his chest. I wanted to experience every contour of his sleek muscles.

Cupping my face, he pulled me toward him. Fingers slipped into my hair, clasping my head as he deepened our kiss. My insides burned and I pushed closer with a blistering need to be as connected to him as possible.

Ethan's fingers curled tight in my hair. I felt the tension in his hold before he broke our kiss. Grasping my waist, he pressed his forehead against mine and exhaled several harsh breaths. "Nara, we need to stop before we both don't want to."

"I don't think I want to," I said, molding myself to him.

Lightning flashed again, highlighting his pained smile. "It's good to know I'm not the only one who lays in bed at night fantasizing about holding you like this."

Before I could respond, he rolled me over and hooked his arm around my waist. Spooning me tight against his body once more, he whispered into my hair, "I love you, Sunshine."

My insides melted, hearing it for real this time. Ethan had shown his love for me in so many ways. Why was my selfish heart locking away the "I love you so much it hurts" silent scream in my mind? I felt the emotions, but why couldn't I say them? Wrapping my arms around his on my waist, tears filled my eyes as I tried my best to tell him what he meant to me. "I don't know what I'd do without you."

"You'd be devastated," he said with a hollow laugh, then slid his leg between mine, locking us together. "I won't be able to prevent you from seeing my dreams, Nara. Just know that you're protected as long as I hold you. If this works, then you'll eventually move on to seeing yourself in the dreams and that's when you'll need to look for the shadow."

It suddenly occurred to me that if Ethan saw my dreams like watching a movie, then he saw…my face heated instantly. "Um, since you see my whole day, where are you when I'm taking a shower?"

His lips touched my ear. "Waiting in your bedroom."

Yeah, right. I groaned in embarrassment. "All my secrets are revealed."

"I don't know exactly how you feel about me, Nara. That secret is still yours. And about the other… I've respected your privacy."

Pleased heat shot down my neck and across my chest. *Now I knew why he hadn't seen Fate attack me in the shower.* "Wow, that's impressive. It would've been so easy to—"

"That's cheating." He kissed the curve of my ear. "If I ever see you without your clothes, it'll be *your* choice and not in some dream."

Ethan's sincere comment, spoken in his deep, husky voice, sent a jolt of pleasure shooting through me. *Tell him you love him, damn it!* What was wrong with me? I quietly sniffed back tears of frustration.

The thunder and lightning were starting to fade to distant rumbles and faint blips, but the gusty wind continued to blow rain in a watery, thrumming rush against my bedroom window. The rhythmic sound, combined with the relaxing sensation of Ethan's fingers sliding through my hair, lulled me. Closing my eyes, I drifted to sleep.

"ETHAN?" I whispered, holding my hands straight out as I stumbled in total darkness. I heard thunder in the distance, but no lightning cut through the blackness. I stepped carefully, hoping to find a door or wall with a light switch.

Something zoomed past, a wave of rotting flesh and sharp

sulfur following its wake. The acrid smell burned my nose and throat, making the tiny hairs on my arms rise up. A scurrying sound preceded a faint hiss. I froze and gulped, hoping it didn't sense me. Claws scrabbled and I heard it turning around. Whatever it was, it had detected my presence. Nails gouged the ground and a grunt echoed in my direction as if it had bolted toward me. I knew I couldn't outrun it, so I jerked my hands up and tensed, ready for the impact.

Lightning illuminated the black space for a split second, but it was long enough to highlight the heinous creature. A thick-barrel chest and powerful arms were closing in on me, claws extended in shredding mode. Its blackened teeth dripped with blood and saliva, the snarling maw ready to devour. I let out a terrified scream just as someone gripped my waist and pulled me backward.

The creature must've reached for me, because searing, knife-like pain suddenly yanked at my left thigh, tearing and ripping at the flesh and muscles. Crying out, I jerked my leg back and gagged when I smelled the iron-rich scent of my blood. Warm liquid spurted down my thigh, a thick whoosh gushing with my rampant heartbeat.

The scene changed. I was standing in a dimly-lit living room I didn't recognize. Thunder popped, followed by flashes of lightning. I glanced down at my thigh and let out a sob of relief. My skin and jeans were intact.

In a nearby room, someone screamed. I started toward the sound, but my left thigh cramped, stopping me cold. Grabbing hold of the fireplace mantel, my fingers bumped a football trophy. The inscription on the brass plate read: *Blue Ridge High School Varsity Football.*

The yelling escalated, a high-pitched voice screeching at ear-piercing decibels. I gritted my teeth, ignoring the dull pain radiating through my leg as I pushed open the swinging door into a kitchen. A two-headed snake monster with a human-like body held an empty steaming pan. The monster hissed at the creature cowering on the floor in a football jersey covered with dripping red liquid. Was that blood?

The smell of burned skin and spaghetti sauce permeated the

air, and yet the attacking monster continued forward, moving toward the bent over figure, swinging the hot pan. Excruciating pain laced across my back while fear immobilized me.

I tried to yell, to demand the snake-monster stop, but tightness cinched around my waist, sucking me out of the room. I screamed and grabbed for the invisible band pulling me back, but my fingers only snagged on my own clothes. Then everything went peacefully black and soft as if I'd been surrounded by silk.

Rubbing my face against the softness, I inhaled the earthy scent, feeling safe and protected. I welcomed the quiet tranquility. Clung to it. Only moments had passed when a faint whisper of pale light began to seep through the darkness. The serenity was about to leave me.

"No," I pleaded, grasping at invisible folds, hoping to keep the dark cloak of safety wrapped around me forever. Music filled my ears and I was in a bedroom, but kind of above it. I frowned at the perspective. I wasn't this tall. I started to take a step but almost lost my balance. Glancing down, I was standing on a chair. This wasn't my room, but it felt like mine.

Razor-sharp fingernails dug into my shoulders, while rough hands shook me hard. My head snapped around, my brain sloshing in my skull. I was so dizzy my head lolled from shoulder to shoulder. Then cruel words poured in, the dam opening full blast.

"We hate you." Voices repeated over and over.

A horrible image blipped in my mind, making me cringe.

"You're acting crazy," a man said in a freaked-out voice.

Another graphic picture flashed. I blinked. "Stop. Go away!"

"You're embarrassing me. What's wrong with you?" a woman's shrill words echoed in my ear.

"Go crawl in a hole and die, you freak!" A guy my age taunted, full of spite and hatred.

My heart pounded hard as if it were trying to burst through my chest. The screeching voices and the terrifying scenes wouldn't stop. Over and over the insults came in loud bursts, as if people were standing all around me, but I was alone in my room. How was this happening? Squeezing my eyes shut, I tried to shake away the horror.

Fingers bit into my shoulders once more. I gasped at the surreal pain. My eyes flew open. A grotesque skeletal creature with red eyes and long curling horns clacked his boney jaw at me. Bits of bloody muscle and sinew were barely keeping its jaw together. He looked like he'd been flayed, yet he stood in front of me, a menacing, powerful force.

"You want to die," he said. "I see it in your eyes."

My stomach churned and I stumbled, almost falling off the chair. I shook my head in violent jerks. "I'm not crazy. I'm not."

A long skeletal arm waved. "You're nuttier than a fruit-cake." The beast glanced down at his clawed, emaciated hand, then his red, hostile eyes jerked to me. "Do you think I'm real?"

I clenched my teeth. "You're not real."

He backhanded me, his boney knuckles cracking against my cheekbone. "Felt real as shit, didn't it?" he mocked, evil laughter echoing.

I glared, trying hard not to shake in front of him. He was enjoying my fear. Feeding off it.

Nodding toward the ceiling fan, he smiled. "Go ahead. If you do it, I'll leave you alone." He shoved his face close to mine and promised with a whisper, "Forever."

His rancid smell gagged me. Salt suddenly burned my cracked lips. *Tears*. I was crying. The creature grinned then, and with a flick of his hand, the head-banging music on my stereo upped a notch, pumping to the rapid beat of my heart.

"I just want it to stop," I whispered.

"Poof and that's it." He snapped his fingers and leered. "For....ev....er."

I wanted to throw up, but exhaustion and hysteria conspired, demanding relief from the constant din barraging my mind. Peace sounded so good. My foot hit the back of the chair, knocking it away.

The room tilted, then jerked and my throat burned as if it were on fire. The need to breathe, to suck in air overwhelmed. I clawed at the tight extension cord, but the skulled beast yanked at my hands, pulling them down. "Don't fight it." He sounded pleased, almost serene. Releasing my hands, he folded his boney fingers inward slowly, the long claws curling toward his fist. With each bend of his knuckles, the room blacked in and out, my throat crushing bit by bit.

Someone grabbed my legs and screamed my name.

Blood rushed back to my brain and I vaguely heard, "No, Ethan! Oh, God please, no!"

The demon beast was gone and Samson had his arms wrapped around my hips. "Help me. I believe you, little brother. I believe you." He pressed his face against my waist. "I'm so sorry. I should've come home sooner. Please, I can't do this without your help. Lift the cord off."

He believed me? My arms felt like ten-pound weights had been tied to them, but I clumsily managed to pull the cord off my neck.

We fell to the carpet and Samson yanked me close with rough, unsteady movements. Tears streaked down his cheeks and his trembling hands felt like a vise on my face as he forced me to look at him. "We're leaving tonight! You're coming to live with me."

When the soft darkness started to surround me once more, this time I fought it. "I want to stay," I croaked. My throat burned and my face felt bloated and puffy with tears, but I wanted to see more of Ethan and Samson. "I'm so sorry, Ethan." I whispered as the wash of silky darkness swept over me, bathing me in instant quietude. Folded in its warmth and assurance of peace, it occurred to me that this darkness was the opposite of white light, yet it held strong positive qualities. It was the brightest kind of darkness. A calming safety net, like my dreams were for Ethan.

A faint flutter reached my ears, and then a pale light began to bleed into the darkness. The peacefulness was about to leave me again. I grabbed at the invisible dark folds of safety, and for a split second, an image rippled across them, distorting with the movement. Was it round? I strained to see, but gasped when it disintegrated in my grasp. I could've sworn my fingers brushed against feathers.

I stood in the sunlight in my kitchen, watching my mom

turn a charred hamburger over in the frying pan. As I scrubbed the tears from my face, a distinct pinging sounded from the island beside me.

Mom called out, "Inara! Phone."

"What?" I heard myself reply from upstairs.

Mom leaned away from the pan, speaking louder. "A message on your phone—" she started to say, then sighed and moved the pan to another burner.

When I realized she was going to pick up my cell phone, I remembered my dad was supposed to contact me. I heard myself coming down the stairs, but I'd be too late to stop her. Before my mom could glance at the display, the dream me stepped in front of her, thinking I could somehow block her view. Her hand went right through my body to pick up the phone. Dream me shuddered at the strange sensation just as I walked into the kitchen.

Mom turned the cell phone toward me. Shock and hurt flickered in her gaze.

The text message from Aunt Sage read, *Am still trying to find your dad.*

CHAPTER 24

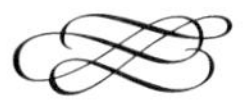

"What does that mean?" Mom asked, pointing to my cell.

Dream me stepped inside my body. I took the phone and as I tried to think of an excuse, the screen saver popped up; it was a picture I'd snapped of Bo, Luke and Duke. "Picture," I blurted.

"Picture?"

"Um, yeah. We're doing a project in Biology about...genetics. We're supposed to bring in pictures of our parents."

Tension eased from her face. "Well, there are plenty of pictures of your father and me." She slowly walked over to the built-in cabinets in our living room, where photo albums were entombed with a film of decade-old dust.

Out of the corner of my eye, I saw a faint shadow appear to my right and felt its oppressive coldness pushing against me. The last thing I wanted was for Mom to look at old family pictures and dwell on the past. Before she could pull out an album, I said, "Actually, I needed a picture of Dad when he was a kid, not an adult. That's why I asked Aunt Sage if she might have some." Holding up my phone, I continued, "Guess she's not having much luck. Do you have any of you when you were little?"

Mom looked disappointed, then her eyes lit up. "Wait. I

think I might have a couple pictures of me when I was in elementary school up in my room. I'll go look."

As soon as she disappeared upstairs, I straightened my spine, turned to the shadow beside me, and spoke in a forceful tone. "I see you hovering around me like a cranky old man with nothing better to do than butt into people's lives. My fate is my own, not yours to swat around at your whim."

The shadow quickly moved away from me, but then the room began to spin and I was suddenly in the middle of a forest. Sun streaked through the trees, while birds chirped and other forest sounds echoed in the dense woods.

The fog grew darker and a little more solid until he resembled the outline of a human form. It was an odd experience to watch dark smoke morph into a face with a menacing expression and empty, soulless space where eyes should be. The shadow glided close. "You're messing in *my* domain, little girl," he said in a cold, hard tone, then spread his arms wide, as if the world were his to command. "*Fate* is my power to wield, not yours!"

The outrage radiating from Fate made my stomach twist, but if I didn't stand up to him, he'd continue to haunt me or worse, kill me.

Narrowing my gaze on the shadow, I glanced upward to the trees where the birds were chirping, then stared into his bottomless eye sockets. "Ravens warned me each time you tried to harm me. Could that be because they knew what you were doing went against nature? That it fell outside the natural order?"

The shadow curled his hands into fists and blipped in and out. He was moving at such a high frequency, I could barely track him. Finally his form settled and solidified again. Staring over my shoulder, he snarled. "You mean those ravens?"

The moment I turned, deep grocks and reverberating croaks flooded my ears. Twenty-five feet away, a huge swarm of ravens had formed a fast-moving cyclone and Ethan was standing in the middle of it with his eyes closed. "Ethan!" I called out, but the birds' cacophony grew even louder. Their swarm spread until the wall of shiny black wings blocked

Ethan from my view. I had no idea what the ravens' presence or their odd behavior meant, nor did I understand why Ethan had finally shown up in my dream. Panic welled. I wanted to run toward him, but my feet wouldn't move, no matter how hard I tried.

"Now I understand how you're able to see me," Fate said, sounding irritated.

When I saw Fate staring at the cyclone of birds, his eye sockets focused in thin slits, I knew he'd prevented me from going to Ethan. He was toying with my emotions and I was sick of it. "You're playing with my fate, defying the laws of nature to suit your need for vengeance."

"And you're not?" he roared, snapping his soulless attention back to me.

"I have this ability for a reason. It *is* my nature."

Fate shot forward, thrusting his misty face directly in front of me. His arctic disdain washed over my features as he narrowed his pitted eyes, sneering, "Ask your father how 'using his nature' worked out for him. Oh, wait…" Leaning back, he crossed his arms, his expression chillingly smug. "You can't, since he didn't care enough to stick around."

"He cares!" I wanted to believe saying the words made them true.

"You probably remember this…hold on, you should dress for this 'special' occasion," Fate said haughtily as he lifted a shadowy hand and suddenly I was wearing a billowy red formal dress and heels. When I glared at Fate, he pointed to my right as a scene materialized in the air.

A dark-haired man laid a book on the nightstand, then leaned over a young blonde-headed girl and pulled her covers up around her.

My heart pounded as I gobbled each movement, taking in every nuance between my dad and me. It must've been soon after the accident, because I had the butterfly bandage on my forehead.

"That's the last story," Dad said.

I looked at him with adoring eyes. "Night, Daddy. Thank you for taking me to get ice cream today."

He pressed a kiss to the top of my head, then straightened. "You're welcome. I love you, Nari."

I snuggled under my covers, answering without hesitation, "I love you, too, Daddy. See you in the morning."

As the picture faded away, a lump knotted my throat. I didn't remember this particular night between my father and me. I must've blocked it out, because it was too painful. That was the last time I'd seen my dad.

"So touching, I think I feel tears coming on," Fate said with a snicker.

As Fate's solid shape morphed into a patch of rain, creating puddles at my feet, I lifted the dress's hem to keep it from getting wet. At least I knew why I hated ice cream and why I had such a hard time saying 'I love you'. Both were the last memories I had with my dad.

Solidifying once more, Fate's tone hardened. "Here's a dose of reality, Nara."

A flick of his hand and a new scene materialized. My father stood in the doorway of our house. As he glanced back inside, I half-expected to see my younger self run up and hug his leg. Instead, my father took a step to the right, lifted a suitcase and then walked out with an impassive look on his face. Loading the suitcase in his car, he drove off and never once looked back.

As the scene dissolved, I lowered the dress to the damp ground, searing hurt knifing through me. I wanted to punch Fate for obliterating the sweet memory between my father and me. Fate wanted me to witness how easy it was for him to desert us. I ached, but I wasn't going to let Fate's twisted mental games distract me from my goal—forcing him to back off.

Clenching my fists, I stepped forward and shoved my face into his shadowy features, disturbing the solid shape. I felt perverse pleasure in wiping the condescension off his face as I spoke into his dark, misty form. "You might be Fate—"

"Might be?" he snarled, cinching tight around me.

My breath whooshed out like a sponge being squeezed dry, but I'd had plenty of practice with Fate's tactics. Gritting my teeth, I wheezed, "I know what you're doing is wrong. You can't—"

Cold hands snaked around my neck, cutting off my words as he dug deep into my windpipe. "I *am* Fate!" he snarled and pressed harder.

As my vision blurred, I tried to pull his shadowy hands off my throat, but my fingers went right through him. Somehow I knew that if I died in this dream, I wouldn't wake up.

"Want to know the beauty of this scenario?" Fate whispered in my ear as I tried to hold onto consciousness.

His eye sockets moved to look at me. "What? No response? You'll have a crushed larynx and bruises around your throat, and yet there'll be only one person who could've done it."

God, no. He intended to kill me in my sleep and for Ethan to take the blame for my death. My heart pounded and my chest burned. I tried to struggle harder, but I was losing the ability to stand on my own.

A sudden blur of black drew across my vision right before the pressure on my throat stopped. Coughing in a lungful of air, I stumbled back and rubbed my throat as an invisible force shoved Fate away.

Snarling, Fate rushed toward me once more, but a wall of ravens swooped between us. Fate bounced off them like they were an electrified force field.

My hair blew wildly as the birds turned to circle around me like they'd done Ethan. This time they were completely silent. Only the flapping of their wings sounded in the woods.

An arrogant smirk registered on Fate's face right before he disintegrated into mist, then moved through the wall of birds.

I blinked in shock as he began to reform in front of me.

Effugio! A commanding voice shot through my mind. I didn't understand the word, but I felt the urgency.

The order spurred me into action. Just as Fate finished reanimating, I grabbed the voluminous skirt's hem and shot away.

The hair on the back of my neck rose and my breath escaped in frantic pants as I ran through the dense woods, the heels dragging at the thick leaves coating the forest floor. Everywhere I looked, the forest seemed to go on forever, nothing but long lines of trees and endless darkness. I gulped in more air. I wouldn't be able to keep up this pace forever.

Just when my legs started to tremble, something shoved me hard from behind. Flying through the air, I missed a thick tree by mere inches when I landed with a bone-jarring thump among the slippery leaves. Damp earth filled my nose and wet leaves stuck to my hands and arms as I painfully rolled to my back and tried to regain my breath.

Fate approached, menace emanating off him in a display of vivid red sparks surrounding his dense frame. "I will not be overridden anymore!"

I struggled to get up, but couldn't move. An invisible weight held me pinned to the ground. The swarm of birds returned, this time diving straight for Fate, disintegrating his form. But as each bird passed through Fate, I heard screeches of pain, while the smell of burning feathers and flesh wafted in the wind.

As the ravens' bodies hit the forest floor in burning clumps of ash and bone, tears brimmed my eyes. I sobbed, begging the birds to stop.

Nara! The same strange voice drew my attention.

Ethan squatted beside me. His expression was calm, but his eyes weren't Ethan's deep blue—they shined black, like obsidian. He said something I couldn't decipher. I blinked, trying to understand. When I realized he was speaking Latin, the words began to align in my mind.

Focus on me, he'd commanded. His lips never moved, yet I heard his voice speaking in my head, full of authority. It sounded like Ethan, but different—it sounded ancient and slightly out of sync, as if the words entering my thoughts were a collection of many speaking at once.

Curved dark shapes on either side of Ethan's head blocked out the forest, and as he glanced at the birds battling with Fate, the two shadowy arches flanking him seemed to flutter with repressed fury. His dark eyes cut to me. *They're giving their lives for you. Listen to me.*

Choked with fear and confusion, I could only nod.

You must speak *of free will. I cannot tell you more. Hurry.*

Warm wind blew across my face and then Ethan was gone.

"Ethan," I reached for him, grasping air. Fate was winning the battle with the ravens. *You must* speak *of free will*, Ethan had said. That was why Fate had tried to choke me earlier—to keep me from talking. My voice croaked, but I forced myself to speak as loud as I could.

"I exercise my *free will*. Stop screwing around with my fate!" As soon as the words "free will" left my mouth, the few remaining birds scattered among the trees.

An angry hiss reverberated throughout the woods and the heavy weight lifted off my chest. As I sat up, gasping for breath, Fate's powerful energy began to fade. Before his form fully disintegrated, he shot close. I cringed when he bumped against me, sliding his cold breath along my cheekbone in an icy lick of disdain. "I might not know *his* fate, but I know yours."

He was talking about Ethan. *Why wouldn't he know Ethan's fate?*

Fate continued, "I'm the least of your worries, Nara. You'll come to me again one day."

"Never!" I hissed.

Fate smirked. "And I will ask for something in return." As the last remnants of his misty form faded away, assured laughter echoed eerily through the woods, sending a shiver rocking through me.

I AWOKE, calling Ethan's name in a ragged whisper. He lay face down beside me, his hand locked around my wrist. Moving to wake him, I paused to stare at the tattoo on his back. My hand hovered over the image, fingers trembling.

Not only had the feather doubled in length, but it now decorated the center of sword's blade. The sword's hilt started at the top of Ethan's right shoulder, then angled across his spine, its sharp tip ending just above his left hip. A black and silver circular symbol was etched near the hilt, while swaths of purple and green iridescence glimmered along the center of the feather, standing vividly against the feather's darkness and the backdrop of shiny metal.

I studied the black and silver insignia; the two curved halves faced each other, making a complete circle. The black half looked like a raven and the other half was its twin in silver. *Why did the symbol look so familiar?*

"Hey," Ethan said, releasing my wrist to move to his side.

I rolled to face him and smiled when I didn't feel any crackly static in my covers. My triumph quickly faded as my line of sight caught on the red scarring along his neck. I couldn't tear my eyes away.

"I rarely have my own dreams. I wish you hadn't seen that," he said quietly.

He looked so upset, I leaned over and kissed the marks. "I don't know anyone who could've handled that kind of constant torture," I rasped. Leaning back, I met his self-conscious gaze. "Samson is my new favorite person."

The deep grooves around his mouth smoothed into a quick smile as he slid his fingers into my hair. "Did it work?"

I frowned, surprised by his question. "You didn't see my dream?"

His brows drew together. "I saw you talking to your mom in the kitchen about the text your aunt sent, then everything went blank."

"My aunt's having trouble finding my dad."

"Maybe he's out of town. Don't worry. She'll get in touch with him." He ran his thumb along my cheek, concern in his gaze. "Do you think it worked?"

I rubbed my hands across the covers, then ruffled my hair for good measure. "No more static."

Ethan stared at me pensively. "How was Fate?"

Why didn't he see me talking to Fate? Maybe only I could see myself talking to *my* Fate. Clasping his hand, I threaded our fingers together. "He's nasty and manipulative. You were right. He showed himself when I made up a story about Aunt Sage's text to keep Mom from freaking."

His fingers tightened around mine. "Why are you hoarse?"

"I told him he was cheating, which pissed him off. I think

screaming at him that I had free will and he needed to stop messing with my fate did the trick."

Ethan exhaled a sigh of relief and wrapped his arm around my waist. "Thank God. I'm glad it worked," he said, burying his nose in my hair.

There'd been no recognition on Ethan's face. He didn't have a clue that he'd helped me with Fate. *How was that possible?*

Burying my nose against his sleep-warmed chest, I murmured, "Me, too." Yet, I couldn't help but wonder about Fate's parting words. They'd been purposeful and mocking—he'd said just enough to leave me wondering what my future held.

Fate had seemed annoyed by the ravens' appearance in my dream, but he didn't see them as a threat, at least not until they'd tipped the scales by keeping him away from me. Why *had* the ravens sacrificed themselves to save me? Were they responsible for Ethan's presence in my dream as well? Is that why Ethan didn't remember helping me?

There was only one fact I was certain, the feather on Ethan's back *was* a raven's feather.

I trailed my fingers over his tattoo, worried how he would react when he learned it had changed again in a *big* way.

He touched my cheek, his blue eyes on alert. "What is it?"

I loved him so much.

"Come with me." Clasping his hand, I pulled him over to the mirror above my dresser.

When he saw the new tattoo on his back, the color drained from his face. "What the hell is that—"

"It's a sword." I turned his face toward me. He felt tense under my palms and his eyes were glazed over in disbelieving fury. As he gripped his forearm, rubbing his fingers hard along the dragon, I'd never seen him look so angry and scared.

"Ethan!" When he focused, I cupped his jaw. "I love you. I love *every* part of you."

Emotion flitted across his face as he pulled me close. Resting his lips against my hair, he exhaled a ragged, desperate whisper, "How can you love me? From one day to the next, I don't know what's going on with me."

"You're still *you*, Ethan." I pressed my face into his warm neck and wrapped my arms around his back to show him I wasn't going anywhere. "I think part of the answer to what's going on with you was in my dream."

"I was in your dream?"

"You weren't in my dream about my day, but when Fate zapped me into the woods to talk, you were there in the background, surrounded by a circle of flying ravens."

"Ravens?"

"Your eyes were closed and you looked relaxed, almost peaceful among them. I believe the feather on your back is a raven's feather. Don't forget, the ravens helped when Fate was going all vigilante on me." My eyes misted as I continued, "Many of them gave their lives to save me from him in my dream."

Ethan tensed once more. "Fate attacked you?"

"He tried to choke me, but a swarm of ravens threw him back."

Lifting my chin, Ethan rubbed his fingers along my throat, worry and guilt creasing his forehead. "I didn't think he could hurt you in a dream."

"The ravens protected me. But you were the one who told me what to say to make Fate back off."

Shock rolled across his features. "*I* told you what to say?"

"Yeah, in Latin."

He frowned. "I don't know Latin." Raking his hand through his hair, he blew out a breath of frustration. "God, I wish I could've seen your dream."

"It was you, but different."

Shaking his head, he sighed. "Maybe there's some connection with the ravens. I can't explain their sudden appearance in our lives any other way." His expression of wonder turned grim. "But a sword's not very peaceful, Nara."

"A sword can be defensive as well as offensive." Turning him around so his back faced the mirror, I pointed to the circular symbol above the feather near the hilt. "Can you see what this is?"

Ethan moved closer to see. "Is that a raven?"

I nodded. "The black raven is one half of the curve and the other half is the same, but in silver. They fit together like a puzzle. It reminds me of a Yin Yang symbol, a symbol of balance."

When he didn't respond, I continued, "I think the tattoo on your back is somehow connected to *your* dreams. I saw this symbol that night I wore the necklace and shared your dreams and then again last night."

Surprise flickered across his face. "You did? Why haven't I ever seen it?"

"I don't know, but whatever's happening with your tattoo… with you, we'll face it together."

He looked at me, his gaze swirling with love and turmoil. "Promise?"

Even though some parts of Ethan were still a dark mystery, I felt closer to him now more than ever. Pressing my chest to his, I drew a diagonal line from his left shoulder blade to his right hip. Moving my fingers to his right shoulder blade, I trailed them to his left hip, touching his entire tattoo. "Cross my heart. Together, 'til the wheels fall off."

* * *

Thank you for reading **BRIGHTEST KIND OF DARKNESS! LUCID (BRIGHTEST KIND OF DARKNESS, Book 2) is NOW AVAILABLE!**

LUCID

Once Nara combines her prophetic ability with Ethan's power to outsmart Fate at his own deadly cat-and-mouse game, she's more determined than ever to help Ethan learn the meaning behind the raven sword tattoo that suddenly appeared on his back after their confrontation with Fate.

During her quest to uncover the tattoo's secrets, Nara enlists the help of some new friends and discovers her own surprising connection to Ethan.

While Nara digs deeper into the

mystery, her desire for answers leads her down a dangerous path full of powerful and ruthless enemies. Swept into an age-old battle, Nara quickly learns that keeping one's enemies close can be a necessary evil, making an intangible enemy she can control far more preferable to the human enemies she can't.

Keep flipping the pages to read an excerpt from LUCID.

If you found BRIGHTEST KIND OF DARKNESS an entertaining and enjoyable read, I hope you'll consider taking the time to leave a review and share your thoughts in the online bookstore where you purchased it. Your review could be the one to help another reader decide to read **BRIGHTEST KIND OF DARKNESS** and the other books in the **BRIGHTEST KIND OF DARKNESS** series! While you're on the store, grab **LUCID** to continue with Ethan and Nara's epic love story!

BRIGHTEST KIND OF DARKNESS reading order

Reading Order

Brightest Kind of Darkness (Book 1)
Ethan (Prequel) *
Lucid (Book 2)
Destiny (Book 3)
Desire (Book 4)
Awaken (Book 5)

*** The Prequel ETHAN is best read *after* book 1, BRIGHTEST KIND OF DARKNESS.**

To keep up-to-date when the next **P.T. Michelle** book will release, join my free newsletter http://bit.ly/11tqAQN . An email will come straight to your inbox on the day a new book releases.

If you haven't already, be sure to read the novella prequel **ETHAN** for a deeper insight into Ethan's backstory before moving on to **LUCID**!

LUCID EXCERPT

BOOK 2

Excerpt

Ethan stood just inside the entrance of the gym with his arms folded. A sour look creased his face as I approached.

"I don't like him touching you, Nara."

"I know." I sighed and breezed past, leaving him with nothing to do but follow me out of the entrance and into the cool night air.

Before I'd taken more than ten steps, he grasped my elbow and pulled me to the side. Taking the shawl out of my hands, he said, "It's freezing out here," then wrapped it around my shoulders the way I'd worn it earlier.

Once he finished tying it, he said, "What'd he say to you?"

I tilted my head and decided to tell him the truth. "He thinks you're bad for me. That you'll consume me."

Ethan's gaze narrowed and his jaw muscle jumped as he gazed back toward the gym with sheer dislike.

I ran my finger along the twitching muscle. "Do you plan to consume me, Ethan?"

His gaze snapped back to mine and he clasped my shoulders, pulling me so close I had to crane my neck to meet his darkened gaze. "Not in the way he meant."

Every bone in my body melted at the heated look in his gaze as he stared at my lips with hungry intent. But instead of kissing me, he pressed his lips tenderly to my forehead and spoke in a desperate whisper, "You totally break me apart, Nara. You're the only one who has the power to do that. *You* consume me."

One-Click LUCID now!

OTHER BOOKS BY P.T. MICHELLE

In the Shadows
(Contemporary Romance, 18+)
Mister Black (Book 1 - Talia & Sebastian, Part 1)
Scarlett Red (Book 2 - Talia & Sebastian, Part 2)
Blackest Red (Book 3 - Talia & Sebastian, Part 3)
Gold Shimmer (Book 4 - Cass & Calder, Part 1)
Steel Rush (Book 5 - Cass & Calder, Part 2)
Black Platinum (Book 6 - Talia & Sebastian, Stand Alone Novel)
Reddest Black (Book 7 - Talia & Sebastian, Stand Alone Novel)
Blood Rose (Book 8 - Cass & Calder, Stand Alone Novel)
Noble Brit (Book 9 - Mina & Den, Stand Alone Novel - Coming March 2019)

Brightest Kind of Darkness Series
(YA/New Adult Paranormal Romance, 16+)
Ethan (Prequel)
Brightest Kind of Darkness (Book 1)
Lucid (Book 2)
Destiny (Book 3)
Desire (Book 4)
Awaken (Book 5)

Other works by P.T. Michelle writing as Patrice Michelle

Bad in Boots series
(Contemporary Romance, 18+)
Harm's Hunger
Ty's Temptation
Colt's Choice

Josh's Justice

Kendrian Vampires series
(Paranormal Romance, 18+)
A Taste for Passion
A Taste for Revenge
A Taste for Control

Stay up-to-date on her latest releases:

Join P.T's Newsletter:
http://bit.ly/11tqAQN

Visit P.T. :
Website: http://www.ptmichelle.com
Twitter: https://twitter.com/PT_Michelle
Facebook: https://www.facebook.com/PTMichelleAuthor
Instagram: http://instagram.com/p.t.michelle
Goodreads:
http://www.goodreads.com/author/show/4862274.P_T_Michelle

P.T. Michelle's Facebook Readers' Group:
https://www.facebook.com/groups/PTMichelleReadersGroup/

ACKNOWLEDGMENTS

A tremendous "thank you" goes out to the following people who read *Brightest Kind of Darkness* in various stages and gave helpful critiques and feedback.

Pam Berehulke
Cassandra Bird
Rinda Elliott
Stacey Jay
Marcy Posner
Charlene Teglia

To my critique partners, Jeri Smith Ready and J.A. Templeton, I can't thank you enough for your invaluable input (the first, second and third time!) during the writing of this book. I couldn't have done it without you.

To my husband, I appreciate you patiently listening to me talk about this story non-stop for three years with the same supportive response, "Get it out there!"

And to my children, you kept me going by always asking the moment you walked in the door from school, "Have you written another chapter yet? What happens next?"

ABOUT THE AUTHOR

P.T. Michelle is the *NEW YORK TIMES, USA TODAY,* and international bestselling author of the New Adult contemporary romance series IN THE SHADOWS, the YA/New Adult crossover series BRIGHTEST KIND OF DARKNESS, and the romance series: BAD IN BOOTS, KENDRIAN VAMPIRES and SCIONS (listed under Patrice Michelle). She keeps a spiral notepad with her at all times, even on her nightstand. When P.T. isn't writing, she can usually be found reading or taking pictures of landscapes, sunsets and anything beautiful or odd in nature.

To learn when the next P.T. Michelle book will release, join her free newsletter http://bit.ly/11tqAQN

Follow P.T. Michelle
www.ptmichelle.com

facebook.com/PTMichelleAuthor

twitter.com/PT_Michelle

instagram.com/p.t.michelle

youtube.com/PTMichelleAuthor

Made in United States
North Haven, CT
18 November 2022